BATHING BEAUTY

"Would you mind washing my back for me?" Zoe said softly.

Mind? Daniel thought his heart was going to burst clear out of his chest. He moved mechanically toward the partially open door.

"Um, darlin', I'm not real decent at the moment," he choked out before he dared cross the threshold.

"That's all right. I'm not feeling the least bit decent myself." The voice was low and husky. Her back was to him, glistening with the water, a rose petal lodged on her shoulder. He knelt and took the soap from her and felt her hand tremble as their fingers met.

With great deliberation, he ran the cake of soap across her back and set it back in the holder. He massaged the streak of soap into a lather and traced the lines of her collarbones. He bent to give her a lingering kiss on the top of her shoulder, right next to a rose petal.

PRAISE FOR PAMELA CALDWELL:

"Ms. Caldwell takes us to a world rarely seen by romance readers and what a treat!"

—*The Literary Times*

ROMANCE FROM JO BEVERLY

DANGEROUS JOY   (0-8217-5129-8, $5.99)

FORBIDDEN   (0-8217-4488-7, $4.99)

THE SHATTERED ROSE   (0-8217-5310-X, $5.99)

TEMPTING FORTUNE   (0-8217-4858-0, $4.99)

Available wherever paperbacks are sold, or order direct from the Publisher. Send cover price plus 50¢ per copy for mailing and handling to Penguin USA, P.O. Box 999, c/o Dept. 17109, Bergenfield, NJ 07621. Residents of New York and Tennessee must include sales tax. DO NOT SEND CASH.

RUNAWAY BRIDE

Pamela Caldwell

Zebra Books
Kensington Publishing Corp.
http://www.zebrabooks.com

ZEBRA BOOKS are published by

Kensington Publishing Corp.
850 Third Avenue
New York, NY 10022

Copyright © 1997 by Pamela Caldwell

All rights reserved. No part of this book may be reproduced in any form or by any means without the prior written consent of the Publisher, excepting brief quotes used in reviews.

If you purchased this book without a cover, you should be aware that this book is stolen property. It was reported as "unsold and destroyed" to the Publisher and neither the Author nor the Publisher has received any payment for this "stripped book."

Zebra and the Z logo Reg. U.S. Pat. & TM Off.

First Printing: July, 1997
10 9 8 7 6 5 4 3 2 1

Printed in the United States of America

One

Territory of New Mexico, 1867

"I reckon if I wanted my shirts ruint, I could have done that all by myself," Walter Connolly grumbled.

Daniel Whittaker surveyed the faded and tattered remains of his deputy's shirts. "No doubt about it, Walter," he said mildly. "They're about as ruined as ruined gets." Daniel held up a shirt and peered through a hole in the back. "This new laundress doesn't appear to be real well acquainted with the use of a sad iron either."

Walter hitched up his pants. "A woman who can't do shirts no better than that has no call settin' up in business as a laundress," he said, punctuating his words with an emphatic but not very well-aimed spit at the cuspidor in the corner. "It's a cryin' shame what she done to them shirts. They was my best ones, too."

Daniel tipped his chair forward. The front legs hit the floor with a whump and the resulting dust drifted into the stream of sunlight coming through the window. "What did she charge you?" he asked.

"Well, now, I reckon that's what saved her skin—she didn't charge me. Said I should go on down to the shebang and pick out three new shirts and she'd pay for 'em. 'Course these three shirts was bought in Abilene and we both know Clarence has got nuthin' to compare to what you can buy in a railhead town that caters to waddies with ninety dollars of trail pay in their pocket."

"No, I reckon Abilene's got about the best of everything a man could want, though I got a pretty nice shirt in Ellsworth on the last drive I made north," Daniel said. He chewed the inside of his cheek reflectively for a moment. "Did this laundry lady look rich to you?"

Walter twitched the huge mustache that nearly covered the lower half of his face. "Hard to say—she mainly looked kinda wet and sort of pink from stirrin' the wash tub. Her hair's shiny, though, and she's got all her teeth." It was as close as Walter had ever come to praising a female.

"Well, things could have been worse," Daniel announced, rising and stretching his long, spare frame. He reached for his battered brown Stetson. With nothing but jailhouse coffee sloshing around in his innards, he was feeling distinctly queasy. "I'm a little on the empty side, Walter. I'm going to go get me some breakfast," he said. "Keep an eye on things, won't you? Stage is due in in half an hour."

Walter uttered some noncommittal reply and Daniel stepped outside. He paused on the plank walkway in front of the jail to give his eyes a chance to adjust to the blazing sun. Where to eat? His favorite place, Elaine's Good Luck Restaurant, had closed the week before, Elaine having married a miner who'd struck it rich. It was an undeniable fact that unmarried women—whether they were good cooks or bad—didn't stay unmarried long in Gila City, what with a hundred miners, gamblers, bartenders, and ranch hands for every female. It made life hard for a man on the lookout for a wife—and a meal.

Daniel ambled off toward the hotel. There was a big morose Swede there who made tolerable flapjacks. You had to be a gambling man if you went to the hotel for dinner because the chances of getting an edible meal out of the Swede at that hour were no better than fifty-fifty. As a former waddie, Daniel had learned to eat just about anything put on a plate in front of him, but the Swede tested even Daniel's forbearance.

RUNAWAY BRIDE

The Swede, like most everyone else in Gila City, was a newcomer, though newcomer was a relative term. Everyone there had started life somewhere else, except for a few babies born to the working girls. People just kept piling into town, lured by the promise of quick riches from panning gold along the Gila River. Anyone who'd come to town the day before you was an old-timer and anyone who'd arrived the day after you was a newcomer, and along with gold, many had come seeking anonymity. A laundress who couldn't do laundry sounded like one of the ones who might have come seeking anonymity, but why?

Working girls sometimes had reason to seek out a new town—boredom, a jealous customer grown unaccountably fond without the emotion being reciprocated, a greedy madam—but a woman with a useful and humble calling like doing laundry rarely had cause to pull up stakes and start over, especially in a godless place like Gila City, unless she was plug ugly and on the lookout for a husband. In that case, she certainly wouldn't be disappointed. Even the dog at the Red Dog Saloon had had a few proposals in its time. Or maybe this laundress thought Gila City was a place where she could make the maximum profit with her talents, in which case she was undoubtedly right.

But a talent for doing laundry seemed conspicuously lacking in the case of this new laundress, one Zoe Smith by name.

Daniel sighed. He couldn't puzzle it out.

The Businessmen's Benevolent Association, which paid his salary, might be content as long as mayhem didn't reign in the streets of Gila City, but Daniel P. Whittaker was a man who liked explanations. If someone had come to Gila City to escape their past, he wanted to know about it, just in case it ever led to him facing down some desperado with a gun and a firm resolve to escape the long arm of the law.

But Daniel also prided himself on being a reasonable man. As long as a man's sins didn't include cold-blooded murder and he kept his nose clean, he had nothing to fear from Gila City's sheriff. Daniel figured that as a lawman he just couldn't ignore murder—and he was sort of partial to straightening out a fellow who'd left a wife and children behind with no means of support. A quiet conversation with a man in the shadow of the newly built jail usually coaxed a few dollars into an envelope on a regular basis.

"How do, Sheriff?"

A figure nearly as wide as it was tall was rolling along toward him.

"How do, Reverend Bob. I'm fine. And you?"

"I'm well, thank you. The Lord has seen fit to bless me with boundless good health."

"I'm glad to hear it," Daniel said politely. A good half inch of dust nestled in the creases of the minister's broad-brimmed hat and also lay thick as fur on his eyelashes and eyebrows. "You look like you've been riding drag, Reverend."

"I beg your pardon?"

"Bringing up the rear on a herd of cattle, Reverend. It's the worst job a waddie can pull—no experienced hand will stand for it."

"Well, Sheriff, the only steer I've been near is Molly, but I'm bound to admit that it was dusty work bringing her home. We were doing fine until Monday afternoon when she commenced to limping and bawling something awful, and I didn't feel in all good conscience that I could make her carry me so I had to walk the whole way back from Down on Your Luck Camp. I've asked Ned to see if he doesn't think Molly should be shod."

"You don't say," Daniel said, shoving his hat back on his forehead and working hard to not laugh.

Molly was a mixed breed cow known around town as Molly B'damn, as in "That Molly has by damn stuck her head in the back door of the shebang and helped herself to a barrel of pickles," and "By damn if that steer ain't been and chewed right through the hitching rail again." Reverend Bob was known for his mortal fear of horses and his devotion to Molly. The only wonder was that the crafty Molly hadn't yet bamboozled the minister into carrying *her.* "Well, Reverend Bob, whatever the problem is, I sure hope Ned can put her right for you," Daniel said amiably. He touched a finger to the brim of his hat as Reverend Bob moved off down the street.

Daniel resumed walking toward the hotel, his thoughts turning again to the matter of a laundress who couldn't do laundry. He had yet to catch a glimpse of the new woman although she'd been in town for over a month. For one person not to see another person in the course of a whole month in a town the size of Gila City suggested that one of the persons was making a considerable effort not to be seen by the other person. He added it to his list of reasons for paying a call on Miss Smith.

Daniel passed the livery stable and the blacksmith glanced up from his work, his lean brown face guarded. Some of the wariness went out of his expression when he saw who it was.

"Sheriff."

Daniel nodded. "Ned."

Molly B'damn was sound asleep in the corner of Ned's little corral, her nose resting in a trough of fodder. From the looks of her bulging sides, she'd eaten herself into a stupor. Several horses were bunched up in an opposing corner, regarding Molly sullenly.

Daniel hitched his chin toward Molly. "Anything wrong with that old cow?"

The corner of Ned's mouth twitched. "Laziness, I expect, same as usual."

"No doubt the good reverend will pray her back into health by Sunday," Daniel said. "Or she'll eat her way there first."

Ned shook his head. *"I* pray that if anything real bad ever goes wrong with Molly, it ain't no fault of mine."

"I reckon that's a wise precaution, Ned, but Reverend Bob's such a pure and holy man, I doubt he'd hold you to blame regardless."

Daniel tipped his hat to the blacksmith before working his way on down Main Street, exchanging greetings with the lawyer who ran a land claims office next to the butcher shop, the assayer who'd set up next door to him, and one of the cathouse girls who was shaking her bedding out a second-story window of the Red Dog Saloon.

"Howdy, Sheriff!"

Daniel squinted up against the early-morning sun. "Morning, Miss Teresa. You're looking mighty fine today."

"Got me an appointment down at the dressmaker's, Sheriff. I feel the pull of spring. Time to rhett up and put my best foot forward. Those boys from the mining camps will be comin' in with the big money now that the water in the creek's not so cold and they can bear to stand in it from morning till night."

"I'm sure you'll look grand," Daniel said.

"You haven't been up to see us in awhile," Teresa said with a sidelong glance beneath her lashes.

"Well, Miss Teresa, I've been busy out at the ranch on my days off, but I guess I could stop by some day soon." In fact, now that the subject had been introduced, Daniel felt a decided inclination to drop by very soon. Miss Teresa's scanty wrapper hid few of her female attributes and that fact was having a rousing effect on him.

"You do that, Sheriff, and I'll be sure and show you my new dress—that is, if you're interested in ladies' clothing." Teresa winked at him in an unabashedly lurid manner. Daniel lifted his hat in tribute and sauntered on.

For all the distractions he'd encountered, laundresses who didn't know how to do laundry were still very much on Daniel's mind when he reached Trilby's General Store. He paused in front of an ornate sign that said, "Everything for Every Occasion" in red letters edged in black and touched here and there with gilt. Clarence Trilby had spared no expense on it.

It was Daniel's practice never to rile a person by letting them know he suspected them of something unlawful—though he didn't give a damn how riled they got once he was sure they were guilty. It usually paid to investigate these matters in a roundabout way, though, and he made up his mind to do just that with the new laundress. He'd take her some shirts to launder as a way of getting to lay eyes on her, but he was damned if he'd offer up any of his own shirts for her dubious ministrations. He was just as shirt-proud as Walter.

Daniel made up his mind to acquire some sacrificial shirts. He went into Clarence Trilby's store, letting the screen door slap closed behind him.

"Morning, Daniel. What'll it be for you today?"

"How do, Clarence. I could do for some shirts, cheapest ones you got."

"Well, the cheapest ones I got are the ones I keep on hand for the undertaker. You don't want them, though—fabric's so stiff and scratchy, a feller might wish he *was* dead wearin' one of them."

"Give me three, please."

Clarence Trilby shook his head and sighed as he took down three white shirts from the cubbyhole marked "Undertaker."

Zenobia Strouss flattened herself in the darkest corner of the general store. A hoe poked her in the back as she contorted herself so that a galvanized bucket hanging from a hook hid her face. He mustn't see her—he *mustn't* see her! Secreted amidst the hardware, her heart pounding so hard that all she could hear was the rush of blood in her ears, Zenobia prayed earnestly that the sheriff of Gila City would walk out again as unexpectedly as he'd walked in. She squeezed her eyes shut, hoping like a child that if she couldn't see him, he couldn't see her either.

"Miz Smith?"

Zenobia nearly leapt out of her skin. "What?" she cried, turning so precipitously that she collided with a slab of ham hanging from an overhead beam. Clarence Trilby grabbed the hunk of meat before it could swing back and knock her down on the rebound.

"Are you all right, ma'am?"

"I'm fine," Zenobia said breathlessly. Peering past the glass jars of striped candy sticks and peppermint balls on the front counter, she could see that Sheriff Daniel Whittaker had left. Zenobia straightened her shoulders and tried hard to look as if she *was* fine. Ladies who had been approved for matriculation from Miss Walther's Swiss Finishing Academy simply did not give way to emotion in public. Zenobia felt sure that Miss Walther would never have relaxed that particular rule, not even for ladies who had accidentally murdered a man.

Only a few men lazed in the rough circle of chairs around the cold potbellied stove at the center of the store, but every one of them was looking in her direction. Although her mother had always made it clear that she was unrelentingly plain and plump—a thing she could see for herself by looking in the mirror—men had seemed drawn to her ever since she'd come to Gila City. She'd been the object of so much doglike admiration that she had to check in the looking glass every night to remind herself that she was indeed plain and plump.

"Was there something special you were looking for, ma'am?" Clarence Trilby asked. "I saw you come in, but then you just sort of disappeared or I'd have waited on you right away."

"I did come in search of something particular," Zenobia replied, lifting her chin in what she hoped was a dignified sort of way. "I came seeking bathing tubs but I do not see any. Do you not stock them or are you sold out?"

"Well, ma'am, it's like this—I don't get much call for them," Clarence said apologetically. "The men, they all bathe over at the barbershop, and most of the girls, well, I mean *ladies,* the ones that have them, they brought their own with them when they came to town, all exceptin' Miz Teresa over at the Red Dog. Now, I can order you one like I did for her. It's a real nice one. I reckon you could go on over and take a look at it if you want to, so's you could see what you'd be getting before you put out good money for it. Money has to go in with the order, you see," he added.

"That's quite all right," Zenobia said hastily. "I'm sure I need not visit the Red Dog Saloon. I can trust your judgment. If you say the bathing tub was satisfactory, then I'm sure it would suit my needs."

The eavesdroppers by the stove were entranced, either by the thought of Zenobia paying a call on a woman of ill repute or by visions of her bathing—and Zenobia didn't care to think which. She straightened her back and clasped her hands over her small purse. "Order me the best bathing tub available if you please, Mr. Trilby."

"Yes, ma'am!" Clarence hastened to his order desk and picked up a pen. "Would you spell your name for me, Miz Smith?"

"Smith?" Zenobia asked, lifting an eyebrow skeptically.

"No, ma'am, the first name. Seein' as how you don't have a husband, I'll have to put your Christian name on the order 'stead of his Christian name."

"Zoe, then," Zenobia said. "Z-o-e."

She had deliberately chosen an alias with the same initial "z" and "s" sounds as her real name, hoping it would help her to respond naturally when addressed by her new name. She had never really cared for the name Zenobia anyway, so giving it up had been no hardship. The name Zoe, common and abrupt-sounding, suited the new person circumstances were forcing her to become in the heat and squalor of Gila City. Such were the wages of sin, she supposed—Gila City definitely had some hell-like qualities.

The storekeeper's pen scratched across the paper in the silence that had fallen over the store. "Let's see—address. 'End of Main Street' I reckon. Mule or oxen, Miz Smith?"

"I beg your pardon?"

"Do you want your tub shipped by mule train or ox train? Mule train's faster but it'll cost you ten cents a pound that way and I seem to recall Miz Teresa's tub weighed thirty-two pounds. You'll end up payin' more for freight than the tub itself if you have it shipped by mule train."

The men around the stove were gazing at her with varying degrees of longing. There could be no doubt now that they were thinking of her using the tub. "Mule train," Zenobia said, looking away quickly. The musty-sweet tang of fresh fabric in bolts reminded her that she had several more items of business to tend to before she could escape. "I'll take a skirt length of that mixy green if you please, and a paper of pins, too. Oh, and I need salsoda, four pounds, and a firkin of soft soap."

"You must be doin' right well for yourself," Clarence Trilby remarked. "That's four pounds of salsoda just this week alone."

"Well, I do run a laundry, Mr. Trilby."

"I reckon I knew that, Miz Smith. All I meant was, it takes a lot of clothes washing to use up that much salsoda. Somebody else make you a better price on the vinegar you need?"

"Excuse me?" Zenobia gazed at him, completely mystified. *What on earth did vinegar have to do with laundry?*

"With all that salsoda you're using, I figure you must be going through a fair amount of vinegar, too—you know, to keep the dyes in the colored clothes from running."

Zenobia swallowed. "Oh." It explained a number of odd results, not the least of which was that dyes that ran out of one article tended to run *into* another article.

"Well, you let me know, Miz Smith, when you want my best price for vinegar, or ammonia and salt, too, for that matter. I reckon you must need a fair amount of all of 'em.

"I expect so, Mr. Trilby." *Oh, Lord—ammonia and salt, too?* "I'll place an order with you very soon, just as soon as I . . . as I . . ." *Figure out what to do with them.* ". . . as I'm able!" Zenobia glanced anxiously toward the door as Calvin Trilby wrapped her order. What with the unexpected appearance of Sheriff Daniel Whittaker and now this, her nerves had had about all they could stand for one day.

"That'll be four dollars and twenty-five cents, Miz Smith."

Zenobia counted the money out rapidly. That was another thing she'd had very little experience with, what with all her purchases being billed first to her father and then her husband, but with so many hands stretching out toward her for money, money, and more money as she'd fled across the country, counting cash into waiting hands was becoming second nature to her by now.

"Sure is nice to see paper money now and again," Clarence Trilby remarked as he aligned the bills in a tidy pile. "Don't get many of these out here. It makes a change from being paid in gold dust, though I guess you're getting used to that by now, ma'am. Got yourself a scale, do you? Or do you just go by a dollar a pinch like everyone else?"

"Oh, a dollar a pinch suits me," Zenobia said airily, deftly avoiding mention of the fact that she'd had very little occasion to collect money for her laundering services yet. Her lack of success as a laundress was beginning to gnaw at her in direct proportion to how fast the money she'd obtained for her jewels in St. Louis was dwindling. Picking up the parcel of fabric and pins, she bravely tackled the other matter that was preying on her mind. "I have told the deputy—Walter Connolly is his name, I believe—that he may choose three shirts from your stock at my expense. I forgot to add vinegar to a tub of washing water and several of his were ruined. I expect I just got distracted—I'm sure you know how that is! Anyway, I'd be much obliged if you'd put his new shirts on my account and I'll pay for them directly."

"Yes, ma'am, I'd be glad to. Seems shirts are in demand—Sheriff Whittaker was just in buying some."

"The sheriff?" Zenobia said in a determinedly offhand way. "Why, how very interesting, to be sure."

"Have you met him yet, miss? He's a real nice fella."

"I don't believe I have," she said, her heart beginning to speed up in alarm at the turn the conversation was taking.

"Well, you will soon—I'm sure of that. He knows everyone. That's one of the reasons he's sheriff. We held elections for mayor last year and there were two tables, one for each candidate. All the fellows was supposed to line up in front of one or the other to show who they was voting for, only some of the fellows, well, they nipped around to the back of the line so as to get counted a second time. Daniel—Sheriff Whittaker, that is—got asked to count votes because he'd recognize which fellows had been up and voted already. I expect you'll like him—everyone does. That's the other reason he's sheriff."

Zenobia smiled wanly. "Since everyone likes him, I expect he's a very nice man." *And I pray to God I never have occasion to find out.*

"When that tub comes, I'll see it's brought up to you, Miz Smith, and tell you what the freight comes to. I'll bring your soap and salsoda along later, when my assistant's here to mind the store. Of course, if you need 'em right now, I expect one of these here fellers would be glad to carry it for you."

The sound of chair legs scraping bare wood filled the store. Five men had half-risen from their chairs and were looking at her hopefully.

"No," Zenobia said, edging toward the door, "thank you, thank you very much. Later today will be soon enough." She turned and fled from the disappointment on five male faces.

There was a collective sigh when the door banged closed behind her.

"Oh, lordy, it sure is nice to look at a woman," said one man.

Subdued murmurs of assent greeted this heartfelt announcement and then silence fell again as each man retreated to the privacy of his own thoughts.

Daniel jumped down and quickly uncinched his saddle from Blue. He turned the buckskin gelding out in the makeshift corral that he and Lester had finally managed to build. Spring was the beginning of the busy season on a ranch and with only a few days a week to spare from his duties as sheriff, Daniel was anxious to put every minute to good use. He and Lester had seen eye to eye on the wisdom of Daniel taking the job as sheriff for the cash it would provide, but it seemed to Daniel that he'd gotten the easy end of the deal most days—as long as you didn't count the wear and tear caused by aggravation—for it was

Lester who was doing most of the hard labor at the D Bar W so far.

He changed into his old work boots inside the unprepossessing plank-and-adobe structure he and Lester called home. It was located on the boundary between their respective claims and it was destined to be Daniel's one day. So far it had just one large room, but in his mind's eye it already had glass windows, a second story with plenty of bedrooms for his sons and daughters, fireplaces made from the handsome red stones he would haul from the faraway canyons of the mighty Colorado, and a broad dining table beneath a chandelier that would light up the room as bright as day.

Of course, before any of that happened, he and Lester would have to work their tails off. They'd built a herd of thirty cattle so far but they needed to sink some more shafts for water and come up with the cash to buy the costly lumber that had to come in by wagon train. Lester would need a homestead, too, before they were done. They shared the kind of big dreams reserved to the young but he and Lester were toughened beyond their years.

Daniel had taken a round ball during the war, he'd nearly perished in a blizzard once during his droving days, and he'd survived snakebites and near starvation during his childhood in Kansas. He'd watched the wind drive savage storms across the plains and snatch up houses and tear them to bits, and rip through a string of cattle three miles long, leaving half of them dead and the other half crazed with fear. He'd seen his mother work herself to sinew and leather under a fierce Kansas sun and his father grow bent and nearsighted pushing a plow by day and studying his beloved books by a low flame each night.

But out of all the hardship had come a seasoned temperament, one that knew when to be patient and when to fight like hell, and at the forefront of everything was a dream. The dream revolved around a woman. There was a strong romantic streak in Daniel that he kept well hidden, but it ran deep within him. While most men would have been happy just to find a wife in this dusty wilderness where women were so scarce, Daniel wanted there to be a blazing love between him and the woman he wed.

He didn't know what his wife would look like but he knew her character. She would share his vision for the future and work by his side to create something out of nothing. She would be someone strong enough to stand up to him when he was wrong but with enough tenderness that he could open his heart to her without fear. She would understand that when the shadow of the dying tree loomed over him in his dreams and he woke up crying, it wasn't weakness and he didn't want pity. It wasn't for himself that he cried but for all the men he'd seen die too young on the field of battle, from Antietam to Atlanta.

The passionate dreamer in him had spent many hours thinking about the woman he would marry. It made him hollow with need to imagine touching and holding and breathing in tandem with the woman he loved, planting his seed in her and feeling her shudder with pleasure as she took it deep inside. The thought that she would bring forth life—his and hers—from her body exhilarated and intimidated him, shook him to the soles of his feet and lifted him to the stars.

He'd lain alone on his bedroll many a night, imagining holding her through the deep, cold nights of winter or lying next to her in the cool twilight of summer, alert for the whimper of a restless child, waiting to come together when darkest night reduced everyone in the house but the two of them to bottomless slumber. He could smell her, and feel her next to him in the shadows even though her face and name remained unknown.

The feel of a muzzle punching him between the shoulder blades jerked Daniel out of his reverie. He usually saved his dreams for nighttime but here he was in broad daylight, sunk in his passionate longing for a romantic love affair and caught out by Blue. Chagrined by the force of his desire, Daniel took a mouthful of water from the bucket of water he'd pumped and spat it out again. Blue pawed the ground impatiently.

"Here you are, boy," he said, pushing the bucket under the

rail. Blue eyed him in a superior way, as if he knew what Daniel had been thinking about and had deliberately brought him back to reality for his own good. It was one thing for a man to be sweet on a girl, the look said, but what Daniel dreamt of was just plain crazy.

Daniel felt his cheeks heat up a bit. Blue seemed too well acquainted with his thoughts for comfort sometimes. He turned his back on the horse and stripped off his shirt. He'd wasted enough time. He took one of Clarence Trilby's shirts out of his saddlebag. The coarse touch of it curdled his innards—the storekeeper hadn't exaggerated the cheapness of the fabric one little bit. He'd thought to dirty the shirts up in the course of digging holes for fence posts but the fabric was bound to rub his skin raw, and damnit—he was prepared to do his duty as sheriff but a man had to draw the line somewhere. Daniel threw the shirt over the top rail and turned his attention to digging post holes.

The sun was going down and the kerchief he'd knotted around his neck was wringing wet when he finally set aside his shovel for the night. He pumped a fresh bucket of water to wash in and dried his bare torso with his shirt before taking a sack full of hotel scraps the Swede had given him to the pigs. They fell on the booty with unbridled greed, jostling one another like miners at a bar. Inspiration struck Daniel with lightning swiftness. It took him something under five minutes per pig to do the deed and then he stood back to admire his handiwork.

With the sleeves rolled back to fit their stubby legs and the top buttons left undone—a concession to the considerable girth of their necks—they looked exceptionally intelligent in the shirts. All three had rolled liberally in the mud and they shimmied inside the shirts every now and then, letting loose ecstatic grunts as the rough fabric scratched them right where they itched.

Daniel saw a hazy column of dust coming toward the homestead long before he heard the soft slip shuffle of Lester's horse as it jogged the last weary yards homeward. Daniel didn't bother to turn around, knowing that Lester would join him. When he did, he, too, leaned on the rails of the pigpen to admire the scene before him.

"Daniel."

"Lester."

It was as formal a greeting as they ever offered each other. Daniel and Lester had been friends for a long time and if there was one thing they'd learned to do, it was not to talk each other to death. Several moments of silence stretched out, accompanied by the sound of pigs getting on the outside of a lot of fodder.

At long last Lester shoved his hat up a notch. "Now there's something you don't see just every day," he remarked.

"Nope," Daniel replied. Several more minutes of silence went by.

"Well, I expect I should be getting some biscuits started for supper," Lester finally said, pushing off the fence. "I've got a right sharp sensation in my middle."

"Me, too, Lester, me too."

Lester ambled off toward the house, secure in the knowledge that Daniel would share the whys and wherefores of the pigs' new clothes in due course.

Two

To Daniel, Gila City loomed ahead through shimmering heat waves but he couldn't seem to get there fast enough.

He squinted into the sun. He could have sworn that town had expanded its boundaries in the two days he'd been absent—but then, it was possible that it had. When he'd come to Gila City himself, intent on panning for gold and striking it rich, the din of hammers had made it hard for a man to think straight. The streets had been stacked high with lumber being dragged hither and yon to various work sites by teams of oxen while men labored frantically with shovels and pickaxes to construct new saloons and hotels as fast as humanly possible.

The sign maker was still the busiest man in town. With butchers, bakers, bootmakers, bankers, and barbers all moving in at a record pace, the sign maker could barely keep up with the demand for his services.

Daniel spied a building with a sign that said: "Thurston and Meyer, Attorneys and Counselors at Law" beneath the second-story windows. Another on the front floor read "Robbins and Weir, Real Estate Brokers." Daniel blinked. The building hadn't been there when he'd ridden out of town two days ago.

Marooned in the midst of stakes marking yet another new building was his hand-lettered sign indicating the city limit of Gila City and proclaiming that all firearms had to be checked at the jail while their owners were in town—"No Exceptions." He'd looked up the spelling of "exception" to be sure he got it right. No one respected an ignorant man. Daniel reined Blue around a heap of temporarily abandoned wheelbarrows, making a mental note to come back later, after he'd gotten rid of the pigs' new clothes, to move the city limit sign.

"Hoo-ee, Sheriff! What the hell's that smell?"

Daniel pulled up. "Howdy, Nathanial. I reckon it's my laundry."

Nathanial grimaced. "I've buried things that smelled better, my leg among 'em."

Daniel smiled. Mordant humor was preferable to none. "Now Nathanial, you don't mean to say they made you southern boys bury your own limbs after an amputation, do you?"

"We weren't coddled like you northern boys," Nathanial shot back.

Daniel rested an elbow on his saddle horn and shook his head. "No, Nathanial, I reckon you weren't. We all left a little of ourselves on the battlefield one way and another, but you were extra special unlucky."

Nathanial stared hard at Daniel. And Daniel could see the dilemma in Nathanial's eyes—accept the sympathy of a man who had once been his sworn enemy or keep the war alive forever?

Today, in the heat and dust of a place two thousand miles removed from where his leg was buried, Nathanial chose to let it be. He stepped back a pace. "Reckon you'd better go and put that laundry out of everyone's misery," he said.

"Reckon I should," Daniel replied. He tipped his hat before moving on. A man was entitled to his dignity and Daniel meant to let Nathanial retain all that he had left.

When Daniel turned the corner, he saw a most unusual sight.

At least ten men stood lined up in the street, hats in hand, staring reverently at a clothesline draped with female underthings. From atop Blue, Daniel had an excellent view of the lacy garments.

He drank it in, instantly seduced by the spectacle of feminine possessions: long drawers with frills to dance around a woman's calves; white petticoats with scalloped hems and elaborate embroidery along the edges; a violet petticoat with braid trim—obviously the sort of petticoat meant to be seen beneath an artfully hitched-up skirt—and a nightdress.

A nightdress. Daniel's mouth went dry. He gazed dumbstruck at the rippling expanse of thin white material. There was scarlet embroidery on the collar and cuffs and a demure ribbon tie at the throat. To see the woman who owned the garment actually wearing it would be a privilege reserved for her husband, a privilege he would exercise in the privacy of their bedroom. Daniel thought longingly about being that husband.

It was Blue who pulled him back from the brink of making a fool of himself. The horse jerked the reins out of his hand as he reached for some grass growing by a water trough. With a start, Daniel remembered why it was that he'd actually come to Miss Zoe Smith's laundry.

Seeing the evidence of female occupation on the line made Zoe Smith into a living, breathing entity, and Daniel found he could hardly wait to meet her. He hoped she wasn't plug ugly because that covered an awful lot of ground and he was on the lookout for a wife he wouldn't mind looking at across the breakfast table.

He looped Blue's reins around a pump handle. Just beyond the clothesline was the faintly lopsided building that housed Miss Zoe Smith's laundry. Daniel thought briefly of saying something official sounding, like, "You men move along now," and then realized he didn't have the heart. They weren't doing any harm and, after all, wasn't it every man's God-given right to worship all things female?

As Daniel walked past the wash line, he resisted the temptation to reach out and touch a soft merino vest and a nainsook camisole. He knew that seeing one man touch the precious things might start a stampede, and so far the fellows were behaving pretty well.

But it sure wasn't easy being good, especially when a little gust of wind flipped a pair of drawers across his arm and the lace caressed his bare skin. Sweat beaded on his upper lip. By the time he walked through the open door into Miss Zoe Smith's laundry, he felt very nearly irrational with suppressed passion. Only the powerful odor of pig manure motivated him to keep moving forward rather than put the encounter off until another day when he felt more in possession of himself.

The front room was filled with heaps of laundry—small piles, large piles, medium-size bundles, big sacks, a basket or two, and one huge hamper. A trail of wet stains led across the plank floor to the back room. There wasn't another single thing in the room—no counter, no sign with a list of charges, no bell to ring for service, no placard pledging satisfaction or your money back. Nothing. The walls were bare, the floors were plain raw planking, and the windows were devoid of shades, shutters, or curtains. Even by Gila City standards it was stark.

There was no sound from the back room. Should he go through? Surely a woman with so much laundry to do should be busy at this time of day. Daniel hesitated, clinging to the reeking bundle in his arms.

And then it occurred to him to wonder whether Miss Zoe Smith, having washed all her underthings, had been left with nothing to wear. The idea that she was hiding in the back in a state of semiundress brought a slow, lazy grin to Daniel's face. And then he realized she must have had *something* left to wear out in public or she couldn't have hung out all the things on the line.

With nervousness born of high expectations, Daniel edged toward the door to the back room. It was dim inside, having only one small window that overlooked the alley. A rocker tub occupied the center of the room, surrounded by empty wooden buckets. In the gloom he could just make out a potbellied stove in the corner, with a cauldron on top that was gently belching steam. A hamper filled with dirty clothes waited for attention and a rough-hewn table was strewn with a dark bundle of clothes.

"Miss Smith?"

The bundle shifted and muttered. Daniel smiled. It wasn't

even high noon yet and here was Miss Zoe Smith already tuckered out from laundering all her pretty lady's things. He removed his hat and coughed politely.

"Miss Smith?"

The bundle made a grumpy sound.

"Miss Smith, I have some laundry I'd like to leave for you to do."

The bundle made a vague gesture toward the front room. "Leave it."

"Well, I can see that you're busy, ma'am, but don't you need to know my name? Ma'am? Miss Smith? My name is Daniel P. Whittaker. You can bring these shirts back along to the jail when they're—"

The bundle of dark clothes sat bolt upright. "Daniel F. Whittaker? *Sheriff* Daniel P. Whittaker?"

"Yes, ma'am." It tickled Daniel that she already knew who he was, and he was moved by the sound of her voice. It was unexpectedly deep and a little bit husky, with a faint accent. He squinted into the gloom trying to make out her features.

She stood up, wiping her hands on a nonexistent apron. Her mouth was nothing but a round shadow in the pale blur of her face. "I . . . I have a lot of orders that are ahead of yours. I mean, I couldn't possibly do your laundry *soon.*"

"Well, ma'am, I can see that you have a lot of work, but as for that, I don't need these shirts back right away."

"Not right away?" she echoed, coming around the table. "But . . . but . . . it might be *weeks!* No, no, I mean it could even take *months* before I get to them!"

Daniel backed into the front room as she bore down on him. The instant the light hit her face, he stopped listening.

Her eyes were china blue, just pure, blindingly stop-your-heart china blue. Daniel felt as if someone had tossed him high up into the air. Her skin was a radiant pink and cream in the morning light. Oh, Lord, how he wanted to touch that skin!

"Sheriff?"

Daniel realized she was staring at him and waiting for him

to say something sensible. "Ma'am!" was the best he could come up with on short notice.

"So you understand you'll have to take your laundry someplace else?"

That would mean being kicked out of paradise! "No, ma'am! That is, there's no particular hurry. Whenever you can get them finished will be soon enough for me."

"But I'm all alone here as you can see, and as I've been trying to explain, it will be . . . oh, Christmas at the very earliest! I just can't accept any more work at the present time."

Daniel was still falling all the way down into the depths of those clear blue eyes. Angels had eyes that color. He wished it was polite to stare, but since it wasn't, he made a stab at getting a hold of himself. He had a vague notion that she'd said when he first walked in that she *would* do his laundry and now she was saying that she wouldn't.

"Is there some reason you'd rather not do my laundry, ma'am?" he asked, thinking that the smell might have put her off. "I mean, mine in particular?"

Some of the pink along her cheekbones faded. "No! I mean, that is, what I'm trying to say is, well—I can't! I just can't! I haven't any maid or . . . or servant to help me. I'm trying to do this all alone. People in this godforsaken place would rather gamble than earn an honest living working in a laundry, and men just keep bringing me more and more dirty clothes, and I have to burn cow dung to heat the water because there's no wood or coal to be had except at exorbitant prices and . . ." She trailed off and stared at Daniel, as if aware that she had begun to babble.

"I didn't mean to distress you, ma'am," he said hastily. "I'd wash them myself to spare you the trouble, but I'm just no darn good at it, ma'am, no good at all." He shrugged and offered up a rueful half-smile while mentally begging his mother's forgiveness for the whopper. The plain truth was that he could do laundry as well as any female alive. His mother had seen to that. *All* her boys had been taught to do so-called woman's work, or she'd have been overwhelmed, what with being the only female in a household of seven men.

Zoe Smith was regarding him unhappily, indecision mixed with desperation on her face. It made him want to hold her close and stroke her hair. Her lower lip wobbled.

"But . . . but . . ."

"I'll just set my shirts down here, ma'am," he said gently, "and don't you worry at all about when you get them back to me." Daniel tipped his hat and eased his way backward out the door before she could think to thrust the filthy shirts back at him. He meant to do business with Zoe Smith no matter what obstacles she tried to put in his way.

He nearly fell down the flimsy front steps of the laundry as he exited. It wasn't poor construction that had him off balance, though. His head was reeling and his heart was hammering and he felt for all the world as if the earth had tilted sharply on its axis.

Blue regarded him cynically as he unlooped the horse's reins from the pump handle. He raised one of what Daniel thought of as his eyebrows—the cluster of long hairs that arched above each brow bone. Daniel could have sworn that Blue knew exactly what he was thinking about at that moment. About shining blue eyes and glowing skin and a perfect, round little female figure.

"Don't you look at me like that," he growled, irritated by what felt like the horse's uncanny intrusion into his thoughts. "I reckon a man's entitled to *some* privacy."

He swung up into the saddle with a grim determination to keep his personal feelings off his face lest a *person* see there what Blue did. The flighty, giddy feeling in his chest was no one's business but his own. He let Blue amble toward Ned's livery stable nice and slow, thinking all sorts of pleasant thoughts about Miss Zoe Smith on the grounds that too much of a good thing often reduces it to only a fair thing.

He thought about the china-blue eyes, the husky voice with the faintly English accent, like an easterner's, and the frilly underthings of the line. Unfortunately, repetition failed to dim the allure of Miss Zoe Smith. By the time he stabled Blue and walked back to the jail, though, he fancied he had mastered his emotions at least well enough to avoid having his mood detected by Walter Connolly.

Zenobia waited until the sheriff had ridden off and then rose. With shaking hands, she closed the crude front door and dropped a plank into the brackets on either side of it. The building was so out of true that even closed, the door admitted a long wedge of sunlight that splayed across the floor.

Zenobia stared at it. She could feel her heart still racing. He knew! He must know!

Wanted for murder: one Zenobia Strouss, a plain and unremarkable female aged twenty-nine years, late of Philadelphia.

She had fled as fast and as far as she could, passing through the towns where good, decent folk lived, where mothers did their marketing with children in tow, towns where they had real plumbing and pretty gardens, not endless balls of sage brush. She might have sought work in one of them, perhaps as a schoolteacher or a companion to a genteel lady—though both would have been humiliating comedowns for the pampered only daughter of Barnabus Strouss—but ultimately, someone would have inquired into her background.

So she had kept going, spending weeks jostling and jouncing in trains and river boats and stagecoaches, from one forlorn outpost to the next, spanning mile after empty mile, and as she traveled, she'd seen the telegraph lines strung all the way across the country. The word of her crime must have traveled over those fragile little wires.

It wasn't fair! Stephen had deserved to die! Stephen had been an odious reptile, a willing partner of her husband in an obscene plot to get her pregnant. She didn't deserve to be punished for defending herself against rape.

But it had all caught up with her. She'd thought she was safe out here in the back of beyond. She'd passed by all the towns where the law was respected, passed through all the towns connected to the East by train where pursuers might reach her more easily, and only stopped when the big Wells Fargo and Company stagecoach rolled to a stop in Gila City one day at dawn. There, where all the signs advertised saloons and liquor and music halls and vice of every sort, where unkempt men slept propped against water troughs and the walls of ramshackle buildings, she felt she might be safe. No one there would be likely to care who she was or where she'd come from.

But that comfortable assumption had changed with Sheriff Whittaker's visit. He'd looked at her very intently, as if trying to memorize her face, as if he *did* care who she was and where she'd come from. Considering he was the law, or what passed for it in Gila City, it was most unsettling. The Territory of New Mexico wasn't part of the United States. It had no courts, no judges, and no need to adhere to the Constitution, but a man could collect a bounty on a fugitive just the same, and she'd come to learn that they did have a rough sort of justice in the Territory—it was just that they made up the rules as they went along.

Sheriff Whittaker looked like a lawman who wouldn't hesitate to hang a murderer. Zenobia had sensed a sort of steely resolve in him, in his grave courtesy and in the gray-green eyes that held her gaze so unwaveringly.

But mainly it manifested itself in the big pistol he wore in a holster halfway between his left hip and the fly of his pants. The bluish gleam of the metal was cold and menacing enough, but add to that the lean hardness of the sheriff's body and she had no doubt that resistance would be futile. Sheriff Daniel Whittaker could probably draw so fast that she would no sooner have formed the intention of running than he would have the mean-looking gun out of its holster.

But what if she was dreaming it all up? What if Sheriff Whittaker *didn't* know about her and only wanted his shirts washed, like he'd said? Zenobia flopped down on the big hamper of laundry the boys from Don't Give a Damn Camp—"begging your pardon for the name, ma'am"—had dropped off.

She didn't know. She just didn't know. The best bet would be to get out of Gila City now, but where else could she go that would be any safer?

Where she *wanted* to go was back home, back to Philadelphia and her lovely house and all her beautiful things. She'd never appreciated the life she'd had more than she did now, living in this cess pit of a town in a building where she wouldn't have stabled horses back home.

Worst of all, it was her favorite night, Friday, when all the best people went to the opera. Ebenezer, her husband—would lead her into the grand foyer of the Philadelphia Opera House, so dark and debonair a man that every female head turned when he entered a room. She would have the satisfaction of wearing an incomparably beautiful gown, perhaps the aquamarine from Worth—a special birthday gift from her father—and the matching pendant earrings and chased silver choker.

Though, of course, the pendant and choker weren't in her possession anymore. They sat in a jeweler's case in St. Louis, traded for cold hard cash, and she sat here in Gila City, tired and smelling awful. Zenobia swallowed. She spent half her time vacillating between self-pity and bone-deep dread of being arrested for murder. She straightened her shoulders, suddenly resolute. She could not—*would* not—go to jail for having killed Stephen. There was no way to go but forward, come what may.

Where was that disgusting odor coming from? Zenobia followed her nose and realized that the horrible smell came from the shirts the sheriff had just dropped off. Well, that settled it—she'd wash his shirts first. That way she'd get rid of the odor and the sheriff, too. Tomorrow she'd march right into the jail and give him his blasted shirts back, all clean and pressed.

With a sigh, Zenobia arose. To wash and press three shirts in one day would be a real challenge. So far, the best she'd managed was to ruin three shirts in a day. She boiled water in the cauldron on the stove and dropped the sheriff's shirts in, recoiling at the smell as they hit the water. She added soap and stirred. A filthy scum soon formed and the water turned a repulsive shade of brown. Zenobia began hauling in water to fill the rinse tub.

Today, like every other day in Gila City, was relentlessly hot. Zenobia's undergarments clung to her skin as she worked. One man had lingered one day when dropping off his laundry and told her that early spring was the best time of year in Gila City, before it got *really* hot. She still couldn't decide if he'd been teasing her but rather thought that he must have been. How could Gila City get any hotter?

And instead of relief from the heat, nightfall only brought more problems, with a sudden drop in temperature that left her shivering in her damp clothing. Zenobia thought derisively of her mother's dictum that men perspired and horses sweat, but a woman glowed. In Gila City, everyone sweated, horses, men, *and* women.

Sheriff Whittaker was no slouch when it came to sweating either, if his shirts were anything to go by. Zenobia sniffed at the lingering malodorous scent. How could a man who appeared so neat give rise to such a smell? The long fingers gripping his hat had been clean, the nails evenly trimmed. The face with its low, hard cheekbones had been clean-shaven, and the shirt he'd been wearing was definitely washed and pressed by someone who knew what they were doing.

Why hadn't he taken these shirts to *that* person? The only explanation Zenobia could think of made her quake. Could it be that he'd just needed to get a glimpse of her to be sure she matched the description on a wanted bulletin? Perhaps when she delivered his shirts to the jail, he'd clap her in irons, or whatever it was they did to criminals when they arrested them.

Zenobia sighed gustily. It was no use thinking about it. There was no stage she could get on between now and tomorrow anyway. She tipped the rinse tub back and forth, her arms aching. For distraction, she thought of the restaurant around the corner, the one that was for sale. Running a laundry had turned out to be infinitely more difficult than she'd imagined when she'd inquired into whether it would yield a reasonable return on her limited funds.

The sale of her jewelry had netted her a fair amount but it was her only capital and capital must never be squandered. Her father had imbued her with a certain amount of business acumen despite her mother's prohibition on talking about his locomotive works at the supper table. While Gila City was undeniably in need of a laundry, the backbreaking labor, all done in an atmosphere of engulfing steam, would be the death of her. Surely there was just as strong a demand for a good restaurant.

And she adored food. Her mother, a dainty woman, had constantly put her daughter on reducing diets of one kind or another, all to no avail. Zenobia's waist was still a horrifying twenty-two inches. None of the eating establishments Zenobia had tried so far produced anything even passably edible, so she guzzled coffee and ate bread and potatoes for every meal. It would do her waistline no good at all, for among the foods that had always been absolutely forbidden to her were bread, butter, milk, sugar, potatoes (sweet and white), molasses, fat meat, Indian corn, pastry, and beer. Despite the confident assurances of Drs. Brinton and Napheys, whom her mother had consulted, Zenobia had never succeeded in reducing much despite denying herself these things.

She hauled in bucket after bucket of water, inspired by fear to new heights of exertion. Seldom had she actually done so much laundry in one day. There was no drain, no plumbing, no running water of any kind to make the job any easier, either. Emptying the cauldron of its hot, dirty water was a special sort of purgatory in the heat. She paused in her labors when the sky outside began to shade to orange and purple and hurried to the nearest bakery for bread. It paid to be off the streets of Gila City before dark, when the men became even more loud and disorderly than they were during the day.

Her last act before locking the door for the night was to bring her own freshly washed clothes in from the line. Besides her traveling dress, they represented everything she'd been able to carry away from Philadelphia. It was remarkable how little one could fit into a small valise. She'd never undertaken a journey before without a maid to pack her numerous trunks, and carriages to lash them to.

She would have given a great deal to be able to go upstairs to her own bedroom tonight, to undress with her maid's help and slip into one of the foulard nightdresses Bridget would have already laid out on the bed. Bridget would comb out her hair and carry away her dress to be brushed clean for another day. How could she ever have snapped at the woman for being clumsy or slow? Bridget had been a paragon, anticipating what she might want before she even knew herself that she wanted it. What luxury she had enjoyed, and she'd never appreciated it even a tenth as much as she should have. Besides Bridget there had been her butler, Sidcup, and a whole army of other servants.

Now *she* was the servant, looking after other peoples needs, and what awful people they were—unwashed and scarcely able to eat with utensils judging by the numerous food stains on their clothes. It was hard to imagine a worse fate for the only daughter of a doting and wealthy industrialist. Except, Zenobia admitted in an instant of utter truthfulness, to be hanged by the neck until dead.

She stared at the sad iron waiting on the stove. Hanging *might* be preferable. She simply could not get the knack of using the thing. With a heavy feeling in her heart, she maneuvered one of the two heated slugs into the iron's inner compartment. The tongs she used to handle it grew hot and nearly burned her fingers. She did pass the iron over her camisole and petticoats, though not very skillfully, but she'd taken so long to get the slug into the iron that it was almost cold when she started so it didn't matter. She replaced the cold slug with a hot one and started over.

When she tried ironing the sheriff's shirts, she saw with dismay that they had retained a murky brown color from the wash water. The light cast by the smelly kerosene lantern wasn't very good, though, and she held out hope that they weren't as dingy as they looked. By the bright light of day, they would no doubt look much better.

But by the time another half hour had passed, the color of the shirts was rendered immaterial, for she had managed to get the metal slugs into the iron before they cooled and the shirts bore singe marks everywhere. Between fatigue and disappointment, Zenobia felt close to tears. Now she would have to go buy three new shirts for Sheriff Whittaker and return *those* to him, all the while praying he didn't notice the difference.

All that was left to her was to go to bed. She bit her lip and sighed. Even the prospect of sleep lacked appeal, for the rickety bed which had been left upstairs by the previous owner had been left for a good reason. It was little better than a torture rack. It didn't even deserve to be called a bed, especially not when compared with the four-postered, chintz-draped extravaganza of comfort she'd had back home.

The thing upstairs was made of some kind of native wood, a gnarled type all riddled with holes. Planks formed a platform for a thin, straw-filled mattress, but they were still rounded in the shape of a tree and bark-covered. She tried in vain each night to fit her hips and bottom and elbows and shoulders into the hollows between the boards, but it felt like sleeping on a piece of corduroy carved out of granite. She had contemplated sleeping on the floor once or twice but she wasn't at all sure the building was vermin free, since she'd heard some suspicious scurrying sounds at night.

No, sleep could wait a little longer. Divesting herself of the day's grime and sweat, on the other hand, had unqualified appeal, despite the fact that without a tub, bathing was something of an ordeal. She'd had to resort to wedging her feet into two buckets and pouring water over herself while standing up, but at least that way she didn't have to mop up as much spilled water afterward.

Covering the small back window with a cloth, she heated

water in the cauldron on the stove and undressed, trying her best to ignore the sound of horse races and wild victory calls on Main Street. The first touch of lukewarm water over her skin was such bliss that she momentarily forgot her fear of having someone burst in on her through the wholly inadequate front door. For the first time since she'd arrived in Gila City, she decided to wash her hair with soap, too. What heaven it would be to be clean!

The only problem was the soap. The glop Clarence Trilby sold her for doing laundry worked all right in boiling water but in her hair it proved gooey and greasy and hard to rinse out. Oh, for a bar of the hard-milled English soap she'd always used back home! Her eyes began to sting as the rinse water flushed soap out of her hair and across her face.

She groped blindly for the last bucket of rinse water. Shots suddenly rang out nearby and she let out a shriek. The sound of men shooting at one another never failed to unnerve her, and here she was, naked as a baby and with soap in her eyes! With unsteady hands she lifted the bucket up and tipped her head back to get the soap out of her eyes.

It proved to be her undoing. With her feet wedged in the buckets and blind to her surroundings, she lost her balance and toppled. She windmilled frantically on the way down but to no avail. The table caught the edge of her face as she fell and she landed in a heap, too dazed to cry at first. She clutched her head, sucking air in through clenched teeth as the pain tried to take her breath away. Other parts of her had taken a beating, too, for she had landed amidst overturned buckets, but nothing hurt as much as her face at the moment.

But there was no blood. Thank God. Zenobia knew she wasn't a beauty but she'd have hated to be disfigured by some gruesome injury caused by her own clumsiness. Relief released the tears she'd been holding back. Feeling like a fool sitting naked among the soap suds and overturned buckets, she struggled to her feet and crying all the while, began to dry herself. She slipped a nightdress over her head and set the room to rights, still hiccupping and shedding an occasional tear.

Zenobia nearly crumpled with alarm when she heard a knock at the front door. The drunken men of Gila City were coming to rape her in her own house!

"Miss Smith?"

Zenobia didn't know whether to laugh or cry. It was Sheriff Whittaker. Was he the threat or the savior? She made her way cautiously to the front room.

"Yes?" She had to clear her throat and try a second time, because all her crying had left her voice raspy.

"Miss Smith? It's Sheriff Whittaker."

"Yes, Sheriff, I know. What do you want?" Not for anything was she going to open the door and let him see her like this!

"I came to see if you were all right, ma'am," he said. "I saw your light on and I thought the gunfire might have alarmed you. If you'll open your door, I think I can set your fears to rest."

Zenobia's knees began to shake. Had he come to arrest her at this time of night because she'd be off guard now? Or had he come to exact some kind of payment from her in exchange for *not* arresting her? She'd read articles about the lawless West that said sheriffs on the frontier had few scruples and even fewer checks on their power.

"Ma'am? Are you all right in there? I sure do wish you'd open up this door." Despite her fevered imaginings, Sheriff Whittaker's baritone voice sounded reassuringly normal.

Because he sounded so sincere, she decided not to risk arousing his suspicions by not opening the door. She lifted the crossbar and the door immediately swung inward on its uneven hinges. Sheriff Whittaker stood there, his face illuminated by the faint light of the kerosene lantern in the back room. He smiled, a lopsided grin that quickly froze.

"Why, Miss Smith, whatever happened?"

Her lower lip wobbled. "I . . . I'm fine," she managed to say. "You needn't worry about me."

"Well, I hate to contradict a lady, but you're not fine. That's one dandy of a bump you've got there." His eyes narrowed. "No one's been in here and gotten rough with you, have they? Because no matter what gripe a man may have about his laundry, I won't allow it."

Zenobia felt a swell of gratitude for his gallantry. "No, Sheriff, nothing like that," she said. "I just fell. I'm clumsy. I always have been."

Sheriff Whittaker cocked his head to one side. "What you need to do is get a cold, wet cloth on that, ma'am. Have you got fresh water in the back?"

Zenobia shook her head. "No, I used it all."

"Well, why don't you go sit down and I'll pump a new bucket and we'll see if we can get you fixed up?"

Zenobia nodded and turned away quickly. Daniel Whittaker's kindness was touching. It threatened what little composure she had. She righted the only chair she possessed, a rickety affair, and sat down, thinking what an unattractive sight she must present, with her reddened eyes and skin all blotchy from crying, never mind the swelling on her face.

Sheriff Whittaker reappeared and set down a sloshing bucket. "Here you are, ma'am." He withdrew a clean handkerchief—neatly pressed and folded and spanking white, she noticed—and dipped it in the water. "Now put this right on the bump and keep it there. Cold water's the best thing short of a fresh piece of meat for something like that. It's too bad all the meat in this town is brought in overland already pickled. You're going to have a dandy of a shiner."

Zenobia held the compress gingerly against the painful area around her eye. "This will be wonderful, really, thank you. I'm sorry to have taken so much of your time away from official duties."

He smiled, the white lines at the corners of his eyes disappearing into tanned creases. "There isn't a man in town who wouldn't agree that my official duties include protecting the women. We don't have so many that we can afford to get careless about them." He set his hat on the table and nodded toward the coffeepot on the stove. "Reckon I could get some coffee heated up for you."

Zenobia shook her head quickly. She had let him in to allay suspicion but she hadn't meant for him to stay too long. Now was the time to begin getting rid of him.

"It helps when a person has had the bejabbers knocked out of them to have something warm put back in," he said, ignoring her refusal of the coffee. "I'm speaking from experience, ma'am, not just good intentions."

It was his good intentions that were undoing her. So much sympathy and concern after a long draught was about to loosen her tears again. "I don't think that coffee is fit for man or beast," she said around the lump in her throat.

He lifted the lid and sniffed. "You may be right about that. I'll just nip on down to the jail and get you some fresh coffee. My deputy, Walter, generally keeps a pot going when he has to stay awake, which he has to on Friday and Saturday nights especially, to check in the guns the fellows bring to town. It won't take me but a minute."

"No, no, thank you!" She had to discourage him. He had to go away and stay away. "I don't much care for coffee at night—it keeps me awake."

"Well, if your mind's made up on the matter, I won't say otherwise." He held out one hand. "Here, let me wet that for you again. You don't want to bend over with a shiner like that. It'll hurt something fierce if you do."

He hunkered down by the bucket and dipped the hanky, wringing it out and refolding it meticulously with his long, blunt-tipped fingers. She took the handkerchief back, trying to avoid eye contact as he studied her face.

"I'll be fine, really," she said with as much conviction as she could muster. Being looked after had an appeal that she was finding difficult to resist, but resist it she did. "There's no need for you to stay any longer."

"I know you'll forgive me for saying so, Miss Smith, but you look a mite worse for wear. I'll feel better if you'll just let me abide here a little while longer, until you get some better color to you."

For a soft-spoken man, he was extraordinarily hard-headed. He smiled up at her, balanced easily on the balls of his feet, his elbows resting on his knees. An old leather vest hung in comfortable conformity to his body, its only adornment a plain gold shield embossed with the words Sheriff and Gila City.

"Are you sure I can't change your mind about that coffee?" he asked pleasantly.

Zenobia shook her head and immediately regretted it. The area around her eye throbbed with the motion. Seeing her wince, Sheriff Whittaker took the cloth away again and rewetted it.

"Seems I'll have to add you to the list of injured in this town tonight. It's going to be a mighty long list. A whole bunch of fellows got roughed up pretty good down at the Red Dog Saloon owing to a troop of traveling actors. Never did like actors much, anyway, and now I like them even less."

It seemed to Zenobia that he was making a concerted effort to entertain and distract her. She smiled in spite of herself. "And why is that, Sheriff?"

"Well, you remember I told you I could explain the gunfire? It came from down at the Red Dog. The actors were doing *Uncle Tom's Cabin,* and when it came time for Eliza to cross the river, a man behind the curtain let a trained bloodhound loose to chase her. The fellows were rooting for Miss Eliza to escape and they got so upset when that dog went after her that one of the boys up and shot him."

"Shot the bloodhound?" Zenobia was horrified—she loved dogs.

Sheriff Whittaker nodded. "Just grazed him, though. This fellow had just sort of 'forgotten' to turn in his gun and he'd had a bit too much to drink. Most men aren't great shots when they're sober, but when they're liquored up, they're really bad."

"So those were the shots I heard?" As sorry as she was to

hear about the dog being hurt, Zenobia found comfort in the thought that nothing worse had happened.

"Well, those were only the first few. Seems that when the actress playing Eliza realized what had happened, it occurred to her that she'd come mighty close to being shot herself and fainted dead away. That's when all hell broke loose, with half the fellows wanting to go to her aid and the other half wanting to beat the daylights out of the fellow who had fired the shots and scared her so."

"But you managed to restore order?"

"It wasn't too hard. The lady actor came around pretty fast and I told the fellows that if they wanted to see the rest of the play, everyone had to sit down and shut up. That sorted things out right quick."

"And then you came here and sorted things out for me," she said. "Well, I want to thank you, Sheriff. I appreciate your concern, but I'm sure you need to be getting back to work now."

"I can stay awhile longer, ma'am, if you're feeling like you're dizzy or need some help getting upstairs to bed."

Oh, Lord, no, that was the last thing she wanted! What she wanted was for him to leave. Nice as he seemed, he was still the sheriff and she was still a murderer on the run.

"No, that won't be necessary. I don't want to detain you, not when men might be out there shooting at each other or robbing banks or something."

Daniel knew she thought he was slow to take the hint. He was well aware that however much he desired to remain in her presence, Miss Zoe Smith, with equal fervor, desired to be rid of him. He rose and quickly retrieved his hat from the table. She just looked so adorable, all wet and pale and vulnerable. He'd never wanted to gather a woman up in his arms and soothe her and take care of her the way he did Miss Zoe Smith at this moment. Her effect on him would have been painfully evident had it not been for his old Stetson. He'd knelt down in front of her to keep his condition hidden from her notice, but now that he was standing up again, the uncomfortable bulge would be right on a level with her eyes. He felt sure she wouldn't welcome such proof of her attractiveness.

He kept his hat in front of him as he bid her good night. Back in the street, he walked slowly toward the jail without sticking his head into any of the saloons he passed. Someone was always quick enough to find him when real trouble developed. He didn't need to go looking for it just now.

And he wanted a chance to be alone with his thoughts about Zoe Smith. There was something about her that just bewitched him, from her curvaceous outlines in the damp nightdress that concealed almost nothing—like the lovely thighs, the pretty little knees, and the full, round breasts with a taut peak at the center of each—to the china-blue eyes that just drew him right in.

It wasn't putting it too strongly to say that he had just barely prevented himself from proposing to her tonight. What a fool she would have thought him—or unstable or just plain dangerous—and who would blame her? What man first set eyes on a woman at eleven in the morning and by eleven that same night had their future together all mapped out?

But *he* had. There was no question in his mind that she was the woman he was going to marry. He wanted to make lots of babies with her and grow into old age with her by his side, but she'd think he was a lunatic if he even hinted at such things before they got to know each other a little better.

He'd never met anyone before who'd made his heart go all funny and his breath dry up in his throat. He'd always wanted to find his one true love, but now that he had, he feared that the very intensity of his wanting might make him crazy. He wanted to sit with her and hold her hands and look into her eyes and then maybe kiss her.

Hell, who was he kidding? He wanted to marry her and start the honeymoon tonight.

He'd almost been to the point where he could put his hat back on his head where it belonged, but thoughts of a honeymoon with Zoe Smith compelled him to keep the Stetson where it was until he reached the jail.

Three

Every time the dream came, all the same emotions surged to the fore, exactly as if it were happening again for the first time.

The evening that had ended in disaster started out promisingly enough, with a kiss good-bye from her husband as he left to attend yet another political meeting. Zenobia had retired to an upstairs sitting room to read a romantic novel. Eben would have made sport of her if he had seen her reading Edward Bulwer-Lytton's *The Last Days of Pompeii*, so she seized on the time alone to enjoy it.

It wasn't until the fire burned low and no servant appeared to relay the coal in the grate that Zenobia rang the bell. It had been very quiet all evening. It usually was when Eben went out, but that night it had been exceptionally quiet. When Zenobia went in search of a servant when none responded to the bell, she discovered why: she was alone in the house.

She remembered thinking how curious it was that Eben should have given all the servants the evening off. Normally he never concerned himself with household arrangements, beyond mentioning when he considered the bill for food belowstairs excessive, or when his three-minute egg was runny. At such times, he would remind her that the running of the household was her primary duty and inquire why she could not make a better job of it.

So it had struck her as very odd that he had given the servants time off without at least consulting her. Even on the Fourth of July when the whole staff customarily had off, the butler had always remained if either the master or mistress was at home, but now even Sidcup was gone.

For Sidcup to have left without bidding her good evening or asking if there was anything else she required before he went seemed out of character for him. Sidcup was not so much older than she, but he seemed to have been born with a permanent mantle of dignity firmly in place. If he had gone out, it could only be because he had been given explicit orders to leave, which was how Zenobia came to the conclusion that Eben must have told the staff to take the night off, for she certainly hadn't and no one else had the authority to do so.

Zenobia went upstairs and added more coal to the grate herself, after first checking that the doors and windows on the ground floor were secure. It was unusual for her to be all alone, and yet she found the prospect of being alone with Eben when he came home appealing, for she so rarely had him entirely to herself. Even when he dined at home, the table was likely to be filled with friends and political supporters.

Eben had made no secret of the fact that if his father-in-law would only free him from the day-to-day drudgery of running a locomotive works, he would fling himself into politics full time. He had tried many times to persuade Barnabus Strouss that having a son-in-law elected to high office would benefit the business more effectively than tying him to a desk.

But Barnabus Strouss could not be moved. He wanted an heir to his empire before he excused Eben from learning the business. Without one, he would not endorse Eben for office nor finance the campaign it would take to make him a congressman, on the grounds, as he put it rather indelicately, that Eben would then be absent from the marital bed even more than he already was. Barnabus Strouss knew the value of his name, and knew also that the smell of his money could envelop Eben in a sweet perfume that would attract more supporters and build bridges to those already in power. There was a time for subtlety and a time for bluntness, and on this issue, he chose bluntness. His price, he said, was a grandson, to whom he could teach the business. Only when he had a grandson would he release Eben from servitude to Mammon so that he might fulfill his true destiny.

And Barnabus Strouss was a man used to getting what he wanted. He had kept Zenobia on the shelf for many years past her coming out, waiting for just the right man for her. It wasn't that many men hadn't courted her before Eben—they had. Plain and plump she might be, but her father's wealth made her irresistibly attractive to certain men.

Eben Sinclair had quite clearly been everything her father could want for her, a graduate of Harvard College from a fine, old Boston family, with the kind of social credentials that even the Strouss family could not claim. As for Zenobia, she had watched Eben at a cotillion held to raise money for the boys in blue during the war, watched him and held her breath as he made his way around the room, being introduced and feted, and why not? In the dress uniform of a captain in the 1st Massachusetts Cavalry, he dazzled everyone.

To watch him was to dream. She saw a look on the face of every unattached woman in the ballroom that said they were all thinking what it might be like to claim him for their own. Zenobia didn't dare let herself think what it would be like, not even after he raised her hand to his lips when they were introduced and invited her to join him in a schottish, not even after he came to call the following week, and not even when he began writing to her regularly when his orders took him elsewhere.

Not until he had paid court to her for a whole year, mainly from a distance owing to the war, did he approach her father to ask for her hand. Then and only then did Zenobia allow herself to contemplate the bliss that could be hers if only she were Mrs. Ebenezer Sinclair. It was no hardship, therefore, when her mother deemed it advisable that Zenobia and Eben marry immediately.

No one could say in 1864 that the war was going well and would soon end. Indeed, in July things looked very grim indeed, when Confederate troops entered the District of Columbia and all but captured Washington. Barnabus Strouss protested that his daughter might be a bride and then a widow in quick succession but his wife made clear that for a woman of Zenobia's age, it was better to have been married, even if only for a day, than never to have been married at all.

They married, spent two nights in a house lent to them as a substitute for the luxury suite they would otherwise have occupied on a honeymoon cruise to Europe, and then Eben was gone again. It seemed to Zenobia as if she'd held her breath for a whole year as the tide of the war turned and Union troops pressed farther and farther south, always with the cavalry in the forefront, until matters came to a head at Appomattox and Eben emerged unscathed. Except for one brief bout of fever that caused her no end of anxiety, he had made it through the war hale and hearty, unlike the many hundreds of thousands of men who succumbed to wounds and disease. She had been the happiest woman in the world when he walked back into the magnificent house her father had built for them during the last year of the war.

Eben seemed changed when he returned, though, somehow hardened, less inclined to indulge her passion for parlor games, no longer willing to sing a song at an evening musicale. There was less fun and tomfoolery in him, qualities she had loved during their courtship. Zenobia preferred to think that he had matured under the stress of combat, become more a man than a boy, but the truth was that she would have preferred to have the old Eben back rather than this new sobersides.

Eben began carefully crafting a home life and a social life that served the image he wished to project. Zenobia marveled that this magnetically handsome man who cast a spell over men and women alike was hers to claim when each day ended. She was as awed as anyone by his brilliance, as charmed and flattered by his attention and his conversation, but as he gained in stature and power, something seemed to go out of their marriage.

He needed a wife, a charming and pliant wife to take to

public functions and to private parties, and Zenobia was happy to fill that role, but it seemed that they had less and less time alone. Eben was always busy, his appointment book filled with commitments. There was only one respect in which he absolutely needed her, and that was to bear him a son.

Zenobia had done her best to comply, but no child had come despite his almost nightly visits to her bed. The physical side of their relationship, which he approached with a good deal of enthusiasm in the beginning, turned cool. He had never spent much time addressing her pleasure, but as time went by, he merely lifted her nightgown and spread her legs. Zenobia felt like a piece of real estate that he inhabited briefly at night. Her mother had made plain that sex was a man's pleasure but a woman's duty, and Zenobia had to concede that her mother had been right.

A year went by, then two, then three, and still there was no child. It was all Eben asked of her in exchange for allowing her to live in his wonderful shadow—to see his extraordinary face opposite her at the supper table, to entertain his bright and influential friends, and to receive the fruits of his supple intellect—and she had failed him. She felt barren, less than a woman and a wife should be. It created an emptiness in her life and in their marriage that she didn't know how to fill.

But she remained hopeful that she would conceive before too much more time passed, and she kept busy with the house and entertaining and social events. She managed to create a veneer of happiness over the core of emptiness within, and she tried hard not to fault Eben for focusing on his career. He was, after all, exactly the sort of man her father was, for in his single-minded devotion to his goals, Eben was a match for Barnabus Strouss.

Such were the circumstances of her life leading up to that fateful night, when everything she had held dear came tumbling down. She had fallen once again under the spell of Edward Bulwer-Lytton's book when she heard the key in the latch of the front door. She set her book aside immediately. Eben was home and she meant to make the most of their time alone. She went to the landing and brushed the wrinkles out of her dress and patted her hair smooth while waiting for him to appear.

But the figure that emerged from the second set of doors in the front entryway was not Eben's.

"Stephen?" Zenobia's happiness slipped away. She had never been able to bring herself to like her husband's best friend.

"Good evening, Zenobia. How lovely you look."

It was the sort of obviously insincere comment that gave her a mistrust of Stephen. She knew she didn't look lovely. She never looked lovely, merely passable. She tried to appear welcoming in spite of her feelings. Stephen had gone to Harvard with Eben, so his relationship with her husband went back further than hers. Unlike many brides, she had not insisted that Eben give up his friends from before his marriage and form new friendships as part of a married couple. She doubted Eben would have complied in any case, at least where Stephen was concerned.

"Thank you, Stephen. Have you come home with Eben? I didn't hear the carriage."

Stephen grinned up at her, carelessly laying aside his overcoat and hat on a side chair. "No, I'm quite alone."

"I see." Zenobia felt her poise slipping. It was almost ten o'clock, not late by society standards. Eben might not be in for another hour or two and she didn't feel like entertaining Stephen for that length of time. In fact, something in his expression made her feel like turning and running. She chided herself for the impulse. Stephen might be a womanizer and ride on his friend's coattails but he had never menaced her. The worst he had done was to pay her overly fulsome compliments, and stare at her with something a little in excess of platonic love. Most women would not have considered it a problem, since Stephen was as handsome in his own way as Eben was in his.

Stephen crossed the black-and-white marble floor and rested one hand on the banister below. "Aren't you going to offer me a drink?"

Zenobia felt sure by the glassy look in his eyes that Stephen had already had too much to drink for one evening. "Eben gave the servants the evening off, but if you would care to serve yourself, you know where everything is."

Her impulse to keep distance between herself and Stephen was growing stronger. Something in his manner alarmed her as it never had before.

"Actually, I haven't really come to socialize," he said. "Or rather, I have, but in a special way. Eben needs for you to have a baby so he can get on with his life and I am here to help him solve his problem."

"I don't believe that's any concern of yours," Zenobia responded coldly.

"But of course it is. Eben is my friend. He does what he can to help me, I do what I can to help him, and since I seem to be forever getting my mistresses with child, it naturally occurred to both of us that I might do the same for you. Of course, Eben will continue to try, too. We shall both do our utmost until success is achieved. If not me, then him. If not him, then me, and you the charming beneficiary of all our efforts."

Zenobia clasped her hands together to still the nervous trembling that had begun. Stephen must be much more drunk than he appeared to be. "Get out, now!"

Stephen cocked his head to one side.

"You love Eben, don't you?" he asked.

"Yes, of course I do." Her voice shook with fear.

"Do this for him then," Stephen said, a sly smile on his face.

"Eben would never agree to such a foul plan!"

"We were a bit the worse for drink when the idea first arose, but he endorsed the idea wholeheartedly. In fact, I believe it originated with him."

"He was joking then," Zenobia said sharply, "and it was in very poor taste. The very idea is obscene! I am in no position to censor your conversations when you are both drunk, but I do not deserve to have such filth repeated to my face. Get out of my house!"

But Stephen refused to be daunted. "If he was joking, why did he send the servants away tonight? Was he drunk then? He wasn't drunk when I saw him at the club just now. He's waiting, Zenobia, waiting for us to make a baby."

Stephen let out a soft laugh and began climbing the stairs.

Oh, God, oh, God, oh, God. How fast could she run? She could see the color of Stephen's eyes. They were a neutral, fathomless gray, the eyes of a predator. Zenobia began sliding backward on the landing, feeling for the edge of the step behind her.

But Stephen had read her intention in her eyes. He swiftly mounted the remaining steps and seized her wrist.

"Let me go!" She spun away and banged her hip into the railing, thrashing at him with closed fists. Stephen laughed, as if he found her resistance amusing.

"What a tigress! Who would have thought it?"

He turned her so that she was facing him and pulled her close. He grasped her face and tried to kiss her, a mocking smile on his lips. Zenobia turned her head away violently and Stephen laughed.

"Well, there's no need for kissing if you don't wish it," he said, grinning. His words came in uneven little spurts as he wrestled with her. "I can do what I came here to do without kissing you."

Zenobia was nearly sobbing with impotent fury. Nothing she did seemed to dislodge him. "Take your hands off me!" she raged.

"Not until I'm through," he replied, and held her effortlessly with one hand as he pulled at the neckline of her dress with the other.

Zenobia clawed and kicked at him in panic. The force of it caught Stephen off guard and he staggered backward on the landing. Beyond his shoulder, in a blur, Zenobia saw the black and white of the floor below. In desperation, she raised her free hand and raked her nails across his cheek.

"Ow! Little bitch!" Stephen lifted his arm to strike her and lost his balance.

Zenobia saw it as her last chance for escape. She pushed at him with maniacal strength and Stephen's foot slipped off the edge of the landing. He toppled out into open air, the rage on his face transforming to naked astonishment. His eyes widened with shock as he flailed at empty air. Time slowed to a crawl. It seemed to take minutes rather than seconds for him to reach the hall below, bouncing off the steps, caroming between the wall and the handrail. He finally hit the floor and his head snapped back against the marble floor with an awful sound.

The hall fell silent.

Zenobia stared at Stephen's body splayed across her foyer floor, at the oddly vacant expression on his face. From the excruciatingly sharp angle of his head to his neck, she knew that he would never rise again. She stood there, unable to react, until the clock began to strike ten. First the quarter, then the half, then the three-quarter hour, and finally the chimes, ten of them. Each sounded louder, more sonorous than the last, beating the message into her head—*Stephen is dead, Stephen is dead, Stephen is dead* . . .

Zenobia came awake abruptly. She was sweating and trembling, her heart hitting her breastbone hard and fast. An oppressive dread pushed all her limbs down into the bed. She always awoke in this state from the dream.

Far away, down the street, she could hear, just faintly, the piano at the Red Dog, and out in the street, the sound of men's loud, harsh laughter. Tears joined the sheen of perspiration on her face and neck. Oh, God, it would never be over. Stephen would live forever in her dreams. She was condemned to kill him over and over and over, and to look down on his lifeless body.

She had fled that night with only a small bag filled with her jewelry wrapped in underclothes.

No one would believe the truth. No one would ever believe that Stephen had come to her and said those vile things. And what husband in his right mind would collude in sharing his wife with another man? *She* didn't believe it and she had been there and heard every word. People would say there had been an affair, that she must have let Stephen into the house and then they'd had a lover's quarrel.

She didn't dare turn to her parents. They thought Eben a paragon. They would never believe that he had arranged for his best friend to rape her! Most likely, it would be more logical to believe that *she* had tried to seduce *Stephen* and killed him in a fit of pique for rejecting her.

And even if she could have made her parents believe her, could their wealth have protected her from being tried for murder? The mere thought terrified her. Win, lose, or draw, the scandal would rip them all apart before it was over. Even if she took the enormous risk of remaining and was acquitted, her marriage would be in shambles, she would be talked about by high and low alike with varying degrees of pity and contempt, and society would never open its doors to her again.

And so she had fled, unable to face the shame and humiliation. But worse than anything else was the prospect that she might end up in prison or even forfeit her life for having defended herself against rape.

Zenobia finally found the strength to sit up in the rickety, uneven bed. She shook all over. Sleep would not come again for hours. She hated the dream, but no amount of wishing things were otherwise could ever change the outcome of it. She blotted herself dry with the coarse linen sheet and felt her way across the room, following the trail of moonlight on the floor. The window was permanently stuck halfway up so she had fresh air whether she wanted it or not.

She knelt and leaned her chin on the windowsill, letting the night air dry her tears. Beyond the edge of town, the desert landscape looked chilly and still in the moonlight, but just along down Main Street where all the saloons stood, life boiled over, full of vigor and heat. Zenobia rested her chin on her hands to protect it from the splintery windowsill. Tired and feeling more alone than she ever had in her life, she let the cool breeze pass over her skin.

For a time after fleeing Philadelphia, she had cried bitter tears for Eben and for what she, in her besotted naiveté, had thought they were to each other. She'd cried over him as if he were dead, though the truth was that the man she'd thought he was had never existed. That man had existed only in her mind, but she mourned him nonetheless, and wondered how the other Eben, the real Eben, could have thought so little of her that he would send his best friend to rape her just to satisfy his father-in-law's wish for a grandson.

And then her sadness had gradually been replaced by a terrible hatred. Eben *had* given the servants the night off. She knew deep inside that Stephen had told the truth, that *Eben* had concocted the scheme. It was so like Eben—the *real* Eben—to manipulate those around him to his own ends. She became convinced that he'd never loved her at all, but had only married her out of ruthless self-interest. Zenobia was afraid she might shatter into a thousand tiny pieces if she thought about it too much.

Still shivering in the cool night air of the desert, she wiped away a lingering tear and forcibly turned her mind away from anymore useless dwelling on the past.

Tomorrow she would apply herself to finding a better bed. This awful torture rack would give Saint Peter nightmares and she needed no extra help in that direction. What she needed was a bed that would allow her to relax into deep and dreamless slumber.

And just as important, she'd go buy three new shirts for Sheriff Daniel Whittaker and get the man who personified the law in Gila City out of her life.

Zenobia dressed the next morning and did her hair. She avoided looking at herself in the broken piece of looking glass she kept propped atop the empty packing crates that served as her dresser. She had no desire to look at the bruise on her face, but when it came time to leave, she made herself check to see how bad it was. It was very bad. She, who had never had a mark on her before, was appalled by the angry purple and red skin around her eye and the puffed-up lid.

Zenobia jammed her hat on her head and pulled down the veil. Thank God she'd worn a hat with a heavy veil to conceal her identity when she fled Philadelphia. It would suit the current situation well. Pulling on her gloves, she tucked in runaway strands of hair frizzed by the constantly boiling cauldron. She did her best to look respectable, for she had some important calls to make today.

Buying three new shirts for Daniel Whittaker was only the first of them. Second, she would deliver the shirts to him and maintain an air of calm competence as she did so. Third, and here she took considerable pride in the solution she had arrived at, she would call on Miss Teresa, last name unknown, at the Red Dog Saloon, for advice on where to buy a bed.

It had come to her as she dressed. It stood to reason that if one wanted a comfortable bed, the best person to advise one on where to get such an article was someone accustomed to spending a great deal of time in bed—ergo Miss Teresa, the same discriminating individual who'd ordered a bathing tub. The fact that she even knew the name of a woman who sold her body for a living still sent shock waves through Zenobia.

Back home she'd have crossed the street to avoid women of the sort who entertained men upstairs at the Red Dog, but her respect for women who worked for a living was growing by leaps and bounds. To be able to make enough money to support oneself had come to seem to Zenobia like the highest good on the planet. Coming in an extremely close second was getting a decent night's sleep.

Gila City presented its usual hot, dusty face to her as she made her way awkwardly down Main Street. Piles of planks, missing boards in the walkway, walkways missing altogether in front of some buildings, and other sundry obstacles put themselves in her way but she kept on, doggedly ignoring the butterflies in her stomach as she passed the jail. She would cross *that* bridge when she came to it.

Clarence Trilby hurried around the counter to greet her when she walked into his store, apparently sure it was her despite the heavy veil. She supposed she was the only woman in Gila City who arose before noon, so by process of elimination, it must be her.

"Mornin', Miss Smith."

"Good morning, Mr. Trilby. I require three white gentlemen's shirts, please."

"What size, ma'am?"

Zenobia blinked. Why did Clarence Trilby always ask her questions she didn't know the answers to? Every man of her acquaintance had always had his shirts tailor-made, so it wasn't at all clear to her in what sizes they might come. "What are the choices?" she asked as blithely as she could, glancing toward a barrel of salt pork as if she were already contemplating other, more important purchases.

Clarence Trilby rubbed his chin reflectively. "Well, I suppose you might say small—they'd be all right for a boy, too—and medium and large."

Zenobia pictured Daniel Whittaker. Long-bodied, narrow through the waist, and lean in the hips and seat. He looked like a man who could stand to eat a lot more than he did, but then, that fact was neither here nor there at the moment. She started over again. Wide-shouldered, at least seven or eight inches taller than herself. Beyond a certain point it became difficult for her to say just how much taller someone else was. All she knew was that it gave her a crick in the neck to look up at Daniel Whittaker. That probably meant he was a good six foot.

"Large," she said decisively.

"I expect you'll be wanting the regular quality?" Clarence Trilby said hopefully.

Oh, saints alive! It never failed that he offered her choices she had no clue about. For a hodge-podge sort of place,

Clarence Trilby's general store certainly had a lot of merchandise, and a great deal more than she knew how to choose between intelligently.

"Cotton?" she guessed. That, too, was likely wrong.

"Oh, no, ma'am!" Clarence Trilby looked truly shocked. "I haven't had any cotton shirts in stock since the first year of the war. Even a miner who's struck it rich wouldn't want to pay what it costs for cotton shirts these days!"

No, of course not. Silly her. Glad for the veil that hid her flaming cheeks, Zenobia tried again. "Well, your usual, of course. That's what I meant to say."

"Well, that's a good decision, ma'am. Some of the fellows tries to get by with the shirts I keep for the undertaker, but they're always sorry they did. They're cheap, ma'am, cheap and nasty, but then they ain't made for the living, if you see what I mean."

She certainly did. Just the thought of buying a shirt for a dead man sent a chill through Zenobia. As Clarence Trilby wrapped the shirts, she congratulated herself. They looked as white as white could be, and were folded with precision. *That* would convince Daniel Whittaker she knew her business!

When Zenobia came within a few feet of the jail, she paused, some of her confidence evaporating. Sheriff Whittaker had a way of looking at her, as if he wanted to know a whole lot more about her, that took the starch right out of her backbone.

"Pardon me, ma'am."

Zenobia jumped. A man stood in front of her, hat in hand. "Yes?"

The man looked down at the ground, turning his hat by its brim. "Well, ma'am, it's just that I was wondering, meaning no disrespect at all, ma'am, if you would mind lifting your veil and letting me see your face." He looked up again, regarding her with an earnest look. He looked to have just had a shave and a haircut after some period of abstinence from same, for the newly uncovered skin was a pasty white in contrast to his deeply tanned neck.

"Certainly not!" Zenobia said. "You are very rude to even suggest such a thing."

"Oh, I know that, ma'am, truly I do," the man said quickly, "only it's been so long since I seen a lady, I, well . . . I decided to ask anyway. Just for a minute, ma'am, please?"

Zenobia could see that although he towered over her, the man was hardly more than a boy. He looked a decent type, the sort of boy she had seen time and again during the war, legions of them marching off proudly in formation in flaring wool greatcoats, never to return. If not for her eye, she might simply have lifted her veil. "I'm sorry," she said, softening her tone, "but I couldn't possibly. Now, good day to you."

"I'd pay you, ma'am!" he said, as she began to go around him. "Five dollars!"

The crass suggestion that he pay her when she had been thinking kindly, altruistic thoughts about him ruffled Zenobia. She turned. "I say to you plainly that I cannot! Would you expect your mother or sister to reveal their faces to a strange man on a public street?"

A slow flush crept up the man's neck. "I reckon they'd do it, ma'am, if they thought the fellow was good-hearted and meant no harm by it."

Zenobia fought her growing irritation. "You said you wished to see a decent woman. Well, I assure you, no decent woman goes about displaying herself to strange men for money, so you cannot hope to see one employing this method! Now please, go away and leave me alone."

"What seems to be the problem?" said a voice behind her.

Zenobia's heart sank. "Why, nothing at all, Sheriff Whittaker." She turned to face him and forced an unconcerned smile before she remembered he wouldn't even be able to see it because of her veil.

He shoved his hat up his forehead. "How do, Tommy," he said to the young man. "You just get into town?"

The man nodded. "This morning."

"Came in for some good times, did you?"

Tommy nodded, his slicked-back, freshly combed hair gleaming in the sunlight. "Creek's been running good—I got money to spend."

"Well, I expect you'll have no trouble finding a good time provided you look in the right places. As for this lady showing you her face, I expect if she wanted strange men to see her face, she wouldn't be wearing a veil. Isn't that right, Miss Smith?"

Zenobia nodded gratefully.

"Did I hear you say you had five dollars to spare?" Daniel said. "Because there's some new girls up at Fairchild's Dance Hall that'll give you considerably more than a look at them for five dollars. Begging your pardon, ma'am!" he said quickly to Zenobia. "Fine dancers, I tell you, fine, and happy to waltz or polka with a fellow for two bits."

"You don't say!" Tommy replied, looking distinctly interested.

"See if you can spot a little gal named Lucy," Daniel suggested. "She's new to taxi dancing and she'll appreciate a fellow who's gone and gotten himself all cleaned up and shaved for her."

"Well, thank you, thank you very much, Sheriff, and my apologies, ma'am, if I caused any offense. Good day to you!" Tommy hurried off down the street, forgetting to put his hat back on in his rush.

"He didn't mean you any harm," Daniel Whittaker said quietly as they watched him go. "Tommy Daly is a nice fellow. In fact, if you ever found yourself in real trouble, he'd be the first one to come to your aid."

"Do you know absolutely everyone in this town?" Zenobia inquired.

"Well, not actually, no, but those I don't know, I usually get around to knowing soon enough."

"Well," she said, pushing her package at him, "here are your shirts."

"That was awful fast. I didn't reckon to get them back for a while."

"Special service for the sheriff," she said. "I suspected you must need them soon and were just too polite to say so, but I want you to know I won't be able to take in any more washing for you. I'm just too busy." *There! She'd said it.*

He didn't appear to take her assertion to heart, merely pulling the wrapping back on the package and inspecting one corner of an exposed shirt. "No problem getting them clean, I see." He sniffed. "Smell fresh again, too, almost like new."

Zenobia coughed uneasily. "I'm glad you're pleased, Sheriff, and now if you'll excuse me, I'm in a hurry." Zenobia took off like a shot.

"Miss Smith!"

"Yes?" she said, reluctantly turning back to face him.

"I didn't pay you," he said, smiling that devastating lopsided smile of his. "How much do I owe you?"

"Oh!" And just when she thought she'd made good her escape! But what was she to charge? She'd never reached this moment in a laundress's career before. Inspiration struck. "Two bits," she declared.

"Won't you step inside for a minute?" he said with a sweep of his arm toward the jailhouse door. "I'll get the money for you."

Zenobia slowly retraced her steps, feeling utterly, utterly doomed. Sheriff Whittaker ushered her in and sat down behind a plain desk. He withdrew a poke from a drawer.

Zenobia tried not to look around—her imagination needed no help from reality—but she couldn't help noticing the sturdy-looking cells on the left-hand wall. They had heavy bars, absurdly huge locks on the doors, nasty-looking shackles attached to the walls, and plank shelves with thin gray blankets on them. If Sheriff Whittaker *did* know the truth about her, it was only a matter of time before she was locked up in one of them.

"I assume gold dust *is* okay?" Sheriff Whittaker was saying.

"Oh . . . yes!"

He held out the poke in one sun-browned hand. "Why don't you just take a full pinch? I'm sure I owe you extra for the fast service."

Zenobia stared at the poke in horror. The fact that she'd never done this before seemed painfully obvious. Daniel Whittaker waited, the corners of his mouth lifted and the gray-green eyes amused. She hastily dipped her fingers in and withdrew a pinch, but clumsily, so that a small cascade of gold flecks fluttered toward the floor.

"Oh," Zenobia said, horribly embarrassed, "I'm terribly sorry."

"Never mind," he said. "Now how about letting me give you that cup of jailhouse coffee I offered you last night?"

"Oh, I can't! I'm already late for—"

He grinned. "The first thing easterners have to learn when they come out West, Miss Smith, is that we never rush around like time was money."

Zenobia felt the blood drain from her cheeks. He knew she was from the East! She sat down abruptly.

"That's more like it," he said, and handed her a cup of coffee.

Zenobia accepted the cup, still holding the gold dust between her fingers since she had nothing to put it in. Daniel Whittaker settled back against his desk, half leaning, half sitting. His faded blue linsey-woolsey pants hugged him close, outlining lean hips and substantial leg muscles. The mean-looking blue metal pistol lurked right in her line of vision, too. Zenobia clutched the hot tin cup, forgetting to drink.

"Well," she said brightly, "this has been very nice, but I really must be getting on about my—"

"You haven't tasted it," he said, nodding toward the cup. Zenobia felt herself immobilized by that look. The man had a way of filling up a room that made it hard to concentrate on anything but him. "Here, why don't you just borrow my handkerchief so's you'll have some place to keep that gold dust?"

Forced to surrender her gold dust into his immaculate white hanky, Zenobia felt even more foolish. "Thank you," she muttered as graciously as she could, and stuffed the hanky into her reticule. She lifted her veil just high enough to take a cursory sip of the coffee. "Mmmm. Delicious! I must get your recipe sometime." Zenobia stood up quickly and plonked the still-full cup down on the desk. "It's time I was going."

"I hope you'll pardon my saying so, Miss Smith, but you seem a mite jumpy today. You didn't have anymore trouble after I left last night, did you?"

Zenobia shook her head vehemently. She didn't want him to think he should check up on her every night. "None at all!"

"Well, I sure hope that bruise will be all better soon. I count it a sin for you to have to go around with that veil and deprive all us men a glimpse of those beautiful eyes."

Zenobia felt faintly dizzy. The man was sincerely complimenting her—not because her father had a fortune that he'd like to get his hands on, but because he actually found her attractive! The warmth of his gaze and the smile in his eyes enthralled her. Zenobia swayed a little.

"Miss Smith! Are you all right?"

Suddenly he was there with one long, strong arm wrapped around her shoulder and the other bracing her elbow. Zenobia gazed up through her veil into the gray-green eyes, her heart melting. She almost let herself be folded against his chest but instead found the strength to lay a gloved hand on his forearm.

"I . . . I'm fine," she said tremulously. She felt as limp as the first time she'd ever been kissed. "I don't know what came over me."

"Well, ma'am," he said with a grin, "I'd like to think that I have that effect on you, but I'm not vain enough to believe a woman like you would go all weak in the knees over a fellow like me."

Shameless, that's what he was. Shameless and charming. Zenobia wished with all her might that she was unmarried and that he was a suitor and not a sheriff. What an amazing feeling it was to have a man flirt with her and flatter her because he liked her for herself!

"Sheriff, you know perfectly well that you are handsome and kind and just exactly the sort of man who could make a girl lose her head. You can't wonder at my feeling a bit faint over such a fulsome compliment as you've just paid me."

"Why, Miss Smith, if you didn't have that veil on, I believe I'd kiss you." Daniel Whittaker's grin deepened. Zenobia swayed toward him, wishing she dared give him some encouragement—but of course, she *didn't* dare. He *wasn't* a suitor—he was the sheriff, a fact forgotten at the peril of her soul, and a life she felt inclined to keep.

"That would be a very forward and *most* improper thing to do," she said a little breathlessly, "even for a man from the West." Oh, he was the handsomest thing, especially up close like this!

"Well, Miss Smith, in a new place, a man's got to make up the rules as he goes along. I reckon when a fellow tells a pretty girl he's going to kiss her and she doesn't say he'd better not, he'd better just get on with it before she—"

Suddenly there were loud, ringing footsteps on the plank sidewalk outside. A robust string of curse words accompanied them.

Zenobia, who had been staring in dewy-eyed fascination at Sheriff Daniel Whittaker as he started to lift her veil, got hold of herself sufficiently to step quickly out of his embrace. Walter Connolly came through the door in a swirl of dust.

"Well, Daniel," he announced, "as if we didn't already have enough men who pick a fight just because they've been beat at cards, now we got us a Chinaman and someone's gone and beat him half silly 'cause they didn't like how he looked!"

Four

Daniel accepted that being sheriff meant that duty could and sometimes did claim his every waking moment, but Walter's interruption nettled him in a major way just the same. It forced him to turn his attention away from what was most important to him. He knew when a woman wanted to be kissed and he knew when one didn't, and despite the gray veil obscuring Miss Zoe Smith's face, he just knew her expression had been one of glad acceptance as he bent to kiss her.

Damn! He'd been on the verge of lifting that veil when Walter interrupted them, and not only had he been deprived of a kiss, he'd also missed a chance to find out a few more things about her.

The faint English accent had made him think yesterday that she might actually be English, but their meeting today had modified his opinion. Seeing her dressed for the street, with her exquisitely correct posture and manners, he'd concluded that she probably just hailed from back East where such accents were easily come by. But was she a member of a good family that naturally spoke with such an accent or merely a servant to one?

He supposed it was just possible she'd been a servant, but he didn't think so. Something about the way she held her head, the chin at a certain angle, whispered to him of someone a mistress, not a servant. And if she *had* been a servant, she certainly hadn't been a laundress, more like a lady's maid. It gave Daniel a chuckle to think of the shirts she'd brought him. Brand new, and not even the same type he'd taken to her. As a practitioner of deception, she had a lot to learn. The obvious attempt to dupe him only strengthened the already plausible reasons he had for pursuing an acquaintance with her—personally *and* professionally.

On a personal level, he needed no excuses. He was in love. He'd lain awake the night before thinking up names for their children. He had written down ten this morning, five for boys and five for girls.

But the questions in his mind, the practical ones, had to be sorted out apart from the rich fantasy life he'd been leading. Why hadn't she taken off her veil when she came into the jail? After all, he'd seen the worst of her black eye the previous night. Was there more damage? Maybe she had a lover slipping in the back door, a man who took advantage of her size to push her around. The thought of some other man having a claim on Zoe Smith just about killed Daniel. If she was a little red-eyed from crying today, he'd sure like to know about it so he could take care of the fellow who was treating her badly and send him on his way.

She sure was flighty around him. It seemed certain that there was *something* about herself she'd rather he not know. She'd taken advantage of his momentary distraction when Walter walked in to pull away from him, and it occurred to him that she had been awful anxious to get rid of him the night before. Speediness didn't arise naturally in him, so it always forced itself on his awareness when others hurried for no good reason he could see.

But there'd been no redeeming the moment when haste took hold of her after Walter walked in. Daniel had had to walk her to the door and then he'd whispered, for her ears alone, that he meant to finish what he'd started the very first chance he got.

She had looked down, the soft gauze of her veil gathering up on her shoulders. "I don't think that would be a good idea," she whispered back. "After all, I'm—I'm . . . and . . . you're . . . well, you're . . ." And then she'd stopped, gathered herself up, and in a strong, clear voice, wished him a brisk good morning before flying out the door.

He let Walter lead the way to the north side of town where they found the Chinaman right where Walter had left him, still slumped in an alley behind Dolly's Arcade. Along the way, Walter told him what he'd been able to piece together about the Chinaman.

He'd been summarily relieved of his claim and Daniel didn't even have to ask why; he must have started to sieve out significant amounts of gold. There were fellows who didn't take kindly to another man's luck. If it befell a foreigner, especially a Chinaman, it struck the dishonest and the disgruntled as even more of a personal affront.

The Chinaman flinched when Daniel's shadow fell over him. Seldom had Daniel seen a sorrier sight. Both the man's eyes were swollen shut, one lip and both eyebrows were split open, and his clothes were half torn away.

Daniel hunkered down beside him. "What's your name, son?" he asked.

It took a minute for the man to conjure up enough spit to speak.

"Wing Loo . . . and I am not your son."

The words emerged slow and distinct from between the swollen lips. Bits of dried blood flaked downward. Despite his condition, the Chinaman had a dignity about him. Well, that was all to the good, thought Daniel—he was going to need it. In this town, as well as in the placer camps and on the railroads, a man who buckled when bullied could look for plenty more bullying. Judging by the look of him, though, Wing Loo had attracted more bullies at one time than a man could possibly stand up to without losing an untoward quantity of blood.

Hopeful that Wing Loo's English extended to more than just the few words he'd already spoken, Daniel said, "I'm the sheriff of Gila City, Daniel Whittaker by name. I think we'd better take you on down to the jailhouse."

"No jail." Wing Loo turned his face in the direction of

Daniel's voice in a fair imitation of a man who could actually see what he was looking at. "Not do anything wrong."

"No," Daniel admitted, "never said you did, but no one's going to rent you a room and you need somewhere to bunk down while you heal. Besides, whoever did this to you will think twice before they finish off the job if you're staying at the jailhouse."

Wing Loo appeared to think it over. "Yes. Thank you. I go."

Well, thought Daniel, that had been reasonably easy. Wing Loo spoke better English than most drunks and possessed considerably more sense. Now to get him out of harm's way. Wing Loo was solid—thick limbed and well muscled, with big wrist bones and a big, heavy skull, which was probably what had saved his life.

"Give me a hand getting him up, Walter," Daniel said, wrapping an arm around Wing Loo.

"Now up you go, Wing Woo, nice and slow."

Walter looped his arm around the Chinaman. As they started slowly down the alley, Walter said, "Hey, this Chinee, he's not doin' so bad."

Wing Loo *was* holding up surprisingly well, taking most of his own weight, though he shook noticeably. They came to the corner of the first main thoroughfare, right where the bouncer for Dolly's Arcade sat in a chair watching the street for signs of trouble.

"Where do you hail from, Mr. Loo?" Daniel said conversationally as several men eyed them suspiciously. Dolly's attracted a rough crowd, even in the daytime, and if anyone suspected they were helping a Chinaman, it would attract more trouble. A little casual conversation might mask what was going on.

"Kwangtung Province," the Chinaman said, "and beg pardon, but if you say 'mister' me, you say Mr. Wing, not Mr. Loo, same as for you Mr. Whittaker, not Mr. Daniel."

Daniel suppressed a grin. "Is that so?" For a man who was blind for all intents and purposes and being led by someone he didn't know from Adam through hostile territory, the man had backbone. "Well, I'll just keep that in mind," Daniel replied.

"If Wing's your last name, whyn't you say it last?" Walter asked irritably.

"Is not the way . . . in China."

He sounded breathless, the air forcing its way in and out through battered nostrils. Daniel nodded to a man peering at Wing Loo.

"Got bucked off his horse," Daniel said. "Big old chestnut. Spread the word, won't you, to bring it over to the jailhouse if anyone sees it running loose?"

The man backed off, bloodshot eyes glaring, and let out a discordant belch. Daniel interpreted it as a sign that the man would rather not assist an officer of the law.

"Thank you kindly," he said. "Appreciate it."

Waving a big filthy hand at the others who'd followed him out of Dolly's to see what the sheriff was up to, the man said, "Ah, drover got his face busted up by a horse is all."

It wasn't nearly as interesting as someone getting arrested for shooting someone, or beat up for cheating at dice. The ragged assembly muttered the story from one to the next and soon lost interest, fading back into the arcade and another dusty saloon where the swinging door hung by one hinge. Owing to the condition of his face and the absence of his queue—which Daniel had tactfully refrained from mentioning—Wing Loo didn't look particularly Chinese at the moment or the bluff wouldn't have worked. Daniel had a deep and abiding aversion for the habitually mean-spirited, but just at the moment he had to get Wing Loo to safety, not take on a mess of ugly-minded men.

Daniel said something inconsequential to Walter and Walter had the sense to answer back with something equally inane, lending an air of normality to their progress down the street, which discouraged any other curiosity seekers from inquiring into what was going on. They passed through another narrow, filth-strewn alley and hove into sight of the jailhouse.

"Almost there now, Mr. Wing," Daniel said cheerfully.

"Thank you most humbly."

"Where'd you learn English?" Daniel asked as they made their way down Main Street, one painful step at a time.

"On boat, with book. One sailor, he help."

"You do pretty good," Walter said, surprising Daniel. In the midst of the deputy's constant complaining, it was easy to forget that he possessed a decent heart. "Except for Whittaker. You didn't say that right at all."

Wing Loo almost smiled, the corners of his bruised mouth turning up ever so slightly. "I do better soon."

A flash of motion way up ahead caught Daniel's eye, a drab quick-moving figure making its way along the plank walkway in front of the Red Dog Saloon. The figure stopped by the stairway and darted a quick look left and right, and apparently reassured that no one was looking, mounted the steps, dove-gray veil fluttering.

Well, that was a stumper, Daniel decided. What possible business could Miss Zoe Smith have with the girls at the Red Dog?

Zenobia felt as if she'd blushed all she could blush for one day, with no more blushes left even if she should suddenly see a naked man. But she was one step closer to having a decent bed.

She'd walked into the Red Dog Saloon with her chin held high and her heart thumping. Being morning, no one was about, but the saloon had a mascot, evidently to keep an eye on things when human eyes were absent. A low gurgle from a furry throat alerted her to the dog's presence.

The big dog, which sat on the bar, had a big blunt head and solemn, wide-spaced eyes. Zoe had naively supposed that the name Red Dog stood for some type of liquor, but now she wondered if the place hadn't been named for this animal ensconced on the bar. Except for the fact that the dog had not a hint of strawberry or chestnut in its coat, it would have been a tempting explanation, but the dog was a mixture of gray and black, and its deep golden eyes shifted expressively as it watched Zoe's progress toward the bar.

A hand-lettered sign behind the bar—nailed rather thoughtlessly, Zenobia thought, into a beautiful mahogany mirror frame—announced that the Reverend Robert Johnson's topic for the forthcoming Sunday was *"Let us lay aside every weight and the sin that doth so easily beset us."* When the topic alone was so long-winded, Zenobia assumed that the sermon itself was bound to go on for hours. Zenobia cleared her throat and said a tentative hello.

Red Dog jumped down and disappeared into the back. Zenobia cleared her throat loudly a few more times but couldn't hear a sound once the clicking of the dog's nails on the wooden floor faded away. Unobserved, she stared at the pictures of naked women on the walls. Curvy big bottoms and improbably firm breasts were rendered in lush tones, all quite unadorned by so much as a drapery, their owners recumbent on divans like fruit offered up on a platter. Zenobia had never thought of herself as particularly shy or prudish but was now forced to acknowledge a streak of modesty in herself that left her cheeks hot. She fanned herself with one gloved hand, largely without effect owing to the veil. She turned and stared upward, the only vista left to her not embellished with naked females.

Sheets of tin, nearly as large as the pictures, papered the ceiling, but Zenobia cast about in vain as to what purpose they served—not to keep out the rain certainly, for a second floor topped the saloon. Even odder, each sheet bore the name of a woman.

"I see you've noticed our armor plating," said a voice. A small man with dirty red hair stood behind the bar, a wry smile on his face. Red Dog sat beside him.

"Oh! Yes, yes, I did."

"Keeps bullets from flying on through to the bedrooms when the boys get a little too high-spirited. Nailed one right beneath each bed." The man wiped his hands on a rag laying on the bar.

" 'Course now with Sheriff Whittaker in charge, we don't have nearly so many gun fights as we used to, and those we do have are mostly with small caliber weapons, derringers mainly, that a man can hide in his boot. They seldom have the power to pierce wood but we leave those up just to be safe. Can't have the girls getting shot while they're working."

"Yes, well—thank you. That was most edifying." Despite his lack of cleanliness, the man spoke with a surprisingly cultured voice, something of the schoolmaster in it and more than a little of Scotland.

"Looking for work?"

"Why, no, though it's about a job. I am seeking a Miss Teresa . . ." Zenobia waved her gloved hand helplessly. "I'm afraid I don't know her last name."

"Oh, *that* kind of work." The man's smile widened and he came around the end of the counter. He wore a union suit with pants and braces, but no shirt. Red Dog clicked after him and leapt up to the bar again. "She's upstairs." He inclined his head toward the door. "Outside and to the right. Good luck."

Blushing furiously, Zenobia decided against correcting the man's erroneous supposition. Hurrying outside, she mounted the steps. A tiny sitting room opened off the top of the landing. A vivid purple curtain divided it from the narrow corridor beyond. Zenobia knocked vigorously on the first door.

"Miss Teresa?"

"End of the hall," said a voice thick with sleep. "Alley side."

A long runner muffled her footsteps. Brightly patterned in yellow and green, it ran several inches up the wall on either side. Although it was too wide for the corridor, it wasn't quite long enough. A knotted fringe marked its end a few feet before the last door. Zenobia's last few steps echoed loudly, as if the carpet ending prematurely was a deliberate device to alert the occupant of the last room.

Zenobia knocked. "Miss Teresa?"

"Come back tonight. I'm sleeping now," said a bored but fairly awake voice.

"I do apologize. I wonder if I might just ask you a quick question."

"Room across from mine's available, house takes fifty cents on the dollar."

And just when her face had finally cooled down. "No," Zenobia said hastily, "you misunderstand. Mr. Trilby at the general store said you had ordered a nice bathing tub, and since you seem to be a discriminating person, I wondered if you might know where I could obtain a comfortable bed."

"Like I said, room across the hall is free."

"Oh, dear, this is very awkward. What I mean is, do you know someone I might hire to *make* me a bed, one that I could use in my *own* bedroom?"

Shuffling noises preceded the opening of the door. A blond woman stood there, loosely clad in a silk wrapper. Miss Teresa appeared a good deal younger than the whiskey-deep voice had suggested. She looked Zenobia up and down, frowning when she got to the veil.

"You thinking of setting up your own house?" she asked.

Zenobia feared her cheeks were going to be permanently scarlet. "No, I want a bed to sleep in alone, in my house, but not the sort of house you . . ." She took a deep breath. "Perhaps I had better start again."

"Is this going to take a long time, honey? Because if it is—well, never mind." The madam of the Red Dog bent down, took off one spool-heeled slipper and banged the floor twice. Replacing the slipper, she straightened. "Why don't you come in and sit?"

Trying not to gawk, Zenobia took the chair indicated, the only chair in fact. Flocked paper covered the wall and dark-colored drapes hung at the window. The bed was in disarray, but the rest of what Zenobia could see without craning around too obviously was tidy. A framed and tinted lithograph of a cocker spaniel hung on the wall and several miniature portraits were grouped on a small dresser. The smell of lilac permeated the air, masking stronger scents like beer and sweat.

Teresa eyed Zenobia. "I'm not just exactly at my best in the morning so why don't you say what you've got to say slow and easy, and don't leave anything out, all right?"

"Yes, of course. It's really very simple. My name is Zoe Smith and I run the laundry up the street. There was—is—a bed there, but it's not at all satisfactory. I was wondering—"

A scratch at the door was followed by the appearance of the gray-and-black dog from the bar. A stretched-out sock dangled from its mouth, dragged down by something heavy inside.

"Thank you, Dog," Teresa said. She slid a bottle out of the sock and scooted a saucer out from under the bed with one toe. She poured a few drops onto the dish and the dog lapped them up. "Now, off you go." She shooed him away with one hand.

Teresa poured herself a drink and indicated the other glass with one eyebrow. Zenobia shook her head.

"Didn't think so somehow," Teresa said, and tossed off the shot. "Now, you were saying?"

"I need a bed," Zenobia said, cutting to the heart of the matter before she could be interrupted again. "A comfortable bed. Do you know where I might buy one?"

Teresa laughed. "Is that what all this is about? Well, honey, why didn't you just say so in the first place?"

"I did try to."

Teresa poured another shot and sipped at it slowly this time. Her hair hung in tangles, working loose from a ribbon and pins, but she was very pretty in spite of giving the impression of hard usage. If there was one thing Zenobia hadn't come prepared for, it was to be envious of a whore, but she was. Surely men had proposed to Teresa. Why on earth did she do *this* for a living?

Teresa seemed to divine Zoe's thoughts—and her pity. She lifted the shot glass with a cynical look. "Don't feel sorry for me. Men like me, but I always liked liquor better. All it took was figuring out how to make the one pay for the other."

Zenobia ducked her head, flushing. How could Teresa have inferred her thoughts despite the veil?

"That's quite a shiner you got there, honey."

Startled, Zenobia glanced up, her hand coming up instinctively to cover her eye.

"Light's coming in behind you, honey. Veils don't hide too much when the sun hits them right." Teresa's eyes narrowed and she studied Zenobia shrewdly. "You got a husband?"

Zenobia wrestled with the answer to that. From a legal standpoint, the answer could only be yes, but as a practical matter, she did not. "Well," she said hesitantly, "not exactly."

"A man, then?"

Zenobia shook her head, filled with the sudden cold realization that she would never have a man again, not ever, not while Eben lived. He would never give her a divorce, not after she'd killed Stephen and not with her father's money hanging in the balance—even assuming she could take the risk of going back East and *asking* him for a divorce. And she certainly couldn't contract a second marriage without ending the first. Then she'd be a murderer *and* a bigamist. She had no hope for children, no hope for love, ever. With unexpected swiftness, tears collected in her eyes.

A drawer screeched and a lilac-scented hanky appeared under her chin.

"There, use that," Teresa said. She drew Zenobia to sit next to her on the bed. "I didn't mean nothing by asking. I just wondered where the black eye come from is all."

Zenobia battled the tears but accepted the bourbon-fumed comfort of Teresa's embrace. Her nose ran like a tap, and before long the linen square was drenched. "I . . . I'm sorry," she hiccupped. "I don't know what's come over me."

"The truth, likely enough. Sometimes the liquor shows it to me and I just bawl my eyes out, can't stop for nothing. I think the same happens to men every now and again, but when the truth gets a good hold on them, most men do their damnedest to avoid it. They go out and pick a fight instead of crying."

"Well, that's, that's . . . an interesting theory," Zenobia said, her breath steadying. Teresa squeezed her before letting go.

"It fits the facts." Teresa leaned down and rapped on the floor with her slipper again. Pouring water out of a flowered pitcher into the ewer, she invited Zenobia to freshen up. She slipped the bottle of bourbon into the sock on the dresser just as a black nose pushed the door wide.

"Here you go, Dog." Teresa held the free end of the sock so that the huge jaws could clamp down on it. She saw Zenobia watching the exchange in the reflection of the looking glass and shrugged. "If I keep the bottle in my room, I just drink till it's all gone. It's too early in the day for that."

"Is Red Dog yours then?" Zenobia asked as the feathery black tail disappeared through the door.

"Red Dog? Oh, you mean Dog! Red's the guy downstairs."

"Oh." Even the most obvious theories fell apart in Gila City. "Red and his dog—Red Dog. I see. Well, again, I do apologize for . . . for breaking down the way I did."

"Don't give it another thought, honey," Teresa said with a wry smile. "I've always thought we women have so much to cry over in this world it's a wonder we don't just bawl all day long. Now as for that bed, there are a few fellows who come by fairly regular who are handy with a hammer and nails. Provided you buy the wood, I expect they'd be happy to make you a bed in exchange for getting some laundry done."

"Of course," Zenobia said, greatly relieved to avoid a further drain on her cash reserves. "I wouldn't expect them to do it for nothing."

Teresa grinned, exposing a missing top tooth halfway toward the back. "I'll be sure and explain to whatever fellow I send down to you that you'll be barterin' laundry, not yourself."

Zenobia dropped her veil to hide what she fervently hoped would be her last blush of the day. With a grateful heart, she took her leave of the madam of the Red Dog Saloon.

Five

A man's troubles were nobody's business but his own. Daniel glumly stowed away his dinner in silence, wishing it weren't so, because Lester sat across the table, also eating diligently, and if there were any man on earth Daniel would trust on a delicate matter, it would be Lester.

He'd gotten the welcome news from Teresa that Miss Zoe Smith needed a bed and had promptly appointed himself for the job of making it, but for a woman who'd damn near walked on hot coals—calling on Teresa and all—to see to getting one, Zoe Smith had showed a marked lack of enthusiasm for having *him* make it.

"Oh, I'm sure I never could allow it," she exclaimed when he showed up on her door step offering his services as a carpenter.

The string of objections she offered up in quick succession put him in mind of her reaction when he'd asked her to wash his shirts. She stood prepared to wash anyone else's clothes, but when he arrived, suddenly she found herself overcommitted.

Likewise with the bed. Well, yes, she *did* want a bed, only she hadn't any wood for it yet, and she hadn't thought to get one quite so soon, and she thought she might not have the money handy to pay for the wood for a little while yet, and besides, he was the sheriff and had far more important things to do, she was sure.

Daniel lifted a forkful of beans halfway to his mouth and then lowered it again. The memory of the encounter just plain robbed him of his appetite. He'd had to work hard to keep a smile on his face as he stood on her doorstep. He couldn't stop wondering what it was about him that put her off so badly, not when all *he* wanted was to pull her down on his lap and kiss her silly. There she was, a little bitty thing, all round, going in and out in the middle so nicely, those pretty blue eyes all lively and wide—and all of it was just tearing his heart out. He stared at his plate, feeling as if he might bring up what he'd already eaten.

"You going to eat the rest of that?"

Daniel pushed his plate toward Lester without a word. Still debating whether to share his woes with his partner, Daniel pulled papers and a pouch of tobacco out of the worn inner pocket of his vest. He looked at Lester and at the tobacco. Lester nodded.

Daniel took his time rolling, thinking how to explain all about Miss Zoe Smith to his partner. Sometimes these practice conversations with Lester, back and forth in his head, solved a problem with never any need for having the actual out-loud talk. He'd been through high and low with Lester, from near death in a snowdrift to as good a visit to a cathouse as two men had ever had, and he could predict with reasonable certainty how Lester would respond. Of course, Lester surprised him every now and again, so when in doubt it paid to do the thing proper and pass it by Lester—if he could muster the words to put the thing to him right. Daniel handed one rumpled cigarette to Lester and started a second.

The grunts and shuffles and scraping of utensils on tin plates and the clinking of spoons in pottery mugs made a comforting backdrop for thought. Klingensmith's Eatery served up the same menu every night—hog jowls, black-eyed peas, some form of "Texas meat," either marrow, guts, or sweetbreads, and fried potatoes and rice, all smothered in gravy, with rice pudding to finish, provided a man still had room—but Daniel didn't care for it all that much.

Lester, whose parents had walked the freedom road to Kansas, retained a love of all foods reminiscent of Dixie, so Daniel never had to ask where his partner wanted to eat when he came to town. What it lacked in atmosphere—and it lacked a lot—Klingensmith's made up for in quantity. Plain tables of pine planks, many warped for lack of curing, backless plank benches to sit on, grimy curtains limp at the grimier windows—no, no atmosphere at all. The place was full up all the same, with more men outside waiting their turn to eat in the harsh glare of the kerosene lanterns hanging overhead. Lester mopped up the last rivulet of gravy on his plate.

"Good grub."

Daniel nodded. "Not bad."

Daniel had quizzed Teresa up one side and down the other about her visit from Miss Zoe Smith and then ridden out to the ranch, full of how he was going to build the new laundress a bed. Daniel had carefully chosen some fine oak pieces from his precious stores, enough to make a large bed—a good size for two people to wrestle around in if they were of a mind. He'd been collecting special pieces of wood for some time against the day when he could start making furniture for his ranch house.

He'd asked Lester to bring the wood in with him the next time he drove the buckboard to town for supplies. Daniel was going to have to tell him *something* about how matters stood in a minute or two, especially if they weren't going to go to the laundry and drop off the wood.

"You want a hand taking that wood along down now?"

Daniel glanced up. Lester was pushing for some reason. Ordinarily he'd have let Daniel enjoy his smoke in peace.

"Reckon so." Daniel stood up reluctantly.

A plate flew across the room and hit the wall, spraying five or six men toward the back with gravy-soaked potatoes. The men sprang to their feet and the atmosphere shifted instantly from relaxation and gratification to outright hostility. Hands went by instinct to nicked-up, gouged-out leather holsters, but every hand came up empty thanks to the ruthless enforcement of Gila City's no-weapons policy. Daniel was the only man in the room who was armed but he resisted drawing. He liked to have a few words with a man before he shot him.

"Well, there's something I hate to see," he remarked loudly, "—good food going to waste." Every eye went to the glop still sliding down the wall. Daniel let his own gaze drift, trying to pinpoint the source of trouble, which party was squared off against which other party in the yellow circles of light. None was readily apparent so he decided to try another tack. "You know, I *liked* those fried potatoes. I'd sure like to know who took exception to them."

"He's the one who threw 'em," said a voice.

All heads turned toward the speaker. He pointed at another man. Nathanial Evans swayed in his seat, apparently speechless with rage. Nathanial stabbed an accusing finger toward a man at the back of the room.

"D-d-damned Indian, eating off the same plates as the rest of us!" he said, finding his tongue.

The Indian returned Nathanial's stare, his eyes glittering. He wore the clothes of a drover and appeared to Daniel to be Yaqui. He seemed to recall that a Yaqui Indian worked for James Archer, a rancher who'd built up a sizable enough operation to need paid hands. Chances were, the man was in town to pick up mail and supplies for Archer's spread. The Indian held himself tensely but made no move to retaliate.

Daniel nodded to him. "I thank you for excusing Nathanial's behavior," he said pleasantly. "I'm afraid he's had a good deal to drink and likely doesn't mean any harm. You give Mr. Archer my regards, won't you?"

The Indian, who hadn't once looked away from Nathanial, finally let his glance flick to Daniel. By a barely perceptible nod he indicated his willingness to let the matter rest if Daniel was going to step in.

"Len, I guess those fellows could use a wet rag to wipe off that gravy," Daniel said.

Len Klingensmith, relieved that his place wasn't going to be busted up after all, scuttled across to the injured parties and handed them a rag. "Here you are, gentlemen."

Men began to murmur among themselves again. Daniel collected his hat from a peg by the door. Nathanial Evans hadn't moved, his face still suffused with rage. Daniel knew it would be like handling a powder keg to get him out of Klingensmith's but he had to or risk the whole mess blowing up again the instant he turned his back.

"Hello, Nathanial. Care to join me for some coffee over at the jailhouse?"

"Indian lover!"

A few men nearby laughed uneasily.

"Well, Nathanial, I reckon you've had a bit too much of whatever it is you're using to ease your pain today. Let's get you out into the fresh air, shall we?"

Enough men saw the advantages of getting rid of Nathanial that they made short work of handing him on down the row. Between his artificial leg and too much drink, Nathanial couldn't mount an effective resistance. Daniel was on the verge of heaving a sigh of relief when Nathanial came within reach of him and lunged for the Colt at his hip.

Men scattered, bowls went flying, and a cup bounced heavily off the wooden floor. Its contents scalded Daniel's leg. Lester, who had been waiting inconspicuously in the doorway, dove into the fray and came up under Nathanial, a slick and graceful move that proved how fast a big man could move when he had to. The shock of it appeared to knock Nathanial Evans's breath out of him. Without missing a beat, Daniel pushed the door open, revealing a sea of gaping faces.

"Pardon us," he announced. "We got a man here who isn't feeling so good. Just make way and you can go on in and have our seats." The promise of seats dissipated any curiosity the men in line might have harbored over what was going on. Competition to be the first through the door broke out as soon as Lester passed by with his burden. Daniel followed without haste.

"Where to?" Lester asked in an undertone.

"Jail. Let him sober up."

Lester strode along as if he weren't packing a hundred and fifty pounds on his back. The sun had disappeared into the west a little while before, leaving a hot pink horizon tinged with gold. Daniel squinted against the brilliance of it and drew a deep breath.

"Fine sunset," he remarked.

Lester just kept walking but Daniel hadn't expected a reply. Lester had never been one to waste words. The incident at Klingensmith's Eatery had cheered Daniel up in a perverse sort of way, reminding him that every problem had a solution. Sometimes all it took was a glib tongue and a little decisive action. Love changed a lot but it didn't change that. Daniel realized he could solve this little problem with Miss Zoe with one hand tied behind his back if only he used the right words accompanied by the right attitude. He felt no further need of a talk with Lester.

Happy to have rediscovered his misplaced confidence, Daniel whistled softly as he opened the door of the front cell and Lester tipped Nathanial onto the bunk. Wing Loo, who had been bunking down in the back cell, raised his head and watched the proceedings.

Walter hooked his thumbs in his belt and set right in to complaining. "Aw, can't Nathanial sleep it off somewheres else? Now we're all full up, Daniel. What are we going to do if we get us some real trouble tonight?"

"Put the troublemakers in the livery stable, like we used to before we built the jailhouse. Now, Nathanial, you get yourself a little sleep and when you wake up, we'll send you on home."

Nathanial was sitting on the edge of the bunk, glaring at Lester. "Eating with Indians and getting hauled away by a darkie," he said contemptuously. He spat on the floor. "I ain't never seen such a place."

The planes of Lester's wide, handsome face altered subtly. "I'm no one's darkie, mister, and never was. I was born a free man." The words came out slow and strong. "I fought with the 1st Kansas to make sure no man had the right to call me darkie or nigger ever again. You keep in mind which side won the war and I'll try to forget that men like you bought and sold my parents."

Lester turned, parade ground sharp, and walked out. Daniel looked Nathanial in the eyes and nodded toward the desk. "There's a badge in there, Nathanial, and Lester's entitled to wear it. He's sworn to uphold the peace, same as me. He was just doing his job. I reckon he kept you out of big trouble tonight. There's no call for you to be sayin' the things you did about him."

Nathanial spat again, his face sullen. "It ain't a crime to call a man what he is, Sheriff, at least not where I come from."

"Well, in Gila City it's a crime to disturb the peace and it's sure as hell a crime to assault the sheriff. Lester saved you from being charged with both. I'd thank him next time I see him if I were you, not call him names." Daniel turned to Walter. "Well, that's the long and short of it. I'll be along down at Smith's Laundry if you need me."

"You got more dirty shirts already?" Walter said, thick eyebrows riding high and a twist to his mouth that said Daniel was bit bad and Walter was sorry to see it.

"Just lending a hand is all," Daniel replied in a tone of sweet reason. "Miss Smith's got a business and it's the Businessmen's Benevolent Association that pays our salaries, so I see it as my duty to lend her a helping hand."

Walter rolled his eyes but wisely kept his mouth shut.

"You think maybe she need help?"

Daniel shoved his hat up. "You reckon to work at a laundry, Wing Loo?"

The Chinaman nodded. "I do good laundry. I came looking for Gum Sahn, you say Gold Mountain. I think I have more luck find dirty clothes mountain. Time I find job, make money, pay you for all food and help."

Daniel smiled. "No charge, Wing Loo. I'll talk to Miss Smith tomorrow about you working at the laundry."

Daniel saw the disappointment in his eyes, but the Oriental bowed his head, palms together. Daniel could appreciate that Wing Loo was anxious to make a fresh start, but he wasn't about to give up his private audience with Miss Zoe tonight so that Wing Loo could use the time to apply for a job.

Lester was waiting in the buckboard behind the jail. Daniel climbed up and Lester clapped the reins across their old workhorse's back. They drove in silence for a few minutes. Finally Daniel spoke.

"I gave Nathanial a piece of my mind, in case you're wondering. 'Course it wasn't nearly so good as the piece of mind you gave him."

Lester made a derisive sound that reached Daniel's ear despite the rattling of the wagon.

Daniel propped a foot on the buckboard and responded to the unspoken comment. "Well, I expect you're right, Lester. He bears watching. Truth is, he hates some men more than others, but what he mainly hates is any man who's got two legs."

"Well, that gives him a lot of men to pick on then," Lester said quietly. "He'd best not bother *me* again."

"Don't worry," Daniel said. "If he does, I'll just shoot his good leg out from under him."

Lester shook his head but by the last strands of daylight fanned across the horizon, Daniel could see the corners of his mouth turn up.

"You never would. You sure are turning into one fine liar, Daniel."

"Well, Lester, I been practicing a lot lately."

Zenobia bit off the end of a thread. This skirt would take forever to make. With a machine, any seamstress could have done it in a day, but here she was, stitching yard after yard of seams in the cheap green wool, and with yards more yet to go.

The lovely superfine skirt she'd been wearing when she fled Philadelphia had never been meant for the kind of treatment it had been subjected to—hard benches in trains, seats in coaches no wider than fifteen inches so that her traveling companions constantly chafed her garments not to mention herself, and then hauling and fetching and bending and scrubbing in it ever since.

A faint thump down below made her lift her head. She edged toward the window in the front room. She had gotten chary of windows. With men so desperate for the sight of a woman, it seemed she hardly ever ventured near one without catching a glimpse of some expectant male hoping to see her.

In the filtered pink light of sundown she saw a wagon and the outlines of two men in the street below, the brims of their hats obscuring their faces. The one shook the driver's hand and withdrew a cloth bag from beneath the wagon's seat before the wagon drove away. What on earth? The bag was too small to be filled with laundry. A patient knock at the door downstairs caused her heart to beat faster. She knew that knock!

And sure enough, when she opened the door, there stood Daniel Whittaker, *Sheriff* Daniel Whittaker.

"Good evening to you, ma'am," he said, grinning lopsidedly. He handed her his hat. "If you wouldn't mind holding that, ma'am, I've got to bring in the wood for your bed."

Before Zenobia could utter a word of protest, he ducked out of sight and reappeared an instant later carrying several long boards.

"I'm just going to take these right on upstairs, ma'am," he said smoothly. Her own powers of speech, by contrast, seemed to have fled. "No point in having to heft it all a second time—just take it where it's supposed to be straight off." Zenobia gaped as his long legs and muscled backside disappeared up her stairs. "Which room, ma'am?" he yelled down.

At first she couldn't speak at all and then she started to say "What bed?", but what came out was, "Back!" Practicality had waged a brief war with her objection to having Daniel Whittaker on the premises and practicality had won.

"Well, ma'am, I do believe I can commiserate with you for wanting a new bed," he yelled down. "Does this thing feel as bad as it looks. Before she could answer, there came a suspicious creaking sound from upstairs and Zenobia hurried up the steps.

"What do you mean by lying on my bed?" she demanded when she rounded the corner and found him stretched out flat with his feet hanging off the end. He grinned up at her impudently.

"Well, I figure I should get a feel for what it is you *don't* like in a bed so's I can make you one you *will* like."

"There's no need for you to make me a bed at all," she said with asperity. "I've already told you that. Why you wouldn't listen is beyond my power to understand." His devilish smile merely widened and she had to work hard at completing the thought. "And if you're not building me a bed, then there's no reason at all for you to test the one I already have."

"Yes, ma'am, but as it happens, I've got the wood and the willingness to do it for you." He stood up. "I'll just get the rest of the wood."

He left her standing slack-jawed in the tiny bedroom. He was back almost before she could remember to close her mouth.

"Now, ma'am, I was figuring on a bed for two, because I've got enough matching oak to make it that size. Divided in half, it wouldn't be quite enough for two smaller beds so it seems to me the only practical thing is to make it double width so as to put the wood to best use." He gave her another disarming grin. "It's just odd how it works out sometimes when you're building things."

"But—"

He set the second load of planks down on top of the first. "Now, I'll just fetch up my tools and maybe we can work out what exact style you'd like. I've got a little leeway for some trim and whatnot. I have an extra piece or two with some grain that's going to come up real nice with some oiling."

"But, Sheriff!" Zenobia wailed.

He looked up from sorting through the boards. "Ma'am?"

"I don't want you here!" Zenobia clapped her hands to her mouth the instant the words came out. Blood rushed up her neck and across her cheeks.

Daniel Whittaker stood up, an amused glint in his eye. "Well, you know, ma'am, there have been one or two moments when I sort of got that impression. Would you mind telling me why?"

Zenobia shook her head vehemently, hands still clapped to her mouth.

"Well, ma'am, ordinarily I'm not a man who feels the need to pry into what another person thinks, but in this case I'd sure look on it as a kindness if you'd elaborate. Do I scare you, ma'am, is that it?"

Zenobia shook her head, still dumb with horror over her gaffe. How could she have been so thoughtlessly, horribly blunt? Now he would certainly grow more suspicious about her!

"Ma'am? Would you feel better if I took off this badge?"

She stared at him over her fingers, completely unable to craft a response that would explain her behavior without making matters worse.

He gave her an encouraging smile and shucked off his vest and the badge with it. "Because I know some people who are intimidated by a badge, even if they haven't done the least thing wrong, especially ladies." He folded the vest and laid it across the bottom of her bed. "Or maybe it's the gun. Is it the gun, ma'am? My mother's a wonderful woman, a good Christian soul, and she won't stand for me wearing it in her house, says it makes her heart do funny things to see such a wicked piece of metal strapped to me, with only one purpose and that to deprive another man of his life." He lowered his chin and peered up at her through his lashes, clearly intending to beguile her with his charm, and heaven help her, he possessed it in abundance. "If it's the gun, ma'am, I can take it off."

Daniel Whittaker slid his hands to the buckle on the scarred-up leather belt slowly, as if she were a horse that might startle if he moved abruptly. With great deliberation, he pulled back the free end and released the tongue from one smooth worn hole, darker than the rest. Ever so gently, supporting the weight of the holster and pistol with one hand, he pulled the belt free of his waist.

"Now, I'm just going to take it out and hang it on the post at the top of the stairs, all right? You understand I can't put it too much further away from me or I wouldn't be ready in case I hear some trouble and have to get it back quick."

Zenobia nodded, her heart slowly settling. He didn't seem to have taken offense at her absurd outburst, nor wondered if she had a *personal* reason rather than a general one to dislike lawmen around her. He smiled reassuringly, the gray-green of his eyes especially intense tonight. She heard a soft creak of leather bending on itself and then he came back in, hands held out to show that the lean hips were free of weaponry. His pants were creased just where the gun belt usually rode.

"Is that better, ma'am?"

"It is," she said. And it was. He looked less threatening and she decided to take the easy way out. "I guess the gun did make me a little uneasy."

"It has that effect on some people. I tend to forget that unless I'm reminded of it. I've worn a sidearm ever since I was sixteen, so it just feels like a part of me."

"Have you ever shot anyone?" A shiver of morbid fascination went up her spine at the thought.

"Well, not with that particular pistol, ma'am," he said, "and never before breakfast."

Zenobia smiled. She knew well enough when she was being teased. "I m not accustomed to men wearing pistols as a matter of course," she said. "I suppose I feel like your mother does about them."

"It's a sentiment that does you credit, ma'am." His grin bored into a place somewhere close to her heart.

Zenobia swallowed. "Do you . . . that is, have you had many occasions to pull it out and point it at someone, or whatever it is they call it?"

"It's called drawing, ma'am, and I don't draw it often. I don't find there's a lot of use pulling a gun out unless you mean to use it. So I try to leave it in my holster most of the time."

An irrational vision popped into Zenobia's head. She saw Daniel Whittaker lying on Main Street in a puddle of his own blood. "I hope you wouldn't hesitate to use it if your life were in danger," she said a little breathlessly.

"I can pretty much set your mind to rest on that score, ma'am. I've faced that situation and fired when I had to, but I don't ever mean to kill a man as the result of a misunderstanding if I can help it."

Zenobia smiled in relief at the thought that despite his gentle, considerate nature, he wouldn't hesitate to defend himself. He smiled back, producing that queer tightening in her chest again.

"Well, I can see that the gun was the problem, ma'am. I'm awful glad you've relaxed. I sure never meant to scare you. That's the last thing I want to do. How about if we just agree that I'll keep my gun to one side when I'm here? Let's shake on it."

He held out one strong tanned hand. Zenobia suddenly felt something akin to panic after having let herself be swept up in the glow of his presence. Too many good reasons for not encouraging his friendship sprang to mind. Still, she couldn't help liking him.

"Yes, all right," she said, raising her hand to meet his. It felt hard and warm against hers. Something warm and magnetic seemed to flow from him, something that reversed the poles and turned earth into sky and vice versa. Never, not even with Eben in the beginning, had she ever felt such a peculiar and stirring attraction. It took her breath away. She told herself she needed something to put some distance between them again.

"You know, Sheriff, it's not proper for a gentleman to offer his hand to a lady," she said, adopting her best drawing-room manner. "He should always wait for the lady to offer *her* hand first."

"Is that so?" he replied earnestly, still not letting go of her hand. His strong level brows drew together across the bridge of his nose. "And why is that?"

Zenobia glanced at their joined hands. "Because it obliges the lady to either allow the man the intimacy of touching her or risk giving offense by refusing to do so rather pointedly."

"I see." He looked at their two hands and up again with a spark of mischief in his eyes. "Do you know, I think I might have heard something of the sort before, ma'am, but sometimes a fellow doesn't care to take the chance that a lady won't offer him her hand so he just forges on ahead."

Zenobia wiggled her hand free from his large, warm grasp. "Well, yes, I suppose some bold ones might, but one day they'll get a slap for their troubles."

He grinned, not at all troubled, it seemed, by the implied threat. "Somehow I just can't imagine you ever slapping me, ma'am. Now, answer me this, do you like to dance, Miss Smith?" he asked.

"Yes, I do. Why?"

He rubbed his palms on his pants legs, as if they had suddenly begun to perspire. "There's a dance, ma'am, on the Fourth of July," he said. "I was just thinking that maybe I could . . . well, that we could sort of keep each other company at it, if you know what I mean." A faint pinkness appeared on the tanned cheeks.

Well, this she understood at least. The sheriff of Gila City was as starved for a woman's company as all the rest of them. She didn't have to have committed a murder to draw his attention.

Daniel Whittaker's eyes drifted to her hand, hanging at her side, as if he regretted having let her wrest it away from him. "I know it's more than four months away and I daresay you think I'm a bit peculiar for bringing it up so far in advance, but it's about the biggest celebration we ever have in Gila City, so fellows who want a lady to go with them need to ask early. I'd sure be honored if you'd accompany me."

Zenobia had had at least twenty stock phrases drilled into

her, some for accepting invitations, some for declining them, and others for doing neither but doing it politely. She chose the third option. "I can't say whether I will be going to the dance, Mr. Whittaker, but if I do, I will surely keep your kind invitation in mind."

He let out a breath he'd evidently been holding and nodded. "Thank you, Miss Smith. I can't ask for more than that." He withdrew a carefully folded piece of foolscap from his back pocket. It curved in the shape of his buttock from being in his pocket. "Now, about this bed. I drew up an idea I had. How would this suit you?"

Zenobia stared in wonder at the sketch. "You could make a bed that looked like this?" It might not compare to the custom-crafted pieces she'd grown up with, made by European cabinet-makers and shipped across the sea in crates lined with cotton quilting, but at this moment and in this place, it looked like a little piece of heaven. She darted a glance back up at Daniel Whittaker, who looked undeniably pleased by her reaction.

"I could. It would take me some little time, you understand, but I believe it would be worth the wait. In the meantime, I might be able to knot you a sling bottom for this other bed, if Clarence Trilby has some good stout sisal in stock."

Zenobia felt her cheeks flame. She might be plump but she didn't weigh *that* much! Daniel Whittaker could take his good stout sisal and go hang!

"I don't believe it need be all that strong to support me," she said stiffly.

"No, ma'am, I don't think so either. Why, you're just a little slip of a thing, Miss Smith, but it's hard to make a knot that'll hold in the cheap stuff and you might take it in your head one night to just run up the stairs and fly into that bed. Didn't you over do that, when it was so cold you thought something might freeze and fall off if you didn't get under the covers and warmed up fast?"

Zenobia smiled, somewhat mollified. "I guess I might have, but not since I was a child, and my—" *My nurse became cross if I ran indoors.* No, *that* she could not say, for it gave away something of her past. ". . . and besides, my feet would pick up splinters if I ran up the stairs here."

He glanced toward the landing. "I could have a look at those stairs for you, ma'am, see about sanding them smooth. The thought of you getting splinters in your feet makes me feel real bad."

Zenobia thrust the drawing of the bed back at him, uncomfortably aware that she had given him numerous openings tonight to insinuate himself into her life. If she didn't guard her tongue and get rid of him fast, things could only go from bad to worse.

"This is lovely, really lovely. Why don't you give me some time to think it over? I'm busy and I know you're busy. Maybe we can talk again in, oh, say a month." She stifled a mock yawn. "It must be getting terribly late. You'll have to excuse me, Sheriff. I'm tired and I have some more work to do before I turn in."

"I didn't realize I was keeping you from more important things, ma'am," he said, clearly disappointed at being shown the way out.

"I do so much appreciate your kindness," she said, as she led him out to the landing.

He pursed his mouth as if he had something else to say. Evidently thinking better of it, he lifted his gun belt off the newel post and went down the narrow staircase. Zenobia remained on the landing, arms drawn tight around herself. When Daniel Whittaker was near her, she veered between wanting to melt into his kind, gentle presence and realizing how much danger she could be in if she ever did.

She heard his footsteps fading toward the front door and then all was silent. The building settled back into calmness, the place creaking on its foundations as the heat of the day oozed out of the wood. Zenobia could still smell, just faintly, the aroma of Daniel Whittaker around her—the dust on his hat and the dry, sun-browned smell of his skin, and the odor of tobacco smoke, sharp and pleasant.

If anything could send her to a gibbet, it would be the simple kindness of a man who drew her too close to him, the open, good-natured face luring her to trust him. Certain that he had long since left, she started when she heard his voice drifting up from just inside the front door.

"Good night, Miss Smith."

He *was* persistent.

Zenobia sighed. "Good night, Sheriff Whittaker."

Six

Zenobia awoke the next morning to the sound of banging on the door below. The brilliant light of morning sun filled the room. It was a wonder that it had taken the knocking to awake her. Feeling grouchy in the extreme, Zenobia groaned as the knocking resumed. She knew that knock. It *had* to be Daniel Whittaker.

Zenobia stumbled to the front room where the window overlooked the street. Directly beneath, she could see the sheriff's dusty brown hat, but there was someone else with him, too, someone hatless and with hair the color of midnight.

She yelled loud enough to be heard through the rippled panes of glass. "I'm not up for the day!"

Daniel Whittaker hesitated in the act of raising his clenched fist to knock again. When his wandering gaze found her, he grinned and pulled off his hat.

"Sorry to disturb you so early, ma'am," he yelled up at her, "but there's someone here who's real anxious to meet you." He added a shrug as his grin widened. Apparently she needn't have suffered agonies of embarrassment the previous night for having blurted out that she'd rather he stay away from her. It hadn't deterred him in the least.

Zenobia exhaled moodily. The man certainly had charm, but did he *have* to inflict it on her in the morning? And if there was one man in town who was going to call on her incessantly, did it have to be the sheriff?

Zenobia tried to raise the window but it stuck firmly in the closed position, as firmly as the window in the back room where she slept was stuck in the open position. She yanked and pulled at it in an exaggerated fashion for Daniel Whittaker's benefit.

"It won't open and I can't come down!" she bellowed.

Daniel Whittaker pantomimed toward her front door, and a minute later his cheerful baritone drifted up the staircase. "I'll have a look at that window for you later, ma'am, but right now I have some business to tend to elsewhere. This fellow with me, he'd like to speak to you about a job here at the laundry."

"He'll just have to come back later," Zenobia snapped. Morning was not her best time of day, and most especially not *early* morning.

"I'll tell him you said so, ma'am," Sheriff Whittaker replied politely. His footsteps retreated before she could unleash her exasperation over the early-morning disturbance fully.

Zenobia strained for any sound that would indicate he hadn't really left. She just couldn't seem to get rid of the man! Stomping back into her room, her glance fell on the oak planks he'd delivered last night. It added to her seething mood. Charming, soft-spoken, kind, considerate, and helpful he might be, but Daniel Whittaker had an uncanny knack for getting his way. He *was* going to make that bed, and nothing she said or did would stop him.

Yanking her nightdress over her head, Zenobia began the annoying business of dressing herself for the day. With Bridget standing by to latch, hook, button, and tie, she'd never realized what a beastly business it was to dress oneself. She had to wrench this way and that and contort herself to fasten everything. Each fastener seemed just a bit past the farthest reach of her hand. Blast! A tie she'd thought secure fell apart the moment she released the ends.

Faint whooshes and thumps from below caused her to stop in her tracks several times, motionless and trying to identify the odd sounds. But for as long as she stood still, nothing could be heard. She went to work on the equally tedious and frustrating business of dressing her own hair and decided the sounds below must be a trick of the wind or perhaps street noises creating a percussive shock against the side of the building.

But when she descended, she peered in wonder at the front room. All the dirty laundry had been sorted and folded in precise piles, each pile just the right size to fill the wash cauldron.

More revelations awaited her in the back room. The fire in the stove glowed, the cauldron emitted wisps of steam, and five wooden buckets full of water stood neatly aligned, ready to refill the cauldron. The rocker tub brimmed with water, too, its hinged lid propped open awaiting the first load to be rinsed. It looked like nothing so much as a baby bird—a large dumpy wooden baby bird—waiting for its first meal of the day.

The floor had been swept, the slugs to fill the iron nested at the back of the stovetop, the soleplate of the iron scrubbed, the table straightened, and a fresh muslin pinned securely to the ironing stand. Quite unable to absorb it all, Zenobia stared around her in gratified astonishment. If her regular laundresses from back in Philadelphia had suddenly materialized and dropped her a curtsey, she could not have been more amazed.

Groping for an explanation, Zenobia wandered out the front door, wondering if it was all some huge prank concocted by Daniel Whittaker. Had he organized all this and then stepped out of sight to savor her stupefaction? It seemed more than a little plausible. Who else on earth would have done such a thing?

"You just wait until I get my hands on you, you . . . you . . ." What were some of the more colorful descriptions she'd heard since coming West? Varmint? Coyote? Hornswoggler?

"Good morning, missy."

Zenobia shrieked and pivoted. An Oriental man arose from a squatting position and bowed. He wore loose black trousers and a white shirt with the cuffs turned back several times, revealing strong hands and thick wristbones. She clutched at her chest, her heart hammering.

"You nearly scared me to death!" she cried.

"I very sorry, missy." He gestured to the spot where he'd

been hunkered against the wall. "I wait for missy in shade, is cool." He bowed again, his palms pressed together.

"Oh! Are you the one who's looking for work?"

"Yes. My name is Wing Loo and I do laundry good. Not ask for much money."

"You'll be the first one west of the Mississippi not to," Zenobia muttered.

"Beg pardon?"

Zenobia shook her head quickly. "Never mind. Where are you from?"

"Kwangtung Province in Celestial Kingdom, what you call China. Live in Sunwei district, where Canton River end, in place call Szu Yup. Many come from there, look for fortune in this land."

Zenobia sighed. Exasperating men seemed to populate her life these days. "No, I mean where were you before you came to Gila City?"

"Ah. I come from mining camp. I not like look for Gum Sahn no more, what you call gold."

Zenobia noticed with alarm the green-and-yellow bruises on his face and the half-healed cuts. "I see. Are you prone to drink liquor and get in fights?" It seemed to her the sort of question her butler would have asked a prospective servant who presented himself in such a condition.

The man in front of her drew himself up to his full height, slightly taller than she. "Wing Loo not drink liquor." He made a disdainful gesture. "All bad—rotgut, tangleleg, redeye. Only foolish man drink them. Men from Celestial Kingdom make tea from green leaves. Make all right inside, clean head and other parts, not like liquor, taste bad and make head hurt."

That sounded promising. "In that case, do you really know how to do laundry?"

Wing Loo fluttered a hand in the direction of the front door. "Let Wing Loo show."

Zenobia could find no fault with that plan. She tried to think as she followed him inside what other stern questions Sidcup asked prospective employees. He possessed a seemingly endless fund of pointed inquiries about personal habits, past positions, and performance of duties that made applicants shiver and blanch their way through interviews with him as she sat by uncomfortably. When he would turn to inquire whether madam had any further questions for the quaking wretch standing before them, she could never think of any, quite sure that she and the applicant would be equally relieved when the interview ended.

Now she had no Sidcup to oversee the hiring process. Wing Loo, however, measured up to her requirements so far. Immaculately clean, polite, respectful—could he be all that he seemed? Zenobia decided to stop looking for trouble as it had recently demonstrated an unerring knack for finding her first. Let this strange man from the Celestial Kingdom show that he could do the job and she would be satisfied. Well, more than satisfied—joyous, in fact.

Two hours later, Zenobia felt nearly rapturous as Wing Loo staggered forth to hang a third load of laundry on the line. White shirts scaled new heights in whiteness, blue pants departed the wash tub the same color as when they'd gone in, red shirts were still red, and each and every other color remained true, too, while—miraculously!—the dirt vanished into the wash water. If Wing Loo had produced rabbits out of a hat she could not have been more impressed.

Wing Loo politely negotiated the terms of his employment, beginning with the necessity that missy buy him a wringer. Zenobia assured him that she, too, had felt the lack of one, and would immediately go buy one at the shebang if they had one in stock. Otherwise she would order one. All the while she cringed with embarrassment. She'd *known* clothes shouldn't be so horribly wet that they dragged on the ground when hung out to dry, but only now did she recall the four-spindled wringer sitting out on laundry days back home.

"I see that you have no shoes," she remarked to cover her chagrin. "Shall I purchase some for you while I am at the store?"

For the first time Wing Loo's composure appeared to slip a little. His color heightened as he bowed deeply. "Beg pardon, missy, but have no money. I buy soon—if get job."

Zenobia briskly pulled on her gloves. "You do indeed have the position. I intend to buy you the shoes as part of your first week's salary. Gila City's streets are not very clean."

Wing Loo grimaced "No, not clean. Men very dirty, and horses, too," he said. The horses seemed like an afterthought. Zenobia knew precisely what Wing Loo was too polite to say, that many of the men of Gila City stank to high heaven.

"What would be a fair wage, do you think?" Zenobia inquired casually. She greatly feared that Wing Loo would want an exorbitant salary, given his talent and the dearth of workers in Gila City.

"Wage?"

"Money, pay."

"Ten dollar a week."

Sidcup would have fainted dead away. Zenobia discovered she was made of sterner stuff. In a boom town, ten dollars a week seemed very reasonable, and even if income from the laundry kept only slightly ahead of costs, it would be like a little slice of heaven, for she was making nothing right now, even though a good deal of her capital was irrevocably committed to the building.

"And I sleep here, on the floor," Wing Loo added, "no trouble to missy." He waved toward a corner of the front room.

Zenobia actually liked the idea of Wing Loo living there. It would provide a convenient buffer between herself and the omnipresent Sheriff Whittaker. "Yes, very well, only you may as well have the front room upstairs. It's empty. Now, before I leave, is there anything else you require from the store?"

"Ammonia, vinegar, salt, washboard, brush." Wing Loo ticked off the items on his fingers. "And wringer."

"Yes, naturally a wringer." Another thought occurred to her. "Do you iron as well?"

"Very good," Wing Loo assured her. He stroked a hand back and forth in the air. "All time, best around."

"Wonderful!"

Zenobia drifted out the door in a haze of happiness. Just when she had despaired of ever making a go of her laundry, she had snatched victory from the jaws of defeat—with a little help from Daniel Whittaker.

Daniel could not say later with any degree of certainty how it was that he ended up driving Miss Zoe Smith and Wing Loo out to Hangtown Camp, but drive them he did. Hangtown Camp, falling outside Gila City limits, could not be said to be in his jurisdiction at all—mining camps had their own form of law, if you wanted to call it that—but an irate Zoe Smith was not to be tampered with. There were erupting volcanoes that had discharged less heat than she did when she learned through Clarence Trilby that Wing Loo had been forcibly dispossessed of his mining claim.

And so Daniel had borrowed a light wagon from Ned at the livery stable and now they rattled along, paralleling the Gila River. With Zoe Smith perched beside him, Daniel reckoned that the probable difficulties ahead were a small price to pay for the pleasure of her company. She sat straight as a ramrod, a parasol jouncing above her head and seemingly indifferent to the heat of the flats. He doubted the fires of hell could have deterred her in her fanatical determination to see justice done.

"Imagine! To pummel a man like that for no other reason than that his diligence has borne fruit," she declared indignantly. "Detestable louts!"

It was one of many heartfelt outbursts from her since they'd left town. Daniel nodded. He'd long since run out of things he could say in response. Men could be cruel, life wasn't fair—that sort of thing. For a woman who made her own way in the world, Zoe Smith seemed a little naive about the ways of that world.

"You put me in mind of my mother at this moment," he remarked, more to himself than to her.

She turned and regarded him curiously. "In what way?"

"Well, it's your righteous indignation, I guess. My mother had it, too. Back when the border ruffians used to ride up out of Louisiana and blue devil the free Negro community near us. They set fire to their crops and looted and destroyed whatever they could lay their hands on. She took it to heart, same as if they'd done it to our place."

Daniel paused, thinking back. It had come as a hard lesson in the heart of a child that men could hate so virulently over such a thing as another man's color. It was a lesson Zoe Smith seemed to be learning just now.

"I think men are beastly to one another. Did your mother make them stop?"

"No, that was beyond her power, but she saw the smoke when the ruffians rode through and she'd hitch up the mule and go clean and help set houses to rights until my father dragged her back home, fearing she'd make herself ill with all the work. She'd start in to baking then, and keep taking canned goods and preserved food she'd set by for our family to the Negro families who had been left with nothing."

"I would have been so angry," Zoe Smith declared. "Couldn't you call in the sheriff to stop those men, the ruffians?"

"We didn't really have a sheriff. Besides, the ruffians struck and ran, mainly at night. By the time anyone got there, it would have been too late. It came down to the Negroes defending themselves as best they could and neighbor helping neighbor afterward."

"They were lucky, then, to have neighbors like your mother."

"She was a woman of strong convictions, that's for sure. She gave so much of our food away the first year the ruffians started raiding that we came close to starving that winter. After that, my father formed a charity committee at church. Baptists are strong antislavers and contributions ran high. It sorely aggravated the ruffians that white folks were helping the Negroes. They began to target the folks who helped the Negroes."

"Did they ever come to your house?"

Daniel shook his head. "Those boys were too cowardly to try and take revenge on a house with six armed men. We even loaded a gun for little Jesse—he was only seven then. No, they found easier targets."

Zoe Smith made a satisfied sound. "Good! I hope you ran everyone of them straight back to Louisiana."

"Well, ma'am, not quite, but I reckon we made them think once or twice about coming back to Peachtree, Kansas."

The gritty dust borne on the breeze crunched between his teeth as they rolled on under a sky the color of Zoe Smith's eyes. Daniel glanced at her as often as wouldn't be considered rude. Damp tendrils of hair clung to her temples and the grim set of her lips reminded him that he hadn't written to his mother in a while.

Zoe Smith exhibited a lot of spunk. She'd cornered Daniel at the jail and questioned him intently on how it was that Wing Loo could have been run off his claim, and was that legal, and somewhere between that moment and this, he'd been shanghaied for the trip to Hangtown. Much to his relief, Wing Loo persuaded her that he didn't *want* his claim back, although he admitted to missing his writing box and the mementoes of home it contained. That was all the inducement Zoe Smith had needed to organize this little expedition.

Daniel clucked the horse up into a trot. The Hangtown boys, he felt sure, were brothers under the skin to the border ruffians when it came to meanness. He hoped he could satisfy Zoe Smith's burning desire for justice and extract them all safely from Hangtown Camp again. Wing Loo sat behind them in the back of the wagon, slumping down further the closer they got to Hangtown.

Although it was petty of him, it nagged at Daniel how the woman he loved had come to idolize the Chinaman. Wing Loo could do no wrong in her sight. Not for the first time, Daniel regretted not having offered to help her do the laundry when he'd had a chance, for it was Wing Loo's talent for washing and ironing that had won him her undying admiration. Daniel resolved that he would not let such an opportunity pass him by again. If she needed help, she was going to get it from *him*—and not any of the other men in Gila City who gawked and sighed over her when she went out in public.

Hangtown appeared deserted as they approached it. The motley assortment of tents looked like ungainly beige animals dozing in the heat. Daniel nudged around under the buckboard seat with his toe until it connected with the Winchester rifle stowed there. Like the Colt in his holster, it took .44 caliber bullets, and he'd brought a great big box along. He'd attempted to show Wing Loo how to load and fire a gun but the man insisted that "Celestials" would not dream of using such barbaric things. Daniel began to understand why he might have lost his claim.

All the Hangtown boys would have guns, though, that was certain. Daniel stopped at the edge of the little tent city and men who'd been dozing away the hottest part of the day emerged into the sunlight blinking and stretching. Before he could stop her, Zoe Smith alit from the wagon and demanded that Wing Loo accompany her to his abandoned tent. Daniel tied off the reins and jumped down to follow them.

All that remained of Wing Loo's tent were tatters of canvas anchored to the ground. Other odds and ends fluttered in the slow breeze—a shoe, bits of paper caught on the tent stakes, the cover of a rice paper book. Zoe Smith picked through it all, the very picture of vexation. Miners gathered to watch, studying her with great interest as she retrieved pieces of paper and cloth like a chicken pecking for grain. Wing Loo cast apologetic looks in Daniel's direction. He'd made it plain to Daniel that it hadn't been *his* idea to come to Hangtown.

At last Zoe Smith realized she had an audience. With blue eyes snapping, she shook her umbrella at them. "How dare you all just stand and watch as I undo the damage you did? You, pick up those papers, and you, give me that tin of food! You should all be ashamed of what you did, beating a man merely because his hard work paid off!"

The man she singled out gaped at her. Looks of amusement and admiration gave way to confusion.

"You left Mr. Loo without even any shoes. Do you not know what it says in the Bible, that whatsoever you do unto the least of my creatures, you do unto me?" The men exchanged uneasy looks as she brandished the umbrella at them. "What do you think God would say if you'd taken *His* shoes?"

A few of the claim stakers gingerly handed her bits of things culled from the windswept ground. She thanked them, not graciously but with enough courtesy to suggest that they were on the right track to redeeming themselves. Wing Loo hastened to collect everything from her, including the crushed remains of a wooden box.

"Well, I believe I have said all that can profitably be said to men of such poor character," she finally announced. "I hope you are all thoroughly ashamed of yourselves. Sheriff Whittaker, if you please."

Daniel assisted her back to the wagon and onto the seat, thoroughly enjoying the brief contact with her round little figure. She snapped her umbrella open again, her breathing agitated in the hot afternoon air. Wing Loo clambered into the back and Daniel noticed that he didn't bother to correct *her* about the order of his name—Mr. Wing, not Mr. Loo. As they drove away, he glanced in the back and suppressed a guffaw of laughter.

Wing Loo was clearly engaged in some sort of heartfelt prayer—probably thanking providence for Miss Zoe Smith.

Daniel knew just how he felt.

The sheriff of Gila City leaned back in his chair, his hat down over his face and his arms folded across his chest. He wiggled one toe in his boot, trying to scratch an itch without expending too much effort. A lone fly buzzed listlessly on the windowsill. Midday generally brought few problems, so he tended to use that time for rest and cogitation.

He'd been devoting a lot of time to cogitating about Miss Zoe Smith. Oftentimes, the thinking consisted of what his father would have called decidedly impure thoughts. Out at the ranch the past two days, he'd rolled up in a buffalo hide at night, and with Lester gently snoring on the other side of the room, watched embers glowing in the fireplace they'd built from rocks hauled down from the mountains.

He had let his mind drift all dreamy and hazy around the thought of sharing his blanket with Zoe Smith. That was what the Indians called it—"sharing a blanket"—and he had to concede that it went right to the heart of the matter and described the urge fairly.

Daniel shifted uncomfortably as the thought of her spreading out naked beneath him on the buffalo robe, the delicate wrists beneath his hands, the white thighs opening to him. Daydreams like that could leave a fellow in a miserable condition, and the jail lacked enough privacy for him to settle the matter single-handed.

But he couldn't stop thinking about her. He hadn't seen her since he'd brought her back from Hangtown the previous week. He'd fixed the windows upstairs at the laundry for her, and knotted a new rope support for her bed. She'd fluttered all around him while he worked, suddenly anxious to be rid of him. She'd repeated that she needed more time to think about letting him make her a new bed, but Daniel knew a dodge when he heard one. He could tell hemming and hawing from a mile off. It only served to strengthen his impression that Miss Zoe Smith had some kind of secret that she was afraid he would find out about.

He didn't mind, though, not at all. He figured it gave him a kind of leverage with her, and besides, whatever she'd done, it couldn't be all *that* bad. She was too well brought up. With posture like a soldier from a crack company and well-spoken in that quick, clipped way of hers, she was clearly the product of a good background. She instinctively played by the rules of polite society. No, she wasn't one of those who'd been born low and liked to adopt a polished manner—she was the real thing.

Only why was she doing laundry, and why was she doing it in a place like Gila City? Probably her guilty secret had to do with a transgression no one here would think twice about, like using the wrong fork at a fancy dinner party or insulting some interfering old society matron. Now, if she'd come to town with a baby on her hip and no husband in sight, it would have been different. *That* kind of disgrace he could understand, though it wouldn't have dampened his ardor for her one bit.

The other reason he knew she couldn't have done anything too awful was her fundamental kindness. She was fair-minded and she didn't have a mean or vicious bone in her body—quite the contrary. One day—probably when they were both old and gray—he'd finally tease her little secret out of her and he'd find out what silly little mix-up had made her come to Gila City. Whatever it was, he was glad it had happened because it had brought them together. The very notion that she could ever have broken a law made him chuckle out loud.

Daniel anchored his heels more securely on the edge of the desk and let his breathing deepen. Oh, lordy, he loved that girl! It took an effort to stay away from her, but he'd made a decision to give her some breathing room. He hoped that she might miss him, even if only a little, and be that much more glad to see him when he did show up again. She'd see that nothing bad had come of letting him through her door and she'd relax.

The next stage of his plan was to begin wriggling into her life again in subtle ways, the way prairie dogs burrowed under a storage shed and emptied every sack of grain. By the time you realized they'd been there, it was already too late—the grain was gone. He'd quietly install himself in her daily routine, and one of these days, if he was very lucky, he'd get a chance to see those pretty feet of hers bare again. He'd seen them the night she came to the door with her hair dripping all over the nightdress she wore, bare feet peeping out, just dainty and about as gorgeous a pair of feet as had ever trod this earth. Until that night, Daniel had never given much thought to a woman's feet, but as she had in so many other ways, Zoe Smith had considerably rearranged his thinking on the matter.

But Daniel found over the days that followed his deliberate decision to give Zoe Smith some breathing room that he was increasingly anxious to stake a more public claim on her. Too many men nosed around her, especially the customers at the laundry. He heard about it in painful detail from Wing Loo.

Wing Loo was Daniel's spy in her camp. Every day, following Daniel's suggestion, Wing Loo would take himself off to the bakery for something to eat, and every day he would just happen to pass by the jail on his way back and let Daniel know how things were going at the laundry—what sort of mood Zoe Smith was in, what she looked like that day, who was trying to turn her up sweet—all the crucial facts.

So far the arrangement had netted him the very useful information that Miss Zoe Smith loved roses. Of course, he hated the gambler who'd brought her a sachet of them, dried out petals tied up in a net bag that she could put under her pillow. According to Wing Loo, she'd exclaimed over the little sack as if it were filled with gold. Daniel bristled at the very thought of another man discussing with the love of his life what she put under her pillow at night, but it did give him an idea.

Daniel abruptly swung his feet down from the desk. He reached for his hat, deep in thought. His mother had endured a lot of hardship, lonely days on the prairie while his father worked the land, keeping house in a soddy where the roof leaked and snakes dropped down from the rafters where they lived, enjoying the dank darkness of a soddy as much as the people deplored it. His mother and father were Ohio born and raised and they'd had no idea how difficult homesteading would be when they headed west, but they'd persevered.

Daniel didn't care if poverty *was* a virtue that built character. He vowed that Zoe would have better. He would see to it. Not for her a life of ceaseless drudgery with nothing of beauty. She wouldn't have to wait until the last years of *her* life for a nice house. He was damned determined on that point.

And she'd have a garden, too, one where she could grow roses. Daniel headed out the door and ambled off toward the shebang to order up some supplies for the continuation of his campaign to woo Miss Zoe Smith. He'd see that she had roses no matter what it took.

It was starting to work a hardship on her nerves, this benign watching. He tipped his hat to her in the street, and once or twice, when she rounded a corner and nearly tripped over him, he'd greet her cordially and offer to carry a package for her. He'd inquire after her health, ask if she'd made up her mind about the bed, and all the while they talked, she got the impression that he scarcely heard a word she said. She felt watched. She'd asked for a month to think over the matter of the bed and it appeared he was going to give it to her, but now she felt more unnerved by him *not* calling on her than she had when he called on her, and that was saying something.

Toward the end of April, however, something happened to distract her from the dilemma of Daniel Whittaker, absent or present. She was coming back from delivering laundry one morning when the big Concord coach emblazoned with the ornate black-and-gold lettering of Wells Fargo and Company rolled to a halt on Main Street. That in itself wasn't unusual, but when Wing Loo appeared and greeted a large contingent of Chinamen who detached themselves from the coach's roof and interior, she began to suspect that her life was about to change dramatically.

Curiosity drove her to Wing Loo's side, but he was too busy directing the activity of the new arrivals to answer her questions. He led them all up Main Street and around the corner like some Oriental parade, small round sacks bobbing at the ends of sticks balanced over their shoulders. They also carried cooking pots and chests and a live rooster and several hens in a bamboo cage suspended on a pole between two of them. Goodness only knew where *those* particular bits of luggage had been stowed during the journey, Zenobia thought.

Zenobia bided her time until they reached the laundry and then, seeing as how they all evidently intended to stop there, inquired of Wing Loo just exactly who they were and what they were doing there. The men hunkered down patiently on the sidewalk in front of the laundry while Wing Loo explained it to her. The explanation was delivered in English but with a good deal of Chinese mixed in, along with wide elliptical motions of his arms which didn't clarify his meaning very much.

The story, when she finally deciphered it, was simple enough. Wing Loo had summoned them all to come work at Smith's laundry. Zenobia recalled watching Wing Loo labor over his meticulously repaired writing box on numerous evenings, sketching delicate Chinese characters in vertical columns. Zenobia had naively assumed he was writing to relatives back in China. It turned out that he *had* been writing to his relatives, but these relatives had already been in America. All were broad and sturdy like Wing Loo, and they appeared to accept him as a sort of *paterfamilias* even though he was clearly younger than some of them.

Zenobia rubbed her aching temples and tried to count heads. Ten men sat on their heels, arms resting on knees, regarding her with polite expectation. Their good-natured faces echoed Wing Loo's with only minor variations, although he assured her that some of them came not from his district but from Sunwei and Toishan. Since she hadn't a clue where either Toishan or Sunwei might be, it hardly mattered, but it seemed important to Wing Loo so she tried to listen carefully.

He explained that this one had been in San Francisco working in a barroom, those five had been working together on the railroad but were happy to leave because the swaggering, blustering white crews, enraged by the skill and speed of the Chinese at laying track, had continually threatened to skin them alive, and called them women because they washed after each day's work in bathtubs made from empty whiskey kegs.

The others had gone prospecting, like Wing Loo, for although they were the sons of farmers and sailors, they were a pugnacious people and had embraced the challenge of the unknown. Their native districts—and here it became a little clearer why it was so important to Wing Loo to delineate their origins—had bred China's adventurers for centuries, so the lure of foreign exploits was a part of their nature.

"Well, I hope these adventures they envision don't include beds to sleep in," Zenobia said, focusing on the practical, "because we haven't any."

"Oh, no, missy, not expect beds," Wing Loo hastily assured her. He spoke to the men in rapid Chinese and they all wagged their heads back and forth. No, their expressions said, they didn't expect beds. In fact, they would be positively *shocked* to be offered beds. "All want work hard, make money," Wing Loo declared.

"Well, I suppose I can promise them hard work," Zenobia admitted, trying to calculate how she might corner the market in laundry in Gila City. "I could accept all the laundry that's brought in instead of turning some away, and I'll have to try to get even more business. The hotels and saloons must all have laundry. The trick is to set prices just low enough that it makes more sense for them to bring it to us rather than do it themselves. And I suppose we'll need another stove and cauldron and rocker tub and wringer and . . ."

Her Chinese audience smiled and nodded encouragingly as she mused aloud, even though they had no idea what she was saying. Her brain churned numbers around. She *could* buy more supplies, she supposed, but how could ten more Chinamen live under her roof? They would have to sleep on pallets downstairs. Would they mind?

She looked up and down the line of polite faces. Some very young, some an indeterminate sort of middle age. None looked the sort to complain, and from what Wing Loo had said, they'd all known a fair amount of hardship.

Wing Loo had managed to do most of the laundry with not much help from her. She supposed he could manage this as well, although she couldn't envision having much privacy left for herself. Still, if that was the price for success, it was a price she would pay. Entrenched habits—such as having a household revolve around her convenience—would just have to be unentrenched, that was all.

Zenobia straightened her shoulders and led the way through the front door. This was a new life—she would cope.

Seven

"And you can see there's plenty of room up here. These are good-size rooms, so you'd have no trouble renting them out for a sizable amount if you wanted to. Most men in this town aren't too fussy—just a bed in each room will make them ready for paying guests."

"Yes, Mr. Merrick, I can see that." Zenobia wandered away from the real estate broker. If there was one thing she detested, it was being told the obvious. Of course the potential income from renting out these rooms was great—provided she didn't mind sharing her living quarters with yet another group of men. In the two months since Wing Loo's relations had moved into the laundry, she'd grown somewhat weary of battling for her privacy amidst a veritable sea of men.

Her footsteps echoed down the center hall on the second floor of what had once been Elaine's Good Luck Restaurant. She peered into each of the four bedrooms in turn and then into the small middle chamber by the stairs. It was obviously meant to be the lavatory, except there was only a small rudimentary bench to hold a concealed chamber pot in it. Heaven only knew when flush toilets might come to Gila City—if ever. Zenobia played with the idea of turning one of the small side rooms into a bathing room with her bathing tub in it. That would be almost too wonderful.

There were no beds in any of the bedrooms, as Charles Merrick had pointed out. Elaine had taken her own bed and sold the rest, one supposed. Beds were a ridiculously valuable commodity in Gila City. Anything made of wood was, really, owing to its having to be freighted in. No doubt that was also the reason everyone burned those repulsive cow patties in the stove instead of using wood or coal. Availability rewrote the rules in this dustball of a town.

Irritated by the heat of midday, Zenobia paced off the dimensions of the bedrooms, her every step coming back to meet her off the bare walls. Hot and airless though it might be at the moment, the building had a comforting solidity under foot when compared to the laundry. She eyed the large back bedroom which faced west, away from the damnable clamoring sunrises with which she had been greeted every day so far in Gila City. If a rain cloud ever opened up over Gila City, she planned to go out and dance under it, possibly naked. Despite the dust and the emptiness, the one undeniable charm of Elaine's was that not a single other person lived in it.

The laundry was thriving and she had begun to fantasize about having a place to be alone again, away from all the communal camaraderie of Wing Loo and his industrious relations. Apart from counting the cash drawer each day and paying out wages, she'd spent all her time soliciting new business for the laundry recently. Now that she'd done that with considerable success, it left her too much free time again. The vacant restaurant just around the corner had plucked at the edges of her boredom and teased at her commercial instincts, which told her that it could be just as lucrative as the laundry.

Zenobia turned to Charles Merrick. "I'll take it. You may write to the owner and tell her that I will pay her the price she asks, but in twelve equal installments over the forthcoming year. If I find I am able, I will discharge the debt earlier, but that is my best offer."

Zenobia turned to inspect a window frame, as if the offer she had just made was not at all unusual. In fact, offering to pay in installments constituted a rather bold deviation, for cash on the barrel head was the custom in Gila City. Her father had cleverly structured deals in this way to make important purchases without risking his capital—or to seize a timely chance to make money when he had no capital to risk. Zenobia thanked providence that her father had so often ignored her mother's prohibitions on talking business at the dinner table.

Merrick considered the offer, his eyes narrowing. Older and more urbane than most of Gila City's residents, he treated Zenobia with courtesy and a certain respect—as opposed to the unbridled admiration and libidinous suggestions she'd come to expect from nearly every other male in Gila City. Charles Merrick had made no overtures of that sort, at least not yet. Zenobia had concluded that Charles Merrick's first love was strong drink, but so long as he did not conduct business in a drunken stupor, she had no complaint with him.

"Had you anticipated paying any interest on the outstanding balance?" Charles Merrick inquired.

Pulling her gloves on more securely, Zenobia said, "I do not, Mr. Merrick, and I suspect that you have full authority to act for the owner in this matter. Why don't you concede that my offer is a reasonable one and we can simply adjourn to your office and draw up a contract containing the details of the sale?"

A ghost of a smile whisked across Charles Merrick's face. "Why not indeed? I hope I shall have the honor of being your first customer."

But as things turned out, Sheriff Daniel Whittaker was the first to eat at the newly renamed Smith's Good Luck Restaurant. Zenobia left the laundry every day—after nodding and smiling her way past eleven bowing Chinamen whose names she could almost pronounce correctly now—and went to the shuttered-up restaurant. There she scrubbed and polished and dusted and swept from dawn until dusk to get the place ready to open. Everything she needed was more or less supplied, from pepper boxes and vinegar cruets on the tables to plates and tin cups and huge cooking pots all stacked in the rear, but dust had seeped in through every crevice and coated it all. Everything was filthy beneath the desert sand, too, thick with encrusted food and greasy residue. Elaine's wedding party had been held there and no one had bothered to clean anything before they left Gila City.

Feeling exhausted and overwhelmed by the end of the week, Zenobia began to regret her purchase. The fact of the matter was that she had no more idea how to run a restaurant than she'd had about running a laundry. She had absolutely no practical skills that counted for anything here in Gila City. Playing refined airs on the pianoforte, singing, drawing, and riding to hounds were not in great demand here, and those accomplishments—as well as an excruciatingly rigorous training in social etiquette—comprised the sum total of her education. It was as well that the fear of failure pushed her onward with a kind of quiet desperation.

The stove at the restaurant proved no easier to light and keep burning than the one at the laundry. Her lack of experience in actually doing any sort of domestic work manifested itself in other ways, too. Her knuckles were scraped raw from wielding a scrub brush and she had yet to try her hand at cooking, though she remained fairly optimistic that she would prove quite adept at it. Her love of food and the absolutely appalling fare offered by the other eateries in town assured her success. Anything she cooked would necessarily be an improvement.

She spent Friday morning scrubbing the big rubber ponchos cut to use as tablecloths. Elaine had been nothing if not practical. The ponchos were unwieldy and smelled of decomposed food, but they had to be dealt with. She tied her hair back with a clean strip of cloth, too impatient to dress it or pin the mass of it on her head. Thick, waving tendrils escaped at regular intervals, cascading over her neck and face, sticking to her skin and tickling her nose. At noon she set aside the final poncho, hanging it over a bench to drip dry.

The door creaked and yet another man peered in. "Are you open yet? Can a man buy some dinner?"

"No," Zenobia said tiredly. "Next week."

She hoped it was true. So much remained to be done. Clarence Trilby had delivered supplies to get her started—a half barrel of corned beef, a half keg each of farina and hominy, four gallons of molasses, a firkin of butter, and a half barrel of sugar—but at that very moment she had only one thing on her mind, and that was eating her own lunch, not cooking for others. She had only picked at the morning rice and tea before leaving the laundry. The repetitive nature of their breakfasts didn't seem to bother Wing Loo and his relatives but it did her. In the midst of wiping down and straightening the shelves behind the kitchen, she'd come across a can of Ambassador brand yellow peaches with a red and white label that proclaimed them to be "second to none." It was the first morsel of food she'd seen in a long time that promised to please her palate.

All through the tedious labor of the morning, she'd held on to the tantalizing prospect of eating the peaches for lunch. Wiping her hands on her apron, Zenobia eagerly took a knife to the can. It wiggled around in her grasp and the knife didn't pierce the lid at first. She had to resort to stabbing it repeatedly and then trying to connect the small triangular holes she'd made.

A shadow fell across the floor as she struggled with the can. Glancing at the darkened silhouette in the door, she said crossly, "I'm not open yet. Please go away. I do wish everyone would read my sign."

"Well, ma'am. I did see your sign," said a deep, pleasant voice she recognized instantly as Daniel Whittaker's. Her heart was inexplicably buoyed up by it. "It looks nice, and I think having the sign maker add that message by the door about admitting no intoxicated persons was a good idea, but since I'm sober as a judge, I was kind of hoping that the other part, about being closed, didn't apply to me."

"Sheriff Whittaker! Do come in."

"Thank you, ma'am." She could hear the smile in his voice although the sun behind him still obscured his expression. He took off his hat and she gestured to the can of peaches.

"I was just going to have something to eat, but I haven't had much luck opening this can."

"Well, maybe I can lend a hand."

She fell back a pace, her hands clutched behind her, and regarded him a little shyly. His presence was having a most peculiar effect on her, making her heart beat faster and her hands tremble. He took out his own knife and separated the lid from the can with a series of swift cuts.

"There you go."

"Will you join me?" Her pulse would not slow down. Zenobia was loath to admit it, but this was more than mere gladness to see a friendly face. She gestured toward the peaches to cover her disquiet.

"No, ma'am, I won't. My partner, Lester—I don't believe you've met him yet—is in town and we just ate down at Klingensmith's."

"You have a partner? I thought sheriffs had deputies."

He smiled. "Well, I do, ma'am, but I also have a ranch, and Lester and me, well, we're partners inasmuch as we staked claim to land right next to each other. We plan to just do everything twice, like build stock pens and run-ins until both of us have a going concern."

"Oh! I had no idea. Well, I hate to be rude, but I've got such a lot of work to do that I really mustn't put off eating any longer. Won't you stay and talk while I eat?"

The smile that was never far away surfaced again. There could be no doubt that he was pleased she'd asked him to stay. He set his hat down and folded his long legs to fit under the table opposite her. Almost as an afterthought, he reached up and combed his fingers through his hair to obscure the imprint left by his hat. The rich brown curls, streaked with blond by the sun, flopped into attractive disorder. He shrugged sheepishly. "My hair has a will of its own, I'm afraid."

Zenobia gestured to a lock of her own errant hair. "I know what you mean," she said. She picked out a peach slice and nibbled at it as it dangled on the end of the knife. She cast a sidelong glance at Daniel Whittaker as she realized that there was no ladylike way to eat peaches with a knife. Daniel Whittaker grinned and Zenobia dabbed at her chin, embarrassed.

"I'm so sorry," she stammered. "I don't usually make such a . . . such a *spectacle* of myself when I eat."

"I like to see a woman who enjoys her food," he declared. "Too many females pick and paw at it." He pulled out his handkerchief as she searched futilely in her apron pocket for a clean rag. "Use this, why don't you?"

"Oh, thank you." She dabbed at her chin, feeling foolishly happy. Eben would have lifted one faintly disapproving eyebrow if she'd ever eaten so untidily in *his* vicinity.

If Daniel Whittaker hadn't been the sheriff, she would have been able to relax and appreciate his company. He was a very handsome man, only she had been far too nervous of him until this moment to appreciate just how handsome. She'd noticed the striking gray-green eyes, of course, the light clear color set off by dark lashes tipped with gold. Dark brows rode the browbone straight out to the temple, but there was a cheerful, quiet masculinity to the whole face that could still a woman's heart. He was regarding her steadily, a grin lurking on the wide, generous mouth, and she could not look anywhere but at him. She swallowed another piece of peach hastily, before she could choke on it. "I'll have Wing Loo return your handkerchief the moment he's washed it."

"There's no hurry. I sort of like the idea of it riding around in your pocket."

Zenobia quickly looked down. He was attracted to her as surely as she was attracted to him! That Daniel Whittaker was not only attracted to her but was also romantic enough that he wished her to carry something of his left Zenobia quite unable to think straight.

"How's everything going with Wing Loo and the others?"

"Oh, as well as can be expected," Zenobia managed to say. "They are very civil people but my being unable to converse with them necessarily creates a barrier between us. They make every effort to include me in their conversations, but the simple fact is that I cannot speak their language. Wing Loo's cousin, Ah Tup, has kindly tried to teach me a few words, but Chinese is most difficult. Did you know that it has four different tones which alter the meanings of the same word most alarmingly?"

"Why, no, ma'am, I didn't," Daniel replied, hoping she would just go on talking and talking so he could look at her. He could hardly conceal the pleasure it gave him. Her cheeks were pink from some emotion and her hair created a puffy halo around her head that caught the light from the window and lit up her face.

"Well, it does," she was saying. Daniel made an earnest attempt to follow what she was saying. "The same word can mean four different things depending on which tone one uses, only I cannot, for the life of me, hear the difference between all four nor reproduce the sounds properly. I have provided Wing Loo and his relations with a good deal of entertainment in my endeavor to speak even a few words of Chinese but they are too polite to laugh out loud at me. I suppose I must be thankful I was not born in China, else I would not be able to make myself understood, I assure you."

Daniel laughed. "I expect if someone had spoken it to you all your life, you might have learned it."

"I very much doubt it. I *would* enjoy understanding what it is they all talk about, however. It all sounds rather raucous, all quick, sharp sounds, and absolute gales of laughter to go with it. For all that they are so polite and insist that I share in their meals, I feel rather left out. I do envy them their closeness."

"It is nice to have somebody to talk to." He tilted his head to one side, studying her, and Zenobia tried in vain not to stare back. Fine lines radiated from the corners of his eyes, white against his tan, where his skin creased when he smiled.

Zenobia nodded agreement. "When I go up to bed at night, I can't help hearing them downstairs still. They all hush their voices out of consideration for my rest, but I actually strain to hear them. It sometimes makes me wish I—" *Wish I still belonged somewhere, with someone.*

He tilted his head. "It makes you wish—?"

She shook her head quickly. "It's nothing. Oh, well, I expect

I had better get back to work. I have a great deal left to do if I'm going to open next week."

"Will you be doing the cooking?"

"I'll be doing everything."

"That's a fearsome amount of work, ma'am. Have you ever cooked for a big group before?"

Not for anything would Zenobia admit that she'd hardly ever set foot in a kitchen, let alone cooked. "I don't anticipate many difficulties," she said confidently. She noted the twitch at one corner of his mouth but decided against asking the cause of it. "Let me rinse your knife blade in some hot water to get the peach juice off of it."

"I'd appreciate that. A sticky blade isn't much use."

Zenobia retreated to the stove against the back wall, behind the half-height counter that separated the kitchen from the serving area. "Oh, drat!"

"What seems to be the problem?"

Zenobia started violently. Daniel Whittaker had followed her. He certainly did move quietly! She took a deep breath to steady herself. "The fire died out." She opened the black metal door that covered the stove's belly and knelt to peer inside. "There's plenty of fuel here," she announced, refusing to call it what it really was. "I heaped in extra just so this wouldn't happen."

Daniel Whittaker had hunkered down behind her and was looking over her shoulder. "Yes, ma'am, but I think too much fuel is what caused your problem."

He was so near that she could smell the leather of his vest mingled with the salty odor of horse and a pleasant, faint odor that she fancied must be his own skin. She stared sightlessly at the stove's interior, transfixed by his nearness. She was careful to keep from leaning back, for then she would come in contact with the wide chest.

"You want to tend it, see," he said, his voice close to her ear. "Start with a few patties and get it burning nice and steady, and then you add a few more every so often, depending on how dried out the patties are, but you can't heap so many in at once or it just smothers the fire." He reached for the poker but instead of taking it from her, he grasped her hand, poker and all.

Zenobia stared in bemused fascination at his hand surrounding hers so that only her fingertips showed. A thin scar traced across his wrist, white against the honey-colored skin, and short golden brown hairs, curling and stiff, showed at the cuff of his shirt. They tapered to a light scattering across the back of his hand, catching the light of the fire as he poked at the embers and they rekindled. He stirred them around until the edges of other patties began to smoke and burn. His chest touched her back as he leaned forward, the motion of his arm transferring itself so that her whole body was stirred in small circles by his, held captive against the hard torso behind her. The air suddenly felt curiously difficult to breathe.

Zenobia started to lose her balance but Daniel Whittaker reached with his free hand to cup her shoulder and brace her firmly against his chest. "You see how it's done?" he asked. "You get it real hot in the center and then keep pushing the new pieces into it a little at a time." His voice seemed to rumble right through her. "Now, you just keep an eye on it and every so often, you toss on another patty. It should burn nice and steady for you then. You think you can do that?"

"Oh, my, yes," she managed to say, not sure anymore exactly what it was they were talking about. It felt remarkably as if *she* were the one being kindled by Daniel Whittaker's expert ministrations. His embrace was so intimate and yet so utilitarian, so practical and yet so . . . erotic.

The simple desire to see a friendly face had metamorphosed into desire of another kind, a breathless longing that went beyond, far beyond, what was proper, and carried with it risks she could ill afford to take.

"Thank you, Sheriff Whittaker," she said, still speaking to the stove. She didn't dare look over her shoulder to see what might be in those gray-green eyes, nor risk him seeing what was in hers. "I'm sure I shall manage better from now on." She disengaged her hand from his in a decided manner and set the poker up against the stove.

He sensed her dismissal and stood up in one fluid movement. The contact was broken so quickly that she wondered for an instant if she had only imagined the delicious and dangerous closeness of their bodies. But when she rose and turned, she saw by the dark, intent look in his eyes that she had not been mistaken. It had happened, and he was as affected by it as she. Zenobia attempted to regain control of herself. To be wooed was dangerous enough; to respond would be madness.

She found her voice and used it to inject a note of ordinariness. "Please, won't you eat the rest of the peaches? I'm quite full and I don't want them to go to waste."

His easy smile returned, softening the tension between his brows. "Well, I don't mind if I do, ma'am, if you've had your fill. I confess, I'm partial to peaches. In fact, watching you eat them gave me quite an appetite." The sidelong grin said more than his words, enough to make her lower her eyes.

He took his knife back from her—with only the most benign brushing of fingertips this time—and speared a peach from the can. He dropped a slice in his mouth and chewed it with relish until they were all gone.

"Thank you, ma am. I enjoyed those. And don't worry about my knife—I'll rinse it off at the jail. I'll just use it to stir my coffee. He sheathed the knife in a scabbard that rode on the hip opposite his gun and started toward the front of the restaurant, collecting his hat from the table on the way. He paused with one hand on the doorknob. "You'll let me know about making that bed for you just the minute you make up your mind, won't you?"

Zenobia nodded and swallowed. A bed big enough for two people, he'd said. "Yes, Sheriff, I certainly will."

"Now, Daniel, what in the hell *is* that thing exactly?"

One of Walter Connolly's better qualities was that you always knew right where you stood with him. Daniel valued that, particularly at the moment when he was spending so much time wondering what Miss Zoe Smith was really feeling. Every so often, he just let himself sink into the luxury of his deputy's company in the sure and certain knowledge that what Walter said was just what Walter was thinking.

"It's a rosebush, Walter." Daniel tugged the guy rope on the miniature sun shade he'd rigged to provide shade for the thing during the hottest part of the day. He scratched at the soil in the sawn-off whiskey keg and added a little more water. Behind him, Walter harumphed.

"I think you been had, Daniel. It don't look like no rosebush I ever seen."

"Well, it will," Daniel said defensively. The very unpromising-looking clump of twigs he'd received in response to his order for a rosebush had taken three weeks to arrive from the mail-order nursery in Missouri and he was bound and determined to get it to grow. "I got a letter with it says it's dormant right now and I should keep an eye on it and water it and it'll start growing soon." He scratched at the bark with one fingernail. "See here, where it shows green underneath? Instructions say that's how you can tell if it's really alive. A dead one wouldn't have any green under the bark, so you just bide your time, Walter. We'll have us a rosebush soon enough."

"Why in hell do we even want us a rosebush? A jailhouse is no place to be growing rosebushes," Walter growled. "May as well just turn in your six-shooter for an apron and a duster."

"Uh-huh." Daniel glanced over the instructions again, listening to Walter with half an ear. If there was something the deputy really wanted him to hear, he knew the remark would always be prefaced by something like, "If you want to know what I think." That way, no important information got lost in the daily give and take.

"Do you mind tellin' me *why* we're growin' roses in front of the jailhouse?" Walter persisted. "It wouldn't have nothin' to do with a certain lady who can't do laundry, would it?"

"Well, it might, Walter, it just might," Daniel conceded.

"Daniel, if you want to know what I think, I think you got it bad." Walter Connolly hawked a big gob of tobacco juice toward the street. "Now, you can keep your compass in your trousers if you want to, but I figure you should go back to keepin' company with the doves if you've got to have a woman. They like you well enough, and you don't have to grow no damned flowers for 'em."

Daniel sat back on his heels. It was the longest, most impassioned speech he'd ever heard his deputy make. "I'll bear that in mind, Walter," he said. "I will. Now, you have a care and don't go using this tub for a spittoon by accident, you hear? Or on purpose. I don't care how you feel about roses. I've got a feeling Miss Smith will like them just fine and that's all I care about."

Walter muttered something sulfurous but was spared the necessity of clarifying his feelings when a scrawny youth came pelting around the corner and slid to a halt in front of the jail.

"That one-legged man, that southerner, he picked a big fight with a *vaquero* over at Dolly's place! She said to run and get you quick!"

"Well, hell, that's more like it," Walter declared gleefully. "Let's go, Daniel!"

Zenobia set her broom aside and cast a critical eye over the restaurant. Not bad—a little crude, but it looked quite clean compared to a week ago. Now she had to wash and dry every pot and dish in the back, and then she could begin to experiment with cooking. What exactly one did with corned beef and farina and the other foodstuffs Clarence Trilby had advised her to order she had no idea, but how hard could it be? You mixed a little of this and a little of that and put it in the stove. The servants at home were forever popping things in and out of the stove.

The door hinge creaked. An odd clicking sound came toward

her, moving rapidly, and Zenobia spun around, alarmed. She'd been forced to raise the shades today to see what she was doing, and more men than ever had been thrusting their heads through the door to ask if she was open for business yet. She laughed with relief when she saw who was coming toward her.

"Oh, Dog—you gave me a fright!"

The big black-and-gray animal sat down and regarded her solemnly. Tied to his neck by a ribbon was a rolled-up piece of paper. When Dog nudged closer and whined softly, she bent and gingerly retrieved it. Unfurled, it contained a message from Teresa. Zenobia had approached her for help in contacting other madams about laundry service and the note said that Teresa had an answer for her. It asked whether she preferred to stop in at the Red Dog Saloon or receive a call at the restaurant to hear the outcome.

Zenobia examined her dowdy green handmade skirt with dismay. Despite the snowy white apron Wing Loo had given her to wear over it that morning, she had splashes of dirt and water and grease all over herself. She could not pay a call on anyone looking as she did, not even a prostitute.

Zenobia went back to the kitchen where she had been making an inventory of plates and eating utensils. Heaps of steel forks and knives soaked in a white enamel basin awaiting her attention, next to stack after stack of white plates. A stub of a pencil lay next to her sheaf of papers. She touched it lightly to her tongue, a distasteful necessity to get it started. Forming a good Spenserian script with a balky old pencil proved a challenge, but Zenobia applied herself to the task with diligence. After all, a lady was judged by her hand.

Dog looked at her hopefully as she reattached the letter to him. His brows shifted comically, left, then right, then left again as he studied her. "No, I'm sorry, boy. I haven't any of whatever Teresa gives you as a reward for your services." She held her hands out, palms up, to demonstrate emptiness. Dog sighed and clicked off.

Zenobia was up to her elbows in warm wash water with a

sea of grease on top when she heard a tentative knock at the front door an hour later.

"I'm not open," she shouted.

The door hinge creaked. "Well, who said you were?" A blond head appeared.

"Oh, I beg your pardon, Teresa," Zenobia said, hastily drying her hands on her apron. "I do feel rather put upon by the men in this town continually stopping in to ask if I'm open for business. I'm afraid it's made me somewhat short with people who knock on my door."

Teresa's mouth lifted in a wry smile. "I know exactly how you feel," she said. "I have the same problem."

Zenobia felt color flood her cheeks. "Well," she said awkwardly, "do come in."

But instead of coming in by herself, Teresa held the door open for a procession of gaily dressed working girls, at least fifteen of them. They smiled in her direction a little diffidently, and twirled an assortment of parasols. Bonnets of every description trailed bright streams of ribbon, and lace dripped from sleeves and hems and necklines. They came in all sorts, from thin as six o'clock to quite plump, from strikingly attractive to decidedly plain, from deathly pale to skin tones far deeper than *café au lait,* from barely out of the nursery to grandmotherly.

Teresa made her way through the assemblage and began performing introductions. Although most of the ensembles were tasteless in the extreme and far removed from anything she would ever wear herself, Zenobia still felt rather drably attired as she shook numerous hands. Many of the women were near her own age, what her mother had delicately called "the wrong side of twenty," and some were quite young, which came as a surprise. Zenobia had always assumed that fallen women looked decrepit, aged beyond their natural time owing to their wicked ways, but the wages of sin, at least in Gila City, evidently differed from those elsewhere. These women seemed more or less intact—in all ways but one, of course—and relatively robust.

The introductions to such colorful characters as Silver Sally and Contrary Mary over, Zenobia apologized for having no refreshments to offer them. A few bottles were produced from beneath voluminous skirts, evidently a Gila City variation on presenting your hostess with flowers. Dog, who had been trotting around in a gregarious mood, pushing his big blunt head into various hands in search of attention, seated himself and watched expectantly as bottles were opened. Tin cups and even a few glasses were unearthed from among the clean dishes and, soon enough, the atmosphere became quite festive.

Formal introductions gave way to more candid conversation and Zenobia, who sipped cautiously at the raw whiskey in her glass, gradually realized that each of the whores was really a madam, one representing each of the town's bawdy houses, except for Megan, who they called the Irish Queen, who represented a loose association of girls who worked in the cribs, a succession of small rooms along a plank sidewalk on the south side of town.

Zenobia sent a glance toward Teresa, touched and rather amazed by her powers of persuasion and organization. The only madam who hadn't come, Madame Bettina, fancied herself better than the others but sent word through Teresa that she would no doubt patronize Smith's Laundry provided the prices were satisfactory and the service up to snuff. The other women laughed at this and warned Zoe that the dreadful German madam would drive a hard bargain, and no matter how well the job was done, would no doubt tell her that laundry was done better in Dusseldorf.

In no time at all the whiskey sent a glow straight to Zenobia's bones. Teresa sat down next to her on a bench and amidst the riotous chatter of fifteen madams, inquired as to whether Zenobia had been keeping company with Sheriff Whittaker.

"No, not at all," Zenobia said, so startled by the question that she failed to withdraw her glass in time to avoid having it refilled by a passing whore. She warily sucked at the quivering fluid before it could overflow the glass.

"Is that so?" Teresa eyed her with interest. "I haven't seen him lately either, at least not where it counts." She looked at Zenobia very directly. Apparently deciding she hadn't quite gotten her point across yet, Teresa added, "He used to be a customer of mine, at least before you came to town."

"Oh!" Zenobia felt her cheeks flaring. "You don't think—I mean, you aren't suggesting that he's seeing me instead of . . . that I'm . . . I mean to say, I'm in business but I'm not in *that* business."

Teresa smiled. "I didn't think you were, honey, though I suspect you could make more lying on your back than you do here."

Zenobia sucked in a big breath, horrified.

"Queen Bettina would like to have her," chimed in a woman nearby. "She likes the ones that speak well and look like butter wouldn't melt in their mouths—just like her high-class fillies back in Dusseldorf."

"Saints preserve us all from the forces of uplift," another woman said.

The room erupted in guffaws. "Now hush, Linda," Teresa said reprovingly. "Look at Miss Smith—she's gone all red. Guess that proves some of us still know how to blush." She shooed the others away with a wave. "Did Daniel ever make you that bed you wanted?" she asked.

Comprehension dawned. "It was you who told him I needed one?"

Teresa nodded. "He's a friend and he seems kind of sweet on you, so I put a word in his ear."

"Well, he brought the wood to make it to my laundry, but I wasn't sure I should . . ." Zenobia bit her lower lip. "I think I really must accept his offer, though. I wanted to move my bed from the laundry to this place but Wing Loo informs me that it can't be done."

"Oh, yeah?" Teresa quirked one pale eyebrow. "Why not?"

"It's not quite clear to me," Zenobia admitted, "but I gather it has something to do with the type of wood it's made of. It would have to be taken apart to get it out the door and Wing

Loo says it couldn't be put together a second time. Says the nails wouldn't hold."

"Hmmm." Teresa's murmur conveyed disbelief.

Zenobia looked at her in surprise. "You sound as if you don't think he's telling the truth."

"I think Wing Loo's telling you what he's been told to tell you." She stood up and smoothed her pale-yellow dress down over her cage crinoline. As if her rising were a signal, the other women began to collect glasses and put away bottles. "If I were you, I'd let Daniel make you that bed," Teresa said with a faint smile. "If some fellow was trying to grow roses for me, I'd sure be inclined to encourage him." She looked around brightly. "Well, I expect that's about twenty minutes. That's what the book said for a social call, isn't it—twenty minutes?" Without waiting for an answer, she barked, "That's it, ladies. Time to hit the trail!"

Zenobia found her hand shaken by one after another of the madams. She tried to corner Teresa in the milling, jabbering crowd but Teresa appeared to be avoiding her all of a sudden. With her parasol held high and a cigarette dangling from her lips, she led the rest of the madams out of Smith's Good Luck Restaurant.

Eight

Thank God for the Chinamen's chickens was all Zenobia could think as she scraped burnt hominy from the bottom of a big saucepan. Because of them she would at least have some eggs for dinner, not to mention the chickens' willingness to eat burned things—like the hominy—when no one and nothing else would.

But just because she had something in mind for her own supper didn't relieve Zenobia of the obligation to make something edible from the supplies on hand. She had to keep practicing if she ever expected to produce a meal that others would actually pay for. It was decidedly exasperating, burning dish after dish. After all, it wasn't as if she were trying to produce food that would satisfy an epicure. She just needed to produce *simple* things, only it was proving to be amazingly difficult to cook anything at all.

She rebuilt the fire and consulted the copy of Mrs. Rundell's *Modern Domestic Cookery,* which Contrary Mary had given her as a gift on her way out following what Zenobia had come to think of as the "working girls' social." Contrary Mary said that her mother had sent it to her in the mistaken belief that Mary's reference in a letter home to having met quite a lot of men in America translated into a wedding in the near future. Mary's mother urged her to study Mrs. Rundell's book so as to be able to please her prospective husband.

"I've got the knack of pleasing men all right," Mary confided in Zenobia's ear through the din, "but it don't involve no ambrosia or fluff pastry if you knows what I mean. You have this," she said in a broad Manchester accent and thrust the book into Zenobia's hands. "It only reminds me of what I come here to get away from, cooking and cleaning and serving and the like."

Zenobia turned to the section on sweets—rich, delicious puddings, tarts, creams, and custards. It had been a very long time indeed since she'd sat down to a table laden with the kinds of desserts Mrs. Rundell described so lavishly. Zenobia's mouth watered and her stomach rumbled just reading about them. To think she had ever voluntarily turned aside such desserts at her own table for the sake of her waistline!

Eagerly perusing page after page, she came to a recipe for Dutch pudding billed as a modest dessert suitable for everyday family fare. Judging that something designated everyday fare should be easy to make, Zenobia looked over the ingredients. She had all of them, more or less. If the pudding was a success, it would be the work of a minute to double or treble the recipe for use in the restaurant. Blithely dismissing the burned hominy as a fluke, she confidently set out to make the pudding.

It called for a pound of butter, which she measured out from the firkin rather dubiously, not at all sure that butter should smell quite so unappetizing, but then, she'd been accustomed to the freshest of everything and this, of necessity, had been shipped overland. It was probably fine. But how did one determine how much was a pound? Zenobia spooned it into a white metal basin, adjusting the contents until she judged that it weighed about sixteen ounces.

Melted in a half pint of milk. She rummaged on a shelf and found a tin of condensed, sweetened milk. It only contained four ounces, but the difference between four and eight ounces seemed insignificant, and besides, wasn't it condensed? If it was condensed, it had to be condensed down from *something*, so at one time it had been *more* milk than just four ounces. Pleased by her ability to reason her way through these little obstacles, Zenobia poured the thick, gooey milk into the basin.

Next the recipe called for two pounds of flour. Farina was

the nearest thing she had, but Clarence Trilby had assured her that it made up into nice biscuits so Zenobia decided she could use it interchangeably for regular flour. Eight eggs—*those* she had. Four spoonfuls of yeast—that was a puzzler. Surely the saleratus, which was like baking soda, could be used as a rising agent. It had a faintly metallic smell but that would surely be eclipsed by the other good ingredients once it was cooked.

One pound of currants. She opened the tin of cherries she meant to substitute for the currents and added them, making a note to buy currants the next time she went to the shebang. Last came a pound of sugar, sifted. Zenobia poked at the brown sugar, so dried and hardened in the keg that she had to resort to chipping it out with a sugar auger. Mr. Trilby had assured her that white sugar was almost unobtainable except by special order, so it was no good pining for any. She tossed the coarse lumps of brown sugar into the pan, trusting to the heat of the stove to smooth it out.

The recipe called for cooking the mixture in a quick oven for an hour, but whatever was a "quick" oven? It sounded as if it were meant to cook things quickly, which probably meant higher heat. Using her newly acquired skill with fires, Zenobia built up a rip-roaring blaze and stirred the ingredients vigorously before transferring the basin into the stove of the big Livingstone Range. There! In an hour she would have a delicious pudding, and what didn't get eaten right away warm, Mrs. Rundell assured the reader, would be equally delicious later cold.

Zenobia washed her hands with a good deal of satisfaction and then she remembered again what she had been struggling nervously to put out of her mind all day. Daniel Whittaker was coming by today to start on her new bed.

She'd finally conceded defeat in the battle to persuade Wing Loo to at least *try* bringing her old bed from the laundry to the restaurant. Buttressed by his relatives, who shook their heads mournfully as they crowded around the bed, pointing at various parts of it dolefully, he'd explained at great length—in Chinese—what it was that precluded him from doing as she wished, which was, he assured her—in English—his deepest desire, so that it brought him grievous pain to have to say no to her. Zenobia conceded the point. His relatives beamed and squatted by the planks Daniel Whittaker had brought. They pantomimed rubbing and polishing the boards with exaggerated looks of reverence, by which she knew they meant to reassure her that a bed made out of that wood would be *far* superior to her old one.

Wing Loo and Ah Tup carried her packing crate dresser over to the restaurant with great good humor and put it in the large west-facing bedroom she'd chosen for her own. The hallway stretched from front to back and her room would be across the whole back, in the part of the building farthest from Main Street, where the waddies raced their ponies at all hours of the night, yipping and hollering, and the music and the fights and the sound of breaking glass drifted down from the saloons. After subtle but continuous prodding from Wing Loo, she relented and sent word around to the jail that she would indeed like Daniel Whittaker to make her a bed, only she would be needing it in her new room over the restaurant.

And he'd be there within the hour. Zenobia quelled her panic with an effort and looked around the kitchen, deciding what to do while the pudding cooked. Time to do nothing was a luxury she didn't possess. She smelled the pudding, just beginning to heat up, the odor not quite enticing yet. Flies had settled on the counter in some spilled cherry juice and others were buzzing around her head. The sight of so many flies made her want to stamp and shake like a wild thing.

Zenobia ripped into the box of supplies that had been delivered earlier that day and emerged with a box of Einbinder's Fly Paper. Each little cylinder would unfurl into a long helix of sticky paper to trap the flies. The thought satisfied her soul as she picked at the seal on the first cardboard tube. No one in this godforsaken hole had ever heard of putting mesh over windows to keep insects out, and there would—of course—be a delay of many weeks while the roll she had ordered made its tedious way to Gila City via ox train. In the meantime, the flypaper, which the general store stocked all the time, was her only defense.

It took a knife to wrest the seal off the first tube and then the spiral of paper fell and rebounded upward, sticking to itself. Carrying a bench with her, Zenobia got a small kitchen mallet and a tiny nail to hang the strip from. Her thumb took the first strike but the second connected with the nail. She yanked the strip to disengage it from itself. It tore and fell to the floor, immediately becoming coated with dust.

Fighting back tears of frustration, Zenobia took the fallen length to the counter and had the satisfaction of rolling it over all the flies unwise enough not to depart at her approach. The second cylinder came open without incident. Things began to go a little smoother after that—up onto the bench, tap in the nail, hang the flypaper, and down. She hit her thumb quite a few times, and it took the knife and some sawing to open the tubes—which were, according to the manufacturer, supposed to open like magic—and she wrenched her ankle several times stepping down from the stool, but for once she felt as if she were managing well.

The final flypaper proved especially difficult to open. The knife slipped as she sawed at it, gashing a furrow across her thumb. Zenobia leapt away from the counter with a cry. The cut smarted like a bee's sting. Sucking at it, she succeeded only in making it sting more. Blood trickled down her wrist, making her feel for the edge of a table to sit down. She knew she couldn't die from such an ignominious little cut, but it certainly was making her faint to look at it.

And then she smelled the smoke. It was seeping around the doors of the range in tiny furls, but when she hurriedly opened the door the smoke burst out like a pent-up beast. She beat it away from her face and dove in with mitts to rescue the pudding as smoke gusted around her head. Backing away with the basin in her pincerlike grasp, Zenobia flung it onto the counter and staggered toward a window for fresh air. When she returned, she stared in dismay at the pan, its enamel raised in ugly pustulant black bubbles. Worst of all was the pudding itself, spitting and heaving and crusted over by a charcoal skin. The repulsive smoking mass of it quivered and hissed like an angry cat.

No part of it looked edible. No part of it even looked like food. Zenobia clutched her burned fingers to her breast, lower lip trembling. The sharp report of wood on wood out in the street startled her and triggered the outburst of tears that had been threatening off and on all afternoon. Sinking to her knees, she began sobbing with her hands over her face.

"Darlin'!"

Two strong hands at her elbows scooped her up off the floor. Zenobia couldn't even see who it was through her tears. They squeezed out between her fingers and skidded down the backs of her hands. She hoped whoever was holding her would have the decency to just shoot her and put her out of her misery. It sounded like it might be Daniel Whittaker who had a grip on her, which would be good since he was the one man in town who could be relied on to have a gun handy.

"Come on now, honey, it can't be all that bad," he said gently. "Where's all this blood coming from?"

He pried her hands away from her face. Zenobia wailed louder, knowing how awful she must look with blood and smoke and tears streaking down her plump cheeks. Daniel Whittaker patted at her face and forehead with his handkerchief, going over her like a horse at auction. He turned to her hands next. "Oh, look there, you've got a cut. Is there anything else that's cut, Zoe?" He gave her a little shake. "Are you hurt anywhere else? Tell me, darlin'."

Zenobia shook her head which was all rubbery at the end of her neck. "N-no." Daniel Whittaker flitted in her vision, spangled through the veil of tears.

"Shush then, darlin'," he said, drawing her against his chest and wrapping his arms around her. "You'll be all right in a minute." He patted her back with one large hand and smoothed her hair away from her damp face with the other. To be held by him was a consolation beyond describing. Zenobia buried her head against his chest and cried even harder.

"I . . . I . . . wanted to make some pudding," she sobbed, "and . . . and show you how well I could cook."

"Aw, now that's awful nice, honey," he said.

"And . . . and I wanted to look nice for you, too, and have . . . have the restaurant cl-clean!"

His arms tightened around her. "Well, you know, the place does look good, and I expect we could still get out the heart of that pudding, darlin'," he said. "I'm awful partial to puddings."

Zenobia pulled back enough to look up at his face. "You are?" She hiccupped. "You mean you'd really like to try some? If there's any that's all right to eat, that is?"

He smiled, the corners of his eyes crinkling up with it. "Sure would." He tenderly wiped her cheeks with the hanky. Zenobia smiled back through her tears, admiring his lovely wide mouth and the beautiful gray-green eyes and thinking how much she wished he'd kiss her at that very moment. But he was more of a gentleman than she was a lady and he didn't. She disengaged herself from his embrace, flustered by the direction of her thoughts.

It took some doing but she was able to excavate with a spoon a scant serving of the pudding untouched by blackness, right in the heart of the charred mess, though it looked suspiciously runny and uncooked to her eyes. Daniel Whittaker spooned it up with every appearance of delight, though, and expressed deep regret that there wasn't any more.

"That was dandy, darlin'," he said. "I think you're on your way to being a fine cook."

"I can always make more another time," she said shyly.

He stood up and took her hands in his. "I'd like that, but right now we should worry about your hands. They look a little tender."

She looked at her throbbing fingertips, gone a taut, shiny pink. Seeing the damage brought back the pain. She tried to be brave, though—she'd already been a big enough baby for one evening. "I'll put some cream on them when I go to sleep tonight. They'll be fine by morning."

"Well, no doubt, darlin', but I sure hope you'll be careful the next time you go to handle something hot." The long bones of his finger pressed against her knuckles, the dry heat of his hands soothing as he clasped her small and not very clean hands in his. He lifted one of them and examined it. "You sure do have pretty hands, darlin'. It makes a man mighty sad to see such pretty hands all rough from working."

Zenobia sniffed, brought to the brink of tears again by his show of concern and by the appearance of her hands. They truly did look awful, not manicured and pampered as they should have been, *would* have been if not for Eben and his schemes, and Stephen who'd thought he could come and rape her in her own house. Well, she'd sure shown *him*. She'd killed him rather than be raped. Suddenly Zenobia was struck by terror at the realization of exactly who it was who was holding the same hands that had pushed Stephen to his death.

Daniel Whittaker was the sheriff, for heaven's sake, and she was a murderess! But her treacherous body could not immediately give up the comfort of his touch nor the doting smile he bent on her. It would have been seductive in any circumstances, but here and now, it seemed like the only worthwhile thing under the sun. Ripped apart by conflicting emotions, she began to cry again, silent tears slipping down her cheeks.

"I—I know my hands look frightful," she whispered. "The flypaper and . . . and the hammer and . . . the knife . . . and the pudding. None of it went right, none of it. I feel so useless."

"Now, you're not to think on it, darlin'," he admonished her gently. "They'll be all right and so will you. It's just things don't always go so well. We've all got days like that and this is one of yours. Tomorrow it'll all look different." Music from the Red Dog filtered in past the shades that were slapping softly against the window frames in the evening breeze—the notes of a fiddle and a piano twining together, surprisingly sweet.

"Listen—do you hear that music?" he asked. "That's 'Annie Laurie.' Do you know how it goes?"

Unable to stop the soft weeping that had taken hold of her, Zenobia shook her bowed head although she knew the words to "Annie Laurie" perfectly well. Nobody who had lived through the war could fail to.

Daniel Whittaker tucked her hands against his chest, pulling her close again. He began singing softly. The baritone speaking voice went up in song, lighter and purer. Zenobia went still. He sang just for her, sang the song in a way she had never heard it sung before, as if it were a lullaby. She smiled at the beauty of his voice, clear and controlled. The music faded at last but she remained motionless, his light embrace so heartening. She could not bear to break away from it, nor did he seem inclined to end it either, his arms and his body warm and hard against hers.

The gloom of evening softened the contours inside the restaurant, the plank tables just bumps in the shadows by the saffron glow of the kerosene lantern back in the kitchen. Zenobia stared up at Daniel Whittaker, into the shadowy depths of his eyes that regarded her with such tender intensity that it made her insides curl. Just as the moment stretched out to the insupportable and they began to drift apart by inches, a new tune reached their ears.

" 'Arkansas Traveler!' " Daniel exclaimed, seeming as relieved as she to hear another song during which they could cleave together. He towed her toward the side door of the restaurant and threw it open. "You hear it?"

Zenobia nodded, her hand still clutched in his strong grasp. He held his head in a listening attitude, his foot tapping to the music. He turned to her.

The lantern touched the sharp edges of his jaw with gold and the arrow-straight nose with gold on one side and shadow on the other. Beyond his shoulder, the western sky hummed with gold, arched out across the heavens and encompassing him in the palette by gilding the top of his head. The broad outline of his body above hers created a silhouette against the evening sky.

"Will you do me the honor, Miss Smith?" His grin was less cocksure now, the look in his eyes more hope than certainty.

"Y-yes, yes I will," she said, overcome by the largeness of him and the way the huge western sky seemed to make him a part of itself.

He gathered her decisively, his confidence restored by her acceptance, and set them in motion. His grin widened as he made his steps bigger, their bodies whirling together, aligned an arm's breadth apart. He was easy to follow. It would have been hard *not* to go with him, to resist his strength and size and motion. She felt like a thread being wound onto a spindle, going round and round with him as her center, tall and straight. Zenobia's unbound hair flew out behind her, the cloth tie gone on a pivot. The hair came around to slap her face as he dipped and changed tacks. His smile widened in undiluted pleasure as she flung her head to send her hair back behind her again. It flew along like a banner, weightless and shining.

She felt her heart spinning, racing, tripping to the music, and to the exhilaration Daniel Whittaker exuded, all her fear forgotten, all unhappiness banished in the joy of the music and the motion and his touch. She could hear the music only imperfectly, but he beat out the tempo with his body so definitively that she could not fail to stay in step.

They whirled and turned, powered by his exuberance and her willingness to be drawn into it. His face was flooded with warm honey color when the lantern's light fell on him and then turned to cool gilt again when he spun away to face the sunset, but through it all, his lopsided smile remained constant, just for her, always on her, as if she were something precious and gratifying.

At last he reined them both in, his hand on her side tightening to brake her. They looked at each other for a long moment when they were finally stopped, faces flushed, eyes sparkling, and laughed simultaneously at nothing at all, and then their own unprovoked laughter made them laugh even harder.

"Oh, my, that was a fine dance, Miss Zoe, a fine dance," Daniel Whittaker said emphatically. "Thank you, ma'am."

Zenobia stepped back and bent him a sweeping curtsey, swinging her stained green work skirt aside in a graceful arc. "It was my pleasure, Mr. Whittaker," she said.

The grin faded from the sheriff's face as she rose, his nostrils flaring and the level brows suddenly taut. "That's pretty the way you do that, ma'am." He touched one knuckle to her cheek. "Dancing with you is like dancing with an angel. You're so pretty it makes my heart nearly break."

Zenobia felt her chest tighten. "Thank you," she said. The quiver in her voice betrayed how deeply the compliment had affected her. The most shattering thing was that he so evidently meant what he said as a statement of indisputable truth and not a piece of flummery. She lowered her eyes. A door slammed somewhere and they glanced outside in unison.

Reminded of the outside world, Zenobia removed her hands from his grasp. It was all madness, this flirting and dancing and pretending she had a right to a man's attentions! Daniel Whittaker seemed startled. He stepped back a pace and drove his own hands into his pockets in confusion.

"Well, I expect I should take that wood for your bed on upstairs," Daniel said, "before someone comes running to tell me there's trouble. Wouldn't want to vouch for that wood still being there in the morning if I leave it outside."

"No, I don't suppose one should put human nature to the test. It so often disappoints," she replied. "The room where I want the bed is upstairs," she said, deliberately turning the conversation back to practical matters with an effort. "It's all the way at the back."

"All right, ma'am." His voice notched down a shade, matching her own suddenly cooler tone. If he was disappointed that the intimacy and gaiety of their dance had burned away like the morning mist, he gave no hint of it.

He strode to the outside and brought in three loads of wood altogether, bearing the weight with grace. He moved with ease under the burdens, long legs hard with defining muscle but no bulk to any part of him. He swung the planks to parallel the narrow inside stairway as easily as he had maneuvered her, long body rotating like the towering cranes that unloaded the massive iron locomotive parts her father needed from the ships in the port of Philadelphia. The wide shoulders, built fluidly into the torso, testified to the tensile strength of the man.

Zenobia stood awkwardly silent as he passed her, wondering if he thought her strange for her abrupt shift of mood. Regardless of what he thought, what she must strive for was to get through the next few days while he made the bed, thank him profusely, pay him something despite the protest she was sure would be forthcoming, and usher him out her door for good.

Daniel Whittaker could not be allowed any closer. Her capacity for subterfuge, for concealing what was in her heart and for schooling her face to blandness, was pushed to the limit already. She could not hope to carry on her double life as Zoe Smith if it included being courted by the sheriff of Gila City. Her talent for deception simply wasn't great enough. Ultimately she would almost certainly reveal glimmers of Zenobia Strouss Sinclair beneath the surface. And Zenobia Strouss Sinclair wasn't only a married woman—which was quite bad enough—she was also a murderess.

Daniel Whittaker came down the stairs for the last time, dusting his palms off. "That'll about do it for now, ma'am. I've got to go have a bit of a walk around town, show my face at all the places where the fellows gather, and remind them that Gila City's got a lawman. It seems to set a certain tone if I do it before they get to drinking too much, while they're still able to think straight. It's like ladies having their dance cards filled in—if they make their plans for the evening early, it makes the night go smoother."

Relief that he was about to leave prompted Zenobia to want a last few words with Daniel Whittaker, pleasant words that might erase his memory of the peculiar about-face in her mood earlier. "And what would you know about dance cards, Sheriff Whittaker?" she teased.

He picked up his hat, "Well, my mother—the nice Baptist lady I believe I told you about—she taught me about dance cards, though we never had a dance where I grew up in Kansas that had enough people to make dance cards necessary. All the boys and girls knew who they cared to dance with long before the big night, but during the war, when I was back East, I had occasion to be glad she'd brought me up to know some better manners, because I got invited to a number of dances held by society ladies for the officers of my cavalry regiment." He saw the sudden change in her eyes and grinned. "I see that it surprises you, ma'am, to learn that I was an officer, but I was."

It wasn't the fact of his having been an officer that took her so aback. It was the broader idea, that he had spent time in the East, and had some brushes with society women and balls. It was her world he was talking about, and that meant he might peg her all the more surely for who and what she was. Another alarming thought occurred to Zenobia: what regiment had he served in? For that matter, what *army* had he served in, Confederate or Union? It demonstrated all too clearly how little she knew of him, and how risky it might be to get on closer terms with him. Dear God, if he'd served in the Union army, he might even have met Eben!

"How very nice for you," she murmured, controlling her alarm with greatest difficulty. "I mean about the dances and being an officer, and all."

Once she'd relaxed her manner, he seemed inclined to linger.

"Well, it just sort of came about by chance, ma'am. I surely didn't qualify as officer fodder, not in the usual way, but the North didn't have too many boys who could ride when the war started, not like the southern boys who seemed to have been born astride, so that made being able to stick to a horse a valuable skill. I got put in charge of some raw recruits to teach 'em to ride and it just naturally worked out. It was a knack I had, nothing special, but the fellows they gave me learned to face the right way on a horse pretty quick and that put my company a step ahead of the other companies. I got to be a captain before it was all over and I did take some pride in those boys, but not many of the first troops I commanded made it through." A shadow passed over his face. He turned his hat in his hands. "But now, look here, I said I meant to take my leave and I will. Shall I come tomorrow at the same time?"

"Please," she said, moved by the compassion and the loss and the startling aloneness she had read in his face in that unguarded instant. She'd meant to ask him to come again in the daylight, when intimacy did not enfold them so easily in its shadows, but instead she said quickly, "Come for supper, won't you?"

He jammed his hat on his head and gave her that lopsided smile that made her heart lurch "Yes, ma'am!"

Charles Merrick poured a splash of whiskey into the cut-glass tumbler. The practiced motion of his wrist made clear as nothing else could have how integral a part of his business day the drink was. He paused with the stopper over the decanter, one eyebrow lifted. "Last chance."

Daniel shook his head. "So it's your impression she's made real estate purchases before?" he asked.

"I'd say so," Merrick replied. He rolled a swallow of whiskey around in his mouth. The green-and-blue carpet muffled his steps as he retraced the path to his desk. "Even the first deal, for the laundry, she was asking the right kinds of questions about the economy here in Gila City, the population, and so forth, but she wasn't overly cautious, no nervous Nellie, and the second deal, the one for Elaine's place, well, I take my hat off to her. Many a cleverer investor wouldn't have proposed such a deal, never mind been so cool about it." He chuckled, regarding Daniel wryly. "Wish I'd thought of it myself. Miss Smith assumes no risk at all, and makes no cash expenditure, and best of all, makes the payments out of income. There's no risk to the seller either, because if Miss Smith defaults, the property simply reverts to the first owner, with all payments kept as rent. It's ideal in a situation where there aren't people clamoring to buy the property outright, and nobody was. Elaine wanted too much extra because of all the restaurant supplies, so anybody just looking for a building to make into something else passed it on by or built a new one cheaper."

"So now she's got to make a profit running it as a restaurant," Daniel mused, talking more to himself than the real estate broker.

"Yes, she does, but knowing how she's fared with that laundry, I have no doubt she will turn a profit. Didn't I hear that some Chinamen came in on the stage to work for her?"

Daniel stood up, holding his hat by the pinch in the crown. "That's the case." He examined his hat brim. He had already had an answer to the question he'd come asking initially, but it seemed as if there was some deeper truth buried in all of this. How did a woman who seemed unable to look after herself, who burned shirts and puddings and gave herself black eyes stumbling around her own place, have the savvy to negotiate the purchase of real estate in a way that filled even a professional with admiration?

She'd gotten lucky when it came to the laundry. He knew it and he doubted she'd trouble to deny it. Wing Loo was a hard worker and a good negotiator, too. He'd nudged prices for laundering clothes up and been overheard at Clarence Trilby's place casually citing prices at Jackson's Emporium to get Clarence to lower the prices he charged Zoe Smith.

Settling his hat on his head, Daniel took his leave of Charles Merrick. Part of the deeper truth he'd been looking for, he suspected, lay in the fact that Charles Merrick came from quality—educated back East, extensively read, good in conversation, and all with a mannerly polish. Daniel knew that Zoe Smith had more in common with the lawyer than she did with him, and he heartily disliked the fact that Charles Merrick seemed to have some personal interest in Zoe Smith.

Daniel sighed. He'd been trying to pace himself with her, like he'd pace a herd of cattle on a long, hard drive. If she weren't so skittish, he'd have already asked her to marry him and eliminated the dismal possibility that someone else, someone like Merrick, would steal a march on him. Every other man she looked at or talked to—it all made him nearly irrational with jealousy. He pushed his hat down, scowling. It used up a lot of energy, this being in love and trying hard not to make a fool of himself over it.

He looked up and down Main Street. It appeared fairly peaceful at the moment, but General Beauregard James had ridden into town that morning and announced that he was bivouacking outside town after spending the winter chasing a band of Indians who held two white women captive. He was a short, stocky man, pleasant enough to look at but wily and tenacious in his duty. That duty, he explained, included letting his men blow off a reasonable amount of steam before they set off north again.

"I need your understanding and cooperation, Sheriff Whittaker, if I'm to succeed in my mission. Being a former cavalry yourself, you'll know that discipline has to be relaxed every now and again."

"Well, yes, General, I do, and I expect your boys can find a good time here in Gila City." Such was the general's manner that Daniel had reacted unthinkingly to the uniform and the brass and snapped him a salute when he walked into the jail. From that it had taken only a few gruff questions by General James to establish that Daniel had served in the 15th Kansas Cavalry, and they'd had a mutual friend, Captain Curtis Johnson.

"Another good man we lost. Where was it?"

"Battle of Westport, sir, fall of sixty-four."

"Yes, that was it. Well, gone but not forgotten, eh?" The general, who had looked a little misty-eyed for a moment, pushed back his shoulders. "Now I expect a payroll shipment on today's stage. I'm giving my men six months' pay and two weeks off duty. They can do what they please. I propose to send two dozen six-mule teams hitched to wagons into town every morning to haul the drunks back to camp to sober up. As far as I'm concerned, they're free to start over again the minute they can walk a straight line. Do you have any quarrel with that plan, Sheriff? It'll mean a lot of hard currency in the pockets of businessmen in Gila City."

"And businesswomen."

General James flicked a spot of lint off his sleeve. "No doubt, but in my view, it's no more than these boys deserve. They had scarcely enough clothes all winter and only half rations most of the time."

"I'd be obliged if you'd relieve your men of their weapons before you set them loose, General James. It's the law here in Gila City, no firearms of any kind while in town. I don't have enough deputies to go around evening up every contest if your boys get in dust-ups and decide to draw on unarmed men."

"Done," General James declared.

So a horde of U.S. Army regulars was slated to descend on Gila City right around the time Daniel had looked forward to having dinner with Zoe Smith. Well, maybe looking forward to was too strong a term. He grimaced and rubbed his stomach. It had just about recovered from the pudding of the previous evening.

All in all, it promised to be a long hard night. Best to get some sleep before then. Once the stage arrived and the pay was issued to the troops, he wouldn't have any peace. He found Walter at the jail and explained the situation. Rooting around the drawer in his desk, he came up with two extra badges which he buffed with his sleeve. The sunlight glinted a dull gold off them.

"Here, Walter. I'd be obliged if you'd find Clarence and tell him he's needed. I told Ned we'd likely be using the livery stable tonight for the overflow and sent him out to my place to tell Lester to come on into town and lend a hand."

Walter rumbled and belched.

Daniel put his feet up on the desk and prepared to snooze off after Walter departed. He dimly registered the sound of the

Wells Fargo coach passing the jail some time later and knew that peace, such as it was in Gila City, had only a short time to live.

"I beg your pardon."

Daniel blinked and came awake. A thin man, dark haired and with curls dangling in front of his ears, stood in front of his desk. He wore a black frock coat, torn at one elbow, and his stained cravat bore witness to many days without a change of linen. He held a large envelope in one hand. Daniel swung his feet to the floor and the chair creaked violently in protest.

"What can I do for you?"

"When I asked the jehu, the stagecoach driver, where to find the man in charge in this town, he directed me to you, and asked that I bring this along to you also. It is from the authorities of the United States of America."

"Oh. Must be this month's wanted posters. Thank you kindly."

Daniel reached for the envelope but the stranger held on to it as if reluctant to give up his pretext for being there. "My name is Jacob Aleksandrov."

"I'm pleased to meet you, Mr. Aleksandrov. I'm Sheriff Whittaker, Daniel by name." Daniel was still waiting for the envelope to be passed over the desk. To speed things along, he asked, "Was there anything in particular you wanted to see me about?"

The thin man bowed his head, making the ringlets at his cheeks bob. "I am seeking work of some sort and I wish also to find lodgings, but my chief desire is to determine if there is some place in town where I may conduct religious services."

"Whoa," Daniel said. "Let's work our way through that herd one steer at a time. You want work, is that right?"

"That is so, but it is not so important as finding a place where I can share the word of God with the Jews of Gila City."

Daniel blinked at that. "Well, I know we've got us a few Campbellites, and Reverend Bob always gets a fine turn out for his Methodist services, and every so often, we have a man of the cloth come through who tends to the needs of the Congregationals, but I'm not sure we've got any Jews." The man opposite looked stricken so Daniel said quickly, "That's not to say that some fellows might not want to join up after they've heard you speak a few times. Folks out this way are pretty starved for the word of the Lord and they take kindly to a fellow who can make the Bible come alive."

The thin man said lugubriously, "Unlike Christianity, Judaism is not a proselytizing religion. I would never set out to convert men, but only to share the word of God as it is set forth in the Torah, and only to men of the Jewish faith." He lifted large liquid brown eyes to Daniel. "I studied to be a rabbi in Mother Russia but there are too many rabbis there already, so I came to America to walk in the desert like Moses. I am hoping that here God will reveal his plan for me so that I will know whether I am worthy to lead men."

Jacob Aleksandrov sighed heavily. "Alas, I have been wandering far longer than forty days and forty nights, and yet there is no end in sight—no temples in need of a rabbi, no Jews seeking the counsel of a rabbi, nothing."

Daniel knew about Moses and the desert and all, but he'd never heard of a man feeling compelled to revisit the experience personally. "I'm sorry things haven't worked out for you, Mr. Aleksandrov, but like I said, I don't think we've got any Jews in Gila City. Wish I could help."

The rabbi looked even gloomier than before. "Tell me where I might conduct services. That would be the best remedy for my troubled heart, and in that way we will both discover if there are any Jews in Gila City."

"Well, mostly the saloons are empty on Sunday mornings so that's where services get held. You'll find that if you put up signs, fellows'll come and give you a respectful hearing. Why, even once service is over, when they commence to gambling again, on a Sunday they usually have a swearing cup, two bits a curse, to remind everybody to be on their best behavior.

Money goes to the preacher, of course. You could ask around, see if one of the saloon owners would let you use their place."

"Thank you." Jacob Aleksandrov gave a short bow. "That is what I will do." He picked up his satchel. "And where may a man find lodgings for a reasonable price?"

Daniel thought briefly of Zoe Smith's vacant rooms and immediately decided against directing the young man there. He didn't want her to have the distractions—and protection—of lodgers. "Try Klingensmith's, down the street on the left. I think they've got a room upstairs to let. They might let you have it cheap in exchange for helping in the restaurant, maybe serving meals, if you wouldn't object to that kind of work."

At that, the young Jew's expression softened. "The Holy One, blessed be He, makes every occupation agreeable in the eyes of those who follow it."

"Is that so?" Daniel pressed his lips together and nodded politely.

"Indeed," said Jacob Aleksandrov, "an excellent thing is the study of the Torah combined with some worldly occupation, for the labor demanded by them both makes sin to be forgotten. All study of the Torah without work must in the end be futile and become the cause of sin."

"Well, if you say so," Daniel said.

"I did not say so," Jacob said, smiling and pointing a finger heavenward. *"He* did."

Nine

"Did you *really* like it?"

The rosy smile, the lovely china-blue eyes—what could he do but say it one more time?

"Ma'am, that was one of the most remarkable meals I've eaten in a long time." There, he'd said it, and he hadn't lied, not precisely. It *had* been remarkable. What else could you call corned beef that had been boiled with baked beans and carrot tops until he wouldn't have known what any of it was unless she'd told him?

"Oh, I'm so pleased," she said, looking radiant. "I'm hopeful of making biscuits for you tomorrow night, and there's another pudding recipe I want to try, though of course I shall be *much* more careful with the heat of the stove this time."

Daniel kept his smile in place with a supreme effort. "I look forward to it, ma'am. Shall we get along with the bed making now?"

"Are you sure you won't have some more coffee first?" she asked with the pot poised over his cup.

He quickly shielded it with his hand. "Oh, no, ma'am! I couldn't possibly, though it sure was delicious. You know, my partner, Lester—he has an interesting way of making coffee that turns out real well. You should make him show you how he does it someday, just for variety." *It involves using coffee beans, for one thing,* he was thinking, Daniel was pretty sure her method didn't. The first cup had resembled yellow soap-suds. He'd had coffee doctored with plugs of tobacco that tasted better than hers. "How about you? Aren't you going to eat?"

"Oh, no," she said. "I've got some eggs I'll do up later." She ducked her head so that the mass of her dark brunette hair concealed half her face. "I was so nervous over whether you'd like the stew that I couldn't have eaten a bite anyway."

Lucky girl, he thought, but what he said was, "I'll just go on upstairs then, shall I? You come along when you can. I'll be needing your ideas on how you'd like the bed to be."

She brushed the waving tendrils of hair back out of her eyes. "All right." She glanced over her shoulder toward the kitchen. "Maybe you'd like to take the rest of the stew to the jail later for the deputies?" she asked hopefully. "You did say you had a lot of extra helpers."

"Well, that's awful kind of you, ma'am. Yes, I'll do that. Lester maybe won't have had time to eat since breakfast and I just know he won't believe me when I tell him about this stew— he'll have to try some for himself. He's a fine cook, too. Maybe he'll share a recipe or two with you, especially for biscuits. He makes as fine a biscuit as I ever tasted."

"They do say that men make the best chefs," Zenobia said brightly, "but I believe I may just manage with a bit more practice. And your encouragement," she added shyly.

"I have no doubt of it, ma'am," Daniel said gallantly and made his escape.

The corned beef, carrot tops, and baked beans dueled viciously with the soapy-tasting coffee in his stomach as he bent over the first of the boards, aligning them for headboard, footboard, side rails, and bottom slats. He'd eaten as little as she was likely to believe would sustain a man of his size and he bitterly regretted every mouthful. He began to think that Zoe Smith's secret was that she'd *had* a husband back East but that she'd killed him with her cooking. He heard her footsteps coming upstairs and immediately banished such unkind thoughts as beneath him.

"So how long will the cavalry be in town?"

"About two weeks, ma'am."

"I only wish I could manage to open while they're here. It would be a wonderful beginning. I understand they have been given a goodly sum in back wages by their commanding officer," she said wistfully.

Daniel repressed a shudder. Even six months of chasing Indians on half rations couldn't prepare the boys in blue for Zoe Smith's cooking. He straightened up as another thought struck him.

"Those boys are going to be up to considerable mischief unless I miss my guess, and what one boy in the cavalry doesn't think of, the other boys'll teach him quick enough. You take care not to go out alone on the street while they're here, won't you, not even during daylight?"

"I promise I'll be careful," she said, dimpling up in a smile. It nearly took his breath away.

"Good." He sucked in a lungful of air to clear his head and began measuring and marking points for cuts with the big flat carpenter's pencil. "Now, I need for you to help me out here. See there? That'll be the headboard and down there, that's the footboard. The best thing would be if you could lay down for me so I can make sure it'll be the right length for you."

"Oh, is that how it's done?" Her forehead puckered. "I thought that all beds were the same length. Oh, well, never mind. Right here?"

"That'd be fine, ma'am."

She sat down, carefully arranging her skirt so that her petticoats remained covered. "Now I just lay down?"

"Oh, yes, please." Daniel cursed himself for having the soul of a rutting ox, but he couldn't resist. There was no way she could lay down without showing a bit of ankle, and the state he was in, he needed something to get him through the night. She crossed her hands over her breast, like a corpse in a coffin, and closed her eyes. Framed by the boards, she looked so dainty, with darling little feet sticking out beneath her skirts, pretty hair lying half undone around her head, alabaster skin gleaming in the light of the lamp hanging above. He glanced to her right. There was at least the spread of a steer's horns between her and the other side. He'd manage just fine in that amount of space. "Thank you, ma'am. That tells me just what I need to know."

She got to her feet, revealing an unexpected bonus—a flash of white-stockinged calf. Daniel stared mutely at the spot where it had been.

"Oh, my," she said, looking down. "That looks quite long. Are you sure I need it quite so long?"

"Well, ma'am, you do want a little bit of room to shift around in, now don't you?" *With me,* he thought fervently.

"Why, yes, I suppose I do." She gave him a look of pure happiness. "I can't tell you how I look forward to getting into this bed."

"Is that so, ma'am? It does my heart glad to hear it." And before he could say something else that he'd live to regret, Daniel went back to marking off saw cuts.

Zenobia surveyed the scene in front of her, all the Chinamen clustered around her and the laundry tubs and stove untended. She'd arrived at the laundry unexpectedly and discovered a complete lack of activity so unusual it could only mean that something extraordinary had happened.

Young Fan stood by the wall, cowering. His eyes flew from one relative to the next as they tried to explain to Zenobia what had happened. His shirt hung in tatters and one cheek bore a mottled pink bruise.

"So soldier think Fan have money and try take away, slap him," Wing Loo concluded. "Only Fan, he good boy, not let them take missy's money." He added something sharp sounding in Chinese and the other men nodded, murmuring and clicking their tongues.

"This makes me so angry! I shall get a gun for our protection," Zenobia fumed. "I declare, I shall! Those soldiers have no manners."

"Oh, no, gun would be very bad," Wing Loo protested instantly. "Mr. Whittaker good friend to you, good friend to us, and he not like guns for nobody. You say, please, that you not think about gun no more."

"Well, it's just exactly what they deserve," Zenobia insisted, but she knew Wing Loo was right. Gila City's regular residents had grown accustomed to seeing Wing Loo and his relations out delivering and grudgingly left them alone. Not so the cavalry. "They would not dare to accost *me,* at least not in daylight. We shall deliver together, Fan."

Wing Loo issued rapid-fire directions in Chinese to his young relation and Fan scuttled off.

Head high, chin thrust out, Zenobia set forth a half hour later with Fan in tow, an immense load of bundled laundry in a carrier on his back. Threaten her livelihood, would they? She'd show those cavalrymen who was who in this town!

The first several parcels were for the doves down in the cribs, all those drab little rooms furnished with hardly more than a bed where each girl plied her trade. It seemed best to go there while the day was still young, for the cribs were a notorious trouble spot. She and Fan had to dodge to avoid some drunken soldiers as they delivered along the long rutted alleys where the cribs were located. Fortunately, the soldiers were too intent on knocking on doors until they got an answer to bother Zenobia and Fan.

They made their way back to Main Street, starting at the east end. The long expanse of potholed mud shook off sheets of dust whenever a rider passed by or a wagon rattled over it. Storefronts and saloons alternated weathered gray boards with the startling brightness of brand-new wood. Zenobia savored a sense of achievement when she reflected that no matter how ramshackle Main Street might look, Smith's Laundry did a profitable business with at least half the establishments along its length,

Many of the orders were little—linen towels for one saloon, checked tablecloths for another, and an order of smalls for

Charles Merrick, which made Zenobia blush a little as she accepted his payment. It was indelicate enough to launder a man's underclothes for money, and even more unrefined to put the parcel containing them into his hands one's self. The real estate broker, however, seemed to see nothing at all extraordinary in it. He even paid her a compliment on her hairstyle, which vanity had compelled her to do over before she set forth on the deliveries.

"I wonder, Miss Smith," he said, as she was leaving, "if you would care to read this copy of *Harper's Weekly?* I have finished with it and you seem to me a person of some refinement who might enjoy a magazine that bills itself as the 'Journal of Civilization.' There are so few people, after all, of whom one can say that in Gila City."

"Why, I would enjoy it very much, Mr. Merrick," she said, pleased by his thoughtfulness. "I have had little time of late for reading. I haven't even looked at a newspaper in months."

The broker smiled. "We must strive to keep informed, Miss Smith, and not forget that there is a vast world beyond Gila City, offering multitudinous pleasures and entertainments for the genteel mind. Opera, art, music, ballet! Reading is my solace and my source of inspiration while I am far removed from these things. Perhaps you would care to be the regular recipient of such periodicals as I subscribe to, and to discuss issues of appeal to the refined mind?"

"I would enjoy that, Mr. Merrick," Zenobia said. It *would* be stimulating to talk to someone whose manners and conversation reminded her of the society she had been accustomed to back home.

"I look forward to it with greatest pleasure, Miss Smith." The broker caught up her gloved hand and touched his lips to the back of it.

As Zenobia hurried off, she wondered whether she had made a mistake to encourage Charles Merrick. "We must keep informed about the outside world," he had said, and yet the outside world was precisely what she had come to Gila City to escape.

So deep was she in thought that Zenobia did not at first realize what the soldier in the alley she passed was doing. When she registered the sound of liquid hitting the ground and observed his hands busy in front of him, it provoked a hot blush. She lifted her chin and sailed around another man in a tattered butternut coat lying passed out on the plank sidewalk. How very distressing when men behaved like barnyard animals!

"Come, Fan," she said, "we have aprons and linen wipes for the Empire and then cloths for the Red Dog Saloon to deliver next."

Fan followed obediently, dogging her heels. He spoke virtually no English but it brought Zenobia comfort to talk to him. It kept her from being quite as aware of the soldiers who ogled her from saloon doors as she passed. Gila City's men had always been civil to her, even worshipful, but these men from the cavalry were different. They seemed to think she was just another one of the sporting girls.

Dog was sitting at his usual post atop the end of the bar when she went into the Red Dog Saloon. Unlike the first day she had set foot inside the saloon, the place hummed with activity. Men occupied every seat at the tables devoted to monte, faro, rondo, coolo, and fortune wheels. A man stood in the corner, sawing away at a fiddle next to a placard that said, "Don't shoot the pianist—he's doing his damnedest." The pianist was nowhere in sight, though, suggesting that someone had done him a violence despite the sign.

Zenobia found herself remembering the moment two nights before when Daniel Whittaker had taken her into his arms and they had danced to the faraway strains of the Red Dog's musical twosome. What a strangely abandoned and joyous interlude that had been, she thought, feeling again the rousing sensation of being held in Daniel Whittaker's wide grasp.

Reverie couldn't be sustained for long in the midst of mayhem. The din in the Red Dog brought her back to an awareness of her errand. Red stood behind the bar, pouring as fast as he could.

"I have your laundry for you," Zenobia called out to him. "The charge is one dollar and fifty-three cents."

"Coming up just now," he yelled back, "the instant my hands are free."

"Care for a little company, pretty lady?" A drunken trooper came out of nowhere, relying on the bar to keep him upright. "Got money, lots of money."

"Certainly not!" Zenobia snapped. The trooper took an unsteady step closer.

"You're round in all the right places, jus' the way I like a woman," he said, grinning blearily. His breath reeked of liquor. "Come on—I'll show you a good time and you can show *me* a good time!"

Zenobia drew back. "Don't you dare touch me!"

A deep growl filled the air. The ominous warning emanated from Dog, who had leapt down from the bar like a wraith and now pointed his big blunt head at the trooper. Enormous yellow teeth gaped in an impressive display.

The trooper stared groggily at Dog. "Nice dog," he said unsteadily, sifting his fingers through locks of blond hair cascading into his eyes. He couldn't have been more than eighteen. "Looks like my old dog back home."

"Well, he's not like your old dog back home, laddie, not a bit of it," Red said. "Back off and he'll leave you be. Otherwise your mates'll be taking up a collection to bury what's left of you when Dog gets done."

"Nah," said the young trooper. "Old . . . old . . . Rover here—he wouldn't hurt me, wouldya, boy? Dogs like me." He bent to offer his hand to Dog.

Zenobia sidled toward the door. Dog swung his hindquarters so that he remained squarely between her and the cavalryman. Fan kept right behind her through the maneuver. The trooper suddenly noticed her departing and stumbled in her direction. Dog's growl swelled, attracting the attention of more troopers.

"C'mon, honey, don't be frightened," the young trooper said, too inebriated to see that it was him Dog menaced, not her. He took another step, swaying heavily. Dog's hackles rose.

"For Christ's sake!" yelled another trooper, rapidly weaving his way across the room. "That's a wolf, Murph! Stand where ye be and let the woman leave."

A wolf! It explained the massive head, the rough gray-and-black coat, the air of otherworldliness in the golden eyes with the piercing black pupils. Zenobia caught Red's eye and nodded toward the parcel of laundry sitting on the bar.

"I'll collect the money another day," she said nervously. One of Dog's ears flipped backward momentarily, toward the sound of her unsteady voice.

"Thank you, ma'am." Red nodded pleasantly, but the look in his eye coupled with a lightning glance toward the door eloquently conveyed his belief that she should retire from the saloon, and fast.

When she and Fan reached the door, Zenobia hesitated. Dog remained on the alert, tense and bristling. She inclined her head toward him cautiously and called out to Red. "When I'm gone, would you give him a dish of whatever it is he favors, please? I shall deduct the cost from your bill."

"With pleasure," Red declared, a grin splitting his lined face.

Juliette Archer sat astride her purebred walking horse, studying Daniel Whittaker as he discussed business with her father. It was a boring matter, not at all as interesting as Daniel Whittaker, about rustlers who'd relieved James Archer of some prime steers ranging far from the main house. The Yaqui Indian who worked for Archer had tracked the thieves as far as Mexico before losing them, but one of the rustlers had broken away early, his horse's tracks leading into Gila City.

"He may have been paid off for leading them to my best stock," James Archer was saying. "I'd appreciate it if you'd let me know if you see any fellows in town with a lot of cash and no handy explanation for where it came from." The silver-haired rancher leaned on the horn of his saddle. "If I get hit like that again, I'm in trouble."

"I'm mighty sorry to hear about your loss, sir." Daniel meant it. He'd been a guest at Archer's ranch and seen the quality of stock the older man had imported, and had even harbored a hope of one day putting some of his own cows to Archer's bulls to improve the stock at the D Bar W. "I think you could be right about a local being involved, though."

"Why, have you seen someone suspicious?" Archer asked.

"Well, no. What I meant was, who else would know to hit your place and not mine or Lester's or Sixie's or someone else's? It stands to reason that it's someone who's spent enough time around here to know who's got stock worth stealing, but as for keeping an eye out for someone with money and no good explanation, I'm afraid that covers most every man here in Gila City. I will let you know if I learn anything that might be helpful, though."

"Good man," Archer declared. He wasn't so unreasonable as to suppose that Daniel could go off and recover the cattle, but he appreciated at least the appearance of concern. Gila City had been beset by a succession of disinterested, thieving lawmen prior to Daniel Whittaker.

Impatient with man talk, Juliette Archer said, "Maybe we ought to have Sheriff Whittaker out for Sunday supper, Daddy. We've gotten new bulls since he came out last, you know. It'd be worth your while, Daniel. You never know when you may want to do some breeding." She flashed him a meaningful smile.

"I do appreciate the invitation," Daniel said. "Maybe when winter comes around again, I'll come on out, when work on my ranch lets up."

"Sure," Juliette said offhandedly, but Daniel saw the tightness in her smile. There was also tension across the lightly freckled cheeks, and barely concealed displeasure in the sherry-brown eyes.

"I hope you won't wait that long, son," James Archer was saying. "I know Mrs. Archer enjoys your visits as much as

Juliette and I do. Being confined to the house the way she is, any company we get brightens her day more than I can tell you. Maybe come in August, why don't you, when you can see how our spring calves and foals are shaping up?"

The rancher had a way of supporting his daughter's wishes that didn't leave much room for argument. Some said James Archer had spoiled her because he was never going to have a son because of his wife's chronic illness, and others said he'd made his daughter a substitute for his ailing wife in all ways but one. It hardly mattered which—the effect was the same. She did just as she pleased, from wearing men's trousers and riding astride to lightening her hair to a color not bestowed on her by Mother Nature. Daniel had been flattered when Juliette first showed an interest in him, but it was hard for a fellow to chase a girl who ran toward him.

Daniel nodded. "Thank you, Mr. Archer. I'll look forward to seeing the place in August."

"First Sunday," Juliette said, the expression on her long, handsome face softening now that she'd gotten what she wanted.

Her father glanced down Main Street. "Town looks even more in want of your services than usual, Daniel, what with the cavalry here."

Glad for the change of topic, Daniel turned. "Well, I've pulled all my deputies in and General James understands that I'll have to lock his men up until they're sober if any of them get out of hand, so I expect things will be all right."

As he uttered these confident words, Zoe Smith emerged from the Red Dog Saloon just down the street. Daniel's heart gave the odd little thump it always did when he saw her. She was walking in a most determined fashion, her back straighter than straight. Lord, but he loved the neat way she carried herself! One of the boys from the laundry scurried in her wake.

Five or six amorous cavalrymen lingered at the base of the stairs leading to Teresa's, waiting their turn to go up. Daniel saw that they, too, had noticed Zoe Smith, and he wondered how much they'd had to drink and whether they were likely to cause trouble. All the while he was uneasily aware that Juliette Archer was looking at him, her gaze sharp as she perceived that his attention had been drawn elsewhere.

"Since we can't persuade you to come out to the ranch any earlier than August, how would you like to join Juliette and me for supper today?" James Archer was saying. Archer was one of the leading members of the Businessmen's Benevolent Association, so an invitation to dine with him was difficult to turn down. Daniel had just opened his mouth to accept when he saw one of the cavalrymen start toward Zoe, planting himself on the plank sidewalk so that she couldn't pass without stepping into the street.

Zoe froze. Daniel started toward her without so much as an "excuse me" for either of the Archers. He dodged across Main Street between moving wagons and horses. He could see the soldier grinning down at Zoe, saying something that made her mouth pinch up and her back go even straighter. The trooper spat a stream of tobacco juice toward the street and she watched it go arching over the sidewalk with a disgusted look.

Daniel heard Juliette Archer's dismayed shouts ringing in his ears as he struggled to reach Zoe before things could got out of hand. He felt as if he were moving through glue. His heart hammered, and though he seldom unholstered his gun, he reached across his waist for the butt of his gun without consciously making a decision to do so.

But he was too late to stop what happened next. The soldier grabbed Zoe up in his arms and his wet mouth came down on hers. His long shaggy mustache covered her small rosy lips and one big hand pawed at her breast. Rage seized Daniel's heart.

He began shouting, though he could barely hear his own voice above the rattle of coach wheels. He dodged and weaved past the last few obstacles between him and his love. The soldier staggered drunkenly with her in his grasp, overbalanced by his own weight and hers. Just as quickly as he had seized her, she writhed free and reeled away as his comrades guffawed and slapped their thighs. The cavalryman grinned stupidly and tried to swoop her a bow. By the time Daniel leapt the last few feet to the sidewalk, the soldier lay in a tumbledown heap and Zoe had backed up against the building, wiping her mouth with her gloved hand.

"Get on your feet, you drunken ass!" Daniel snarled. He leveled his gun at the man's head. He saw a swirl of pink at the top of the stairs—Teresa, coming to see what all the commotion was about.

The soldier flopped about a bit, regarding Daniel and the gun in his face with a puzzled expression. Daniel's whole body shook with rage except for the hand that held his gun. The eight-inch barrel pointed unwaveringly at the trooper's head.

"Come on, you lousy mule skinner," Daniel growled. If it had been just him and the trooper, he'd have attacked the man with his bare fists for the pleasure of wiping the stupid look off his face.

The trooper blinked at Daniel. "Why you got a gun? Gen'ral said no guns in town."

"I'm the sheriff of Gila City, you son of a bitch, and I don't like what you just did to that lady! Now, get on your feet before I blow your head off."

"Just a little kiss," the trooper muttered, still looking perplexed by the sudden turn of events. He got to his hands and knees and his comrades looked at Daniel uncertainly, not sure whether to help him up the rest of the way. Daniel warned them off with a sharp shake of his head.

"Get up." Daniel barely recognized his own voice, raw with anger.

The trooper knew the voice of command when he heard it and got to his feet by himself somehow. "I'll pay her for the kiss," he said. He swung around and grinned when he saw Zoe. She stood near the steps with Teresa, pale with outrage. "How 'bout it, honey? I'll pay you for the kiss, and then maybe you and me, we can go upstairs together and get better acquainted?"

Daniel cocked his gun. "Soldier, you've got five seconds to apologize to the lady before I blow you to kingdom come."

"Sheriff, can I be of help?" It was James Archer's deep voice at Daniel's shoulder. "Maybe my hands could take this fellow out to camp and explain to General James that he got a little out of line." He tipped his hat toward Zoe. "Ma'am." She inclined her head to him.

Daniel's desire to hurt the man for what he'd done to Zoe was as strong as ever, but Archer's words cut through his rage. You couldn't kill a man for stealing a kiss but that was exactly what he'd been contemplating.

"It'd be best if you just let him be ridden on out of town, son," James Archer said so quietly that only Daniel could hear him. A crowd had gathered and everyone was staring raptly at Daniel, including Juliette, who had managed to cross the street by now. Daniel slowly lowered his Colt.

"Boys." With a jerk of his head, James Archer dispatched the two hands who accompanied him and Juliette to drag the trooper away. Daniel looked toward Zoe. Some color had returned to her cheeks and he knew he should thank James Archer. Shooting the man in front of Zoe would have brought her no peace—she was too gentle and sweet to witness such a terrible thing. Daniel blinked, stunned at how close he'd come to committing cold-blooded murder. He'd never, not even in the midst of war, felt anything like the visceral anger he'd just experienced. Teresa led Zoe over to him.

"You'd best see her on back to the laundry," she suggested, gently pushing Zoe in his direction.

Daniel looked down into her face, that angel face he so adored. She was recovering quickly from her shock, and in the depths of those clear blue eyes, Daniel saw something that bucked him up enormously. She was grateful to him for coming to her rescue even though he'd created such a scene.

He offered her his arm, his mood altering swiftly. "Miss Zoe, why don't I walk you to the laundry, you and . . ."

"Fan," she said, supplying the name, "and thank you. I would appreciate your escort." Fan, hearing his name, detached himself from the side of the Red Dog Saloon and came to them.

Zoe took Daniel's arm and it was she who turned and took the first step, her head high.

It seemed to Daniel that she possessed uncommon backbone, for he felt the tremors in her hand where it rested on his forearm and yet she gave no outward sign of agitation. When they arrived at the laundry, however, her coolness had worn thin. She stopped in the side yard and raised her face to his. She looked perilously close to tears.

"Thank you, Sheriff," she said. "I appreciate your help. I'm terribly sorry that I caused you such a problem."

He realized with a start of surprise that she expected him to chastise her and dreaded it.

"Zoe—I mean, Miss Smith! You didn't cause me the least problem in the world, ma'am. It was that trooper—he was the troublemaker, not you. You couldn't cause me a problem if you tried."

She pulled a handkerchief out of the small cloth purse at her waist. He was sorry to see that she had one available. Whenever he gave her one of his he felt reassured that he would see her again because he knew she'd always return them.

"But you did warn me about the cavalry," she said softly.

"Well, ma'am, I wanted you to be careful when they were in town, but I never meant that you couldn't go out at all. It's my job to keep the streets safe, and when they aren't, it's up to me to step in. That's all I did today, and I was sure glad I was there to keep that fellow from giving you any more trouble."

She smiled, dark arching brows lifting and the alabaster cheeks rounding. The sight of that angelic face so close to his made Daniel go all funny in the knees.

"Thank you, Sheriff Whittaker," she said fervently. "You are surely the nicest man in Gila City." She held out her hand and when he took it, she shook it firmly and turned to mount the stairs to the laundry.

Daniel watched her rounded backside with profound admiration, thinking an instant too late about how he should have taken advantage of her gratitude to hold her close for a moment and render additional comfort and reassurance. After the door had closed behind her, he started back toward the jail, bemused by the seesawing of his emotions over the past hour. As he walked, he tried to puzzle out whether being the nicest man in Gila City was a good thing or a bad thing for his cause.

Zenobia heard a knock at the side door, and though she felt sure she recognized it, she pulled back the curtain to peek out before opening the door. The brush with the cavalryman had shaken her confidence more than she cared to admit.

Daniel Whittaker stood in the alley, his face in shadow as evening fell. He saw her at the window. "Miss Smith? It's Sheriff Whittaker."

Zenobia smiled. "Yes, I can see that, Sheriff." She dusted hominy flour from her hands and unlocked the door.

"I wanted to see how you were, ma'am," he said, making no move to enter and rotating his hat in his hand as if unsure of his welcome.

"Please, come in. I'm just about to put some biscuits in the oven. Are you hungry? Would you care for some?"

"Oh, no, ma'am," he said hastily. "I ate about an hour ago. Mr. Archer—that man with me today—he sent some food along to the jail for all the deputies for dinner."

Zenobia gestured to the kitchen apologetically. "I must continue with making the biscuits while the oven is hot. Would you care to join me in there so we can talk?" He followed her and she resumed rolling out the dough, feeling flushed all out of proportion to the effort she'd been expending in the kitchen. "Who exactly is Mr. Archer?" she asked, distributing flour over the board the way the book said to.

"He's a rancher. He's got the biggest spread around here, with a big house overlooking a lake he's made by damming a leg of the river."

"I see. And the woman with him?"

"Oh, that's Juliette. She's his daughter."

"She's pretty," Zoe said and waited for Daniel Whittaker's reaction. She had seen the way the girl watched with narrowed eyes as Daniel took her arm to escort her back to the laundry. Did she have some claim on him?

"Well, yes, I suppose she is pretty." Daniel cast about in his memory. For the life of him he couldn't picture what Juliette Archer looked like at that moment, not with Zoe Smith in front of him. At one time he'd thought Juliette Archer was pretty, too, but now his standard for female beauty was embodied by the angel-faced creature in front of him who was sending up clouds of hominy flour as she thumped and pounded at a sodden lump of biscuit dough.

"I guess you'd say Juliette takes after her mother," Daniel added, since Zoe seemed to expect him to say something more. "That's Mrs. Julia Archer. She doesn't leave the ranch much, except to go back East once a year."

Zenobia could detect no sign that he felt anything special for the daughter. Relief assailed her—foolish relief since she had no special relationship with Daniel Whittaker, nor ever would. "Back East? Is that where she's from?" she asked to keep the conversation going.

"Yes, ma'am, only she's been afflicted with illness and can't travel much."

"I'm sorry to hear that."

He shifted his weight, looking as though he felt uneasy about something. "One of the reasons I stopped by tonight was to make sure you're all right, ma'am. I can't tell you how sorry I am about what happened this afternoon." Zoe sneezed without warning as hominy flew upward in a spume from the lump of dough she was pummeling. Daniel swiftly withdrew a handkerchief. "Here you are, ma'am."

She mopped at her nose, sniffling. "Are you ever without a clean handkerchief?"

"Not since I met you, ma'am."

Zenobia looked into the gray-green eyes which had suddenly

become serious and dark with some unspoken emotion. She felt a catch in her middle.

"I don't believe I really thanked you properly for your help this afternoon," she said, staring up at him. "It was dreadfully upsetting, but seeing you come to my defense helped a great deal. It makes a woman feel so much better when she knows that someone cares about her."

Daniel Whittaker ducked his head, staring down at his boot tips as heat crept up his neck. "I wanted to kill him," he admitted sheepishly.

"I knew you wouldn't," she said softly. "You're far too level-headed to kill a man over such a thing."

He lifted his head and studied her, a furrow between the level brows scoring the bridge of his nose. By the light of the kerosene lantern over the counter, Zenobia detected uncertainty in his eyes. It always touched something inside her when this strong, confident man seemed uncertain.

"I . . . I couldn't help but think about what happened all day, ma'am, and . . . and, well, I couldn't help thinking that if anyone's going to steal a kiss from you, I'd like it to be me."

"Oh." Suddenly she felt hollow. The look in his eyes hadn't been uncertainty—it had been desire. She didn't ever recall seeing it on Eben's face when he looked at her, but here was Daniel Whittaker regarding her with that deep longing.

Now she was whirled into the currents herself, drawn into the dance by Daniel Whittaker's improbable hunger for *her*— the drab, the dowdy, the unrelentingly plain, plump Zenobia Strouss. He was looking at her mouth and his own lips were parted. She couldn't remember ever feeling this tangled, restless feeling when Eben looked at her. Daniel Whittaker slowly set his hat aside and reached for her.

Zenobia stood stock-still, letting it happen when all sense screamed out against it. She had never seen a man more beautiful than Daniel Whittaker in that moment. The wide mouth, so often curved in laughter, shifted to stillness, poised on the threshold of kissing her. The dark eyelashes, gold-tipped in the lantern's light, shaded downward as he tilted his head. Zenobia could barely pull in a breath. He bent and kept on bending, to fit his face to hers.

A delicious shiver of anticipation ran through Zenobia and then his mouth was on hers, his male scent rising in her nostrils. She felt the imprint of his flesh on hers, his lips taking hers with gentle possessiveness. Her insides caught the flame, too, turning and leaping with the heat of the touch. He relinquished his tense grip on her arms and slid his hands behind her back, pulling her against him so that she melted everywhere he touched. Zenobia heard herself sigh against his lips, but what a deceptive sound it was! There was no relaxation in it, no letting go, just tautening in every part of her.

The big hands massaging her back made Zenobia surrender more of herself to his touch, savoring that sure, competent stroking up and down her limbs, and on all the parts of her that hadn't been touched in what felt like years. She felt a trembling need deep inside to be held bare against his skin. The images that were leaping into her mind went considerably beyond that, to astonishingly vivid images of twining naked with him and doing things she hadn't ever even thought about until this instant.

Daniel moved his mouth over hers, tasting and stroking her, and Zenobia's breath came faster and faster, in a staccato tempo, her pulse fluttering against the collar of her dress. When at last he pulled away, she dragged in a long breath.

"Oh, darlin'," he whispered in her ear, his own breath as shaky as hers. "You're so sweet to kiss." He pulled her up against him, leaving her standing on tiptoe. He kissed her again, cupping her chin with one strong hand in a way that made her feel as if the bottom of her heart had just dropped out. Zenobia thought she might swoon, but his strength held her up. He sighed against her mouth.

"Darlin', I swear, we could set something on fire."

Zenobia couldn't have agreed more, and she knew just exactly what it was they would ignite—themselves. Drugged and stuporous and floating on the wings of lust, she lifted her face to invite him to kiss her again. She clutched at his plaid shirt, crumpling it in her eager fists. He swiftly accepted her invitation, bending and kissing her, more fiercely this time.

She wound her hands behind his neck and ran her fingers through the hair at the nape of his neck. Oh, Lord, but she wanted every bit of him and in every way! Her insides were turning positively molten. Daniel Whittaker's mouth went on stroking her lips, and she ran her hands along his shoulders, delighting in the feel of strongly corded muscles along his collarbone. She wanted him with an intensity that hurt.

Dimly she registered the sound of his hoarse breathing and then something beyond that, out in the street, also rhythmic. Horses went pounding past and then she recognized the popping sound of revolvers, their loud retorts echoing off bare wood. Daniel Whittaker heard the sound, too.

"Damn cavalry," he whispered.

Zenobia murmured agreement against his mouth, hungrily feeling the upper planes of his arms, hard with muscle. If only he would take off his shirt! She swayed against him to distract him from what was happening out in the street. His hand cupped the fullness of her breast and Zenobia inhaled sharply. It was a start in the right direction, and oh!—how sweet it was. Gunshots echoed outside, louder and more numerous than before.

"Oh, darlin'," Daniel sighed. He pulled away from her a fraction and his hands relented in their exploration.

"No!" Zenobia cried.

"I got to, honey," Daniel said regretfully. He straightened up, giving her one last kiss on the forehead followed by a sigh that came up from deep inside him. "Those boys'll kill one another if I don't go out and talk some sense into them."

Zenobia let out an involuntary sob of pure frustration. "But I don't want you to leave!"

"I know, darlin'," Daniel said as he tenderly stroked a curl back behind her ear. "I don't feel like leaving any more than you want me to leave, but I took an oath, so I got to go and save all those fools from themselves." He lifted her chin with one finger and she stared into the darkness of the gray-green eyes. "This ain't over, darlin', not by a shot, I'm burnin' for you just the same way you're burnin' for me, but it'll have to wait."

Zenobia held tight to his shoulders and pleaded with her eyes for him not to go, to take her upstairs and tear her clothes off and invent new ways to make love. One corner of his mouth curved up.

"Later," he whispered, his eyes full of promises.

Zenobia flopped down on a bench when he was gone and pounded her fist on the table in frustration.

Ten

Daniel drifted hazily between waking and sleeping. He'd spent most of the night chasing down one unruly cavalryman after another, a more difficult assignment than he usually faced in Gila City. Some of the cavalrymen possessed scarcely enough beard to justify shaving, but they were strong and determined young cusses, just great big boys at play. It made them disinclined to respect the authority of the law, especially when the law—in the person of himself—wasn't so much older than they were.

Most of the gamblers, miners, and waddies who passed through Gila City showed Daniel a modicum of deference since he was known as one of the few lawmen in the territory who wasn't on the take. He had earned their regard out of sheer novelty if nothing else.

But the cavalry boys just plain had no sense. They'd been pie-eyed and ready to run from the git-go. General James was *their* bogeyman, not some unknown sheriff with a badge pinned to his chest, and Daniel was opposed to firing off his sidearm just to get their attention.

In the end, neither the gun in his holster nor the badge on his chest had counted for much. The troopers were too riled up to listen to any form of persuasion other than brute force. Wrestling the boys out of fights and out of saloons had been like trying to take down muddy alligators, only alligators didn't bite as hard or vomit all over you. Daniel would have had no compunction about shooting an alligator that put up the kind of resistance the cavalry boys had, but he didn't think General James would appreciate getting his troopers back with holes in them.

At dawn, he and Clarence and Lester and Walter had loaded the boys in blue into the wagons promised by General James, but most of the piss and vinegar had gone out of them by that time. Not one of the soldiers could have made it back to camp under his own steam. Daniel sent his deputies off to a well-deserved rest and threw a clean blanket over one of the bunks in the front cell, but now that he finally had a moment to call his own, he couldn't sleep. All he could do was lie there and think about Zoe Smith.

Kissing the woman he loved for the first time had proved to be a considerably more profound experience than he'd reckoned on. His eyes were gritty with fatigue and every muscle grieved him to the limit, but the memory of her in his arms kept sleep at bay. My God, hadn't she been beautiful! He could still feel her, all ripe and warm and melting against him. It was extraordinary, that was what it was—just extraordinary.

Daniel's hips twitched and the whole length of him stirred to life. He wanted to make love to Zoe Smith in the worst possible way. His groin tightened as he imagined her tangled up in the sheets and in his arms, all wanton and naked and white-skinned. He saw her face again, the blue eyes bright with arousal, the cheeks stained pink, and the rosy lips parted and moist.

With a curse, he rolled over. It caused him pain to think along such lines, but despite his need for sleep he couldn't help himself. He punched the hard little pillow under his head into a lump and settled his cheek against it. He couldn't go on dreaming of his beloved, not now when he badly needed sleep, but the memory of that kiss was like a locomotive screaming out of control on a down grade.

She might be cool and composed and proper, but little Miss Zoe Smith had a heart of molten lava. He could see now that her shyness and seeming discomfort could be overcome. He'd been ready to hang back, give her time to get to know him. He had chafed under the self-imposed restraint, but it was manifest to him now that there was no longer any reason to wait. She wanted to be kissed by him every bit as much as he wanted to kiss her. Women could be strange like that sometimes, seeming to want one thing when they really wanted something else.

He wasn't going to take any chances that she'd like being kissed just as well by another man either. He figured to forestall that possibility by kissing her every chance he got, so well and so thoroughly that given a little time, she wouldn't want another man to so much as shake her hand, never mind kiss her. He had been the recipient of a few lessons in the art of physical love— owing to the generosity of the Widow McCloskey the winter he turned eighteen—and he meant to draw on all the knowledge and experience she had bestowed upon him.

He'd had no real need to practice the art of seduction with the widow or with the working girls he'd visited since. He'd enjoyed some lusty sessions, particularly with Teresa, but they were in the nature of professional transactions, friendly but expeditious. With Miss Zoe Smith it would be an entirely different matter. Courtship and seduction and wooing were all very necessary. If you wanted to build a house that would last, you had to lay down a good foundation first.

A light knock at the jailhouse door interrupted his thoughts. he'd pulled down the shades to discourage all but the most serious requests for his services and he didn't anticipate any of those before nightfall now that General James's troops were moving on. The knock came again, though, a little more determined this time. Daniel lay perfectly still.

"Sheriff Whittaker?"

Daniel's heart skipped a beat. Zoe! He leapt off the bunk and almost tripped over his own feet. "Just a minute, ma'am!"

He eyed his razor but dismissed the idea of shaving before he opened the door—he couldn't stall her that long. He rubbed his palms over his cheeks regretfully. He didn't have a heavy beard, but he worried that to an exquisitely neat person like Zoe

Smith, he'd look slovenly. Although she exceeded his expectations in every way—except possibly with her cooking—he worried that he would fail to meet *her* standards.

Daniel hurried to the front of the jail, alight with happiness. He'd been dreaming of her and longing to see her again and here she was just a heartbeat away. The bright light of morning, which had been tamed considerably by the green shades at the jail's windows, hit him full force when he opened the door. He blinked and drank in the heartwarming spectacle of the angel on his doorstep, with her china-blue eyes as clear as the early morning sky behind her. He grinned foolishly.

"Morning, ma'am." He invited her inside with a gesture.

He saw her take in the full degree of his dishevelment and hesitate before stepping over the threshold. Daniel prayed that the warm flush of embarrassment on his cheeks would subside quickly.

"Oh, you're alone," she said in a startled way as she looked around. "I didn't mean for us to be alone."

Daniel felt his smile slipping. He didn't like the sound of that one little bit.

She faced him with a resolute expression and said, "I don't think it is a good idea for us to be alone with one another again. I have come today expressly for the purpose of asking that you respect my wishes in this matter, and not call on me when no one else is about."

"But, darlin'—"

"Please let me finish," she said, quickly looking down at the floor. The brim of her black bonnet concealed all but the rounded outline of one cheek, which told him nothing at all about what was going on in her mind. "I'm afraid I behaved rather badly last night. I regret if I gave you the wrong impression."

Wrong impression, hell, thought Daniel. She'd given him exactly the *right* impression. If he didn't nip this in the bud, she was going to completely repudiate the beneficial and exhilarating experience they'd shared. He knew what was going on. She was worried what he'd think of her—that she was loose or flirty. Prim Miss Smith might feel obliged to *say* she didn't welcome his amorous attentions, but he knew otherwise. She *wanted* to be touched and kissed and loved. It was just that the light of day had made her shy again.

"Now, darlin'," he said cajolingly, "you didn't give me any wrong impressions. You were awful sweet last night. I really enjoyed being alone with you, and I could have sworn you enjoyed being alone with me." He rubbed one hand up her arm. She shivered, but she didn't pull away. "It about broke my heart to have to leave. I was just lying here thinking about taking up again where we left off." She looked up in alarm, one stray lock of brown hair trembling against her neck. Daniel knew she was close to fleeing so he did the only thing he could think of to keep her there. He kissed her.

Zoe Smith let out an inarticulate sound and dipped in his grasp. Her hat brushed across his forehead and slid off backward until it hung by its ribbon from her neck. He could feel her quivering in his arms, but her lips were warm and steady beneath his. Daniel felt his legs weaken with passion. He maneuvered her until she was resting against the bars of the cell and kissed her without letup, until the pounding of his heart left him breathless and he had to back off for air. He looked down at her tenderly, savoring the heavy-lidded look of surrender on her face.

"Oh, darlin', it was purely sinful last night, what you did to me," he whispered, "and now you're doin' it to me all over again."

"Oh, but I didn't mean to!" she cried. "I never meant for there to be any sin!"

"I was speakin' poetically, darlin'," Daniel said, putting his finger to her lids to silence her. Talking was no remedy. He bent his head and kissed her again.

She made a little fluttery sound beneath his mouth and clutched at his arms. Her body trembled and strained against his and her breasts moved rapidly against his chest. There was no question—she was kissing him back and with considerable feeling. The bars of the cell chilled his fingers where they were pinned behind her. The hat dangling down her back was getting crushed but Daniel didn't give a damn and he was pretty sure she didn't either. He pulled away and smiled down at her.

"I was dreaming of you, darlin', when you came knocking," he said softly. He ran his hands down her arms, capturing a wrist in each one. He could feel the blood pulsing beneath the delicate skin there. He raised her hands until she was pinioned against the bars, her eyes dark with wonder and tremulous anticipation. He bent and took her mouth in a deep, slow rhythm, planting his hips against hers. All thoughts of seducing her gradually disappeared.

She strained against him trying to get closer, whimpering and returning the pressure of his mouth enthusiastically. Not even Alice McCloskey, with years of deprivation and a strong natural liking for sex, had been as eager as this.

Daniel felt like a ray of pure sensuality. No dream he'd ever had could match the reality of this moment. He buried his lips in Zoe's hair and heard her short, gasping breaths at his ear. He moved against her and she lifted herself to meet the motion. He brought his mouth back to hers and Zoe Smith panted and made sounds of surrender as their lips met. It seemed as if whatever he wanted, she wanted it just as much.

Daniel was incapable of resisting the obvious. He released her hands and pulled her toward the cell door where the bunk waited. She followed as he backed around the corner into the cell and braced her up against the inside cell bars and kissed her again.

"This is what I want, darlin'," he murmured against her lips. He moved his hips against her to emphasize his intentions. "Do you want the same thing?"

She gave a quick nod, looking bemused by her own acquiescence. Daniel let his full weight go against her, testing her curves and hollows with his own contours. Boot heels rang out sharply on the plank sidewalk in front of the jail and Daniel paused. He was suddenly appalled by the notion of seducing his beloved where just anybody could walk in on them. The footsteps went past the jail door, but it didn't change the fact that they were in a public place.

"Darlin', I'm sorry," he said softly. "I just can't lay you down here in this jail. It wouldn't be right." He stroked a stray piece of hair off her neck. "I'd love, I would purely love, darlin', to take you right here and now, and I can see that you'd let me, but we can't. It violates my notion of what's right and proper, but you could tempt me past that if you really wanted to. Do you want to try, darlin'?" he asked hopefully.

She shook her head, her eyes wide, as quick now to say no as she had been to say yes before, but she undermined her point by looking at his mouth longingly. Daniel obliged her with a kiss.

"I want to be somewhere private with you real soon," he whispered, pulling away. "I want to just unwrap you like a present, layer by layer, and love every little part of you, Oh, darlin', I'm gonna make you feel so good." He used one hand along her side to demonstrate, making a slow, sensual search of the curves beneath her dress. He brushed lightly over the fullness of one breast where it was pushed up by her corset. It made her gasp, and her hips bucked against his. Daniel gritted his teeth so hard it hurt. He'd said he wasn't going to take her in the jail but it was difficult to muster his restraint when she moved like that.

"One day real soon," he promised, finding his resolve again. He was perilously close to embarrassing himself. "Now, you better get along before we do something we'll both be sorry for later."

"But . . ." It was all she said, staring up at him, flushed and panting.

With greatest reluctance he set her away from him and towed her out of the cell. He did it a little roughly, knowing how close he was to going back on his word. Zoe tumbled after him, her hat bobbing at the ends of the ribbon still tied beneath her chin.

Daniel undid the knot and brusquely punched the hat out to approximately its right shape.

"Go on now," he said, gentling his voice to conceal the war within. She stared at him, her breathing rapid. The bright blue eyes were saying things about capitulation that he knew he was better off not hearing, but he did take advantage of the situation to caress the slope of her waist one last time before he gave her a little push on the fanny which set her cage crinoline to swaying. She took a hesitant step toward the door, looking back over her shoulder at him.

"You do it," he said. "You go. I've got to stay here so you've got to be the one to go, but I guarantee, you and I are going to get private real soon and finish what we started here."

Zoe Smith reached the doorway and cast one last look over her shoulder, a look of fearful longing that matched his own. Daniel stood his ground with an effort, and even managed a token smile.

"I'll see you later, darlin', and when I do, I mean to kiss you proper and tell you a thing or two about how I feel."

"Oh." She stared at him for what felt like forever, with a gaze that melted his bones and chewed away at his reason. "Oh," she said again, and then she slipped out the door.

Daniel sat down at his desk and buried his head in shaking hands. At this rate, love was going to kill him.

Rosita Chavez waited in the shadows of Smith's Good Luck Restaurant. She was called Rosita to distinguish her from her mother Rosa, but there was nothing little about her anymore. Her once tiny waist had thickened rapidly in the past months. She avoided looking at her reflection in the window of the restaurant as she waited. She knew what she would see—a monolithic shape in a serape far too heavy for the coming day's heat.

Despair lay thick on her, like the dust that coated everything in this boom town. A foolish passion for a vaquero who had turned out to be a bandit with a price on his head had forced Rosita to flee her home.

In desperation—lest Mama discover her condition—Rosita had followed General James's troops when they stopped to buy fresh horses in the settlement on the Salt River where she lived with Mama Rosa. It had been hard for Rosita, doing laundry for the soldiers and washing their dishes under primitive conditions, though not much harder than keeping house and caring for her younger brothers and sisters while Mama Rosa worked at the saloon. Rosita had kept to herself, protected by the prejudice the white soldiers had against sleeping with "señoritas." Today, however, the cavalry was moving on and Rosita knew she must make other arrangements for herself.

Rosita tracked up and down Gila City's Main Street with her eyes. It was very early and few people were about, though a number of men were slumped against horse troughs, dead to the world. No doubt the restaurant's owner was still abed. Rosita sighed. It would be hours before the door was unlocked and she could make her plea for a job.

She had left the army camp before dawn and walked the three miles to town, passing the wagons full of hung-over men returning to camp in the breaking light. She was hungry and thirsty and scared. No matter how she tried to conceal it, her condition was going to be apparent soon. Mama Rosa was a huge, fierce woman with a tongue like a barber's razor. She had always preached the straight and narrow for her daughter even though she seldom walked it herself. Rosita shuddered at the very thought of Mama ever catching up with her and learning the truth. The best she could hope for now was to evade Mama Rosa. The baby could not be evaded.

A small woman walking quickly up the street caught Rosita's eye—not a working girl, certainly. She was immaculately turned out, though her bonnet was somewhat the worse for wear. She must have been hurrying for some time, for her cheeks were reddened and her breathing rushed. Rosita shrank back into the shadows.

The small woman stepped up to the restaurant door and fumbled in her reticule for a key. The deep pink on her cheeks extended from her temples to her chin, a vivid stain across flawless skin. She had long lashes that cast shadows across her cheeks in the slanting rays of early morning, but what Rosita was searching for was some clue to the woman's character. Was she kind? Would she speak to a Mexican girl without acting as if she were afraid of getting dirty?

Rosita couldn't tell. All that was certain was that the woman was agitated at not being able to find her key. Her hands shook and Rosita wondered if the woman was a drunkard. She hoped that if she was, she had a mild disposition. That sort of drunk one could work for. It was the ones who turned into rattlesnakes who could make life hell for everyone around them. Mama Rosa could be that way when she drank too much.

This woman had a trace of prettiness to her, though not much. In profile, she had regular features, not dainty, not coarse, but with a conspicuously small, straight nose. Her drab and well-worn black jacket had begun losing its dye, fading to a brownish hue, and her skirt was a dull, dark green. Perhaps dressed in prettier colors she would improve, for she certainly had a buxom figure. Her waist was tiny, her hips and bosom generous. It was the sort of figure Rosita herself had possessed not long ago—the sort of figure that could get a woman in trouble.

The small woman stamped one foot in frustration. Rosita didn't think she was a drunkard. A drunkard would have kicked the flimsy door by now, or punched out the glass. She rehearsed a few English words in her mind and stepped out of the shadows.

"Pardon me, miss. May I speak with you?"

The woman let out a shriek and turned. Rosita could see that she had startled her badly. "I'm sorry," she said, nearly as shaken as the woman herself over this bad beginning. "I did not mean to frighten you."

The woman clutched at her chest. All the pink had fled from her cheeks, leaving them chalky white. She stared at Rosita with eyes an impossible shade of blue, the sort of gringo color one heard about but did not believe existed until one first saw it.

"I am looking for work," Rosita said. "You will be opening this restaurant soon, no?"

"No," Zenobia gasped. "I mean yes!" Zenobia was glad to discover that she could still talk. Somewhere during the course of confronting Daniel Whittaker, she had been rendered speechless. Overwhelming sensations had replaced her usual self-possession to such an extent that it had frightened her. Even now, she still didn't feel quite like herself.

"My name is Rosita Chavez," said the girl. "I can cook and wash dishes. I need work."

Someone who could cook? Zenobia studied the young woman as her heartbeat settled back to normal. The girl was heavily cloaked despite the heat. She wasn't more than sixteen or seventeen, with large features and broad cheekbones. The strong face was framed by neatly braided, glistening black hair, but far more interesting than all that was the girl's claim that she could cook.

Zenobia had begun to suspect that she was not a particularly good cook. Daniel Whittaker always smiled as he ate, but once or twice she had been certain that he grimaced when he swallowed. And the truth was that she didn't enjoy cooking at all—that had been an unwelcome discovery considering she had invested nearly all of her remaining money in a restaurant in a town where help was hard to come by.

"Come in and we'll talk," Zenobia said. She turned to the door and recalled the missing key. "Oh, no, we can't get in."

Rosita stooped and retrieved a brass object from the ground. "You are looking for this, no? I saw it fall from your bag."

Zenobia took the key gratefully. "If you're going to be this helpful, I suppose I had better give you a job. I'm not at all good at looking after myself."

And that, Rosita thought as they walked through the door, would suit her very well.

* * *

Life fell into a pattern after Rosita arrived, a pattern that calmed Zenobia's nerves considerably. No longer did Daniel Whittaker find her alone when he stuck his head around the front door of the restaurant each evening. He would greet Rosita, accept the offer of a cup of coffee and, most humbling of all, eat with noticeable relish whatever Rosita had cooked.

The menu was certainly not traditional, nothing at all along the lines Zenobia had envisioned, but it seemed to suit Daniel just fine. From tamales to frijoles, to carne seca, the spicy dried meat that Rosita sliced into strips and put out as an appetizer, he ate it all.

Rosita practiced making more conventional foods, too, like boiled cabbage and corned beef. With Rosita in the kitchen, engulfed in clouds of steam as she fussed over the contents of various pots, Zenobia used her free time to review accounts. She went over the laundry accounts, too, and saw that Wing Loo's books were in order. He kept notations and figures in the left-hand column in Chinese and in the right-hand column in English. The profits from the laundry were heartening, especially since the restaurant had been nothing but a drain on her resources so far and she now had an employee to pay, too.

Without her actually planning it, Smith's Good Luck Restaurant opened for business in mid-May. At the end of her first week, Rosita pronounced herself ready to cook for a crowd, so Zenobia issued supper invitations to everyone she knew—the working girls, Wing Loo and his assorted relations, Clarence Trilby, Jacob Aleksandrov, the sad-eyed young rabbi who lived over Klingensmith's Restaurant, Ned the blacksmith, Walter Connolly, Daniel's deputy, and Lester, his partner.

To see people eating and enjoying themselves, and to hear Smith's Good Luck Restaurant filled with hearty conversation seemed too good to be true. Miners and gamblers and waddies passing by heard the hubbub and came in. Zenobia tried to turn them away but Rosita assured her that there was plenty of food.

Soon Zenobia was rushed off her feet, delivering bowls and trays to tables, clearing away dirty dishes, and collecting money. By evening's end, her apron pockets were heavy with silver dollars and gold coins and her poke was fattened considerably with gold dust. After that, Smith's Good Luck Restaurant opened promptly at eleven every morning.

By eight each night, Zenobia was ready to drop. The exhilaration of counting money at day's end and watching as profits overtook operating expenses energized her, but the energy was never quite equal to the demand, including washing all the dishes, wiping and setting tables, carting food and utensils back and forth, and keeping track of who'd paid and who was still waiting for a seat. She thanked providence for Rosita, for she now saw that it would have been quite impossible to run the restaurant by herself. Even with two of them, the task was staggering.

Each evening, when it was nearly closing time, Daniel Whittaker would stop by. She enjoyed watching him eat, even if it wasn't her cooking. He would smile at Zenobia whenever he caught her looking at him. She enjoyed watching him, especially his hands, tanned and strong as his fingers curled around a cup. Somehow the intent green gaze didn't throw her into such a tizzy when it wasn't just the two of them alone in the restaurant. Even if he lingered until all the other customers were gone, Zenobia could rest easy in the knowledge that Rosita was back in the kitchen, boiling up water to wash dishes and putting away leftover food.

And so life went on in such a way that Zenobia could keep her attraction to Daniel Whittaker under wraps. It wasn't as good as making a definitive break, but she had begun to think that in such a small town, it would be impossible to simply avoid him. It was an exquisite sort of torture, fear of discovery alternating with the lure of Daniel Whittaker's masculinity. But it wasn't as if she didn't have other matters to distract her.

One night, very late, she saw Rosita, clad only in a thin nightdress, passing along the hall to the lavatory by the stairs. Suddenly, what had only been vague suspicion merged with common sense. Rosita Chavez, cook at Smith's Good Luck Restaurant, was going to have a baby. The next morning, before they were both tired and words tended to come out wrong, Zenobia sat the girl down and asked a few pointed questions. She heard her out without comment, sympathizing with Rosita's tearful confession of how she had been drawn to a young vaquero, to his beautiful face and wide shoulders, his slim hips and powerful legs.

"When he took me into the moonlight and touched me just so, and kissed me—I thought I would die from the pleasure, from all the things he did to me," Rosita sighed, dabbing away a tear.

Zenobia quailed inside. She knew *that* sensation all too well. She, too, could end up with child if she wasn't very, very careful, and then she would have an illegitimate baby *and* be on the run for committing murder, and just to top it all off, she'd also be an adulteress. Between hard work and the example of passion's misbegotten fruit right in front of her every day, Zenobia had even more success in keeping her feelings for Daniel Whittaker in check.

One of the news journals Charles Merrick had passed along to her dashed any faint hope she still cherished that she *wasn't* actually a murderer. In a dim recess of her mind, she had held out hope that perhaps Stephen had merely been knocked unconscious and that he had arisen after she left, bruised and battered but quite alive. The journal swiftly countered that illusion. It contained an account of the mysterious death of a socially prominent man in Philadelphia, and the details surrounding the unsolved case—the heartsore young husband baffled by the discovery of his best friend's lifeless body in his entry hall and the simultaneous disappearance of his young wife from their stately mansion, the grisly pool of blood on the expensive marble floor, society's shock and confusion over what had happened in its midst, and so forth.

Except for the pool of blood, it was correct in every detail. Zenobia thrust it into the stove with a cold feeling around her heart, and resolved to redouble her efforts to remain aloof from the sheriff of Gila City. it began to seem, however, as if all of Gila City was determined to live a part of each day in her restaurant, including its handsome sheriff. Lester, Daniel's partner, began dropping by regularly. Lester said little beyond the usual courtesies, but he always positioned himself so that he had a good view of the kitchen. He would watch Rosita, his strong brown face revealing an intense interest in the cook, but Rosita seemed unaware of his existence.

Dog from the Red Dog Saloon came almost daily. He liked the bean-filled tamales Rosita cooked, and Zenobia reluctantly gave one to him each day, not at all sure that wolves should eat the spicy Mexican food, but he returned for another each day, as hale and hearty as ever, so she relented when faced with his dignified and completely irresistible requests for another handout.

James Archer, the rancher, took to stopping in for lunch every so often, too. He was often accompanied by his daughter Juliette, who sent glances in Zenobia's direction obviously intended to make her feel like leaving town, but if the girl fancied Daniel, Zenobia trusted she would soon realize that Zenobia wasn't a rival.

A lively group of Cornish prospectors—"Cousin Jacks" they called themselves—became regulars. They regaled everyone in earshot with tales of hard rock mining in their native Cornwall and their regrettably poor luck in extracting any wealth from the black sands of the Gila River. Zenobia welcomed their cheerful coarse faces and sly humor, and all her other customers, too, because they kept her from dwelling on how much she wanted to be kissed again by Daniel Whittaker.

Daniel walked into Smith's Good Luck Restaurant one day just before the restaurant opened and received a rude shock.

Charles Merrick was deep in conversation with Zoe, a pile of periodicals on the table between them. She was smiling and nodding, hanging on his every word. The rules for civilized behavior prevented him from slugging Merrick, much to his regret. Instead, Daniel sat down next to Zoe and attempted to make his own contribution to their conversation.

It wasn't easy. Daniel hadn't had much formal education but he did a lot of reading on his own and even a little poetry writing, and he seldom felt outright stupid. Sitting across from the urbane and witty Merrick accomplished that in five minutes flat. Merrick spoke of concerts being offered in St. Louis and operas being performed in Boston, and Zenobia discussed Brahms and Beethoven and Handel with him, singing snatches of their work when Charles Merrick's own hummed renditions faltered. Her singing voice was exquisite, light and clear and with no trace of the seductive huskiness that so beguiled Daniel when she spoke. The whole encounter could not have been better calculated to put Daniel in a sour mood.

When Walter Connolly rushed in to report some trouble at the Empire, Daniel was more than ready to slink off and get rough with some miscreant. He knocked some sense into a few heads and made the rounds of the other saloons and sporting houses looking for more wrongdoers. Several onlookers exchanged looks, but Daniel didn't care whether they thought he was behaving strangely. He didn't stop for supper—the very thought made him ill—and because he couldn't sit still long enough to look at them, he tossed the latest envelope of wanted posters into his desk drawer unread.

Eleven

Groans and thumps in the middle of the night served as Zenobia's only notice that life at Smith's Good Luck Restaurant was about to take a new and significant turn. She rolled over and listened, coming up out of deep sleep slowly. Yes, there it was again. Rosita was awake and making ungodly noises and that could mean only one thing.

Why she'd thought she would be able to deal with childbirth was a thing that astonished Zenobia when she thought about it later on. All women managed to produce babies—how hard could it be? That summed up her attitude in the weeks preceding the birth.

How wrong she was. The sight that greeted her when she walked into Rosita's room, lamp held high, rooted Zenobia to the floor. There was blood all over the sheets, a sopping stain in the center of the bed, and Rosita's normally cheerful self was nowhere in evidence. She was writhing around and praying to the Virgin continuously through clenched teeth in a mixture of English and Spanish, alternating with curses so colorful that Zenobia almost dropped the lamp when she heard the first outburst.

Zenobia thought of what she'd assumed it would be like: serene, with nurses and midwives standing by, with clean white sheets and vats of boiling water and bandages and towels stacked neatly to one side, and someone in charge who knew what to do—but there was only her.

She fled. In her nightdress and cloak and bare feet, Zenobia ran to the jail as fast as she could. She hadn't seen Daniel Whittaker much over the past few days, and when she had, he'd tipped his hat and been polite, but there'd been a curious distance in his manner. It was her own fault, she supposed, for kissing him and then saying it couldn't be allowed to continue, but she didn't think he'd refuse to help her, not at a time like this. She tripped and picked up a splinter on the sidewalk outside the jailhouse but it barely slowed her down. She threw herself through the door and almost fell on the floor.

"Daniel!"

In the dim glow of the single lantern sitting on the desk, she saw a shape disengage itself from a bunk in the first cell. The second cell emitted a few rude words and demands to be left in peace but then it quieted again.

"Miss Smith!" Daniel came out of the first cell, pulling his suspenders up over his shoulders. He had lines on his cheeks from the blanket and his eyes were puffy.

Zenobia knew it must be very, very late, but Rosita's baby didn't care what time it was and neither did she. She grabbed his sleeve. "You've got to come quickly!" she gasped. "It's . . . it's Rosita! She's going to have a baby!"

The alarm on Daniel Whittaker's face turned to confusion. "What is it you want *me* to do?"

All of Zenobia's hopes were crushed. "Why, come and help her of course! You do know what to do, don't you?"

"I'm afraid not, ma'am, but I know someone who does."

And that was how Rosita came to meet the much talked about Madame Bettina. The German madam glided majestically into Smith's Good Luck Restaurant, exquisitely attired despite the hour, and peered down her nose at Zenobia from her equally majestic height. Zenobia did her best not to be offended by the madam's condescending air and ushered her and a statuesque blonde who had accompanied her upstairs. Between them, they took charge of Rosita.

Madame Bettina began issuing orders for hot water and newspapers and boiled potatoes with which to clean her hands.

Cleanliness was paramount she said, fixing Zenobia with a piercing look, and nothing could be relied upon to clean the hands like boiled potatoes.

Zenobia fetched and cleaned and ripped cloths and boiled things for what seemed like hours, but all with deep gratitude in her heart, for what the German madam did *not* ask her to do was to go back into the room with Rosita. Zenobia didn't think she could have faced that prospect again. Not even Madame Bettina could make a frightened sixteen-year-old girl having her first baby be quiet, however, and Zenobia cringed each time Rosita's wailing and weeping reached another crescendo.

Daniel Whittaker lit lanterns, got the stove going, started coffee to brewing, and then sat around looking helpless. By the time Zenobia had come to the end of the tasks assigned to her by Madame Bettina and was about to join him, an ominous silence settled on the place. They sat side by side on a bench, looking upward apprehensively.

"What do you suppose is happening?" Zenobia whispered.

"It's hard to say, ma'am," Daniel Whittaker replied. "Maybe she's given her something."

Zenobia hoped it wasn't a gag. She wouldn't have put it past the German madam. She didn't look like a person who suffered complaining and wailing gladly. Perhaps she'd given Rosita a little laudanum. Zenobia hoped she had, and that the relief it brought Rosita equaled the relief it brought to those within earshot of her.

Daniel looked near to falling asleep and Zenobia felt sorry for him. She'd forgotten that his busiest time was late at night and into the early morning. He'd probably only been asleep for a short time when she'd come for him.

"Why don't you go back to the jail and sleep?" she said. "Or better still, why don't you go up and lay down on my bed? It only seems fair that you should have a chance to try it out at least once."

He smiled, a tired smile that didn't come so automatically to his face as his smiles usually did. "Well, that's awfully kind of you, ma'am, but I'll see it out if you don't mind. Madame will expect me to see her and her girl back to her place when she's done and I reckon once I fall asleep again, I may not be so easy to wake up."

The truth was, Daniel thought, childbirth scared him silly. He'd pull a calf out of a cow even if it meant lying on his side in deep mud and sticking his arm halfway up where it had no business being, and he'd turned more than a few foals so their dams could push them out into the world, but he wanted no part in human birthings.

He sat uselessly, the potato boiling long since finished, and watched Zoe drink some coffee. She held the cup with both hands, like someone very tired. He tried to think of something to say but failed. A muffled groan from upstairs reminded him that women always seemed to suffer more in giving birth than animals did. He hated the thought that Zoe might one day be making noises just like Rosita was, and suffer untold agonies to bring their child into the world. Much to his dismay, his eyes began to water. He quickly turned his back and wiped away the moisture. Men weren't supposed to cry over such things. They were supposed to stand by stoically, waiting to learn the gender of the new baby. To disguise his distress, Daniel heated more water and began busily washing dishes.

"I can do that in the morning," Zoe said. "Don't bother."

"It is morning," Daniel pointed out gruffly.

Despite the coffee, Zenobia grew drowsy and awoke sometime later to find that she had drifted to sleep on Daniel Whittaker's shoulder. He'd drawn one arm around her shoulders to keep her upright. It was a nice way to keep vigil, warm and protected. He smiled down at her, half asleep himself. From upstairs came the sound of soft singing in German, a lullaby. It could only mean one thing.

Zenobia climbed the stairs wearily, Madame Bettina appeared at the door of Rosita's room with a fragrant bundle which she handed to Zenobia without apparently stopping to wonder whether she knew how to hold a baby.

"It is a boy. He is quite beautiful. It is my belief that he will grow up to break many hearts one day, more is the pity for womankind."

Zenobia struggled to find a way to hold the baby that felt natural. "What about Rosita?"

"Ach, tired, too tired to feed her baby. What can one expect? A German girl would be feeding her baby and receiving the family and accepting their gifts and offering refreshments, but what do girls in America know about taking care of themselves so that they will be strong for being a mother? This girl, she will rest and then her baby will eat. It is not the right way, but it is the way of things here. Make him a sop if he fusses in the meantime."

A sop? What on earth was a sop? Before Zenobia could ask, the German madam and her companion took themselves off, as unruffled and perfectly groomed as when they had arrived. By the time Daniel returned—and thank God he did!—the baby was wailing in a manner remarkably reminiscent of Rosita a few hours before.

"What should I do?" Zenobia cried. "It sounds as if he might choke or run out of air, he's crying so! Madame Bettina said something about a sop but—"

"Allow me, ma'am."

Daniel took the baby, made an expert wrap or two to snug up the swaddling cloths, and strode toward the larder. Zenobia massaged her aching temples. It wasn't that the baby cried so loudly, but that his cries were so heartrending. She followed Daniel and found him cradling the baby with assurance as he poured out some of her precious store of fresh milk. It soon turned out that the sheriff of Gila City might not know much about getting babies into the world, but he knew a whole lot more than she did about caring for them once they'd arrived.

He dipped one of his ever-present clean handkerchiefs in a saucer of milk and sugar and offered the twisted end of it to the baby. The crying ceased and little whatever-his-name-was sucked with hard toothless gums at the handkerchief. He whimpered each time Daniel withdrew it to dip it in the saucer again.

"That is quite the most amazing thing I've ever seen," Zenobia confessed, overcome with admiration. The quiet went a long way toward restoring her equilibrium.

"Well, it isn't what he wants, but he'll get by a while on it. It's as well for a man to learn early on that he can't always have what he wants."

"But he's just a baby," Zenobia protested, feeling the first stirrings of maternal feeling toward the baby. It had taken her too much by surprise to see the actual details of childbirth to spare much thought until now for the helpless product of it all. "Here, give him to me," she said, feeling reinvigorated now that she had half an idea what to do to make the baby happy. "I'll see to it that Rosita does right by him as soon as she awakes."

Daniel Whittaker stumbled off into the breaking dawn and Zenobia smiled as she locked the door behind him. How like a man to deliver harsh philosophies about survival to an infant only hours old! She watched through the glass window as the sheriff of Gila City walked away, thinking fondly that somewhere in the night, the reserve between them had been broken down. Whatever had been preying on his mind lately had gone away and they were friends again. She would have hated for it to be any other way.

Rosita proved to be a wonderful mother, despite Madame Bettina's gloomy pronouncement on the quality of mothers in America. Only one day after Zenobia hung a closed sign out so they could all rest up, Rosita arose, bathed, dressed, and was back at work in the kitchen. Her initial plan was to swaddle Paco Xavier Rodrigues Chavez so that he was plastered to her ample breast while she worked, but Zenobia forbade it.

"He'll be burnt," she protested. "The steam from the cooking pots will scald him. He's much closer to it than you are, and, besides, look how tender his skin is. Give him to me."

Zenobia tenderly stroked the baby's cheek and he nuzzled toward her fingers, grasping with his lips for something to clamp on to. He felt like silk, soft and smooth, and he was the color of the tea one made for children still in the nursery, with lots of cream. It made him look so vibrant and robust, not at all like the pallid infants she was used to seeing her friends and acquaintances in Philadelphia display so proudly. Zenobia's heart swelled with love. She'd had no idea how attached one could become—and in so short a time!

"I'll put him on my back instead," Rosita said. "I will like to carry him there for a change."

"You'll do no such thing!" Zenobia said indignantly. "What if you turn away from the stove? Then he will be in the steam, too, only you won't notice! And what if you misjudge a distance? He could be banged into a doorjamb. I won't hear of it! I'll hold him while you cook."

And so she learned to do everything one-armed, for she could not simply sit there and coo over the baby all of the time. She had work of her own to do. While Rosita cooked and washed dishes, Zenobia shifted Paco from one arm to the other, setting out plates and utensils. Sometimes she was forced to put him down temporarily, for not everything could be done without both hands. Then he would kick vigorously and watch her, smiling his brief little grins that Zenobia loved to see.

Weeks went by and all the work got done somehow. Paco became the darling of everyone who ate at Smith's Good Luck Restaurant. Daniel and Lester took especially protective attitudes toward him, and Rosita shyly asked if they would consider becoming his godfathers. Reverend Bob was brought in, the restaurant was converted to a baptismal nave for an hour, and young Paco got off to a rip-roaring start with a party notable by Gila City standards for its complete lack of liquor. Reverend Bob showed welcome restraint in not referring to Rosita's lack of a husband, though he did make a rather pointed remark in the closing prayer about the standard of female chastity being deplorably low in the West.

All the guests brought some modest gift for the baby, and Rosita was so tongue-tied by their generosity that she ceased to speak altogether, able only to nod and blush as she accepted them. Molly B'damn, the reverend's faithful and beloved steer, stuck her head through an open window and consumed a tin of sweets that Contrary Mary brought, but to almost universal regret, the steer did not take ill and die as a result.

Even Dog showed an inclination to like Paco, though it did Zenobia's nerves no good to find the wolf nosing the baby's blankets aside on one of the few occasions she set him down. Teresa assured her that Dog had made an excellent baby-sitter for the infant one girl had had while working over the Red Dog Saloon, but Zenobia could take no comfort from the thought. Daniel came by and offered a cradle he'd obviously made himself, and Zenobia accepted it with enthusiasm, although she still kept Paco in her arms whenever the restaurant was open for business. There were simply too many strangers and too many clumsy people about for her to be at ease unless she had hold of him at times like those.

Life seemed to be working out much better than Zenobia felt she had any right to expect when a shadow fell across their doorway one day. It was the shadow of an enormous woman with snapping black eyes and a ferocious demeanor. She braced her feet wide apart and looked over the noontime crowd at the restaurant until her eyes came to rest on Rosita, back in the kitchen.

"Rosita!"

It was only one word but it was enough to bring conversation to a standstill. The woman's very presence *demanded* attention. She was quite possibly the tallest woman Zenobia had ever seen. Back in the kitchen, Zenobia watched as Rosita turned the color of ash. Zenobia clutched Paco tighter and he let out a wail of protest. The huge woman's gaze swiveled momentarily in her direction and then she stalked toward the back of the room, her fists clenched and meaty forearms bulging.

"Rosita! Por qué no me contestas?"

The voice was like the low rumble of thunder accompanying an approaching storm. Several men stood up, put their hats on, and slipped out the front door. Even the loquacious Cornishmen, the "Cousin Jacks," looked quelled for once. Zenobia hurriedly dipped her finger into a creamer and offered it to Paco to quiet him.

"*Buenos días, madre,*" Rosita whispered. "*¿Como van todos?*"

" 'How are things'?" the woman roared. "You ask me how things are with me when my daughter disappears in the night without a word? How things are with me when I must go to the ends of the earth seeking my firstborn child only to find out that she has been traveling with the army like a *puta?*"

Rosita's mother—for it was now crystal clear that's who the woman was—spat viciously to one side. Zenobia flinched as the wad of spit ricocheted off the spittoon with a sound like a gunshot. Several more customers suddenly remembered pressing business elsewhere. Rosita's mouth was working up and down but no sound came out.

"*Y por que,* why I ask myself, does my daughter do such a thing?"

Rosita burst into tears. Zenobia debated whether and how to intervene between mother and daughter, the one so tall and intimidating and the other so small and craven. Truth be known, Zenobia was more than a little scared of Mama Rosa herself, for Rosita's mother gave a fair imitation of her own mother when outraged over her daughter's transgressions—though to be fair, Mrs. Barnabus Strouss had never been known to spit, so in that particular, the resemblance broke down. Still, being older and more experienced, not to mention the owner of the establishment in which this confrontation was taking place, Zenobia felt under some obligation to take matters in hand. She cleared her throat.

"Excuse me."

Rosita's mother bent her obsidian glare on Zenobia. "Yes?"

"We are trying to serve a meal here, ma'am. If you wish to

speak with my cook, please be seated and have some coffee until after our patrons have all eaten and left."

"Cook!" snorted Rosita's mother. "I did not raise my daughter up to be a cook!"

"My mother did not raise me to run a restaurant," Zenobia said stiffly. "and yet one must earn a living. It is a respectable profession."

"Ha!" Another spit, this time better aimed, made it into the spittoon, but some of the fire had gone out of the enormous woman. She looked Zenobia up and down. "And just who are you that employs my Rosita as a cook?"

"I am Miss Zoe Smith," Zenobia said with as much hauteur as she could summon.

" 'Miss'? Then whose baby is that?" Rosita's mother asked suspiciously, eyeing Paco, now dozing on her shoulder.

Too late did Zenobia see the yawning pit in front of her. She had always heard that the path to perdition was a slippery one but she'd never thought to be able to draw so many illustrations of that truth from her own life. She flicked Paco's blanket over his face, but she'd thought of it a minute too late.

"That baby, it is not a gringo." Rosita's mother declared. She poked a large finger in Zenobia's face, stabbing it menacingly at her nose. "I demand to know whose baby that is! Is that my Rosita's baby? What have you done to my innocent little Rosita?"

Rosita's sobbing made a soft background counterpoint to her mother's budding rage. It was a nightmare. Zenobia said the only thing she could to shield Rosita from Mama Rosa's wrath.

"No, it's my baby."

"Yours?" Mama Rosa said suspiciously. "Then who is the father?"

"I am, ma'am."

Zenobia turned quickly. Daniel Whittaker's partner, Lester Cooper, stood just inside the door. His strong brown face radiated certitude. Without bothering to hang his hat on a peg by the door, he crossed the open floor of the restaurant. With his colossal shoulders and legs like tree trunks, he looked like more than a match for Mama Rosa. Zenobia was so relieved that she forgot to be embarrassed by this very public inquiry into her fictitious private life.

Not quite sure where to pick up the narrative, Zenobia decided to put her trust in Lester. Rosita's mother looked almost intimidated by Lester.

Lester didn't even blink as he said to Zenobia, "I knew you all would be busy so I thought I could take the baby off your hands while I eat. Kill two birds with one stone." Zenobia was filled with admiration. Lying on a grand scale obviously came easily to Lester. It was talent she felt in need of at that particular moment.

"Why, thank you . . . um, Lester. I believe I will take you up on that offer." Her face should have been flaming, but Zenobia was too busy lying to blush. Rosita's mother peered at them through narrowed eyes as Lester took little Paco with the practiced ease of a wet nurse. It lent credence to the lie that Paco was his son, and Zenobia thanked providence for men who knew which end of a baby was which.

"Why is my daughter crying if she has nothing to hide?" Mama Rosa demanded, not ready to be completely mollified yet.

Zenobia wiped her hands briskly on her apron. "I suspect you frightened her. You certainly upset everyone else. Now. I have a restaurant to run." Lester's example had fortified Zenobia no end. She turned her back on Mama Rosa, praying that no one would inadvertently blurt out the truth. She could see any number of regulars who knew perfectly well that Paco wasn't her baby and Lester wasn't her lover. After all, she *had* claimed to be only a "miss." It was too bad that she hadn't claimed to be a "missus" as long as she was lying. "Everyone, sit down," she said. "We'll get you fed just as fast as we can, won't we, Rosita?"

She hazarded a glance in Rosita's direction. The girl stared at her with reddened, swollen eyes and undying gratitude.

Mama Rosa glared at both of them, but deprived of ammunition, she shuffled sullenly off to a corner table to glower at her daughter from afar.

How she got through serving the meal, Zenobia couldn't remember later, but she cast numerous sunny smiles at Lester, of the sort a woman might give the father of her child until even his solemn face lightened up. Later, when Lester had handed the baby back to her and left, with a promise to see her "when I get home tonight," Zenobia put away food and washed dishes with Paco on her hip, fobbing him off with watered-down cream as Rosita sat down with her mother and they talked, or rather her mother harangued and Rosita listened. Zenobia half feared the girl would simply walk out with her mother and then she really *would* be Paco's mother. She waited until she judged Paco would no longer be denied his real supper and interrupted them.

"Rosita, would you take little, um . . . Packwood upstairs for his nap and stay with him while I go to the general store? I know you usually go, but I need to speak to Mr. Trilby personally about those overcharges." Rosita jumped at the excuse to escape from her mother.

"Of course, señora!"

Señora. That meant a married woman. Well, the story would just have to remain a bit vague on that detail. "Thank you, Rosita, and your mother, will she be staying in Gila City long?" Zenobia turned a bland smile on the woman.

Mama Rosa scowled. "I will be here until I know my Rosita is staying with good people."

Which Zenobia hadn't yet proved herself to be. That came through loud and clear. "Well, come have dinner here before you go, but you mustn't frighten our customers again."

Rosita's eyes widened at Zenobia's temerity in speaking to Mama Rosa so. She grabbed Paco and made good her escape up the stairs before her mother could explode. Zenobia made an equally deft retreat out the front door and hummed a little tune as she walked to Calvin Trilby's. Now why hadn't she ever been able to speak to her own mother like that?

Twelve

Once again a crisis had been averted it seemed, but with the heat of summer came a new and wholly unexpected peril. Cholera was reported to have broken out in some of the more remote placer camps. It could come riding into Gila City at any time, and no one would ever know who was a carrier until it was too late to avoid exposure. Some said it came through the air, others said tainted water, but it always started with one person and spread from there. Cholera had swept through whole regiments during the war and struck them down. No one could pretend they were safe when modern medicine had offered so little hope to the fighting men.

Despite worried talk, people in Gila City got on with their lives. Paco thrived and Lester spent hours at Smith's Good Luck Restaurant whenever he was in town—which seemed to be more and more frequently—only now Rosita had apparently registered his existence. Considering that he took Paco from Zenobia and held him almost continually when he was there, it would have been difficult for Rosita not to. Still, she never spoke to him, her shyness a barrier as always. It didn't daunt Lester. His patience never wavered. It was easy to see why Daniel spoke so highly of him—and easier still to see that he was sweet on the young Mexican girl, though not a word had been spoken between them.

As for Daniel Whittaker, he came and went, lending a hand whenever he could, seeking opportunities to find Zenobia alone and seldom succeeding—by design. Zenobia thought of him often, though, especially when she lay in her large new bed. It seemed lonely with just one person in it, and she began to suspect that he had never intended for her to sleep in it by herself. The thought aroused her greatly at night when it was safe to think frank thoughts about him. It wasn't hard to imagine his hard, warm body stretched out next to hers, his weight denting the wool-stuffed mattress and drawing her irresistibly toward him.

And then one day, on the street, she saw the man she *should* have been sharing a bed with. Zenobia's heart turned to stone and her feet ceased moving the instant she saw Eben. Just as fast as she'd caught sight of him, he was gone again in a surge of people around the stagecoach on Main Street. Her mouth went dry and she ducked into an alley in blind panic. She peered around the corner when her breathing had settled but she didn't see him again.

But it *had* been him! One could not be married to someone and share a house and a bed and a life with them and not remember their face in every detail, and the way they moved that set them apart from anyone else. Hair color might be altered, weight might vary, and people might suffer an illness, but a face was a face, and she knew she was right. It *had* been Eben!

God, how she would have liked to have talked herself into believing otherwise. Half the human race seemed to live on wishful thinking. Why couldn't she? Because, came the inevitable answer, half the human race didn't have to worry that they'd be hanged by the neck until dead if they were wrong in their assumptions.

Zenobia hurried back to the restaurant in a state of near terror. The next stage wouldn't arrive until the end of the week so she had no choice but to stay in Gila City. She must remain hidden in the meantime, too, because if *she* couldn't leave until the next stage came, then Eben couldn't either. He was one for creature comforts so she didn't think it likely he'd be traveling the long distances between Western towns on horseback.

She crept through alleys so as not to be seen, her skirt sweeping through dust and layers of garbage. Rats squeaked in alarm as she passed and Zenobia repressed a shudder. She felt physically ill, not because of the rats and the garbage but out of fear. She was every bit as afraid now as she had been the night she fled Philadelphia. She had almost begun to believe that she was safe in her new life. Back at the restaurant, she sagged against a wall in the larder and began to shake all over. What in God's name was Eben doing in Gila City?

But she knew. He was looking for her personally, not content to let an impersonal justice system track her down. He would want revenge for Stephen's death. Zenobia held herself tightly, feeling the tremors go through her. It was a truth she never would have recognized before the murder, but so much that hadn't been clear to her before was now painfully obvious.

But her resolve never to go back and never to face a trial hadn't wavered.

She'd just have to stay out of sight. Zenobia waited until the worst of the shaking passed and tied on an apron to set up the tables for the eleven o'clock opening, but her every move was shaped by terror of seeing Eben again, or worse yet, having him see her. There was nothing to stop Eben from walking in and sitting down to eat like anyone else, and Zenobia made Rosita unlock the front doors at opening time.

"It's time you took a turn out front," she announced.

"But, señora—"

"No, you need to learn my job and I need to learn yours," Zenobia insisted.

Rosita went off unhappily, carrying trays full of food that Zenobia dished up while Paco lay in the cradle on the wall farthest from the stove. He waved and kicked and sucked on a piece of candied orange Zenobia held out to him from time to time.

Zenobia had faithfully played out her role as his mother in public while Rosita did all the actual mothering behind the scenes. It was a situation Paco seemed to accept cheerfully. Mama Rosa had gotten a job at Dolly's Arcade and immediately discovered that she could earn a great deal more in a boom town than in a little cantina back on the Salt River. She sent for Rosita's younger siblings and set up house in a shack on the edge of town where a notoriously lucky gambler had died in an ambush. Since the ambush, no one had felt their own luck sufficient to overcome the curse on the place, until Mama Rosa.

Out front, Rosita kept sending unhappy glances toward the kitchen where Zenobia ducked and bobbed like a ship in high seas, trying to keep her face below the level of the divider as she filled dishes, rinsed plates, and stacked pots.

Daniel Whittaker came for the midday meal, and when he came back at closing time and discovered Rosita still coping single-handed out front, he asked where Zenobia was. Zenobia cowered at the top of the stairs. At night, with the lanterns inside the restaurant lit, anyone walking by could see her so she had scuttled upstairs the minute the last customer left.

"The señora, she is upstairs," she heard Rosita say. Her voice dropped to a whisper, but a trick of the acoustics in the stairwell brought her words to Zenobia's ears. "The señora, she is very strange today, Mr. Whittaker. I do not know why. Tonight, Mr. Merrick wished her to sit down and share his magazines with him, and she would not come out of the kitchen even though we were not busy anymore. She threw plates at me, Mr. Whittaker, to take out to the customers, and walked like this, like a crab, around the kitchen."

"Is she sick?" Daniel sounded puzzled.

"I don't think so."

Zenobia slipped down the hall and into her room, shutting the door softly. She leaned against it, her heart pounding. What was she going to tell Daniel to explain her odd behavior? *My husband is in town to seek revenge for my having murdered his best friend and I don't want him to see me?* She'd better think of something else quickly—she could hear Daniel Whittaker's footsteps approaching her door.

"Zoe?" He was knocking softly. Somehow he had slipped

from calling her Miss Smith in public into calling her Zoe when they were alone together.

Zenobia bit her lip. "Yes?"

"I was hoping to see you tonight," he said.

A sudden, unpleasant thought struck her: What if Eben had come to the jail asking for information about a woman fitting her description? "I'm about to go to sleep," she said, striving to keep her voice calm.

"Well, I'd like to see you for just a moment before you do."

"That's not possible," Zenobia replied. "I've already changed into my nightdress."

"Well, ma'am," he said, falling back into a more formal address, "can't you just crack your door? Rosita says you wouldn't speak to hardly anyone today. Can't you tell me what's the matter?"

Zenobia searched desperately for the words that would convince him to go away. None came.

"Is it the cholera, ma'am?" Daniel Whittaker inquired. "They do say it might be more than a rumor. Is that what's got you so nervous?"

Zenobia leapt at the excuse. "Yes! That's it! I'm deathly afraid of contracting cholera."

"I see." She heard him shift his weight. "Well, ma'am. I can't say as I've heard of any cases here in town yet."

"I don't care," she said firmly. "I'm not taking any chances." *Now* he would go away and leave her in peace.

"If that's the case, ma'am, I have an idea. Why don't you come out to my place with me? I'm set to leave in the morning, me and Lester both. We have to round up spring calves and put our brands on them. You'd be safe from any cholera out there and by the time we came back in four or five days, we'd probably know if there really is cholera coming our way."

Go to Daniel Whittaker's farm, or ranch or spread, or whatever it was they called it out here? Zenobia thought quickly. It would enable her to leave town until after Eben had gone away, and there'd be no chance of him seeing her in the meantime.

The plan fit her needs precisely, although there was a certain nerve-wracking irony in leaving town with the sheriff to elude capture for murder. Zenobia thrust such superfluous considerations from her mind.

"Yes, I would be pleased to go out to your . . . place," she declared. "Yes, thank you!"

She almost heard him smile. "I'll be by with the wagon at ten o'clock sharp."

Of course there had to be one last scene with Mama Rosa, of the very sort Zenobia had dreaded all along. As she stood with her valise by the side door the next morning, skulking in the folds of the curtain so as not to be seen, Zenobia saw the woman striding down Main Street. She kept close tabs on her daughter, reluctant to admit that she was making a living in a completely moral manner. Mama Rosa herself served drinks at Dolly's, and did a show several times daily that involved pulling nails out of the wall with her backside, so her standards for Rosita clearly differed from the ones she felt bound by herself.

"You are going away?" Mama Rosa sniffed when she saw the valise at Zenobia's feet.

"Yes, for a few days."

"I am going to order more hominy while you are out of—" Rosita broke off abruptly when she saw her mother. She stood in the doorway to the kitchen with Paco on her hip. Rosita's face went a shade lighter. "Mama. *Buenos días*. Would you like a cup of coffee?"

Mama Rosa spun around to face Zenobia. "You are going away and leaving your son with my little Rosita?" she demanded. "She is not your servant! She is a cook!" The job had evidently moved up a rung or two on the ladder of respectability since the first time she'd heard about it.

"Well, it's only for a few days," Zenobia faltered. "I'm . . . I'm feeling a little poorly, and I was hoping to get some rest and—"

Mama Rosa shook a finger at her. "You think I don't see, but I do! I know how you rely on my daughter. Why, if it weren't for her, you could not run this restaurant! Whatever you are paying her, she should be earning twice that, and now you expect to go away and she will do *all* the work of the restaurant *and* take care of your baby? Bah! Rosita, give him to me."

Hands shaking, Rosita handed little Paco over to her *mamacita*. She did not dare look at Zenobia, biting her lip hard to hide her distress.

"Now, you, Miss High-and-Mighty, will take your baby with you, and if you are lucky, no one will offer my daughter what she is really worth while you are gone and she will still be here when you return, and you will still have a business."

Paco's mouth puckered up. Mama Rosa was the only thing they'd found that wiped the smile from his face, other than a lack of food. Zenobia hastily jiggled him up and down to distract him from the foghorn voice of his grandmother. Rosita clasped her now empty hands in front of her and stared at the rough plank floor.

"You must not allow this *gringa* to take advantage of you like that, Rosita," Mama Rosa admonished.

Zenobia heard the wheels of a wagon roll up and stop outside. If Daniel was surprised to see her rush outside with Paco clutched to her side, he covered it well when he saw Mama Rosa. He tipped his hat to her and Lester, who'd made no move to get down from the buckboard, jumped to the ground and lifted Zenobia up to the seat like a considerate husband would. It was a wonderful thing if you were going to get caught up in living a lie, thought Zenobia, to have friends ready to back you up. She could still hear Mama Rosita lecturing Rosita as they turned the corner.

Daniel's house, if one could call it that, turned out to be nothing more than one large. all-purpose room made of clay bricks he called adobe. Zenobia regarded it with no small amount of dismay. It was dark inside, with only one window, and that one covered with oiled hide and not real glass, and there was no floor yet, just hard-packed dirt. Outside, under a brilliant blue sky, washing off the dust from their journey in a basin of well water, she felt better. The water was clean and cold unlike Gila City's water, which all came from the river. Poles set into the roofline of the house formed a canopy of shade over a tiny courtyard with a rudimentary stove built from flat rocks.

Daniel seemed so worried about her having a poor opinion of the place that Zenobia, out of politeness alone, praised the charm and simplicity of it. His face creased into a hesitant smile.

"I have plans," he said, "big plans. It'll be a lot different when I'm through."

"I'm sure it will be," Zenobia replied. "If my bed is any measure of your talent for building nice things, then this house will one day be quite wonderful."

His smile widened. Zenobia kept hers in place with an effort. Sitting in the striped shade of the rough-peeled poles overhead, with chickens scratching around her feet and a goat investigating the bonnet she'd set down next to her, she felt like one of the poor souls she'd pitied on her journey across the western scrublands. Each drab little way station had been drearier than the last, and Daniel Whittaker's "homestead" resembled the poorest of them. Still, it was none of her affair. It wasn't as if she would ever have to live there.

Suppertime improved her mood. Lester cooked a wonderful meal, sacrificing one of the miserable-looking chickens to the stew pot and producing biscuits so heavenly they caused Zenobia to make a note in her mind to speak to Rosita about encouraging his attentions.

Before she could stop herself, Zenobia said to Lester, "You know, I believe that Rosita might enjoy making a friend in Gila City—other than me, that is—but she's shy. If you were to, say, go work in the kitchen, doing, oh, I don't know what, maybe making biscuits, you might be able to get her to talk to you."

"Is that a fact?" Lester appeared to consider the idea. "And you wouldn't mind, ma'am, I mean, having a stranger in your kitchen?"

Zenobia waved her hand in airy dismissal. "Well, it would be easier not to have extra people underfoot when we're trying to work, but if you were *making* something, something we could serve, like, well, those biscuits I mentioned, then she'd be glad for the help and so would I. It wouldn't be as if you weren't making yourself useful, and of course, you could make friends with Rosita at the same time. I believe she has said one or two things about hoping to get to know you better."

Zenobia detected a smirk on Daniel Whittaker's lips. "And of course, if you did make biscuits," she added quickly, "why, there'd be no charge for any meals you eat, naturally." Daniel looked as if he thought she were trying to take advantage of Lester!

"Thank you, ma'am," Lester said. "I believe I may just do as you suggest."

Good food always put Zenobia in charity with the world, rather like it did Paco, who made a face but soon accepted the goat's milk as his own supper. With the sun sketching a blue-and-pink palette across the western horizon, and deep blue giving way to a spangle of stars in the east, Zenobia felt life might not be *quite* as intolerable out here as she'd thought—provided the house really did receive the promised improvements. Of course, she reminded herself sternly, what Daniel Whittaker did or did not do to his little mud house did not concern *her*.

When the sun finally disappeared, Lester stood up and allowed as how he would sleep at his place that night. To Zenobia it seemed perfectly natural, but it appeared to take Daniel by surprise. For her own part, she expected Daniel to take himself off to sleep elsewhere, too, but not too far away. She had never slept so far from civilization, out where land stretched away in empty brownness in every direction.

It got surprisingly cool outdoors when the sun went down so they sat by a small fire in the hearth indoors when Lester had gone, drinking coffee. Daniel spread a big bear fur for her to sit on, apologizing for the lack of chairs. Personally, Zenobia thought he would have done well to use some of his precious store of wood to build furniture for himself before he went off making things for someone else but she kept the thought to herself.

Paco drowsed, happy and full, next to her. Zenobia tucked her legs under her skirt, trying to be demure when the situation left such a big opening for more. She suspected Daniel might be a little ill at ease, too, for he took down a bottle of whiskey from a high shelf built into the wall by the fireplace.

"Will you have some?"

"No, thank you all the same."

"I'm not generally a drinking man," he said apologetically, "but I do like to have a drink when I'm out here and don't have to worry about being on duty."

"I would have assumed you were not a heavy imbiber," Zenobia replied to put him at ease. He seemed so anxious for her to think well of him.

"I used to like my liquor too much, ma'am, especially for someone coming from a home that was strictly teetotal. During the war, and when I was a young waddie, well, I could make a lot of redeye disappear. I think it's a gauge of a man's character if he feels the need as he gets older to go on drinking as much as he did when he was a sprout. I'm happy to say I don't."

He made a little show of brushing the dust off the shoulder of the bottle, as if proving that no one had disturbed it in a long time. Zenobia hid her smile by turning her face away. The way the wind blew dust around in this part of the world, the bottle could have picked up a coating like that in a morning. But the fact that he cared what she thought made her feel a certain pleasure.

He poured the whiskey and sat down again. Zenobia picked at the edge of her skirt, trying not to look at his hands holding the cup, or the wide, hard thigh in the corner of her field of vision.

"I've been meaning to ask, what is a waddie exactly?" she

said, to make sure the conversation stayed centered on him and not herself.

"Why, it's a hand, a fellow who rides herd on cattle. That was my first job when I left home. I could barely sit a horse back then, since we'd only owned one old workhorse, but I was looking for adventure. You know how young fellows are."

"You aren't such an old fellow now," Zenobia teased. She'd been wondering how old he really was. He had a quiet authority that made other men look to him for guidance—she'd seen that a number of times—but there was a youthful quality there, too, in spite of the weathering of his face and the solid masculine look of him.

"Well, I'm twenty-five," he said a touch defensively. "I reckon that's old enough."

"Well, certainly, but for what?" Zenobia said it lightly, concealing her surprise. He was four years younger than she was!

"Old enough to know my mind. Why, I left home when I was fifteen and I was riding line by myself by the time I was eighteen. Even Lester didn't ride line by himself until he was twenty. Shoot, he was an old man." Daniel grinned. "He hates when I call him that, says it's just his natural disposition to be a little more serious-minded than I am."

"He *is* a very serious-minded individual," Zenobia agreed. "I confess, I work sometimes at getting a smile out of him just to prove it can be done. I think Rosita could make him happy. It would be nice if they discovered they suited one another. She's a hard worker and a fine person, but she's not good at standing up for herself. He seems to be someone she could lean on."

"That he is, ma'am. Why, I owe my life to Lester. There's no man I trust more in this world."

"He saved your life? Was that during the war?"

Daniel poured himself more whiskey. The lines of his face softened. "No, ma'am, I made it through the war in pretty good order."

He withdrew a small leather folder from his pocket. Zenobia

caught a glimpse of a photograph. Without being too obvious, she tried to see the face in it, but he was handing her a slip of heavy cream-colored paper. It was limp with age and wear.

"I've kept this to remind myself how lucky I was."

Zenobia took it and turned it so the fire's light shone on it. It was a form, with dotted lines to fill in the particulars. She read:

Bible House, Topeka. February 16, *1861. From the Kansas State Bible Society to* Daniel Francis Whittaker *Soldier in* 15th Kansas Cavalry. *Should I die on the battle field or in Hospital, for the sake of humanity, acquaint* M/M John Whittaker *residing at* Peachtree, Kansas *of the fact, and where my remains may be found.*

Zenobia quietly handed it back to him. How bleak it must have been to carry a constant reminder that one could die at any moment.

"Don't look so sorrowful," he said gently. "It's over now. I saw a lot of things I'd as lief I hadn't, not ever in my lifetime, but I never did get busted up too bad, just one round ball, and I was over that in a month. I came a lot closer to dying before I ever signed on with the cavalry."

"When Lester saved your life?"

"That's right." He seemed gratified that she'd remembered. He poured another whiskey. "I was riding line in a blizzard that shouldn't have happened to the devil himself, about as far out from my line shack as I ever went, trying to push some cattle into cover, and my horse went down a slope I didn't know was there until we commenced to sliding in a great big tangle of rope and reins and snow. He rolled over me and broke both my legs. That horse never was very sure-footed but he was willing, and that's a good quality in a horse. He'd broken one of his own legs but I couldn't put him down because my gun belt got twisted around beneath me in the fall, and he ended up on his off side, so the rifle in my saddle boot was under him. I had to listen to him suffer. I learned to wear my gun belt forward after that, so my pistol would always be where I could reach it. I hated not being able to help that horse to leave this world."

"Forget the horse, for heaven's sake!" she exclaimed, thinking how overly devoted to their animals some men were. "What about you?"

He grinned. "You can tell you're from back East, ma'am. Out here, a horse can mean life or death and he's your best friend, too, sometimes. You treat even a second-rate horse the best way you know how."

The last thing Zenobia wanted to do was remind him she was from the East. To cover the gaffe, she said quickly, "What about your own suffering? Weren't you worried about dying, all alone as you were?"

He shrugged. "Well, I pretty much decided after the first day or two that I wasn't long for the world. It didn't bother me so much as you might think. I've nearly died many a time and I was scared every time except that once. The cold numbed up the pain from my legs some, so I watched the snow fall and the light go and come and go again without too much discomfort. I mostly lay there and dreamt of food—big tin pans filled with roasted chickens, a roast goose almost floating in his own rich gravy, a roast pig with an apple in his mouth and a pudding in his belly, apple pies, pumpkin pies, mince pies, white cake and yellow cake, and doughnuts galore, each one as big as a table could hold. I started in to eat one and I'd broken off a big hunk when I heard this man asking me did I want to die or was I going to wake up. I opened my eyes and there was Lester bending over me. I wasn't sure I'd woken all the way up, though, because here was this face the color of fresh-plowed earth in the middle of nothing but snow and whiteness, and an accent that came from somewhere down South, just all soft and slow and hospitable. I remember thinking that if this was heaven, my mother was going to be mighty pleased, for she'd always maintained that Negroes went to heaven, same as white folks."

He took a swig from the cup and grimaced. "The next thing

I knew, he was holding a cup of hot coffee under my nose. The first mouthful hit my belly and that's when I knew for certain I wasn't dreaming or in heaven. Back in those days, Lester couldn't make a good cup of coffee to save his soul. It seared my stomach and everything it touched on the way down. I'd sooner swallow a cannonball than ever be obliged to drink something that bad again, but I confess that on that occasion, it may have been just what I needed, for after he'd made me drink it all, I made up my mind that I wasn't going to leave this earth with that taste in my mouth. No, I determined to get me at least one more good cup of coffee before I departed."

Zenobia wiggled her finger in the dirt, scratching a line in it. Something big was gnawing at her, forcing her to think back. She could see Stephen's face, the stunned surprise in his eyes when his own weight had carried him out into space. She wished she didn't have cause to think so much about how a man might feel when he knew his time might be nigh. She looked at Daniel from beneath her lashes.

"Why weren't you afraid to die? I mean, why all the other times but not that time?"

Daniel thought a moment. "I reckon it was because I figured there was nothing I could do. No amount of effort on my part was going to make the least bit of difference. I couldn't crawl or drag myself anywhere because the snow was so deep, I didn't even have any chance of getting branches to build a signal fire. Every other time I was in a pinch and near to dying, there were things I could do to ward off the end so I had to keep on fighting, no matter how miserable I was. This time was different. I couldn't even shoot myself. It was real peaceful, and I was glad not to be afraid. I remembered how my father read to us from the Bible about peace coming on you when the angels fetch you up yonder and I thought maybe that was how a man knew for certain that his time had come, when he came over all peaceful like that."

Zenobia could take no comfort from his words. Stephen hadn't known peace. She had seen nothing but fear on his face.

He'd struggled the whole way down the staircase, tumbling hideously, between the bannister and the wall. He'd tried to save himself, throwing out an arm, bracing with a leg, wrapping his arms around his head, with short, awful cries as his breath was driven from him with each impact.

"My story upset you, didn't it?"

Zenobia looked up quickly. Daniel Whittaker's concerned green gaze brought her back from the unpleasant place she'd been. "No, not since I know it turned out for the best."

He encouraged her with a smile. "More than you know. It turned out that Lester was riding line for a widow named Alice McCloskey. He'd been following some steers that had wandered off her place in the storm when he came across me. He rigged a sort of litter behind his horse and dragged me down off that range to her place, and between them, they managed to splint my legs straight because there hadn't been much swelling on account of the cold. After that, Mrs. McCloskey looked after me like I was family."

Daniel watched the pale fire send its light across Zoe Smith's face. She was so beautiful! He was filled with love watching her, and filled, too, with earthy thoughts about her, mixed with memories of Alice McCloskey. She was watching him expectantly, so he went on.

"It seems Mr. McCloskey had been dead for six years. That's a long time to spend alone, and Alice McCloskey wasn't a bookish person like her husband had been. She liked conversation more than books, so she was glad of my company seeing as how it was a deep winter. She lent me her husband's books to pass the time when she was busy. It was a long winter—this was way north of here, you mind. The snow started early and just went on and on, but I didn't mind. I like to read and I needed time to heal, and Alice McCloskey, she wasn't *so* very old, maybe forty, and good-looking. We got along fine. I learned one heck of a lot that winter, and not all from books."

He realized he'd said more than he'd meant to and ducked

his head to hide the warming of his cheeks. But Zoe had been watching him intently as he spoke, and her brow furrowed.

"You're not saying that she . . . that you and she . . ."

Daniel felt the heat come up his neck. The whiskey had definitely loosened his tongue, much to his regret, but at least Zoe didn't seem offended—more just *interested*. "Well, yes, ma'am, I guess you could say that we . . . that she . . ."

"But you were so young," she said, frowning.

Daniel chuckled. "Not when Alice McCloskey got through with me. It was an education and a privilege to know her."

Zoe smiled hesitantly and said something completely unexpected.

"What did she teach you exactly?"

Daniel took another long drink of whiskey to clear his ears. "Ma'am?"

"Well, you don't have to tell me if you don't want to. I just wondered, well, you know, what a woman with experience would teach a young man about . . . well, about . . . what to do."

She might be a little tongue-tied but she didn't seem embarrassed. He knew how easily Teresa and the other sporting girls talked about the subject of relations between men and women. Maybe nice women were just as interested, only they didn't have the same chance to educate themselves. Alice McCloskey had opened his eyes to the fact that nice women could be every bit as interested in sex as men.

"Well, mainly the basics of what a woman likes, I guess. Up until that time, I was like most bachelors and didn't have much experience to go by. About all I'd ever had to do with a woman in that way was with professionals, and not even so many of them. The ones I did go to, they just lay down and well, you know, made themselves available. Even if I'd been months on the trail, every night kind of dreaming and hoping about something a bit more . . . well, romantic, it just robs a man of all sense when he's been without a woman and he sees one waiting for him like that. Me and every other young fellow in that situation is going to do what nature tells him to do. Alice McCloskey, she taught me not to be in such a hurry, to use my hands and my mouth to give a woman pleasure, and to watch what she liked and wanted more of."

He glanced over at Zoe. "Sorry, ma'am, if that's too specific for you."

She shook her head. "No, not at all."

Zenobia toyed with the bundle of twigs used to clean the hearth. She wasn't offended. After the first shocking invasion of her modesty on her wedding night, for which no one had bothered to prepare her, astonishment had given way to an understanding that that was how babies were made, that it wasn't enough to just sleep next to each other, or whatever foolish idea she'd had before. It had been a full year before she had come around to the notion that she might ask for more, for she now realized that as a wife, she'd done little more than the professional girls Daniel described, at least at first. Gradually she had begun to talk to Eben when he began, when he rolled toward her and gripped her nightdress to pull it upward.

She slid a sideways look at Daniel, the firelight playing over the hard, tanned planes of his face, the flames reflected in the depths of the silver-green eyes. He'd thought of tenderness and kisses, even when he was paying a stranger for it, even when he'd been in the throes of that same imperative need to couple that Eben had displayed. Eben had taken his rightful due without such thoughts, she knew, anxious to touch her breasts and sink into the heat between her legs.

She'd made Eben slow down, learned to do little things to please him that made him take more interest in her in bed than just the things he could do without her participation. She'd come to like joining with him in a way that was quite apart from the rest of her life with him.

He'd been half shocked by her boldness sometimes, by the way she took his hand and guided it over her skin or reached out to touch him. He couldn't hide his shock from her, not even in the dark, but he'd been unwilling to rebuke her because it would have meant a lessening of his own pleasure, but he'd also been unwilling or unable to show her tenderness, or to tell her in words that he enjoyed being with her in that way. She'd wanted to hear it, to know that the sharing of her body meant *something* to him beyond his need to procreate.

Zenobia considered the few kisses she'd shared with Daniel Whittaker. Having his arms wrapped around her and the hard, lean body moving into hers had awakened her to a sense of the same animal fervor Eben had showed. Zenobia edged her glance downward so that she saw the curve of Daniel Whittaker's buttocks, the slope of his thigh. The thought of having him moving over her and of holding that part of him as he thrust into her body lit a flame between her legs and made her breath catch. She wrapped her arms around shoulders, hugging herself tightly.

"You cold?" he asked. "I could build the fire up."

Zenobia shook her head, her mouth dry. A man who cared. That was the lure. A man who noticed what she flinched from and what she yearned toward, a man who let loose of his innermost thoughts and revealed his true feelings. She hadn't ever come close to having that with Eben.

"No, I'm fine," she said, her voice barely above a whisper. "Tell me what happened with the widow. Did you stay with her long?"

He set his cup aside. as if he'd decided he'd had too much whiskey. The smell of it radiated pleasantly from him, warm on his breath. If he kissed her, she would taste the fumes against her lips, inhale the malty scent as his hands took possession of her flesh. The thought excited her unbearably.

"The widow? Well, like I said, she was good to me, taught me what a young man should know. I can't deny that I took to the instruction. She was a fine, strong woman, with a liking for men. Anyway, I began getting around without crutches when spring came, collecting strays, helping Lester bring cattle down from winter forage. The widow, she put me in charge of all the men, and let me know that I could be her foreman permanently if I cared to go on working for her at night, too."

Zenobia envied the widow passionately. "It sounds like you were doing all right for yourself."

"You might say that, but I wanted to make my own way. I was only eighteen, remember, and not nearly done with seeing the world. She upped the offer to marriage but I didn't want that any more than I wanted to stay on as her foreman. It wasn't that I didn't bear her a strong affection, for I did, but I didn't want to step into a dead man's boots and take over his ranch and his wife. Besides, I knew that other people would have looked on her as foolish for marrying a fellow my age, and if there was one thing Alice McCloskey wasn't, it was a fool. No, we just sort of met at a good time for both of us and made the most of it, but I wanted to build something of my own."

Eben had never really worked a day in his life, but he had demonstrated his willingness to do anything, *anything*, to cement his claim on her father's fortune. Daniel Whittaker, on the other hand, was a good and moral man who believed he should work for what he got. Everything she found out about Daniel Whittaker only made her love him more.

Zenobia's heart missed several beats. Yes, she loved him. This charming man with the hard body and the easy smile—she loved him with all her heart. She could hear the sound of his voice as he went on speaking, but she couldn't make out the words. All of her was consumed with staring at him, reassessing and admiring his face now that she had realized she loved him.

The swell of happiness it brought her to realize she loved him was fleeting. It felt like a deep stroke of cruelty to discover love at this time and in this place and for this man. All the circumstances had been right for the widow McCloskey those many winters ago, but every circumstance conspired against Zenobia Strouss Sinclair in the here and now.

Zenobia bowed her head.

"Now, look here. I've done nothing but talk about me all

evening. I want to hear about you. You never did tell me where back East you come from," Daniel was saying.

She could feel tears threatening. There it was—the reason she couldn't love him. She didn't dare to tell him anything about herself, not even the most rudimentary information. Where had she grown up? Who were her parents? What did her father do for a living? Why had she come west and started a laundry? Even her name, for heaven's sakes. She loved him and she couldn't even tell him her real name.

It was time to avert disaster. Zenobia shifted suddenly, nudging the baby with her hip. Paco whimpered.

"Oh, dear! There, I've woken him up with my clumsiness," she said, quickly sweeping the baby up. The swiftness of the ascent produced a howl of protest from Paco. "Oh, now I'm just upsetting him more. Sometimes I simply cannot think what to do to make him happy! Here, why don't you take him?" She thrust little Paco into a startled Daniel Whittaker's arms. "You're much better at soothing an unhappy infant than I am."

Daniel was as befuddled by the turn of events as Paco. One minute all had been peaceful and calm and now things were all topsy-turvy for no reason that was very clear to either the man or the baby. Zenobia jumped to her feet and announced over the din of Paco's lusty cries her intention of using the privy.

The cold desert air cleared her head and made her aware of the dampness of her eyes, and of the tears she had successfully kept in check. She pulled her shawl around her and stared up at the vast sky, dappled with stars almost liquid in their brightness. She wondered if there could be any truth to the belief that the stars shaped one's destiny.

They must be malevolent indeed to decree that she should murder her husband's best friend and flee for her life to a town so small it didn't even appear on a lot of maps, only to fall in love with the town's sheriff.

Inside the house, she could hear Paco's cries diminishing to soft whimpers, and the deep, almost inaudible crooning of a man's voice. She would stay where she was and fight her tears in private, and hope that when she had mastered herself, Paco would have fallen asleep and Daniel Whittaker, too.

Things worked out the way she'd hoped. When she finally dared—after a chilly half hour pacing to and fro in the desert moonlight—to reenter the house, she discovered Paco draped across Daniel's wide chest as he slept with one arm curled protectively over the baby. Her heart softened to see Daniel in sleep, the sun-bleached brown curls all tousled, the shadow of a beard growing in, the wide, beautifully shaped mouth relaxed.

Zenobia drew a blanket around herself and lay down on the far side of the bear rug, with the baby between them. At least now she didn't have to wrestle with the very strong temptation she'd been feeling to reach out to Daniel Whittaker and invite him to make love to her.

It was a mystery to Zenobia where Lester had slept the previous night, for the next morning when she thought of it, she realized he hadn't ridden away nor were there any other buildings in sight, just a little lean-to. However, it didn't matter a great deal, for it turned out, much to her dismay, that she was destined to spend two days without the comforting presence of either Lester or Daniel. They were off to seek out the spring calves and brand them.

They saddled their horses and loaded supplies onto a pack mule—coffee and cooking pots, branding irons, extra ropes, and blankets. Zenobia watched and wondered whether she should beg Daniel to stay with her, for the possibility of being left alone scared her. Lester had cooked bacon and pone for their breakfast and showed her where he kept everything, including the Dutch oven to parch the coffee beans.

Zenobia sat forlornly at the table while they loaded up, staring at the homely brown tin canister of Arbuckle Company coffee. She traced the white outline of North America on it with her fingernail. What if some horrible natural disaster befell and both she and the baby died? There were tornadoes and earthquakes and floods—anything could happen! A plague of locusts was not inconceivable. There was precious little to eat out in the desert. Locusts would sweep across the desert and come to the little mud house and devour it from the ground up, leaving nothing but the stone hearth and the chimney standing.

Somehow Zenobia overcame her hysteria. Daniel had work to do. It would not be fair to ask him to stay behind with her. In fact, it might be more dangerous than having the coyotes to tea. He had not promised to wait on her hand and foot in any case. He had only promised her safety from exposure to cholera for a few days, and she *did* feel safe from cholera, but only cholera.

All alone, really all alone. The sheer loneliness made Zenobia want to weep after they rode away with a promise to be back as soon as humanly possible. She wandered around the little mud house and then ventured into the tiny courtyard. Outside, beyond the perimeters of the house, felt too open, so she stayed back in the shade. Then Paco began to fuss and she realized his bottom was sore so she took off the napkin pinned around him and left him to dry in the warm air.

The napkins had been laying unused in the larder. Zenobia had ordered a case from Independence, thinking they'd add a nice touch to the utilitarian rubber tablecloths, but none of the customers at Smith's Good Luck Restaurant ever seemed to have seen one before. Most were left unused on the table, or used as handkerchiefs, so they'd stopped putting them out. Each man seemed to have his own remedy for spills anyway, from cuff to sleeve to beard to pant leg.

Paco kicked happily, naked and dry. Paco might be happy but his benefactor, the goat, was not. Daniel had given her a brief demonstration of how to milk it, and suggested she snub the goat up to the fencepost tight when she did, so it couldn't jump around too much and hurt her. Although she'd managed to get the milk out, her touch had been none too gentle and she was sure the goat was just waiting for a chance to get even. It stood just outside the little courtyard watching her with baleful yellow eyes.

She had to venture out for water, to pump it at the well head, and to lead the remaining horses to the trough rather than hauling full buckets to them. When night fell, she heated up water and took advantage of her solitude to bathe. She stood outside, under the peeled pole canopy and poured water over herself. Zenobia felt quite hedonistic, bathing naked by moonlight.

The goat chose that moment to attack. It churned its little cloven hooves to gain momentum and bashed into her hip, sending her reeling. Zenobia flipped over backward, landing her in a pose so undignified she was embarrassed just to be in it. The goat snorted and pawed triumphantly.

"Oh, no, you don't," Zenobia muttered. She disentangled herself and came up fighting. She grabbed the other, still full, water bucket and took aim at the goat's head. It helped enormously that the goat charged her again just as she got the bucket swinging on the right trajectory.

"Ha!" she cried, as the bucket connected with the goat's head. His own momentum added to the force of her own swing made the goat stagger backward dizzily. "You devil! You leave me alone, do you hear?"

The goat turned and tottered away, unable to quite comprehend what had happened to it. Zenobia shook her fist in victory. Only then did she realize that she was covered in dirt that had stuck to her bare wet skin. She didn't care. She had done battle with the evil, yellow-eyed goat and won!

She danced a victory dance, round and round in a circle, naked and mud-covered in the moonlight, whooping with delight. For once she had managed to look after herself with absolutely no help from anyone.

The second day she realized with surprise that she was content to be at the homestead, doing what needed to be done, with the baby on the rug or in her arms. She tidied and sang to the baby and fetched water to the animals and made pancakes, which were wonderful because Daniel had real baking soda—a precious tin of Wilt's Own—and not saleratus, with its awful alkali aftertaste.

She thought of loving Daniel numerous times, but her mind shied away from the thought. Her heart lurched when she thought of how he'd look when he rode in, that easy grin, the teeth showing white in the shadow of his hat brim, and the warm teasing look in his eyes meant just for her. It was impossible not to dream about what it would be like if she were his wife and they lived and loved in this little mud house. She'd sell the yellow-eyed goat, of course, and get another, better-mannered goat, but other than that, the prospect seemed delightful.

When he and Lester did return, her romanticized imaginings were dealt a blow. The two men were dead tired, covered in dust, and hungry in the bargain. Zenobia did her best to warm up corn bread and coffee for them, wishing she'd known the hour of their arrival so she could have had something more ready. They ate what she provided, sketched in the bare-bones details of the round-up, and lay down and fell asleep fully clothed, not to stir again until sunup. It did not at all fit with Zenobia's expectations, which was perhaps for the best, since the lure of playing house with Daniel beckoned her so strongly. Adding insult to disappointment, Paco had one of his rare fussy nights and she spent hours up walking with him.

In the morning. Lester helped hitch the horse to the wagon and waved them off for the return trip to town after a breakfast of biscuits and gravy. He handed Zenobia onto the buckboard seat, put Paco into her arms and asked that she give his regards to Rosita if she did not think the girl would be offended.

"No, Mr. Cooper," Zenobia replied with a smile. "I don't think she'll be offended. I think she'll be flattered."

Daniel apologized on the way to Gila City for not having been a very good host the night before. "I expect you're not accustomed to having your supper companions fall asleep in their plates, I'm afraid Lester and I weren't very good company last night."

"No, in fact you were no company at all, unless one counts snoring as conversation," Zenobia replied.

He sent a glance sidewards toward her, grinning. "Well, ma'am, I suppose I deserved that. Tell me, though—it's a point of honor with me—do I snore off-key? Lester always says I do."

Zenobia laughed. How wonderful it was to be in love—provided she could get away from the object of her affection as soon as possible.

Thirteen

Zenobia alternated the next day between bouts of unhappy tears over what could not be and prolonged periods of loving contemplation of the perfection of Daniel Whittaker, but she did manage to accomplish one useful thing. Wing Loo told her, when she collected the books at the laundry for the weekly accounting, that a strange man had been asking questions pertaining to the whereabouts, appearance, and so forth, of the owner of Smith's Laundry while she'd been out of town. Her breath froze.

"What did he look like?"

Wing Loo described the man. Eben, without a doubt.

"What did you tell him?"

"I say you not here, not see for a long time, would he like to leave address for you to write to him if you ever come back."

Zenobia heaved a sigh of relief.

"I do the right thing?" he inquired, watching her closely. "People come looking for other people, not always a good thing. Think missy want see man, she write, he come back."

"You did exactly the right thing," she said. "Did he give you an address?"

Wing Loo shook his head. "Say not matter if you gone away for good, I say I think so."

But she had to be absolutely sure he'd gone away. She visited the agent for Wells Fargo and Company—who just happened to be a customer of Smith's Laundry—and as she delivered his laundry, mentioned that she thought she might have seen a friend of hers alighting from last week's coach, but then she had never seen him again.

The agent offered her the chance to look at the manifest to see if she saw a familiar name, and sure enough, there was Eben Sinclair listed. She pretended it was another person on the list she was inquiring after and wondered aloud if he was still in town or whether he had perhaps left again. The agent obligingly produced the manifest for the previous day's coaches and, much to her relief, she saw Eben's name again, this time on the eastbound departures side. Bless Wing Loo for knowing to send him packing.

Zenobia suspected that Eben had sent private detectives in search of her and they must have seen her when she was living at the laundry. Eben had followed up by coming himself, to positively identify her and have her arrested, perhaps, but more likely to extract his own vengeance on her for killing Stephen. Wing Loo had forestalled that by persuading him that she was long gone. Now she could stay in Gila City with a lighter heart. Why would Eben look for her there a second time when he'd been told she'd left?

Zenobia set to work in the restaurant feeling as if she had dodged a bullet. When Reverend Bob ambled in and hung up his broad black preacher's hat, she welcomed him cheerfully.

"It does my heart good to see a lovely lady in such spirits," he remarked.

"Indeed, I am in a very good mood," she said. "The sky is a beautiful shade of blue today." *And I'm in love.*

Reverend Bob peered out the window, his forehead furrowed. "It looks the same as it ever does, Miss Smith."

"Then perhaps it is its very constancy that gives me good cheer," she replied.

"I am gratified to find you so determined to be in charity with the world," he said, "because I have a favor to ask of you. As you know, Independence Day will be upon us in a matter of weeks, and I find that the rough-and-tumble men in these parts wax very sentimental over the birth of their nation, or rather the nation they have left behind. It is my intention to organize a celebration day and see that the celebration contains within it some edifying moments, perhaps a speech or two extolling the Constitution and the Declaration of Independence, and another promoting Christian values, to help rein in the excessive imbibing of intoxicating beverages and general licentiousness. I flatter myself that if the observance is handled well, it will elevate the souls of the men of Gila City."

"Um, why, yes," Zenobia murmured. She had been watching Molly B'damn stick her head in through a window, nosing aside the curtain by a serving stand loaded with baskets of rolls while the reverend spoke. He never bothered to tie her up, being a firm believer in her essential goodness. "Pardon me for just a moment, won't you?"

Zenobia hurried to the window, pinched the steer's nose hard to make her back up, and closed the window. Yes, she had definitely grown braver since coming to Gila City.

"Now, Reverend Bob," she said, "what is it that you wish me to do?"

"Would you consent to organizing the preparation and serving of the food for the festivities? I have reckoned up the number of persons permanently residing in town plus those who will likely come in from outlying camps and homesteads for the day at about a thousand."

"A thousand? You want me to feed a thousand people?" Zenobia was aghast. On their busiest day so far, Smith's Good Luck Restaurant had served only seventy-five people at any one meal.

"You mustn't be alarmed, Miss Smith. I expect to solicit donations from all the merchants in town, and all the business establishments, to defray the cost, so you would not be out of pocket."

No, but I'd have to be out of my mind, she thought. "I don't see how Rosita and I could manage the actual work," she said.

"I am of the opinion that all the eateries in town should contribute their labor," Reverend Bob said. He looked quite pleased with himself for thinking of this. "Bear in mind that I am asking you to *organize* this feast, not do all the work yourself."

And much against her better judgment, Zenobia agreed, because as she listened to Reverend Bob prose on, she recalled that Daniel Whittaker had asked her many months ago if she would accompany him to the Fourth of July dance. What better excuse could she offer for not going with him than that she would be too busy cooking and serving food to the whole town?

Daniel scuffed along, dragging his boot heels as he puzzled over what he lacked where Miss Zoe Smith was concerned. He was no closer to winning her; in fact, in his most pessimistic moods, such as now, he had to concede that he'd actually lost ground since the very satisfying exchange of kisses some time before. What he didn't know was why.

He'd spent a good long time contemplating his face in the mirror that morning. He wasn't a bad-looking fellow. Of course, he didn't slick his hair down like Charles Merrick, city-style, and he didn't have the smooth, pale skin of a man who could earn a living with his brains alone, like the real estate broker. No, his skin was tanned because he worked with his hands and his back, but he didn't believe there was any disgrace in that. He didn't think Zoe Smith did either. So he wasn't a handsome sort but he didn't scare horses either.

He continued down the list.

He knew Zoe Smith set store on bathing regularly and he'd been going to the barbershop at least once a week since she'd arrived, so he had that objection covered. She was *nice* to him, no more and no less than she was to all the other fellows who ate at Smith's Good Luck Restaurant and that was anathema to him. If she'd been snappish or ignored him, it would mean he'd done something to displease her and at least he could set out to discover what it was.

He reckoned he might have done his cause a disservice by

drinking too much whiskey when she'd been at the ranch. He'd been wrapped up in the glow of her presence and overlooked how much extra glow was coming from the whiskey. His face burned when he thought of some of the things he'd said to her. What woman wanted to hear about the women who'd come before her? He groaned aloud at the embarrassing memory and a miner passing by looked at him strangely.

In retrospect he felt a fool for being so candid. She'd left the baby with him and disappeared, ostensibly to use the privy, but she'd been gone a very long time and then he'd fallen asleep, helped along considerably by the whiskey. And after the roundup, he'd had not a lick of energy to spare to charm her, and so a second opportunity had been wasted.

She just didn't seem to think of him as anything special, or different from all the other fellows, and that was the long and the short of it. He'd had months to make an impression on her and he didn't think he was any closer to making her his wife. And the rosebush wasn't doing too well either.

Maybe Teresa could shed some light on the situation. He knew she and Zoe had gotten pretty well acquainted. It was worth a try. He'd pour out his troubles to her and she'd understand. She'd once told him that whores spent more time listening to men's sad stories about their lost loves than they spent on their backs servicing them. Yes, he would definitely speak to Teresa and get the female perspective.

"Sheriff, there's trouble at the Silverado."

Daniel blinked and came out of his unhappy musings. "What sort of trouble?" He recognized the man in front of him as the half owner of the Silverado, an ex-Indian scout who could usually handle his own trouble.

"Gambler with a six-shooter. He swears the dealer and everybody else at the table cheated him. He's got a gun and he's already winged the fellow sitting opposite him."

"Aw, hell." Daniel wasn't in the mood for any life or death struggles.

The atmosphere in the Silverado was tense when he walked

in, but most of the patrons were dealing, lying, and cheating with about the usual amount of gusto while keeping a wary eye on the standoff in the center of the room. The customers were rough—bullwhackers, some mule team drivers passing through, a couple of buffalo hunters who stank of the dead hides they were packing, and the usual assortment of miners and waddies. The light toward the back was dim, but Daniel could see plenty more men back there. He hoped none of them was going to side with the gambler who'd held on to his gun.

The holdout was an ugly cuss, and the others around the table would not have won any beauty contests either. Daniel introduced himself to the ugly gambler and got right down to explaining the law about turning in guns while in town, but he got an inelegant cursing out for his trouble.

"Well, look, I can just shoot you and that'll be the end of it," Daniel said wearily.

"Not if I shoot you first," growled the gambler.

"If you do that, you won't get out of town alive," Daniel said. "Why don't you just work out whatever problem you've got with these fellows here and I'll take your gun on down to the jail, and everybody can get on with their lives."

"It is said," came a clear soft voice from the shadows, "that if you have entered a city, conform to its laws."

The gambler turned toward the unseen speaker and laughed. "I make my own laws."

Daniel stared into the gloom. The fellow who was speaking out was either stupid or drunk. But he turned out to be neither. He stepped into the light beneath a kerosene lantern. It was Jacob Aleksandrov, the traveling rabbi, who had spoken.

"A man should never depart from established practice," he said calmly. "Behold, when Moses ascended above, he did not eat, and when the ministering angels descended to earth, they partook of food."

Most of the saloon's patrons fell silent, blinking and frowning. One man seemed to speak for all of them when he said, "Huh?"

The ugly cuss holding the gun looked impatient. "I don't know what in the hell you're talking about, mister, but if you're so all fired up to get into this argument, tell these cheating bastards to give back the money they stole from me and maybe I'll give the sheriff my gun."

"Nobody stole nothing from you," snapped another gambler at the table. "The play was fair and square."

"That's not how I saw it. Now you're gettin' me mad. Now you're gonna have to give me all the money you walked in here with to make me back down," the ugly cuss said. He waved the gun at the others. "Go on, empty out your pockets."

"The Talmud says there are four characters among men," Jacob said tranquilly. Daniel had to admire his coolness if not his sense of self-preservation. "He who says what is mine is mine and what is yours is yours—his is a neutral character. Some say this is a character like that of Sodom. He who says what is mine is yours and what is yours is mine is a boor. He who says what is mine is yours and what is yours is yours is a saint. He who says what is yours is mine and what is mine is mine is a wicked man. One cannot stand aside when a wicked man tries to prevail."

"Is that so?" sneered the gambler. All around him, eyes were glazing over.

"Furthermore, in the Tractate of Aboth, it says—"

"Just give the sheriff the damn gun," yelled a man in the back, "before this fellow talks our ears off."

"Yeah," said another.

The place was filled instantly with loud, rough voices calling for the gambler to hand over his gun.

Daniel sensed the tide turning his way. He stepped toward the table to take the gun. The ugly cuss couldn't shoot *everybody*. Even he seemed to realize that and he made a face as he angrily slammed the gun down on the table.

Daniel saw the muzzle flash and heard the report with particular lucidity since the gun happened to be pointing in his direction when it went off. He heard the spiteful rattle of a bullet passing close to his ear and felt the hot sting as it grazed a path across the top of his shoulder. Daniel looked down and saw a rip in his shirt.

It was one of his favorites, a strong green with pale yellow piping. The half owner of the Silverado, who'd been right behind him, grabbed the gun and quickly ejected the rest of the bullets from the chamber,

"Take him on down to the pokey, boys," he yelled. "Are you all right, Sheriff?"

"I guess so." Daniel peered at his shoulder. Blood flowed freely from it, soaking his shirt. Damn but it hurt! That was the way of things. Sometimes a man was mortally wounded and kept on going like nothing was wrong for a few minutes, but let a bullet plow through skin and a little muscle and you needed some whiskey to keep from crying like a baby.

"Here, Sheriff, here's a cloth to wipe that up with. Want some whiskey?"

"Nah, see to that other fellow there, the one who got shot before I got here." No, no whiskey for him. She wasn't going to smell whiskey on *his* breath again anytime soon.

The Silverado's half owner looked over the gambler who'd been winged. "The barber'll stitch that up quick enough. Come back when he's done," he said to the gambler, "—drinks on the house."

"Sir, if you please, I wish to ask you a question," Jacob Aleksandrov said.

The owner of the Silverado turned. "What can I do for you?"

"I was in your establishment to see if you would grant me permission to hold religious services here."

"Hmm. What denomination? Nah, hell, it doesn't matter. Churching is churching. Is this just a one shot deal or are you in town for a while?"

"For a while. I would hold services each Saturday at sundown."

The man raised an eyebrow. "Saturday? But that's one of my busiest nights!"

Jacob Aleksandrov looked downcast. "Yes, that is what all the saloon owners tell me, and the managers of the music halls. I have been looking for weeks and have found no one who will spare an hour for holiness on a Saturday."

The Silverado's half owner sighed heavily. "Well, I should probably check with my partner first, but there's no doubt I owe you a favor. If not for you, I expect this place would have gotten busted up pretty good. All right, one hour, right? No more?"

The young rabbi was transformed. "Yes, you have my word on it!"

Daniel beckoned to Jacob Aleksandrov. "Come walk along with me a little way."

"Yes, yes, we must take you to the barber," Jacob said. "Let us leave without further delay. I apologize."

"No need." Daniel led the way out of the Silverado. "I was wondering, Mr. Aleksandrov, whether you would consider becoming a deputy for me."

"Jacob, please, you must call me Jacob, and what must I do as your deputy?"

Daniel explained the concept as they walked. "I'd only need to call on you now and again, but I figure a man who can talk a fight out of existence is my kind of lawman."

"I see." Jacob was silent for several minutes. "It is written in the Talmud, 'Be on your guard against the ruling power, for they who exercise it draw no man near to them except for their own interest, appearing as friends when it is to their own advantage.'"

Daniel mulled this over. It didn't seem to be an answer to his question.

Jacob went on. "But what it really means is that one should not shirk the responsibility of office, but not to be motivated to accept out of selfish ambition either."

"Well, does that mean yes?" Daniel said.

"Yes, I would be honored."

"Good. Now, here we are where I mean to get patched up," Daniel said.

They went into Smith's Good Luck Restaurant. The effect of his wound was everything he had hoped for.

"Daniel! You're bleeding!"

Zoe Smith rushed to his side. He grinned, feeling a bit lightheaded. She'd called him Daniel!

"Oh, come and sit down. You look pale!" she cried.

Daniel purely loved the feel of her little hands all over him, drawing him over to a table, pushing him onto a bench, pulling aside his shirt to see the damage. Rosita was practical enough to already be fetching a basin of hot water and clean napkins, Daniel just sat there, thoroughly enjoying having Zoe fuss over him. She *did* care about him! He'd known it all along.

Reverend Bob elicited the details of events from Rabbi Jacob, to whom Daniel tried to introduce him, but Zoe hushed him.

"Don't you dare talk," she scolded. "You must save your strength."

"Yes, ma'am," he said meekly. What an angel she was, all aflutter around him, her bright blue eyes shining with concern. He winced as she dabbed at the wound.

"Oh!" She covered her perfectly round rosy mouth. "I'm so sorry! I hurt you, didn't I?"

"Only a little . . . ma'am." She *had* dug at it pretty good.

"I'm so terrible at anything practical," she cried. "Here, I'll let Rosita do it."

Daniel quickly grabbed her wrist. "Oh, no, you finish. It's just that it . . ." He gave her the most forlorn look he could manage. "Well, it's going to hurt pretty bad no matter who does it, and I'd as lief it was you who hurt me as anybody." That hadn't come out quite right, but she didn't seem to mind. She went back to pawing at him with the wet napkin and he flinched, though he made sure to soften his reaction this time. He'd just had a flash of brilliance that exceeded even the inspiration to come to Zoe rather than the barber to have the wound cleaned and bandaged.

"So if I understand you right, you're going to preach a service at sundown at the Silverado each Saturday night?" Reverend Bob was saying.

"Not preach exactly," Jacob said, "but conduct a service, yes."

"Now, that's some original thinking, preaching on a Saturday. I like it!" Reverend Bob exclaimed. "You teach them the word of God on Saturdays and I'll take over on Sundays. It'll be like hitting them with both barrels!"

Jacob smiled. "I suppose one could say that."

"By golly, we'll clean this town up in no time. Say, I've got another little project I could use your help with. Fourth of July's coming up, Independence Day, and I need . . ." He led Jacob away, gesturing and talking effusively.

Rosita was already back in the kitchen, getting ready for the evening customers after having seen that Daniel's wound wasn't serious. It left Daniel alone with Zoe, just what he'd been hoping for. Her cheeks were all pink from agitation and her hair curled at her temples from the heat of the day. Had there ever been a prettier woman? Daniel had to swallow the lump in his throat before he could speak.

"Miss Smith . . . Zoe, that is . . . I was wondering, do you remember me asking you to go to the Fourth of July dance with me?"

She went still. "Why, yes, I believe I remember something of the sort. However, I have just told Reverend Bob I'll help prepare and serve the food for everyone, so I'm afraid I won't have time for any dancing."

"But you'd go with me otherwise, and not some other fellow?"

She smiled brightly. "Why, of course."

"Then there's no problem, ma'am. You see, we eat around three o'clock, but the dancing doesn't start until later, when it gets cooler."

"Oh."

She slowly wiped her hands dry on her apron, which was

stained with his blood. Daniel knew reluctance when he saw it and pulled out all the stops.

"You wouldn't change your mind, now would you, ma'am? When a fellow's been shot at, he's already had a hard enough day. It sure would mean a lot to me if you'd say yes." Daniel gazed up at her. His mother would have swatted his backside with a rolled-up newspaper if she'd ever seen him give such a performance.

Zoe Smith looked down at the floor and then slowly raised her eyes. "Yes, all right," she said softly.

Daniel grinned. "Why, thank you, ma'am! It will be a pure pleasure to take you to the dance." He glanced down at his shirt, hanging open and pushed off his shoulder. "There's quite a tear in this shirt where the bullet went along. I don't suppose you're any good at mending tears so they don't show?"

Zoe bit her lower lip and shook her head apologetically.

"Well, no matter," Daniel said.

She couldn't do laundry for anything, she was the worst cook he'd ever met, she couldn't mend a tear, and he didn't care one little bit. She was going to the Fourth of July dance with him and that was all that mattered.

The *Gila City Intelligencer* was only a handbill cranked out on a hand press which resided in the overhang next to the hotel, but it garnered as much attention as any big city newspaper. Luckily for Zenobia, by the time the announcements regarding the Independence Day celebration appeared in it, Zenobia had a plan for coping firmly in place. So many men stopped to thank her for taking charge of the cooking and to ask for further particulars of the menu that she could barely get from one end of Main Street to the other in less than half an hour.

She had thought long and hard about how to go about tackling the job and decided against involving the other restaurant owners. She was afraid of looking even stupider than usual if she tried to work side by side with professionals, and besides, it would be a great coup if the owner of Smith's Good Luck Restaurant could snatch all the credit for producing the feast.

So she approached another group of professionals. Teresa called for a meeting of all the sporting girls and they convened at Smith's Good Luck Restaurant. Though it would mean a certain loss of income to them, the doves unanimously agreed to help Zenobia out. The general feeling was that it would give them a chance to meet men while they were fully clothed and on their feet, useful for those wishing to find a husband. It would also allow them a chance to celebrate the Fourth of July like everyone else.

"Hell's bells," said the Irish Queen, summing it up for all of them. "I'm as patriotic as the next girl!"

"And we'd come for the dancing anyway!" said a young whore.

It was Teresa who, in her laconic way, was a demon problem solver. It was she who proposed that they buy several hundred pounds of corn with the money collected by Reverend Bob and apportion it out to the various whorehouses that had parlors.

"Then you girls make your customers, while they're waiting, grind it into meal, and if you're not busy, make 'em grind some anyway as part of the price for your services. That way we'll have enough meal by the Fourth to sink a ship."

A two-hundred-and-fifty-pound hog was ordered up from Bisbee to provide lard, and lumber had been scared up from every nook and cranny to build a weir on the river to pen fish for the fish fry.

"We're going to show those boys we women can do more than lie on our backs!" declared Silver Sally. "You wait and see!"

And that was how Zenobia came to be on the banks of the Gila River on a scorching hot day in June, along with every prostitute in town. The river didn't run all that fast and deep as a rule, but there had been a torrential rainstorm two nights before, with hail the size of peas and lightning enough to make the hair stand up on a person's neck all night, and the Gila now kicked up like an overfed pony. Everyone had taken one look at the site chosen by Silver Sally and begun shucking off their dresses and cage crinolines and corsets—those who bothered to wear them at all—and button boots, since it was clear they were going to get a soaking. Now they were wrestling the planks out of the livery stable wagon and into the water, trying to assemble the weir according to Silver Sally's instructions. The idea to catch the fish had been Teresa's, but it was Silver Sally who turned out to have a talent for carpentry.

Zenobia got tumbled over by the water almost immediately, and one by one, even the few who could keep to their feet, let themselves slip into the water all the way for some relief from the heat. Amazingly enough, Silver Sally's plan worked and a weir began to take shape, allowing water through its slats but holding back fish above a certain size. Contrary Mary screamed when the first fish got diverted into the pen and started leaping all about her, slapping her neck with its fins and tail.

"It's worse than a drunk man's hands," she cried, batting the fish away.

Everyone laughed, including the statuesque blonde from Madame Bettina's, who had arrived at the livery stable to join the work party.

"That's Madame's niece," whispered Teresa. "She's educated just as fine as you please but Madame's never let her out by herself before, thinks she's too good for the likes of us. Madame must think it's all right for Dulcie to come because you're in charge of things."

Though she held herself with poise, the blonde looked slightly ill at ease. Zenobia marched over and shook the girl's hand, extracted a name from her—Miss Dulcie Mueller—and introduced her around with the information that she'd helped deliver Rosita's baby. The girl looked pleased when the doves nodded approvingly. Zenobia realized she'd been wrong the night of Paco's birth. The girl *did* understand English, and she spoke it with a slow, careful precision that hinted at a painstaking tutor somewhere in her past. Dulcie also proved to be a tireless worker and extremely proficient with a hammer and nails, which earned her the admiration of all the working girls as nothing else could have.

As the day went on, they diverted more and more fish into the holding pen. The girls shrieked and giggled at the way they tickled, swimming around their bare shoulders and legs. Zenobia crawled out onto the bank for a rest and to repin her hair, and that's when she saw Daniel Whittaker ride up on his buckskin horse.

"Afternoon, ladies," he said, sweeping off his hat and grinning lopsidedly at the splendor of so many moist, partially clad females.

"How do, Sheriff?" The girls paused in their labors and more than a few dimples appeared.

"I just came to see how you're making out, ladies, make sure everyone's all right."

"Oh, we're doing just dandy, Sheriff," said the young, skinny whore who was looking forward to the dancing on the Fourth. She tipped her head and grinned at him provocatively. "Water's fine—why don't you come in and see for yourself? We could show you a good time, couldn't we, girls?" she said slyly.

Everyone started yelling and waving at him to come on in. Some of the girls swung their hips, others pushed their breasts out provocatively. With an assortment of inviting smiles, sly grins, and outright leers they invited him to join them, each in her own way, and while some were merely being playful or devilish, Zenobia could see that others were serious in their offers to entertain him.

She experienced a flare of self-righteous possessiveness. Didn't they know it was *she* whom he liked? She reacted with horror the instant she realized what she was thinking. Daniel Whittaker was a sharp student of human emotions. She'd better not let him see her face when she was thinking such things! She decided she'd go off into the scrubby little stand of trees upstream to relieve herself and thus avoid the risk of him seeing her face before she got her thoughts back in proper order.

She was halfway to the small grove before she realized Daniel Whittaker had ridden after her. She turned impatiently.

"I need a little privacy, if you please." It came out snappishly, but he only smiled.

"I just thought I'd see to it that you got back safe."

"Well, we've all been using the trees up here all day for . . . for a necessary closet, and we haven't needed an escort." She hitched up her petticoat, all too aware that in addition to it, she wore only her chemise and drawers, and all of it was quite damp. The layers that should have stood between her and Daniel Whittaker lay in a heap with all the others near the livery stable wagon.

"I understand, ma'am," he said. His teeth showed white in the shadow of his hat brim, the way she'd imagined they would. "I'll just tag along all the same." He slipped down off his horse with an easy movement that emphasized his slim hips and muscular legs. "I'll keep my back turned if it makes you feel better."

Zenobia turned and marched away. "Ow!"

He was at her side in an instant. "What is it, darlin'?" he asked, full of concern.

"I stepped on something," she proclaimed angrily. *And it was all his fault for distracting her!*

"Let me see," he said.

He took hold of her bare ankle and turned the sole of her foot skyward before she could stop him. With no alternative to falling down except to grab on to him for balance, she found herself tipped over his bent back with her cheek pressed against his spine.

"Aw, nothing too serious," he said reassuringly.

The sound of his voice came through her ear as a rumble. He pinched her foot hard.

"Ow! That hurt."

"But now that splinter's gone," he said, straightening up and smiling down at her. He held out a cactus spine. "There's the culprit."

Zenobia put her foot to the ground, anxious to end the contact with his long, hard body. Her foot sent her a painful reminder of where the cactus spine had been and she flinched.

"Now, let's sit you down here in the shade for a minute," Daniel Whittaker was saying. "You sure do smell all fresh and clean, what with spending the morning in the river."

"Thank you," she said peevishly. "I do happen to bathe at regular intervals, you know."

"Oh, I know," he said, settling down next to her. His horse sighed and cocked one hind foot. "I recollect real well how you looked after your bath that night I first met you, with a shiner and all, and I realized right then that you were a woman with uncommon dedication to bathing." He pushed her hair back off her face. "I believe it was that night that I first thought about doing this."

Before Zenobia could comprehend what was going on, he was bending down and kissing her. The sheer surprise of it kept her from pushing him away. His hands were large and solid behind her back as he wrapped his arms around her. Her brain caught up with events and she made a sound and kissed him back, hard—not at all what she should have done, but too many daydreams about him had rendered her incapable of resistance when taken by surprise.

She smelled the salt and sun and horse scent on him, and felt his tongue, warm and inviting, across her lips. His chest was wide and arousing, pressing her breasts flat and massaging them. It created heat and friction and delicious sensations that took on a life of their own and went lower down, too.

And saints preserve her, she was massaging his back with her hands, feeling the flat planes of the shoulder blades and the small trough of his spine, moving lightly over the shoulder that had been creased by the bullet. Any part of him would do; she just wanted to touch him.

His thumb stroked the side of her breast and he nuzzled her brow, his heart beating hard and his breath coming quick in her ear.

"Oh, darlin'," he murmured. "Oh, darlin', I do love the way

you feel in my arms. I swear, I don't ever want to let you go. Give me another kiss."

And give him another kiss she did, filled with passion by his invitation for *her* to kiss *him* (set her on fire.) Zenobia felt as if she was melting and turning into different colors of the rainbow beneath her closed lids.

Daniel groaned in appreciation as she stroked his chest. "Darlin', I about want to explode when you touch me like that." He nipped at her neck and then kissed the tops of her breasts just above the damp linen of her chemise.

Zenobia stretched, pushing herself upward hopefully. She wanted more of that. She took his head between her hands and guided it, lower down. Oh, she wanted that quite badly!

He unbuttoned her chemise partway and his lips found one nipple. He tugged at it and she whimpered. It created a bliss between her legs, too, most unexpectedly. She longed to take his hand and pull it to herself. He would know just what to do, and oh, how she wanted it done! With all her heart and her whole body, she wanted him to touch her there, and to go on teasing at her nipple with his lips.

Zenobia eagerly pulled at his shirt, fumbling for the buttons and opening it. He was so smooth and hard to the touch beneath it! She reveled in the feel of him, though her arms felt weak as he bared her other breast and massaged it with his hand.

"Oh, Daniel," she whispered. "That feels . . . ah!"

"I know just what you mean," he said softly, and kissed her again, his hand as busy at her breast as ever.

Zenobia gasped and arched up into his touch. Between them, they managed to slide off the log they'd sat down on without losing contact. Zenobia opened her legs and felt Daniel's weight settle across her. His hips moved against hers and she took a deep breath. She arched to close the distance between his hips and hers and her head fell back into the cradle of his hand. Her naked breasts rubbed across his naked chest and she let out a delirious sound of pleasure.

"Ahem."

Zenobia was clutching at Daniel's hips and pulling him against her when she heard the sound. Her fogged brain could not at first identify it and then she heard it a second time. It was a person, someone other than the two of them. Oh, why didn't they just go away?

But Daniel was tugging her chemise over her breasts. They felt full and swollen, too large to fit back into the confines of the chemise and he reached to retrieve his hat to help cover her. When he shifted, Zenobia was momentarily blinded by the sun coming through the tops of the scrawny trees above. All she could see was the silhouette of someone on horseback. It seemed to be a man, for the figure sat astride, but there was a mass of golden hair around the head that seemed more feminine than masculine.

Daniel rolled off of Zenobia, sitting in front of her. "Why, Miss Archer, what a surprise."

Zenobia struggled to button her chemise. Miss Archer. It must be James Archer's daughter. Without looking up, she knew the girl must be sending daggers her way. The girl had conveyed her dislike for Zenobia whenever she came into Smith's Good Luck Restaurant although her father had always been extremely pleasant.

"Yes, I can see that I've taken you by surprise," Juliette Archer murmured. "I've been looking everywhere for you. They said in town that I might find you out here and I no sooner found those women splashing around in the river over there than I saw your horse. I came into town for a dress fitting and Father said I should bring in the steer he's donating for the Fourth of July celebration. I've left my hand at the livery stable with it."

"Well, that's kind of your father," Daniel said as he scrambled to his feet, trying to keep Zenobia shielded from view.

Zenobia desperately tried to cover herself, but no matter whether she fastened the buttons on her chemise or not, she still wouldn't be decent, not in so little clothing and all of it wet. She wished she could just crawl under a rock and avoid any conversation with Juliette Archer.

"Why, Miss Smith, is that you?" Juliette Archer inquired. For once she sounded like her father, pleasant and civil. "I confess, I hardly recognized you!"

Zenobia had not grown up in the thick of cutthroat society debutantes and matrons without knowing a barb when one was cast. She stood up with dignity and said with equal sweetness, "Why, Miss Archer, I'm sure no one could ever fail to recognize *you*. You have such a distinctive way about you."

Juliette Archer smiled, but it was a glacial thing that only a man could have thought was genuine. "Why, thank you, Miss Smith." She touched her horse with one spur so that it pivoted and she faced Daniel squarely. "Will you come into town with me, Sheriff Whittaker, and tell my hand what to do with the steer?"

Daniel turned to Zenobia. "That would be up to Miss Smith. She's the one who's taking care of all the cooking for the celebration," he said proudly.

"And I understand that all her friends are helping, too," Juliette said.

The gloves were off now. The same women Zenobia had shied away from talking to just months ago *were* her friends, and she wanted to tear out some of Juliette Archer's phony-looking blond hair for implying that the doves were second-class human beings because of what they did for a living. But Daniel hadn't heard the message implicit in Juliette's tone.

"Why, yes, she's got just about everyone in town ready to do something for her," he said. But he wasn't immune to Zenobia's natural discomfort at being caught in an indelicate situation. "However, I'm sure she'd like to get back to the fish penning. Why don't you head into town and I'll be along presently?"

Juliette sketched another frosty smile. "Why, certainly, Daniel. I'll go slowly and maybe we'll meet on the road. It's not as if you're needed here. It looks as if all the *ladies* are doing just fine without a man—for once."

Juliette Archer rode off, throwing one last sunny smile over her shoulder directly at Daniel. Zenobia was so mad she could barely conceal it. She stomped back to the river and waded right in to obliterate the dirt streaks on her chemise and petticoat and refused to meet Teresa's questioning glance. Daniel had to chase his horse, which had wandered, and by the time he arrived at the weir, she had managed to regain possession of her temper.

"What do you want done with that steer from James Archer?" he yelled over the running water and the hammering.

Zenobia rejected several choice replies, chiefly having to do with unnatural acts and Miss Juliette Archer. "You had better ask Reverend Bob to recruit someone who knows how to butcher. I don't think any of my friends do."

And with that she turned her back on the perplexed Daniel and began hammering nails into the weir with a vengeance.

Fourteen

By the time the Fourth of July dawned, Zenobia had so much on her mind that she had no time left over to brood about the spiteful, snide Juliette Archer. And besides, she didn't, wouldn't, *couldn't* have Daniel Whittaker, so Miss Juliette Archer could have him—whether Zenobia liked it or not.

The Reverend Bob had done an admirable job of organizing the town for the big day. Men cleared out the livery stable to serve as a venue for the dancing in case of rain, bunting was draped all around it and an area raked smooth for dancing outside if it stayed dry, and musicians from Fairchild's Dance Hall got together to rehearse a selection of dance music with other musicians from saloons and music halls. A shallow pit was dug and filled with cow chips, then lit and covered with steel plates unscrewed from the ceiling in the Red Dog Saloon for the occasion. Rosita supervised the frying of the fish on the red-hot sheets of metal, and every table at the restaurant used for mixing and tossing and seasoning the other dishes.

Start and finish lines were marked on Main Street for foot races and horse races, an oiled pig stood in Ned the blacksmith's corral for a pig-catching contest, and waddies galloped up and down the side streets with flags stuck in their horse's bridles. A few horses took exception to having the fluttering pennants affixed to them, but none more so than the one that careened sideways trying to get away from his and ended up leaping through the big glass window of the Empire Saloon.

Dog trotted into Smith's Good Luck Restaurant around noon,

sniffing for handouts, and Wing Loo and his relations, whom Zenobia had mercilessly pressed into service, trotted out. Only once Dog had been bribed by Teresa with a half bottle of redeye into leaving would they return. They resumed dipping and breading the fish and carrying it out to Rosita, keeping a wary eye on the wolf who crawled half under the steps and did not stir for the rest of the day.

Despite the appearance of things running as they ought, Zenobia greatly feared a disaster from some unsuspected quarter. She'd ordered in vast quantities of supplies and thought the menu through a thousand times, but it seemed simply too huge an undertaking to go smoothly. She must have forgotten *something*. Feeding a thousand people—the very notion took her breath away. Surely they would run out of food and she would be blamed!

Pans and pans of corn bread and pone to fry with the fish had been baked. The ovens at Smith's Good Luck Restaurant had been in use for days, from early in the morning to late at night, while they served to the public only meals which could be cooked on the stovetop. Ah Tup had shuttled back and forth from the laundry, fetching pans of cake batter to cook in the laundry's oven and returning with the finished products. It had all been stored with great care, stacked and covered with yards of muslin supplied by Clarence Trilby to keep it moist.

Three o'clock was fast approaching, when a thousand people—maybe more—would line up for food. Zenobia rushed from the laundry to the restaurant to the fish fry pit like a sheepdog trying to keep its flock together. Walter Connolly bawled out orders to men to carry tables and benches and chairs out from everyplace in town that had them to Main Street for the feast.

"I just wanted to thank you, ma'am, for everything."

Distracted from her agonizing, Zenobia turned to see Nathanial Evans, the one-legged Confederate Army veteran. He held his hat between his hands, folding the brim back and forth. He'd had more than a few free meals at her restaurant, for he never seemed to have money though he always managed to buy liquor somehow.

"Why, I'm sure you're welcome, Mr. Evans. It promises to be a fine day for a celebration."

"I didn't mean just for today," he muttered, looking at the ground. "I meant for, well, *everything*. I'll pay you one day, if I'm able. I expect I might. I have some plans. I may just get into the cattle business."

"I'm sure I wish you the very best of luck in whatever you do, Mr. Evans."

"Thank you, ma'am." He slapped his hat back on and quickly limped away.

"Now, no one can't sit in the horse trough!" Walter Connolly bellowed nearby. "You fellers, move that table out a little further!"

Several men were using rollers and ropes to move Ned's anvil out into the street, for what purpose Zenobia couldn't imagine, but she saw that Ned, as strong as he was in a lean, wiry way, was easily bested by Lester Cooper for sheer muscle power. The two men seemed to be competing each time they took a turn on the ropes, to see who could outdo the other. They grimaced, their teeth standing out white against warm brown skin, as they put their backs into the job.

Ned was such a quiet man, rarely smiling or speaking unless spoken to, that Zenobia was surprised to see how he seemed to be showing off. Then she saw that both men were sending covert glances toward the pit where Rosita bustled about, turning the frying fish with a long-handled flipper. Rosita, she noted, was looking back every so often, watching them from under her lashes as they heaved and strained. As soon as the anvil was set on the mark made by Reverend Bob, Ned hurried over to take a pan of fish from Rosita. From that point on, he was her devoted helper, ferrying cooked fish to the serving tables.

Lester frowned, his expressive face a study in resentment. He was a handsome man with an awesome physique, but when it came to love, he appeared to lack confidence, for he continued to worship Rosita from afar. He had never come in to the restaurant to make biscuits, more was the pity, for most of Rosita's surreptitious glances were aimed at him. but shy, quiet Ned—who would buy a plate of food at the restaurant to take and eat at his forge but never eat in the restaurant despite urging from Zenobia—had staked his claim.

Zenobia observed that more and more of the whores were appearing, decked out in all their finest. They spread cloths on tables and carried plates and utensils out from the various restaurants. Zenobia had had to concede defeat on that score, for she couldn't provide a thousand plates and cups by herself.

She saw James Archer arrive, with Juliette in an eye-popping dress that drew universal male approval, and Mrs. Archer, too, She was a lovely, pale woman with a demure manner who was tenderly lifted by the rancher into an invalid's chair so she could be wheeled to sit in the shade and observe the festivities. Their carriage, with bunting wound around the horses' harnesses, was led away as Juliette began to receive greetings from men passing by. She laughed and held her hand out for their kisses, smiling coyly and slanting flirtatious looks at them from beneath the perfect fringe of her elaborately dressed golden hair.

Suddenly aware that *her* hair was probably frizzing in the heat and that her face was no doubt shining with oil and perspiration, Zenobia rushed off to change. She'd had the foresight to haul several buckets of water upstairs to fill the hip bath the night before and now it waited, just right at room temperature to cool and refresh her. She washed with a bit of rose glycerin soap, an extravagant purchase at Trilby's General Store, and dusted herself afterward with another extravagant purchase, some violet-scented talcum powder.

With all the bustle all over town, her bedroom felt like a haven of peace and repose. Enjoying the sensation of being cool and dry and knowing it would not last, Zenobia lay down naked and watched the curtains move in the light breeze at the window. They had been another small extravagance, made from polished cotton printed with pink cabbage roses on a leafy green background. She'd stitched a matching coverlet and pillow slips, with dark-green ruffles to trim them, and threaded ribbon through buttonhole borders. It had given her such inordinate pleasure, this modest ensemble that hadn't cost as much as even one of her imported sheets back home. The pride she took in having made it herself added to her pleasure in it—that and the fact that Daniel Whittaker had made the bed, made it with the strong, tanned hands she loved so.

Oh, dear Lord, she'd forgotten about the baked beans! Zenobia leapt off the bed like a scalded cat and flew around pulling on her stockings, garters, drawers, chemise, petticoats, and—and Paco! She'd meant to check on him! Dulcie Mueller had volunteered to keep him with her at Madame Bettina's so they could devote themselves to the preparations, but she should go relieve Rosita so the girl could visit her son and nurse him. And here she'd been, dawdling! It would serve her right if the whole town booed her onto the next stage when things went wrong.

But willing hands had been at work, and the beans discovered and set to heat by the time she dressed her hair and raced down the stairs. Hungry men proved adept at getting food from hither to yon, and almost before Zenobia and Rosita and Teresa and Wing Loo knew it, all the dishes got to where they should go.

Before everyone ate, Reverend Bob asked for and got a moment of silence. He announced a schedule of events and then turned the dais—a plank set on four barrels—over to Jacob Aleksandrov for the blessing. A few men groaned and more than a few rolled their eyes, obviously familiar with his customary verbosity. Jacob, who had been deputized to work for Daniel for the day, cleared his throat to speak and then noticed the badge on his shirt pocket. He hesitated and then removed it.

He cleared his throat a second time. "Let all who occupy themselves with the affairs of the community do so in the name of heaven, for then the merit of their fathers sustains them and their righteousness endures forever." Jacob took out his badge and pinned it on again. "God bless America!"

A roar went up and there was no doubting the sincerity of the thanksgiving, much of it for the brevity of the invocation. Daniel reckoned it might be a new record. He wandered away as the men began to eat and the working girls fluttered amongst them, delivering platters and trays. Daniel was too on edge to eat, for tonight he meant to ask Zoe Smith to be his wife.

He just couldn't put it off any longer. His nerves couldn't take the wondering and the waiting. He loved her with a love that was painful, and he had half an idea that she loved him back. If he was wrong and it was just that she liked his kissing, well, he'd work with that.

The rosebush had finally produced a bloom, though it had a few ragged edges. He'd carefully neatened up the petals with scissors and he planned to take it to her when he picked her up for the dancing. His palms sweated as he thought about putting the big question to her, so he thought instead of his outfit, his very best clothes—a well-ironed cotton shirt in pale blue with a starched white collar attached and a narrow black cravat, his good boots nicely oiled, the tan linsey-woolsey pants he'd had made in Abilene that fit him so well and made him look almost as big a dandy as Charles Merrick, and a jacquard vest in cherry red. He'd washed his hair in a bucket that morning because the barbershop had a line going out the door and around the corner and he couldn't wait for a tub. He'd dressed his unruly curls with pomade that laid them down, but when he arrived at the jail to change at four-thirty, he saw that his hair had sprung back into its usual tousled disorder.

Daniel sighed. Well, she'd seen his hair that way often enough, and if she married him, she'd surely see him that way a great many more times. Maybe for their wedding day he'd ask the barber to put some of that Hamlin's Wizard Oil on it. If there ever *was* a wedding day. His palms began to sweat again and he dried them on a piece of linen towel.

There was no more delaying. He dressed and looked at his pocket watch again. Five o'clock. Hell. He had to wait another twenty-five minutes before he could go get her. He'd sat on his horse in a deep woods during the war, awaiting the order to charge with less turmoil in his heart. He wondered if he should just leave Gila City if she said no. He wasn't sure he could bear to see her day after day, knowing she was never going to be his. Worse still, he might have to watch her marry Charles Merrick. He'd definitely have to leave town if *that* happened. He'd heard California was a nice state to live in.

He'd set Lester the task of corraling all the guns in town, down at Trilby's General Store so Clarence could spell him. He decided to take a stroll in that direction just to pass some time. Lester sat outside the store looking glum, probably as a result of having to wait until later to eat. Like most really big men, his partner liked to eat early and often. The strong planes of his face sagged and his massive shoulders were slumped and rounded. Lester said not a word about Daniel's fine turnout, which disheartened Daniel, for no one knew better than Lester how seldom in his life he dressed up like this.

The two men sat in silence for several minutes.

"Anyone give you any trouble so far?" Daniel asked.

"No."

"Good. Well, give a holler if they do."

Silence fell again, punctuated by yips and yahoos from further down the street. Chinese lanterns had been strung along Main Street, and now men went along, lighting them. Daniel found himself wondering if Lester had any useful ideas on how one should go about framing a proposal of marriage. Maybe he should ask him. But as so often in the past, just thinking about what his partner might say, Daniel felt he knew what his answer would be.

Lester would tell him just to get on with it, to take the bull by the horns. That was Lester's style—no shilly-shallying. He'd never let himself get so tongue-tied and land-locked over approaching a woman. Why, Lester was the very model of confidence where women were concerned. Daniel had seen it for himself dozens of times. Lester might be quiet around him but when he saw a woman he liked, he just sauntered over to her and began chatting away until she was eating out of the palm of his hand. No, no need to ask Lester for *his* advice.

"Well, reckon I'll be getting along," Daniel announced.

Lester said nothing.

"If anyone was to give you a problem, it probably would have been the boys from the placer camps," Daniel added. "Shouldn't have much problem from here on."

Lester grunted.

Daniel began to think as he walked away that Lester had his nose out of joint about something. Well, if Lester cared to mention the cause of it to him, he'd find a sympathetic ear. But then, Lester was a proud and stubborn cuss. He'd be more likely to keep his troubles to himself. Just as well, thought Daniel—he might not be able to deal with anyone else's troubles on top of his own tonight. His palms began to sweat again as he approached Smith's Good Luck Restaurant.

The rose was a sad-looking thing, but when he handed it to her, Zoe reacted as if he had brought her frankincense and myrrh. If Daniel hadn't been so damn nervous, he'd had been much more gratified by how well his long-term effort had paid off.

"I'm glad you like it, ma'am," he said, noting with disgust a faint stutter in his voice, That was all he needed.

She seemed nervous, too. As she put the rose in a tiny glass and set it on a windowsill, he saw that her hands were shaking.

"That sure is a lovely dress," he said. It was a frothy thing, with lace and ruffles and a great big bow drooping across her behind, all in some light color that reminded him of the beginnings of a good sunset. Ladies probably had some elegant name for it, but he just called it "sunset" in his mind.

They left Rosita sitting on the front step of the restaurant holding Paco. Ned sat on a barrel nearby, looking quietly hopeful. Zoe expressed the hope of seeing them both at the dance. Rosita sniffed and said she might be there and then again she might not. It wasn't entirely up to her. Daniel figured she probably meant it would depend on whether or not the baby was fussy.

On the way to the livery stable, Zoe mentioned that she hoped Lester planned to stop by and ask Rosita to come dance with him and that put a different face on things altogether. Certain facts rapidly assimilated in Daniel's brain.

"That dog won't hunt," he concluded.

"Whatever do you mean?" Zoe asked.

"What I mean is, I've just now realized that Lester is so doggone far gone in love with Rosita that he won't get off his rump and go ask her to the dance for fear she'll say no."

"Then he's a coward," Zoe declared.

Daniel didn't like to agree, but he couldn't disagree either. "Well, when a man's in love, sometimes he just doesn't act sensible."

Zoe sighed. "I was afraid of that. What I don't understand is how Lester can be so brave that he won awards for valor in the War—you did say he had, didn't you?—and saved your life, and faces down such a terror as Mama Rosa without batting an eyelash, and yet he can't ask a girl to a dance."

"Love," said Daniel, his palms beginning to sweat again. "Love'll do that to a man."

"I do hope he plucks up his courage," she said a little crossly. She was having to walk quickly to stay with his stride, so Daniel slowed down. "Otherwise he's going to lose out to Ned, and I think Lester is the right man for Rosita."

Daniel was spared from further discussion of how stupidly men behaved when they were in love by their arrival at the livery stable. The band sat outside since the sky was clear, and played a jaunty air as the ribbons were pinned on the winners of the last foot race. Reverend Bob cleared his throat and patted his belly reflectively. It was evident that he meant to hold the dancing hostage to one more round of speech-making. Everyone sighed and more than a few slipped off for a bit of liquid refreshment.

He began by raising his eyes upward and begging the Almighty's intercession on behalf of the sinners of Gila City, "and you know, Lord, how very many there are," and gradually worked his way around to admonitions against vice in every form, from gambling and drinking to fornication. Since he'd just named the three favorite pastimes of Gila City's residents, it was inevitable that the audience ran out of patience and began to talk to each other so that Reverend Bob ended by shouting the last few words of his oration.

The mayor, a tall, plain fellow, turned out to be considerably more popular, quoting phrases from the Constitution and reminding everyone present that although they were not formally part of the United States, the residents of the Territory should sanctify and recognize the rule of law.

Daniel saw Juliette watching him and supposed he'd better ask her to dance at least once. He knew dozens of fellows would try to steal Zoe from him and he'd have to relinquish her now and again. He'd approach Juliette then, when he had nothing better to do. It had dawned on him—unkind thought though it might be—that she had a tendency to pout just the tiniest bit when she didn't get what she wanted.

The mayor finished with a story about George Washington and then sent an assistant out with a jar for men to draw lots to see who would assume the role of females for the first round of dancing. Soon those who'd drawn the short straws were tying handkerchiefs around one arm. All the working girls were there, but the ratio of men to real women was still thirty to one. All the men who hoped to have a dance with a real female had snowy white handkerchiefs ready to lay between their bare hands and the ladies' dainty dresses. Daniel clutched Zoe's arm closer to his side. He didn't feel at all inclined to share her whether these other fellows knew better then to stain her dress with their big sweaty paws or not.

There was a grand march to open and he thought his heart would burst with pride and love when he saw how beautifully Zoe carried herself, and how graceful she was. Why, there wasn't another woman there who could touch her. There was a polka to follow, and he couldn't stop grinning down at her as they whirled and spun. Next there was a square dance. A tall, skinny waddie got pressed into service, pushed by his friends onto the plank dais. He wore chaps and spurs, a red silk neckerchief and a big Stetson and was evidently known for his prowess at calling.

"Git your partners fer a quadrille," he bawled. Those who stood around the area raked smooth for dancing began to clap and the band launched into a tune.

"Spit out your tobaccy and everybody dance," the waddie chanted. The dancers formed up, but Daniel could see Zoe wasn't at all sure what to do. They promenaded by pairs, sketching a big circle, turning and linking arms, and then the order came to make a square, one couple at each corner.

"Swing the other gal, swing her sweet! Paw dirt, doggies, stomp your feet." Now Zoe was really lost. Daniel did the step called, a sort of jig with the feet lifted high, but so many people there were uninitiated that no one had to feel embarrassed if they didn't know what to do until they saw someone else do it.

"Ladies in the center, gents round 'em run, swing yer rope, cowpoke, and get yo' one!" Daniel circled and retrieved Zoe and tried to show her what to do next, but she was picking up fast, watching and imitating the other two "females" plus the one real one in their square.

"Swing and march, first couple lead, clear round the hall and then stampede." There was a lot of cheering and laughing then, for the order to "stampede" was a puzzler to just about everyone. The men on the sidelines took advantage of the confusion to move in and swipe partners separated from their men.

Zoe disappeared into the arms of Charles Merrick and Daniel felt his blood boil. Not on this night of all nights! But he was helpless to do anything, not unless he wanted to pull rank by drawing his Colt and firing shots overhead to bring everything to a standstill. The crowd thickened, but Daniel did have the satisfaction of seeing Zoe, who was now in the center dancing a galop with the real estate broker, look in his direction and send him a regretful look. It did wonders for Daniel's temper. He tapped his foot and bided his time with more patience then, until he could reclaim Zoe for a schottische.

The sun began to set, and though it was an especially nice evening, not even the sky could compare to Zoe Smith in her sunset-color dress. Daniel could never recall so wonderful an evening. Even though his ranch wasn't nearly what he hoped it would be one day, he felt as if all his dreams were on the verge of coming true. Nothing could make a dent in his happiness, not unless Zoe said no to his proposal, but he felt just as sure as he could that she would say yes.

Reverend Bob got on the dais and announced a special treat, courtesy of Mr. Wing Loo from Smith's Laundry. Daniel could see that Zoe was surprised, so she must not have known about the fireworks display. The preacher had come to Daniel for permission, and so Daniel wouldn't think a gunfight had broken out when they began. The Reverend asked everyone to step back from the area around Ned's anvil and join in the singing of some patriotic songs while the treat was prepared. Mama Rosa loomed out of the crowd as they were waiting and made straight for Zoe.

"Why for are you out here dancing in your fancy dress while my Rosita looks after your baby?" she demanded. Zoe cringed and Daniel drew her closer.

"Now see here—" he began.

Mama Rosa focused her piercing black eyes on him. "And where is the father of that little boy? This is not the man who says he is your husband!"

Daniel felt his neck heating up as the men around them enjoyed the scene. Mama Rosa turned to Zoe again.

"How is my daughter ever going to find herself a good husband? Look at all these men! My Rosita would be dancing and getting offers of marriage if not for you making her stay at the restaurant with *your* baby!"

Fortunately, the band struck up with a flourish just then, and men were sent out to extinguish the Chinese lanterns nearby.

Wing Loo bowed to the mayor. Daniel had never seen him look so regal. He wore a loose black silk coat with a high collar, and his hair had grown out just enough since his unlucky arrival in Gila City to enable him to plait a small queue. Several family members stood by, holding a medium-size chest.

Wing Loo bowed again and addressed the crowd. "In Celestial Kingdom, fireworks are very great tradition. I proud to show them—hope you enjoy."

With a solemn air, Wing Loo withdrew items from the chest which he unwrapped and arranged on the anvil. With the touch of a match, they began to splutter. Wing Loo stepped away and the crowd gasped as a rocket exploded upward and burst overhead, throwing out a shower of gold and purple sparks. The response was overwhelming applause. Wing Loo allowed himself a small, satisfied smile and bowed toward those assembled before he went on, methodically setting up rockets and launching them.

Daniel had never seen any fireworks to rival them. A sulphurous smell permeated the area and smoke drifted down over the watchers like mist, but they were so entranced by the display overhead that they scarcely noticed. At last the Chinaman directed his crew to set out a string of rockets along the ground away from the spectators while he himself picked up a huge mallet. Young Fan, bare-chested and oiled for the occasion, took the mallet as his uncle set packets of gunpowder on the anvil.

The band began to play "The Star-Spangled Banner" at Wing Loo's signal. Fan wielded the mallet to strike the gunpowder packets, which produced a sound so uncannily like a cannon being fired that several men hit the dirt, while Wing Loo set the rockets off in sequence. Mouths hung open and more than a few tears were shed at the sheer beauty of the spectacle. By the time the music ended and the last sparks faded overhead, it would have been difficult to find a group more popular in Gila City than Wing Loo and his ten relatives, who smiled and bowed over and over again in response to the thunderous applause.

Amazingly enough, none of the rowdier residents felt they

had to uncork their six-shooters to add to the celebration, although Daniel did see Nathanial Evans lurking near the edge of the crowd with a sour look on his face. No doubt he wished the band had been playing a tune to honor the Stars and Bars, not the Stars and Stripes.

The moon was well up now, and Daniel took the liberty of putting his arm around Zoe as they strolled away from the dancing in search of something to drink. James Archer beckoned as they passed and Daniel realized with an unpleasant jolt that he'd been so absorbed with Zoe that he hadn't once approached Juliette for a dance.

"Good evening, Mr. Archer, Mrs. Archer. It's a pleasure to see you in town, ma'am."

Mrs. Julia Archer inclined her head. "Won't you introduce your lady friend, Daniel?"

"With pleasure. Ma'am, may I present Miss Zoe Smith?" How Daniel wished he could introduce her as his bride-to-be, but that would have to wait.

Juliette smiled at him, waving her fan back and forth. "I didn't see any beef served, Daniel. Did you forget about it after our little, well, our little 'encounter' at the livery stable?"

Daniel stared at her. What did she mean, their little encounter? She'd showed him the steer and that had been the end of it. "Um, no, ma'am. I guess I left it to Miss Smith what to do with it."

Zoe smiled ever so sweetly at Juliette. "Why, do you know, my 'friends' and I caught so many fish and had so many other donations, I just forgot about that steer completely." She turned to James Archer and her expression grew softer. "It was most kind of you, sir. I'm most awfully sorry I overlooked your gift."

James Archer nodded. "I can well believe you forgot, young lady, with everything else you had on your mind. It was very resourceful of you to catch so many fish. Fresh food is greatly appreciated in these parts, especially when it's well prepared."

"Indeed, the meal was wonderful," said Mrs. Archer. "You

were very brave to take on such a job. My husband tells me your restaurant and laundry are doing very, very well."

"I've been wondering," Juliette murmured, "where a woman comes by the money it takes to buy businesses like that? I mean, what sort of business was she in first to have come by such a large sum?"

Daniel felt Zoe go tense beside him.

Mrs. Archer said, "Why, Juliette, I believe that's Miss Smith's private business. I'm surprised at you asking a question like that."

"Why, I meant nothing by it," Juliette said, her eyes wide and innocent.

Daniel felt caught in undercurrents he didn't understand. It seemed the two younger women were on a collision course, but over what? Rather than take a chance on things turning unpleasant, Daniel gathered Zoe's hand over his arm and wished the Archers a good evening. As they walked away, he thought of finding the exact moment to ask Zoe to marry him and his heart thudded.

Closer to the restaurant, the street grew quieter. It had been a very successful and remarkably peaceful sort of Fourth of July for Gila City, thanks to Reverend Bob and, he suspected, the planning genius of Rabbi Jacob. The genius lay in not letting the boring speeches stretch out so long so that too many men drifted off to saloons and gambling tables and away from the organized activities. And, of course, there was Zoe and the working girls with the wonderful food, and Wing Loo and his relations and their spectacular contribution.

When they came to the restaurant, Daniel drew Zoe into the shadows of the doorway. Inside, only one low lantern burned and there was no sign of Rosita. He didn't have any flowery speech planned, and he had no parlor to use where he could go down on one bended knee while Zoe posed prettily on a settee, so Daniel decided to start the proposal with his strong suit. He took Zoe into his arms and kissed her.

He pulled her against him and she went all pliant and made

happy sounds of acquiescence. His heart beat hard and his body went into a state of longing, tense with wanting to touch her and hold her and daring to think whether she might invite him upstairs to spend the night in *their* bed once she'd agreed to marry him. He cradled her neck and slipped his fingers into the soft hair she had pulled into an elaborate swirl on top of her head. He wanted to find the pins and loosen them one by one, and have the silken mass of it come tumbling down over his hands and face as he kissed her.

She was raising herself on tiptoe, clutching at his shoulders, and Daniel lifted her round little figure so that she pressed even more firmly against him. He wanted to see every lovely inch of her, and find out if the rest of her skin glowed with the same ivory light as her cheeks and chin and forehead. He felt as if time might stop and just the two of them could step off the edge of the world together.

"Oh, Zoe," he whispered, "you feel like a dream come true. I want to make love to you so bad."

"I want you, too," she panted, putting quick fervent little kisses along his cheek. "Oh, maybe just this once . . ." She twined her head along his shoulder and turned it so that she could touch his earlobe with her tongue.

Daniel shuddered, holding on to his sanity with an effort. "Maybe just this once what, darlin'?" he prompted.

"You could, you could, we could . . . go upstairs and . . ."

"I'd love that, darlin', I really would," he said hoarsely. "I love you, Zoe, I love you as much as a man can love a woman. I want to be with you tonight."

She pulled back and he could see the faintest glimmer of light reflecting off the lovely high cheekbones. "I . . . I shouldn't, but I want to so much, Daniel."

He kissed her tenderly. "Darlin', let's make it right between us and then maybe you'll feel you should. Zoe, will you marry me?"

She went taut in his arms, her body stiffening. It must be the surprise. He'd shocked her. He felt her pushing against his shoulders and reluctantly let the contact of their bodies loosen as she slid to stand on her own two feet. She stared up at him, her eyes wide, the blue turned to silver by the moon.

"Daniel, I . . . no," she whispered. "No, not now, not . . . I can't, not ever."

She stepped back but Daniel didn't move, transfixed by the awful look on her face. She was shaking her head wordlessly, and then, without warning, she turned and dashed into the restaurant, slamming the door behind her. Daniel felt as if something heavy had fallen on him.

He grabbed the doorknob and tried to turn it, but although she had left like something shot out of a cannon, she had managed to lock it behind her. He rattled it in disbelief, so hard that it made the windows shake.

"Zoe!"

He shook the door again. Something had gone horribly wrong and he hadn't the least idea what it was.

"Zoe!"

The faint light of the lantern back on the kitchen counter disappeared. Daniel ran to the side door in the alley, but it was locked, too. He fell back against the building, breathing hard. The center of his chest hurt, as bad as if young Fan had swung his mallet with all his might and hit him dead center on the breastbone.

Oh, God. His legs went out from under him and he collapsed to the ground, his back to the wall of Smith's Good Luck Restaurant. He couldn't forget the look on her face. She'd looked so . . . so *revolted*. But why, why?

Later, it seemed like hours but he knew it was only minutes, Daniel staggered to his feet. He stood there, weaving from the shock of what had happened. But what had happened? She'd kissed him, passionately, and she had even suggested that he might spend the night with her, and then?

And then he'd asked her to marry him and she'd run like hell. Daniel shook his head from side to side, unable to bear the pain.

Fifteen

Juliette Archer waited in the shade outside the only dressmaker in Gila City. She was hot, she was furious, and she wanted to inflict suffering on Miss Zoe Smith the likes of which she had never known. No one could have seen what she had seen the day by the river, when that woman had rolled around in the dirt with Daniel Whittaker, and not have known what she was before she had transformed herself into the oh-so-respectable Miss Zoe Smith. Only a man blinded by lust could fail to see the obvious. Anyone looking at Daniel Whittaker at the Independence Day celebration could *tell* he was blinded by lust.

It would cost some money to find out the truth about Miss Zoe Smith, but all she'd had to do was tell Daddy she needed some new dresses and he'd given her an open line of credit at the bank. It wouldn't take too long to get to the bottom of things where Zoe Smith was concerned. A woman like that must have left a trail behind her that stank to high heaven.

She saw the man she was waiting for and stepped deeper into the shadows. He walked with an uneven gait, so it took him longer to reach her than it would have taken someone else, but Juliette found that for once she could be patient. The man she was waiting for had no liking for Daniel Whittaker or Zoe Smith. He thought they were both do-gooders. He would be glad to search out information to wreck their happiness, and all he wanted in return was money. Money was the key. It was a good thing, thought Juliette, that she had plenty of it.

* * *

Teresa straightened out her bed and sat down on it to roll a cigarette. It was early in the evening of a hot day, so she hoped there wouldn't be too many of her regulars climbing the stairs for her tonight. One of them, a Cousin Jack, had just been and gone. She had always liked the Cornishmen, most of whom had started life as hard rock miners, laboring underground with good cheer from an early age.

They were affable and used the language interestingly, and always called everyone by some term of endearment, like "my son" or " 'andsome." She'd grubstaked this particular Cousin Jack, Sell Tarr as he had finally told her his real name was, because he always amused her, and she had reached a stage in life where she appreciated that quality in a man almost more than any other. He'd lie beside her and tell her amusing stories when he was done, and she would listen, which was rare. When a man had spent himself, she usually saw to it that he left soon afterward.

But Sell was different. He put himself out for her pleasure, and tried to cheer her up after he was done. He'd stroke her back and chuckle when asked whether he'd had any luck on his claim recently. "Well, my beautay," he'd replied once, "where gold is, it is, and where it ain't, there be I."

She liked Sell's humor and his tough, muscular body, but her favorite customer for a long time had been Daniel Whittaker. She'd have had to be a fool, though, not to notice that when Zoe Smith came to town, Daniel Whittaker's heart had been taken prisoner, so she had begun to think more on Sell. She didn't mean to spend the rest of her life whoring. It wore a body out.

Teresa lit her cigarette and hung out the window to catch whatever breeze there might be. Daniel hadn't been to see her in a long time, at least not that way. Teresa could have loved Daniel very easily, but she'd gotten a tip a long time ago from an older whore.

"Don't give your heart away, dearie," she'd warned. "Wait to see which ones fall in love with you and then, when the time is right for getting respectable, choose one of them. If you can't keep a tight rein on your heart, then get into another line of work."

So Teresa had learned not to give her heart away. From the look of him, though, Daniel Whittaker had not. He'd been walking around town the last few days looking like a man who'd eaten some spoiled food. Nothing could make you feel like that faster than love gone bad. Zoe Smith didn't look too chipper either. Something must have gone wrong between them the night of the Fourth.

Teresa sighed. Just then she saw the sheriff of Gila City. He turned slowly and began the climb up to the second story of the Red Dog. She didn't think Daniel was coming to her for sex, which meant that he might be coming as a friend. The heaviness of his tread as he approached her door was all the confirmation she needed that Daniel Whittaker needed a friend. He stopped in her open doorway, shoulders sagging, like a man who was carrying too much weight. She gestured to the chair.

"Sit," she said, and got up to pour them both a bourbon.

He sprawled in the chair, eyes dull, and finished the shot in one gulp. Teresa refilled his glass.

"Life stinks," he said.

"Yeah," she said, "and then you die."

He rubbed his eyes. They were bloodshot and underlaid by dark circles. "I know I look like hell at the moment," he said, his voice a low gravel, "but from where you sit, how do I rate as husband material?"

Teresa snorted. "For looks? Passable, real passable."

"I didn't mean that," he said, leaning back and closing his eyes. The long, taut planes of his cheeks looked hollowed. "I meant, do I seem like I'd take care of a woman and treat her right?"

"Hell, if it's just compliments you want, Daniel, I'll get one of the other girls. I need more of a challenge." He opened his eyes and looked at her with misery on his face. Teresa, who'd been trying to fun him out of his mood, softened. "Sure, Daniel. I can't imagine too many women who wouldn't be happy to say 'I do' to you."

He let his eyes close again and drew a weighty breath. "It's too damn bad you're not the one I asked." He held out his glass with a shaky hand. "Pour me another, will you?"

Teresa smiled ruefully. "Well, I gather I'm not or we wouldn't be having this conversation." She put her hand over his to hold the glass steady while she refilled it. "Zoe?"

His expression grew pinched, as if the very sound of her voice caused him pain. "She won't have me, Teresa, and I don't know why. I swear, it's going to kill me."

"Nah, it's not going to. You just hurt so bad you wish it would."

He finished the bourbon without even opening his eyes to look at the glass. "What do I do, Teresa?" he asked.

"You ask her why, I guess."

"She won't talk to me." She could see that the liquor on top of misery and lack of sleep was sending him toward a good drunk fast. He wasn't much of a drinker, but Teresa swore by liquor for dulling life's little pains. Hell, in his situation it wasn't going to make things any *worse*.

"But you asked her why when she turned you down, right?"

"Sure I asked her, but she looked at me like I was some kind of crazy. She just said she couldn't marry me, not ever. I'll never forget that look on her face, like I had a hell of a nerve for even bringing it up. Now she won't even talk to me. I don't get it, Teresa. What do women want?"

"You're askin' the wrong one, Daniel." Teresa refilled his glass and he tossed it off. Even *she* didn't drink that fast. "I know women and I know men, but I don't begin to understand what makes 'em get together and what pulls 'em apart."

"If you were Zoe, though—what do you think she wants? Why'd she look at me like something that needed stepping on?"

Teresa stood up. "This ain't gettin' us nowhere. Lay down on the bed."

He shook his head. "That's not what I came for."

"Well, talk about knowing how to make a girl feel wanted." She took the empty glass from him. "I meant, lay down and sleep. You look about halfway to death."

He tottered and swayed when he stood up. Teresa nudged him in the right direction and he fell on the bed. She rolled him away from the edge and pulled off his boots. He laid one arm across his eyes so that all she could see was the wide, beautiful mouth.

"It hurts bad, Teresa. It hurts real bad." His mouth tightened and she thought he might be on the verge of tears.

"I know, sweetheart," she said softly. "I'll see what I can find out."

She retrieved her kidskin boots from under the bed and left him to sleep it off, thinking what good advice that old whore had given her.

Teresa hushed the assembled doves and lit the small lantern she'd borrowed from Ned. Daylight showed through the cracks in the door of the livery stable, but otherwise the place was nearly dark. They were trying to keep the meeting a secret, closing the doors to avoid curious eyes, and meeting in the morning. If all the whores in Gila City had suddenly disappeared at night, it would have been noticed. It was ironic, thought Teresa, that the working girls of Gila City had never met all in one place until the arrival of Miss Zoe Smith, after which they got together regularly for one thing and another, and now here they were joining together on her behalf.

"All right, girls," Teresa said, keeping her voice low to force everyone to keep quiet and pay attention. "There's a problem and it's got to do with someone we all owe a lot to."

"Who?" said a young whore from the cribs. "I don't owe nobody nothing."

"Ya owe *me* twenty dollars rent," snapped the Irish Queen.

"None of that," Teresa said. "Look, it's Zoe Smith, and it's Daniel Whittaker, the sheriff, too."

"I wouldn't mind owin' him," someone said. "Ow! Whadya do that for?"

"Teresa's tryin' to talk, and I want to get this over with so I can get me some sleep," Contrary Mary said. "Now, pipe down."

"I need some ideas," said Teresa. "Now, I know some of you believe in true love and some of you think it's a crock. Either way, it doesn't matter. What does matter is that we've got two people that are in love and they don't seem to be able to get any closer to saying 'I do' than two porcupines with their quills out."

"What do you want *us* to do about it?" someone asked.

"I'm getting to that. Daniel Whittaker is sincere in love and he wants to marry Zoe Smith, but she won't have him. Now, even if you don't think you owe Zoe Smith for helping us to be a respectable part of this town, you've got to admit that Daniel Whittaker deserves our help. I never worked in a town where the sheriff didn't take a piece of your earnings, and free services, too, if he felt like it. Any of you other girls, I expect it was the same where you came from before this." There was a chorus of assent. "He treats us right and we should help him out of his misery. I'm not going to lie to you ladies—he's got it real bad."

"But if she won't have him, she won't have him. Not all of us hankers after marriage. Maybe she don't love him."

"Well, that's the tricky part. She loves him, all right. I went and talked to her and I'm sure as I can be about that."

"Howsomever that might be, what do you expect us to do about it?" Silver Sally said.

"I'm looking for ideas," Teresa admitted. "I'm fresh out. They're both so miserable I can't stand it. Even Rosita, Zoe's cook, has about had it. She said she's going to move in with her mother if Zoe doesn't stop moping around, says her milk's going dry up or go sour."

"Hell, there's your answer—give the sheriff a clear field to call on Zoe and court her and spend time with her. Can't nobody talk nobody round to their point of view unless they spend time together," said the Irish Queen.

"Yeah, you got somethin' there," Teresa said slowly. "Only just because Rosita clears out doesn't mean that Daniel Whittaker gets to move in."

There was a rustling in the back. "Ain't this straw makin' anybody else itch? I swear, it's gonna drive me crazy."

"Hush up, Daisy," someone said.

Silver Sally spoke again. "This ain't that tough, girls. Now think on it, where does Daniel Whittaker sleep?"

"At the jailhouse?" one girl ventured.

"Yeah, and what if the jailhouse burned down?"

Silence greeted this question, silence punctuated by the rustling of straw and the buzzing of flies.

"You ain't suggesting we should . . . burn down the . . . the *jailhouse* . . . are you?" one girl asked.

"Solves the problem," said Silver Sally, sounding bored.

Teresa found herself thinking out loud. "It just might work."

"What's to stop him taking a room over at the hotel, or above one of the saloons?" Contrary Mary asked.

"We get to the owners first, tell 'em we don't want the sheriff bunkin' in where we do business," Silver Sally said impatiently. "It might make the customers nervous havin' the law so close by. They can't make money if we don't make money. Can't any of you girls string two thoughts together?"

"We don't all have a brain like yours," one girl complained. "It was you thought up how to catch all them fish and make a pen and now this, Sally."

"Yeah, you shouldn't be makin' us feel bad just 'cause we ain't as smart as you," said the girl named Daisy.

"All right now, girls, that'll do," Teresa said. "Anybody see any problems with the plan before we get down to exactly how we're going to do it?"

"What if Sheriff Whittaker comes and beds down here?" asked a mulatto girl named Lucy.

"He won't be able to—he'll have to use this for a jail if we burn the real one down."

"Oh." Lucy sounded disappointed. "I was thinking I might volunteer to keep Ned company at night so's he wouldn't want the sheriff around." She paused and added in her soft Louisiana drawl, "I mean, what happens in case the sheriff doesn't *have* any prisoners?"

"Well, hell, Lucy, knock yourself out. You don't need *our* permission if you're sweet on Ned and want to go after him."

"Well, Lucy's got a point," said Daisy. "If she takes care of Ned, we don't have to worry that the sheriff will sleep here."

"That's settled then. Now, we've got to wait for a time when nobody's inside the jailhouse—"

"Someone's bound to always be in there, like that deputy with the big mustache," said the Irish Queen.

"I'll take care of him," said Contrary Mary. "He fancies me."

"And we have to make sure the jail really gets burning good," Teresa went on. "There can't be any walls left."

"Use some of this damn straw," said Daisy, who was now scratching uncontrollably. "Throw some bundles in and let it get started good from the inside."

"We've got to set fire to the jail at night so we got the darkness to work by," said Silver Sally, "and we'll have to create a diversion to make sure nobody sees us. I have an idea that'll do the trick . . ."

Daniel surveyed the stinking burned-out ruins of the jailhouse. Only the heavy metal bars that Ned had labored to make still stood, poking up from the ashes like the leftover spines of a dead saguaro cactus. He pushed his hat up on his forehead. It hadn't been six months since he'd talked the Businessmen's

Benevolent Association into building it in the first place so the law would have a more impressive presence in Gila City. Daniel heaved a sigh—and just when he'd thought his life couldn't get any worse.

And what had those crazy whores over at the Empire been up to? The word had gone out that they were stripping down naked and dancing on the tables, laughing and singing, drunk as all hell to get out. Every gambling house and arcade and music hall had emptied out in record time, and while they'd all gawked—himself included—the jail had gone up like it had been soaked in kerosene.

But it hadn't. Daniel had smelled an arson fire or two in his time, and this one had no lingering odor, no blaze of soot where something flammable had been poured around the outside or tossed in the door.

And Walter Connolly hadn't been there either. He'd told Daniel some cock-and-bull story about having to go "relieve" himself, with no very good explanation as to why he couldn't just use the pot back in the corner like they usually did.

Daniel resigned himself to using the livery stable to hold drunks and other unruly prisoners again, like they had before the jailhouse got built, but for some unaccountable reason, Ned allowed as how he'd prefer if Daniel found another place to bed down till the jail got rebuilt. He said it with great reluctance, refusing to look Daniel in the eye, but he was fixed on it nonetheless. And nowhere else Daniel tried had a room to let or an open bed. It stumped him, but there it was.

He could think of only one place in town with plenty of unoccupied bedrooms, and that was Smith's Good Luck Restaurant. There was no place he'd rather sleep, but seeing as how the restaurant's owner wasn't speaking to him and shied away from him on the street like a sagebrush in front of a high wind, it looked like a fool's errand to even ask if he could rent a room there.

Instead he tried sleeping on the floor of Walter Connolly's tiny room, but by the time morning rolled around, he'd learned at great cost to his well-being that the big man snored even louder than he complained. Daniel's eyes were as red as the sky at sunset by the time he conceded defeat and went into the restaurant the following evening.

It was after closing and the lanterns had been turned back and the tables cleared and wiped clean. Rosita and Zoe sat at one of the tables, finishing their own dinners. Zoe glanced up to see who had come in.

Their eyes met and Daniel's heart did something painful in his chest. Her eyes were just as blue, the skin still fair, the beautiful hair just as shiny as ever. He couldn't think of anything to say. He felt he might be best off staying right on the spot where he stood. At least she hadn't run away. There was no welcome in her eyes, though, only cool neutrality.

It was Rosita who stood up and broke the stalemate. "I must be on my way," she said with a quick glance in Daniel's direction. Daniel began to feel as if he had some sort of disease.

"Where are you going?" he asked, trying for a conversational tone.

"Madame Bettina's place to pick up Paco, and then to Mamacita's," she said. "I stay there now, with her."

"With the baby, too?"

Rosita nodded. "I told her the truth. She was angry, but it was better to get it over with. Now she is pleased to have a grandson."

Daniel nodded. He wanted to ask if she and Zoe had quarreled, if that had provoked her to move in with her mother. But the two women had been sitting companionably enough when he walked in. No, he was the one who had disturbed the balance. The door closed softly and Rosita was gone, and he was alone with Zoe. She stood up and began bustling around, making a lot of fuss over clearing away the two tin plates and pottery mugs they'd been using.

He followed her to the kitchen. He knew what disease it was that he felt like he had: leprosy. There was nothing for her to do beyond putting the dishes in the washing-up basin, but she tried to draw it out. When she could no longer think of anything else to do with her hands, she turned and faced him warily, her hands braced against the stand behind her.

"I . . . uh . . . I guess you heard the jailhouse burned down," he said.

She nodded, not quite looking at him. God, how he hated that! It was if he wasn't quite there as far as she was concerned. He felt a strong inclination to run from the pain it gave him, but he steeled himself to go on.

"I checked all over town for someplace else to stay, but no one's got any vacancies," he said. "I was hoping I could rent one of your rooms." He hitched his head upward, as if she wouldn't otherwise be sure which rooms he meant.

Her gaze flew up to meet his at last. "No." She shook her head nervously. "No, that's not possible. I can't have you here."

She was scared of him for some reason. That was better than having her act like he didn't exist, at least. Scared he could work with.

"Zoe, darlin'," he said gently, "whatever it was that happened between us, I'm sorry. I never meant to give you a fright. You know me well enough by now to know that I wouldn't do a thing, not the least little thing, to hurt you."

Her head was bent, but he could see her biting her lower lip. Her shoulders trembled, too, She was gripped by some strong emotion, but he figured if he could just make his case for staying there, it would be enough for one night. All the rest of what was going on in her head he could work on in the days to come—if he could only persuade her to rent him a room.

"Now, look here," he went on, "you shouldn't be here all on your own anyway. No one's going to bother you if they know I'm staying upstairs, and I'm not going to say another word to you about marriage if you don't want me to, all right? Zoe? Now are you going to rent me that room or not?"

She raised her head slowly and he saw the shimmer of moisture in her eyes. Poor little darlin'—she was about on the verge of tears, but why? Daniel wanted to go to her and take her in his arms, but he forced himself to stay right where he was.

"Yes, all right," she whispered.

Daniel felt a little like crying himself. Somehow he had managed to talk his way back into her life. And he hadn't promised not to kiss her and hold her and make love to her. He'd only said he wouldn't ask her to marry him again. He'd abide by that as long as he could, but he sure was going to work on her other weaknesses in the meantime.

If he could get her to let him make love to her, surely it would be a short step from there to getting her to marry him. He sure hoped he was right about that. He had his heart and the whole rest of his life set on it.

Sixteen

It was insanity, pure and simple. Absolute madness. Daniel Whittaker, with his gray-green eyes and tousled hair and strong tanned hands, was living under the same roof with her. Every day she watched him come down for wash water and carry it back upstairs in the flowered jug that matched the basin in Rosita's old room where he slept.

It made her mouth dry out and her breath come quick—out of fear when she was thinking straight and out of desire when she wasn't. He wore no undergarment under his shirt now that the weather had grown so hot, and he'd leave his suspenders down, riding over his pants and against the hard narrow hips. He'd fasten only a few bottom buttons on his shirt, revealing the sculpting of muscles across his chest and down below his breastbone.

She stared. She knew she did. As she scrubbed and wiped and laid out plates, he'd walk past her to the pump by the wet sink, fill the pitcher and go back upstairs. He was out late patrolling the streets of Gila City so he came in after she'd gone to bed and got up after she did. She was always dressed and working by the time he appeared and sauntered past her with a good-natured smile and a cheery "good morning."

And no matter how hard she tried, she couldn't make herself stop looking at him. The dark growth of beard tipped with gold, the flat planes of his face, the lazy grin, the way he held his coffee cup—it all did odd little twisting things to her insides. In the new, more informal setting, she saw other features of his body, too. He rolled up his sleeves in the morning before he washed to keep them dry. She couldn't help noticing the curling brown hair on his forearms, and it struck her as amazing, so . . . so *masculine*.

The thoughts she was beginning to harbor about him were all quite shockingly detailed and lurid. She needed to be touched by him. Her dreadful deep longing to have him in her bed was surpassed only by her deep desire not to hang for murder. She should never have let him back into her life. She'd been so miserable to live with when she kept her distance from him that Rosita had moved out, but at least she'd been spared the temptations engendered by proximity—until now.

She needed more chaperons, especially someone who would be there early in the day, since Rosita had breakfast with her mother now and took Paco to Dulcie at Madame Bettina's before she came to work. As much as she missed Paco, Zenobia had to admit that Rosita was right to leave him with Dulcie. He was getting too big to carry around all day, and Dulcie played with him and was tenderly attentive to his needs.

All of which left her alone with Daniel Whittaker in the mornings. She went to pick up the account books at the laundry one morning—one of her many forays designed to leave the restaurant rather than be there alone with Daniel—and found Wing Loo and his relatives still eating breakfast. They all stood up, smiling and bowing, setting aside their bowls of rice and the endless cups of green tea they consumed throughout the day. Ah Tup bowed, too, but did not leave his place by the stove, where he was deftly frying slivers of pork to round out the meal.

Smith's Good Luck Restaurant had so much business now that it was all they could do to stay ahead of demand. If someone like Ah Tup could learn how to prepare ingredients for western food, it would free Rosita to do just the final mixing and cooking. Zenobia had nicked and bloodied herself so many times trying to help that by mutual agreement, she had ceased handling sharp instruments.

"Wing Loo, I was wondering," she began, "do you think Ah Tup might like to come and work for me at the restaurant?"

Ah Tup paused in his work at the stove. Wing Loo said, "You want ask him? I teach him speak good English, same as me."

"Really, Ah Tup? That would be very helpful. Are you interested in a job at the restaurant?"

"I like help, missy," he said, smiling broadly.

And that was how she solved the problem of the mornings alone with Daniel, because Ah Tup appeared promptly at eight each morning and his efforts increased the restaurant's capacity to serve meals by at least twofold. Ah Tup, with his swift economy of motion, put even Rosita to shame when it came to peeling and chopping and slicing, and his was a cheerful presence.

Lester still came by at least two or three days a week for the midday meal and Zenobia grew impatient with his reticence and his longing glances toward the kitchen. When he asked her where Paco was one day, she snapped, "Go ask his mother."

She was up to her hips in customers and trying to maneuver a heavy tray to a table between two benches filled to overflowing with men, and something in her had had its fill of frustration. She deposited the tray almost on the heads of the customers nearest her and yelled, "Pass it down!" It got to its destination far faster than she could have gotten it there. She wiped her hands on her apron. Well, why hadn't she thought of *that* a long time ago?

"Come with me," she said to Lester. She took him by the shirtsleeve and dragged him toward the kitchen.

"But, Miss Zoe—"

"Don't you 'But, Miss Zoe' me," she said. "I've had enough of this admiring from afar. For all you know, Rosita might have the temper of a mountain lion and the brains of a pudding. Go!" She pushed him through the kitchen door and yelled to Rosita over the half-counter, "This is Lester Cooper. That's Rosita Chavez. Rosita, Lester's going to make some biscuits. Show him where the flour is!"

Miss Walther at the finishing school would have keeled over.

Never had an introduction been made so gracelessly. Zenobia didn't care. A body could only take so much.

Rosita dropped the spoon she'd been stirring with. It promptly sank out of sight into the contents of the cooking pot. *"Madre de Dios,"* she said, staring up at Lester, "you're so tall. I didn't realize . . ."

A hot blush came up on Lester's cheeks, the brown going a deep ruddy color. "Ah, well, um, my daddy's a big fellow."

"Good. Now ask her to marry you," Zenobia said impatiently. "I've got a restaurant to run."

Ah Tup grinned, never missing a stroke as he sliced potatoes into neat strips. Lester swallowed hard.

"Um, Miss Chavez, I was wondering whether you would—"

"Say yes, Rosita, whatever he asks," Zenobia shouted and turned back to deal with the crowd out front. Some people! If she came back and found that they hadn't managed to at least keep the conversation going, she'd strangle them.

But at closing time, Lester, who'd never left, proudly escorted Rosita to the door. "We're going to go pick up Paco over at Madame Bettina's," he explained, "and then I'm going to go meet Mama Rosa, only this time we're going to get it right."

"Oh, good," sighed Zenobia. She wondered whether Mama Rosa still thought Lester was the baby's father, but decided it didn't matter one way or another to her. Let *them* deal with it.

Ah Tup, who somehow managed to wash plates and cups and pots and pans as fast as they were brought to him, took his apron off and wished her a good night before leaving.

"Thank you, Ah Tup. By the way, I'm giving you a raise starting next week."

"Raise?" He paused in the doorway.

Zenobia rubbed her neck tiredly. She still had to count all the money on the table and weigh the gold dust and enter the amounts in the ledger and record the number of customers and whom she'd extended credit to and draw up a list of supplies she needed to order from Clarence Trilby tomorrow.

"Yes, more money. You do very good work. We make more

now that you work here, serve more people." She waved at the pile of money.

"Oh!" Ah Tup's face brightened. "Restaurant make more money?"

"Yes," she said carefully, "and I'm going to pay *you* more money, too."

"Restaurant make plenty money," he said, smiling, "same as laundry. Good!"

Zenobia just nodded and smiled back. He'd find out what she meant when she gave him his next pay packet. When he had bowed his way out the door, she resumed counting. Her neck and shoulders ached from all the trays she'd carried that day. There were *some* disadvantages to having more customers.

She was halfway through counting when she heard the side door open. Daniel Whittaker came in and took his hat off.

"Evening," Daniel said. He smiled. She looked so pretty, her cheeks all pink from the heat and her beautiful hair working its way loose from the knot on top of her head. "Thought I might come by for some coffee. It's pretty quiet out there tonight."

"Oh." Her eyes were large and blue, and she looked all worn out, like she so often did at the end of a night.

He could tell that she wasn't all that comfortable having him there when no one else was around, but it was time to start reminding her that she wanted him to make love to her. He stirred the chips in the stove to heat them up again for boiling water.

"Was the coffee cold already? I heard you—" She stopped, taking in the fact that he was carrying a tray.

"Coffee's fine. It's just that I know you like tea better, so I made you some." He enjoyed the surprise and pleasure on her face as she watched him set down the tray. He put the strainer across her cup and carefully poured the tea. "Cream? Sugar?"

"Both," she replied, looking shy.

He added them and handed her the cup. "Books coming out right?"

"Oh!" She glanced at the forgotten ledger. "They seem to

be all right. Unless I'm very poor at arithmetic, things are going quite well."

He loved to hear her speak, the husky voice, the quick, clipped speech with the faint accent. She rubbed her neck wearily. "Here," he said, "let me do that for you."

Before she could protest, he pushed her collar down and began to carefully knead her neck. She let out a sound and gradually fell back into the touch of his hands. Her shoulders were tight, the muscles hard beneath his fingers as he expanded the territory he felt she'd let him touch.

"You should let me do this for you every night," he said, feeling very cheered up. It was the first time he'd managed to get his hands on her since the Fourth of July, and she was putting up no resistance at all.

She made another sound and let her head go limp on her neck. The red-and-gold highlights in her dark-brown hair caught the light and shimmered and Daniel slid his hands up, threading his fingers through it, squeezing his fingertips over her scalp. Her neck was so slender and delicate, her hair soft as an angel's wings. His heart filled with love. *His* angel!

He let his hands communicate his feelings, tenderly massaging her weary shoulders. The tops of her arms, the sides of her neck, across the slim back, down the spine. He could feel the stiff line where her corset started, just below her shoulder blades, and the outlines of her chemise. She was smooth and warm and soft beneath his palms now, limber and relaxed wherever his hands roved.

"Oh, Daniel, that feels so good."

"Doesn't it, darlin'? I swear, there's nothing that makes me feel as good as making you feel good."

He kept his touch light, but his whole body was stirring to life, exulting in the contact. He began to wonder if he could get her upstairs for a continuation. He could do her feet and ankles and calves and thighs and . . . Daniel stopped himself there. He couldn't think about it or he would lose control, and control was at the heart of his plan.

That and the fact that the shades were up at the windows and men walking by would get an eyeful if he started kissing her right there. No, he'd take it by easy stages. Give her a neck and back rub here and there over the next few days and then waylay her upstairs where he could reacquaint her with his kisses, and she could remember how much she liked them.

"Better?" he said, taking his hands away.

She opened her eyes and looked around, seeming dazed. She craned around and found his face. And smiled, a soft, amazingly sensual smile, eyes heavy-lidded and shining beneath the dark sweep of long lashes. Daniel's whole body ached at the implied message in that smile.

"That was wonderful," she sighed.

With more self-restraint than he'd ever exercised in his life, he said lightly, "Anytime you want me to do it again, just say the word. . . . Oops, I think I heard some shots. Now, you have another cup of tea and get on up to bed, you hear? You need your rest."

"Yes, Daniel," she said dreamily.

Daniel walked out briskly, grabbing his hat by the door. Oh, lordy, he wanted that little girl way too much! He stopped outside in the darkness to collect his wits. At the moment they were scattered all over Smith's Good Luck Restaurant, like clothes torn off and flung aside by lovers in a frenzy to mate. He hadn't heard any shots; what he'd heard was his self-control shredding.

His pulse gradually calmed and his heart settled back into a normal rhythm. He'd done it! He'd set out to reintroduce Zoe to his touch and give her pleasure without alarming her or pushing her beyond the point that she was comfortable with—and he'd done it! And he had managed to hold back all his own overwhelming desires.

And because he had, now there would be a next time, and a next.

* * *

My word, she was starting to have quite a bit of money! Zenobia closed the books and sat back with a satisfied feeling. Seeing how well she was doing, Madame Bettina had come to her and inquired about investing in her businesses, but Zenobia had politely turned the German madam away. She needed no more capital—hers was growing by leaps and bounds. Her father, had he but known, would have been proud, and would no doubt have given her sound advice on what to do with it.

Zenobia celebrated by ordering a new dress at Sally Guthries's Modes. Sally, like so many women in Gila City, was too fond of something, but in her case it seemed to be a patent nostrum which she frequently sipped straight from the bottle, claiming it helped her cough. It certainly must, for Zenobia had yet to hear her cough once. Her work was vastly inferior to the modistes Zenobia had patronized back East but infinitely superior to what she herself could produce.

What else she might do with her excess capital, Zenobia decided to wait and see.

If money could have bought her divorce, she would have been a happy woman, but no amount of money *she* could offer Eben could rival the fortune he would inherit as the deserted and long-suffering spouse of Barnabus Strouss's only daughter. Money couldn't buy her exoneration from the crime of murder either, or freedom from the specter of the gallows that loomed over her in darker moments.

All of which meant it could not buy her Daniel Whittaker. She knew how ardently he desired marriage and children. What a cruel and immoral piece of business it would be if she pretended she wasn't already married and said yes to him just for her own selfish pleasure.

It was her love for him that kept her from doing what she must not. Their marriage would be a sham and their children illegitimate. The fear of discovery that haunted her would then extend to him and them. It would never go away, never be over, and as bad as it was for her, how much more it would hurt to see those she loved suffer if she should ever be found out.

But she did wonder whether perhaps she dared share the pleasures of the flesh with Daniel Whittaker, just once, or perhaps a few times, to quench the flame that built higher and higher in her each day until she thought she might go mad with desire.

Just in the last week alone, he'd met her in the shadowy upper hallway at night and kissed her into submission at least three times. He always claimed he'd just come back to get something he'd forgotten, and hearing footsteps when she expected to be alone roused her from sleep and sent her out to investigate. That's when he would tenderly gather her into his arms and tell her not to be alarmed, that all was well, and kiss her.

He always took off his gun belt before he came upstairs and hung it on a nail he'd hammered in, up high, so she wouldn't ever be snagged by it on her way up the stairs. Sometimes, now that it was still so hot at night, she could feel the dampness at his side where he had sweated against it. When he pulled her close, she felt that, and his ribs, and a good many other things. Her searching hands had learned how his waist felt, and touched the tautness of the skin across his belly and the lean bundle of muscle toward the sides of him, and the hard roundness of his upper arms.

He was so tender and his body moved so sinuously against hers, never rough or forceful. His very restraint was making her crazy. It made Zenobia's toes curl just to think about him. The hot weather would have justified wearing the thinnest nightdress she possessed, but hunger for Daniel Whittaker had pushed her past even that.

The first night she thought of leaving it off altogether, she felt her cheeks warm up, but modesty gave way to her baser urges in just under a minute. She kept her wrapper handy, across the bottom of the bed, in case she heard him out in the hallway, but she could not deceive herself. As she slipped naked between the sheets, she hoped that he would just happen to forget something that night. If he did and they met in the hallway, and he kissed her senseless again, she hoped he would discover her nakedness beneath the wrapper and take from it the message she meant to send.

The ultimate seduction of Zoe Smith happened much sooner than Daniel had foreseen, but not a moment too soon where his sanity was concerned. It had gotten so that he couldn't even think about her without breaking into a sweat. He had an idea that his nocturnal kissing raids had yielded dividends, but never more so than the night when his wandering hand slipped beneath her wrapper and discovered bare flesh. Just *remembering* it made him break into a sweat.

He arranged for Walter Connolly and Jacob Aleksandrov to take the usual night hours the very next day—with the understanding that he was at Smith's Good Luck Restaurant if a problem arose that was so monumental that Gila City might disappear from the map unless they came and got him. Quite a few gamblers had left town for some high stakes tournaments in Tucson and Bisbee, and the miners were mostly out in the placer camps, since standing in a river looked pretty inviting when summer arrived in the desert.

In other words, as he explained to Walter and Jacob, he really didn't expect them to need him. Really, *really* didn't expect them to need him. He ambled toward the restaurant shortly after nine o'clock. He was surprised and disappointed to see Wing Loo and his relations all sitting at a table in the otherwise empty restaurant, and Zoe with them, listening and nodding and looking thoughtful.

He sat down on the small veranda, hidden from view, and bided his time. Two roses scented the night air. They had opened that day on the little bush that had looked so unlikely to survive—never mind bear flowers—when he had first received it from Missouri so many months ago. For some strange reason, it had escaped destruction when the jailhouse burned down. It was discovered the next day sitting unharmed outside the livery stable, as if someone had deliberately relocated it before the fire began.

Without meaning to, Daniel became an eavesdropper. Wing Loo was making Zoe an offer for the purchase of the laundry and explaining that he and his relatives had been saving every cent toward that end, and also toward the fare of brides they hoped to bring over from China. Wing Loo begged her forgiveness if she thought it impolite for them to try and buy the business after she had done so much for them and promised that they would never open a laundry to compete with hers if she said no. But sweet, generous woman that he knew her to be, she assured Wing Loo that she was happy to consider their offer.

Daniel waited until they'd left and the light had been on in Zoe's bedroom for some time, long enough for her to undress he hoped, before he went in and stoked up the banked fire in the stove to heat water for a bath.

"Is that you, Daniel?"

"Yeah, it's me, darlin'," he yelled up the stairs. "There's not a thing goin' on tonight that needs my attention, and it was so awful hot today, I thought I'd come back early and take a bath."

A minute of silence passed.

"Barbershop closed before I could get there today. You don't mind if I use your tub, do you?"

"Oh. Oh, no," she stammered. "It's up here, in the side room."

"All right. Thanks." How he managed to sound so calm when he was so damn nervous, he didn't know.

Her door was closed when he went up. He made several trips to fill the tub, two buckets per trip, and stripped down. He was so ready for her that the air on his naked skin made him rise. He sat down quickly. The water was more cold than hot, since he'd been in such a hurry that he hadn't waited for the hot water to actually boil, but that was fine since it solved his problem temporarily.

Now how was he going to get her out here? He washed and rinsed and dried off and wrapped the toweling around his hips without any sparks of brilliance coming to him. She still hadn't appeared. Daniel knocked softly on her door.

"Zoe? You still awake?"

"Yes." The word conveyed a wealth of information. She sounded all on edge, just like him. Good.

"Um . . . I was wondering if you'd like a bath, too? I'd be happy to bring the water up for you."

There was a slight rustling inside the room. When she answered, her voice was right on the other side of the door, soft and whispery and not more than six inches away. "That . . . that would be lovely. Yes . . . thank you."

Daniel felt like letting out a "yahoo." He hoped he wasn't reading too much into it, but it sure sounded like she was panting for him like he was panting for her. He was pretty sure she liked looking at his body, so he decided to stay in just the towel. He hauled his own used water downstairs and brought fresh water back up—after taking care to pull down all the shades in the restaurant.

His towel didn't cover much and it sure as hell didn't go far toward concealing his urgent interest in being with Zoe Smith. His final inspiration was to take his knife down on the last trip for water and saw the two roses off the bush. He snuffed the lantern first, so there'd be no one later who could say they'd seen the sheriff prancing around outside on the veranda in nothing but a towel.

He couldn't find anything but a pottery cup to put the flowers in, and even a greenhorn knew a little atmosphere was called for. The water steamed in the hip bath and he stared around helplessly for ideas. Then he thought of the little rose sachet that damn gambler had given her, the one that had charmed her so and given him the idea to send for a rosebush in the first place.

If dried rose petals were good, shouldn't fresh ones be even better? He carefully pulled the bigger of the two flowers apart, petal by petal, and dropped them gently on the surface of the water. The effect was pretty darn nice, even to his eye. He turned the lantern back a little and things began to look even more promising. He went to her door again.

"Miss . . . I mean, Zoe? I got your bath ready."

"I'll be right out." The voice was low and husky, not so clipped as usual, and she sounded shy.

Daniel stood there with the other rose in his hand, ready to give it to her. It seemed like a romantic gesture and also relieved him of the necessity of finding something to put it in. Love and lust were building up in him in about equal amounts until Daniel wasn't sure he could handle this whole business with just the right touch.

Her door opened. The light behind her was shining just right for him to see the outline of her body underneath her wrapper. She was naked beneath it. Daniel sucked in a big breath and tried to disguise it as a cough.

"Here you are, ma'am, I mean, Zoe," he said. The frog in his throat spoiled the effect of the presentation somewhat.

She took the rose and looked up at him, her eyes wide. "Thank you."

"This way, please, for your bath," he said, feeling foolishly pleased by her pleasure. He held out an arm and he saw her eyes widen still further as she took in his lack of attire. Her mouth went round and soft as she let her gaze wander across his chest and down, stopping at his waist before snapping up to meet his again.

But she didn't seem offended. Oh, lordy, he'd been so afraid for a minute that wearing only the towel was a miscalculation, but she was breathing sharply, her nostrils quivering faintly. He stood paralyzed as she passed him and went into the side room where the tub was. She pushed the door closed, but only halfway. It had to be seen as an invitation of sorts. Any fool knew that.

He felt his arousal lifting the towel away from his body. Maybe he'd better just stand there for a bit, although the likelihood that he would become any *less* aroused the way matters were progressing was somewhere between slim and nothing.

Oh, lordy. Daniel licked his dry lips. He hadn't thought to set it up that way because he'd never thought she'd leave the door partway open, but the lantern was positioned just right so that it cast her shadow on the wall he could see. Oh, lordy.

She took off the wrapper and he wiped his sweating palms against the towel. Oh, she was sweet. He saw the outline of her breasts, so big and round, as she lifted her arms overhead to fasten her hair more securely. He was going to die of the pleasure of watching her, he just knew it. That slim little ribcage, that dainty little waist, the full hips flaring out below, and legs, just perfect, perfect legs, with the sweetest, roundest thighs, and knees he could tell must have dimples. He was going to kiss those dimples before he died!

Below that the shadow of the tub intervened. Daniel ran his tongue around his mouth to wet it. She was stretching and preening and turning and, by God, it began to dawn on him that maybe she *knew* her shadow was on that wall. Oh, lordy.

She stepped into the tub ever so daintily, lovely full calves and sweet little feet outlined for an instant as she did so. She settled into the tub, but unlike him, she didn't lounge against the back but sat bolt upright. Her breasts stood out proud of her and she began to scoop water up with her hands and slide it over her neck and shoulders, slowly, slowly. Daniel was starting to be in a lot of pain.

"Mmmm, I like the rose petals," she murmured, speaking over her shoulder to the gap in the door.

He cleared his throat. "I was hopeful you would." His voice cracked, but only a little. Of course, she'd realize now if she hadn't already that he hadn't budged from the spot where she'd left him.

But he was coming around to thinking she knew that well enough, because now she was arching her back so that her breasts jutted out. She took the soap from the wire holder and began to lather herself, touching her breasts and cupping them with her hands and tilting her head back. It was all outlined on the wall in dazzling detail.

At this rate he was just going to have to leave a stain on the floor and start over. She saved him from it by scant seconds.

"Would you mind washing my back for me?" she said softly.

Mind? Daniel thought his heart was going to burst clear out of his chest. He moved mechanically toward the partially open door.

"Um, darlin', I'm not real decent at the moment," he choked out before he dared to cross the threshold.

"That's all right. I'm not feeling the least bit decent myself."

The voice was low and husky. Daniel swallowed and slowly pushed the door all the way open. Her back was to him, glistening with the water, a rose petal lodged on her shoulder. He knelt and took the soap from her and felt her hand tremble as their fingers met.

With great deliberation, he ran the cake of soap across her back and set it back in the holder. He massaged the streak of soap into a lather and traced the lines of her collarbones and ran his fingers down the middle of her back, realigning the delicate hairs there. He soothed the soap over the evenly spaced bumps of her ribs and she exhaled quietly. Heartened, he bent to give her a lingering kiss on the top of her shoulder, right next to a rose petal.

"Oh." The sound she made was filled with arousal and pleasure.

Daniel slipped his hand around to cup one large silky wet breast, feeling as if he were moving through a fog. He didn't know for certain yet who he might meet in it, friend or lover. He kissed Zoe's neck and she moaned as his hand found her nipple. The soap on his fingers made it slick to the touch as it formed into a stiff point. He boldly manipulated it and she flowed into the sensation with an exclamation.

He recklessly slid his other hand around so that he could hold both her breasts, heavy and taut and slippery. Heat rushed through him, down to the soles of his feet and up again. She pushed against him, beginning to breathe faster. The lather on her back touched his chest and then was crushed between their two bodies.

His hands tingled, exquisitely alive to the heft and mass of the pendulous breasts. She was moving, moaning, pressing into the contact, making tiny waves form and slap the sides of the tub. Her breasts were so large that he could barely contain them in his hands, and so firm, so incredibly firm.

"Oh. Daniel, that feels so good." She sounded astonished and breathless with pleasure.

He leaned forward so that he could reach her cheek with a kiss and she swiftly turned her face, her lips seeking his. He tried to remember to go slowly. She was so sweet, after all. He urged her mouth open with the edge of his tongue. It had been new to her, that idea, when he'd first done it to her just a few days ago, he could tell, but she had learned with incredible quickness how to meld her mouth to his. Now he felt, with a flame of pure pleasure, her tongue meeting his, thrusting into his mouth and seeking the fullest contact she could. He slipped one hand down her belly, over the soft womanly fullness of it, and into the water.

She didn't seem at all shy and Daniel had no restraint left in him either, despite his earlier worries over how inexperienced she might be. He found the soft hair over the mound at the top of her legs, and parted it with his fingers, combing through it and letting his fingertips graze the soft flesh below.

She reached out with her chin, pushing her head back. The back of it came to rest on his shoulder but she didn't even seem to notice. Her lips were parted, her eyes closed in concentration.

"Do you like that, darlin'?" he asked quietly. "Do you want more?"

Before he'd finished the question, she made a sound and parted her full white thighs as far as she could in the confines of the tub. He slid his hand down, separating the folds and opening her to the warm water. A hiss of air escaped her. He pulled away, trying to see her expression. Had he hurt her? He had to ask her, and had to have some idea of how experienced she was, whether she was a—

"Touch me there," she said urgently. "Oh, Daniel, I'm burning for you. I want you, I want you! Touch me, yes, oh, lower—" She moved against his hand and tipped her head back more, her cheeks taut as he found her inner folds and caressed her deeply.

"Oh, Daniel—" She surged against his hand and water splashed up over the edges of the tub. "Take me to bed, Daniel—take me to bed right now!"

It seemed as if his questions could just wait until later. When the object of his affections was shouting out instructions like a waddie trying to get cattle across a flooded river, it suggested that not quite so much moderation was required on his part.

Daniel hastily got his arms under Zoe and pulled her out of the water. It sucked at her greedily and fell back in angry waves as he stole her from its embrace. Her hair fell down over his arm and rose petals were stuck all over her. She took his face between her hands and kissed him deeply and he was so overpowered by the feel of her naked body against him that he just staggered around in a small circle for a space of time. When he finally found the door, he started down the hall.

"Not that way," she whispered, licking his ear. "The other way—to *our* bed."

Hearing her call it what he'd always thought of it nearly undid him, that and having her hip rubbing against him right where it counted. He nearly flung her across the bed and then lay down across her, seizing the small hands and lacing his fingers through hers. He stretched her arms up past her head and kissed her, his buttocks clenching and trying to drive into her.

"No, no!"

Oh, lordy, she couldn't call it off now! She pulled her hands out of his with surprising strength and wrenched the towel away from his hips. Daniel nearly shouted with relief. He pushed his hips against her, trying to get himself between her legs. He took what seemed the last opportunity to make a tender declaration of love and commitment before they consummated their relationship.

"Oh, darlin', I do love you and I want to—"

His tongue froze as she grabbed his manhood and guided him to the place he'd been looking for.

"I love you, too," she gasped, "but I want you, right now! Oh, please, Daniel."

He answered her plea and his own prayers with a decisive thrust. She answered him with a thrust of her own that about sent him over the edge, but she was right there with him, crying out and saying things about how he was making her feel that made it impossible to do anything but go for the ride with her. She bucked and writhed against him in a frenzy and just when he couldn't hold himself any longer, she cried out and kept crying out and he exploded, too, just like gunpowder on the Fourth of July.

Love could certainly make a person do foolish things, thought Zenobia as she stretched and turned luxuriously. A few rose petals still clung to her, but most of them were smeared across her sheets, and one or two were caught up in Daniel Whittaker's hair. He was still asleep, the broad upper half of him curled around a pillow. The narrow hips and long, muscled legs were tangled in the part of the sheet she hadn't drawn over herself.

The sun hadn't begun to clear the horizon yet, but the sky lightened as she lay there. She turned on her side to really enjoy looking at him without subterfuge for once. The smooth planes of his face, from low-angled cheekbones to determined jaw, were darkly stubbled with a new day's growth of beard. He was white-skinned below his waist and tan above, with even deeper color on his neck and face.

She picked a rose petal off her breast and rolled its velvet limpness between her fingers. As handsome as he was, she thought that the part of him she liked best might be his buttocks. The skin on them was so smooth, every bit as soft as a day-old rose petal, and it was so sensual when the muscles there tensed beneath her palms as he brought that radiant burst of pleasure into her center.

Zenobia sighed. So *that* was what sex was supposed to be like! A man's pleasure and a woman's duty—only a woman who had never experienced what she had the night before could ever say sex was a duty. But perhaps many women never *did* know that pleasure. She had sensed that there was more to it, but it was Daniel who had opened the door for her. It was Daniel, with his patience and his slow hands and his sensual appreciation of her body, who had brought her to a boil by degrees.

And then she'd boiled over. And boiled over, and boiled over some more. It was no wonder Daniel was still sleeping soundly. She'd had so little sleep that she couldn't believe she was awake either.

But then she had things on her mind. Her conscience was not untrammeled like his. She'd thought of that the night before, when she'd realized she could display herself in shadow on the wall. The exhilaration engendered by it aroused her enormously but didn't constitute actual capitulation. Right until she had invited him to wash her back, she'd vacillated. She'd told herself that she was a murderess and he was a lawman, that it would be a sin to sleep with Daniel because she was a married woman, and every other thing she could think of to keep her feelings under lock and key.

But when she'd opened her door and seen him there, holding a rose and wearing nothing but a towel, it had crumpled her defenses. It might be a sin for a married woman to cohabit with a man other than her husband, but hell couldn't be any worse than what she was already experiencing. She'd fought the good fight but the war had actually ended when she opened that door; she could see that now.

She was going to regret it. She was *probably* going to regret it, she amended as she rolled over and Daniel stirred and smiled and reached for her.

Seventeen

"Daniel, wake up! Daniel."

"Huh?"

"Wake up!" Someone was punching him in the upper arm, and not playfully either. He had half an idea that it might be Zoe, but he rejected the notion that the love of his life would use her fists on him. On the other hand, it might be Walter Connolly. Daniel sat up suddenly. What if something bad was happening?

"What is it?" he demanded, and realized too late that the volume was all wrong, far too loud in the comfortable bedroom, better suited to a saloon where a fistfight had erupted.

"It's me, silly," said a soft, whispery voice that turned to a giggle. "Who did *you* think it was?"

Daniel looked down and the alarm drained slowly out of his body. It was Zoe. He fell back on the pillows and threw his arm over his eyes. "What time is it?"

"Seven." She began gliding her hand across his chest in the slow, even strokes she knew he liked. "I have to get up soon."

"Well, I don't." He tried to sound grumpy, but he never could with her. "Why did you wake me?"

She kissed his chest and drew her nails down his side, also slowly, the way she knew he couldn't resist. "Because you were asleep."

The conversation seemed to be going in a circle. He shivered as she touched one of his nipples with her small wet tongue.

"Oh!" This time he awoke in more than body. The dawning

of his wits now coincided with the dawning of the day. He rolled over and smiled at her. "Why, little darlin', are you waking me up for what I think you're waking me up for?"

She pushed the sheet down his chest and past his waist and reached beneath it to run her finger along the narrow line of hair that started below his navel. He shivered and saw the gleam in her eyes.

"Why do you *think* I'm waking you up?" She was slowly disappearing in the direction of her hand, her head moving lower and lower, her lips teasing along the same line of hair. He grasped her head as the mass of coppery brunette hair flowed over his stomach.

"Because—" It came out more as strangled sound than intelligible word. "Because you want me to make you a cup of tea before you have to get out of bed?"

She hummed a noncommittal answer. Owing to the contact of her mouth with certain sensitive parts, it had a distinctly rousing effect. He had hauled four men sliced up in a fight to the barber last night, broken up another fight that erupted at Fairchild's Dance Hall, and had emptied out the Silverado and made the owners close up for the night after another fight smoldered and reignited three times there. Sometimes the best you could do was shuffle the deck and redistribute the participants. He felt leaden with fatigue.

But a man had to rise to the occasion, and when someone was as quick a study as Zoe Smith had proved to be, well, a man had to do more than just rise to the occasion. He had to work at being inexhaustible, too. Daniel twined himself around her delectable body and began kissing the first patch of skin he came to. Her hands were busy at work, lingering along his thighs as her cheek grazed his belly. Her tongue began to do something quite amazing, which, ever since she'd discovered he enjoyed it, he could count on her doing at least once a day.

"Oh, that's good, darlin', real good," he murmured, and it was. Powerless to keep his hips still, he put himself into her hands. She had learned very, very quickly how to wrest control from him. Her determination to experiment in bed could not be denied, and he'd discovered it behooved him to cede power gracefully. Even now, he could tell from her breathing that she had aroused herself as much as him by her actions. *That* was when he could effectively take charge again. He writhed under her sweet hands and mouth and got a loose hold of her shoulders. In a strangled voice, he said, "Why don't you let me take over now, darlin'?"

"Oh, good," she said, panting as she reappeared from under the sheet all bright-eyed and beautiful. "Oh, Daniel, I was so worried."

"Why, darlin'?" he asked, anxious to put her fears to rest.

"I was so afraid I wouldn't be able to wake you up."

Oh, lordy, to be in love and loved in return and to discover that your beloved had an appetite for physical pleasure that *almost* exceeded your own—well, the word "hardship" certainly didn't apply, thought Daniel.

Zenobia thought long and hard about selling the laundry and then made up her mind to do it. Wing Loo deserved it, and besides, she had the restaurant and that was quite enough to keep her busy. She worked out a deal with Wing Loo for a down payment in cash and the rest to be paid in monthly installments over the next two years.

She went to the law offices of Thurston and Meyer rather than let Charles Merrick handle the contract. She wanted to make sure the agreement was as binding as she could make it, not because she thought Wing Loo would try to break it, but because she greatly feared that some slick bully would come up with a way someday to con him out of his hard-earned property if she didn't. She didn't intend for there to be a repetition of the Hang Town Camp confiscation. She relied on the lawyer's obligation not to discuss his client's business, too, so that Wing Loo could take over the laundry without anyone knowing a Chinaman now owned it.

Ah Tup inquired ever so delicately one day about perhaps bringing young Fan to help at the restaurant. He was a good, conscientious boy, and Zenobia readily agreed. She knew her own contribution to the daily workload had declined, though she tried at first to pretend otherwise. She also tried to conceal her preoccupation with the splendid secret life she lived abovestairs with Daniel Whittaker, drunk on love and pleasure, but even if she had succeeded, Daniel Whittaker was so obviously a man in love that no one with eyes in their head could fail to put two and two together. Her secret life, in short, failed the secrecy test.

The same observers were drawing conclusions about Lester and Rosita. Her moving out had proved a great boon for Zenobia, both because of the privacy it afforded her and Daniel and also because it spared Zenobia the necessity of chaperoning Rosita now that Lester had begun pursuing her in earnest. That task fell to Mama Rosa. Rosita's first brush with love had made a mockery of Mama Rosa's custodial powers. Now that Mama Rosa had a chance to reclaim the moral high ground for her daughter, she pursued it single-mindedly. Zenobia hoped Lester was equal to the test. She wouldn't have put it past the by-now famed strong woman of Gila City to inspect behind Lester's ears to see if he'd washed there before coming to call on her daughter.

Rosita chattered a great deal more now, and Lester's habitual somber facial expression metamorphosed whenever he was around her, to a sort of fascinated admiration. He managed to be in town almost every day and Zenobia pitied his horse for all the extra miles it had to carry the big man. Lester's world revolved around Rosita and Paco. The baby now recognized him and reacted with delight when Lester fussed over him. He regarded the baby as no less a miracle than Rosita herself, and appeared to marvel over his good fortune in having both of them.

Zenobia took every opportunity to wish them well, shuddering when she thought of the constraints that having Mama Rosa dogging your footsteps would place on a romance. She rejoiced in the freedom she enjoyed with Daniel, with no one but themselves to please.

In only one respect had she been far wide of the mark when she had imagined how it might be to share a bed with Daniel. As days turned into weeks and weeks became a month, Zenobia rued the simple-minded assumption she'd made that sleeping with Daniel Whittaker would somehow satiate her desire for him. If anything, her need for him intensified with each passing day. In the dark of night, before he came in from walking the rowdy streets, she fantasized about what they might do with each other, refining on it until she wriggled with wanting.

He had been true to his word, not mentioning marriage to her again, which propped up her comfortable fantasy that no future existed, only today. She turned a blind eye to any potential consequences, filled with bright good humor and a general satisfaction with the world that would have made the average optimist look like a prophet of doom.

And then, one ghastly day, the bubble burst.

She had been hurrying around, readying the restaurant to open, when there came a knock on the door. A lady's elaborate hat floated above the demi-curtain hung across the glass in the front doors. Zenobia couldn't imagine who it was, but since Rosita, Ah Tup, and Fan were all busy in the kitchen, she unlocked the door herself.

Ribbons and gauze trim on the pale-yellow confection fluttered as the hat's owner turned.

"Oh!" Zenobia said. "May I help you? Did you wish to eat? We're not quite ready to—"

Juliette Archer strolled past Zenobia without comment, surveying the restaurant with a haughty glance. There was a pent-up quality to her, a sense of containment, like a cat eyeing a mouse. Zenobia tried to recall whether she had always given that impression, or whether her flamboyantly feminine ensemble had somehow changed the effect she created.

"Is your father coming along soon?" she said to the girl's

back. "I can set aside a table just for the two so that you needn't worry about your lovely dress being spoiled."

Juliette rotated, like some stately child's doll on display. "It is my father's choice to eat here, not mine. Since he's not with me today, I'm free to tell you that I detest the food here."

Zenobia stared. Juliette had always cloaked her words with at least a degree of politeness, even if she meant to be unkind. "Then why are you here?" Zenobia kept the strain out of her voice with an effort.

Juliette sent another disdainful look around the room. "I need to talk to you, but not here. It's too noisy and it smells."

"Very well," Zenobia said, careful to keep her voice calm. Returning rudeness for rudeness would accomplish nothing in view of the girl's obvious intent to insult. "We'll go out on the veranda."

Juliette laughed, a hard, thin laugh that didn't carry. "All those dirty, disgusting men you welcome into your little establishment will be gathering there soon. I don't think you want what I have to say to be overheard."

Alarm bells were starting to go off in Zenobia's head. "Very well, we can go upstairs."

The taller girl studied the staircase, as if judging the likelihood of it sullying her sublime yellow dress on the climb upward. "If we must," she sniffed.

But upstairs was evidently where she'd meant to go all along, for she made no effort to disguise her curiosity when they reached the second floor. She sashayed down the hallway, peering into Rosita's former room first, the empty bedroom behind it, then the side room with the bathing tub, and finally, Zenobia's own room.

"Why, what a sweet little love nest," she mocked. "I'll bet all the men just love it." She lifted the edge of the trim on one of the pillows with the tip of her parasol. "How quaint."

"What is it you want, Miss Archer?" Zenobia demanded, growing angry.

"Oh, I hardly know where to start." Juliette wandered across the room and flicked back the curtain to peer out the window. "There's such a lot we have to discuss. For instance," she said, wheeling and fixing a superior look on Zenobia, "what do you prefer to be called, miss or madam? I know we've long since dispensed with scarlet letters, but what is the correct form of address these days for an adulteress?"

The walls of the room tilted around Zenobia's head and her heart pounded at her breastbone. For all her tortured speculation, no one—*no one*—had actually come close to knowing the truth about her until now. But all could not be surrendered on the strength of so little. Perhaps the girl had only made a lucky guess,

"I'm sure I wouldn't know," she replied coldly.

"Oh, but you *are* an adulteress, are you not?" Juliette strolled to the bed and used the point of her parasol to poke at something. A boot fell over, its soft leather top slapping the floor.

Zenobia stared. It belonged to Daniel, one of his good pair, left there by accident instead of being put away in Rosita's room with the rest of his things. It had been their small and now apparently pointless concession to propriety. Zenobia hadn't even seen the boots there when she'd tidied that morning, but years of outdoor living had conferred the vision of a hawk on Juliette Archer.

But in a combat of this sort, one granted no concessions, yielded no ground without a fierce struggle. Zenobia lifted her chin.

"I have not the least idea what you're talking about," she replied sharply. "I suppose that . . . *item* must have been left there by the previous owner."

Juliette blew a harsh breath out her nostrils. "Don't waste my time! I saw Daniel Whittaker wearing them at the Fourth of July dance. You're wasting *his* time, too, aren't you?" Her derisive gaze swept around the room, taking in the chintz drapes, the ribbon-trimmed coverlet, and most damning of all, the bed so clearly meant for two. She pinned Zenobia with a taunting look. "You're a married woman. How does he feel about that? Does it bother him?"

Zenobia kept her lips firmly pressed together to prevent herself from answering. The question intended to trap; there was no answer that did not incriminate.

"Miss Archer, I have a restaurant to run. I am needed downstairs. I am not wasting your time—*you* are wasting mine. I have no idea where you have come by the idea that I am married, and I do not care. Whatever wrong-headed notions you harbor concerning me are your problem." It paid to face one's enemies bravely, defiantly. "I will not ask you to excuse me since I do not feel I owe you that courtesy. I must insist that you leave immediately."

The sherry-gold eyes bore into Zenobia's. "Daniel might also be interested to learn that a man was found dead in your house when you disappeared."

Because she'd been preparing herself for the worst, Zenobia did not betray any emotion, but a chill went through her. As many times as Zenobia had repeated the truth to herself, she had never actually heard the words spoken aloud. She wished that someone would come bustling up the stairs imploring her to hurry down and help, but no such reprieve came.

"I fear that you have a taste for the macabre, Miss Archer. I believe many females whose talents and energies are underused develop hysterical leanings, or perhaps you find that the popular pastime of conducting seances fills your leisure hours nicely. Wherever it is that you have come by your information, I assure you, you are mistaken. I did not leave my home. This is my home, and I do not now—nor have I ever—detected any deceased men lying about the place."

Aplomb alone could save her. Or could it? Juliette Archer examined Zenobia intently as she came a step closer.

"You're lying. You know it and I know it," she hissed. "Give up Daniel Whittaker and leave town or I'll tell him everything, do you hear me? He deserves a good wife, someone like me, who won't drag him through the muck. You can't marry him—

you can only ruin his life! Tell him you're tired of him, tell him you've fallen in love with someone else. Tell him whatever you want, but walk away from him or I'll see to it that you pay a heavy price."

Juliette Archer strode to the door and gave Zenobia a last, lingering look filled with contempt. "Even if you weren't already married, you're not good enough for him. I thought you were just a slut, but you're worse than that, You're no good at all."

The girl marched down the hallway in a whirl of skirts. She cut the corner to the stairs too close and her cage crinoline glanced off the banister, creating a bright wobble of yellow just before she vanished down the stairwell.

Zenobia watched numbly, thinking utterly inconsequential thoughts in the midst of her paralysis. Anyone who wore dresses all the time would have judged the clearance better.

He came in earlier than usual that night and surprised her, sitting at the window, the room in darkness, still dressed. Considering that she usually waited for him naked under a sheet, or pounced on him from behind the door, kissing him and laughing, or concocted some other way to entice him into making love to her—as if he needed urging!—finding her so still and pensive unnerved him.

His first thought was that she might be ill, but she brushed off his inquiry with a brief denial. She fell strangely silent again, her withdrawal from him palpable. Thinking she might have a headache, he offered to go brew tea for her, but she didn't even reply, just staring into the night. He couldn't say for sure that she had even heard him. A cold pain built around his heart. She had never behaved like this before.

He took his boots off and unbuttoned his shirt. Because he didn't know what else to do, he thought he might try an encore of their first night together, taking a bath first himself and them preparing one for her.

It proved to be a success in that it broke through the barrier she had erected between herself and the world. At first he feared his strategy wasn't working, when he came in clad only in the towel and announced that she might like to know that warm water waited for her. She stood like someone in thrall and undressed, slipping out of her clothes and letting them drop to the floor heedlessly. He placed her wrapper around her, not because she'd been excessively modest since he'd moved in, but because she seemed so vulnerable in her blankness, in need of protection and succor.

He bathed her like a small child, gently sudsing her neck and back, oddly unaroused by her flesh, perhaps because she seemed to have reverted to an infantile state of mind. Lifting her hand so that she would follow his touch and rise from the bath, he kept up a soothing stream of nonchalant remarks to entice her back from wherever she was. The cold place around his heart expanded as she allowed him to dry her and take her to the bed without resistance. If they'd had a reputable medical man in town instead of just the barber, he would have consulted him without delay. A nasty thought occurred to him, that she might be a laudanum abuser, but he whiffed her face and shoulders and couldn't detect any of its sickly odor on her breath.

"Oh, darlin'," he said to her as they sat on the edge of the bed together, "you're startin' to scare me. You got to tell me what's got you in such a bad way. C'mon now, it's me, Daniel. I love you—you can tell me. No matter what it is, I'll understand."

She looked at him them, really looked at him for the first time. The blue eyes were luminous, clear and soft and full of unspoken emotion. She inhaled. "Oh, Daniel, yes, you do love me, don't you?"

The tension in Daniel's chest slackened. "Indeed I do, darlin', and that's not gonna change." He took her face in his hands and rubbed his thumbs across the tender patch of skin between the corners of her eyes and her temples. "There's nothing in this whole world that could change that."

She quickly bowed her head and hid it against his neck. A hot splash on his chest alerted him to the fact that she was crying.

"Now, now, what's this, darlin'?" He lifted her chin and made her look at him again. "A man could get to thinking that you don't *want* him to love you. That's not what you want, is it, darlin', for me not to love you?" Although he'd asked the question to tease her out of her mood, he held his breath as he waited for a response. The wrong answer could come winging back to him.

"No, oh, no, Daniel," she cried. She threw her arms around his neck and clung with such ferocity that he winced. "I *do* want you to love me. Daniel," she said breathlessly, "make love to me. Show me how you love me."

She said it not in the often playful way that she gave him orders when they made love, but in a desperate way that tore at his heart. For some reason she doubted his love. Daniel gathered her to him and held her tight. "I love you, darlin', I do. Don't you ever doubt it."

She took his kisses, receptive to whatever he did rather than making her own contributions as she normally did. He used every tender trick and lavish touch he knew to draw out her pleasure, using her body with reverence. Twining against him, breathing softly, she did a dance with him, one in which she shadowed his movements, and he in turn absorbed into himself her mood, which seemed to him to be an urgent requirement for intimacy.

When she reached the height of pleasure, he pushed into her, feeling her collect around him, and whispered his love over and over as she cried out faintly and clutched at him. He took her to one side after he spent himself, cradling her as his heart slid back from the peak and thinking how powerful his pleasure had been. She sighed and pushed her face into his shoulder. She seemed all sweet delicacy in the darkness, not like her usual self, but so, so sweet.

He had sweated with the intensity of the experience. Pulling the sheet toward them, he dabbed at her face and swiped it across his chest and neck where she touched him.

"Don't," she said in a muffled voice, "I want it to be just the way it is, everything. It's all perfect, just as we are right now."

He paused. Ordinarily she'd throw her head back and laughingly order him to dry off when they'd finished and she realized that he was smearing his sweat all over her. Daniel let the sheet drop over them. He settled into the pillow and held the woman he loved, fragile creature that she was in this moment, next to him. If she wanted everything to stay just the way it was, he wasn't going to be the one to change it.

But it confused him, this change in her, and caused him to wonder, long after she fell into a soft slumber, what had occurred to make her think he didn't love her.

He watched her the next morning as she dressed, for any sign that she retained the odd insecurity of the night.

One thing Daniel had never done with a woman and that was to dress, or more specifically, watch her dress. It had become one of the unexpected pleasures of his cohabitation with Zoe Smith. He lay back in bed and watch her shimmy into her camisole and drawers, and roll the stockings up her full, rounded calves and slip on the garters with their small satin bows to secure them.

It produced an effect on him that straddled the line between desire and completeness, which were really the opposite of each other. Depending on her mood, he could be propelled either way on any given day, inspired to undo all that she had just done and make love to her, or lay back in utter contentment, not wishing for a single thing except to watch her moving about, hooking her corset in the front, stepping into the cage crinoline and drawing it up so that it opened like an accordion from the floor to her waist, dropping petticoats over it and securing the fasteners on the front of her dress bodice.

Sometimes he'd drift off to sleep again, feeling that he'd just witnessed paradise and nothing else he could see before he crawled back into the bed that night could rival it, but the temptation to drop back to sleep deserted him that morning. He propped his head on one hand and tried to read her mood. He could detect nothing at all out of the ordinary, neither the quiet, desperate passion of the night before or the melancholy that had preceded it.

She smiled at him whenever she caught his eye and he allowed himself to relax. Her seeming failure to believe in his devotion to her still gnawed at him. He wanted to disprove it by the simple expedient of asking her again to marry him, but he lacked confidence in the moment. Had last night been an indication that she yearned for him to make the offer, to bind them permanently? Or did she need more time to believe in his constancy before she could say yes to marriage?

The consequences of the first proposal had been so disastrous that he decided against asking her a second time until he knew she would welcome it.

She found the letter stuffed under the door of Smith's Good Luck Restaurant three weeks after Juliette's first visit. The young woman minced no more words in print than she did in person:

Do what we talked about or I will go to him. He will hate you if he finds out the truth. Is that what you want? J.

Zenobia stumbled against the nearest table, crumpling the sheet of paper in her fist. Devastation washed through her. The inevitable loomed just ahead now instead of in some vague, faraway future. She had lived in fear that her past would catch up with her and it had, in the person of Juliette Archer. The way it had happened had taken her by surprise, but that didn't matter. Her experiment in wishful thinking had failed dismally. Juliette was not going to vanish.

She had frantically juggled all the possibilities, but Juliette had left her no room to maneuver. She couldn't bear the thought of seeing the disappointment on Daniel's face when she told him she was through with him—that she didn't love him, or whatever bald-faced lie she ended up telling him, but if she just left town without saying anything, chances were strong that he would pursue her. He would succeed in finding her where others had failed, and in his pursuit he would draw the attention of others to her. Her second flight might thus produce the outcome she'd succeeded in avoiding the first time.

And Juliette had protected herself well. Zenobia could see why the girl had demanded she tell Daniel she was leaving him, instead of simply telling Daniel the truth herself. If she told Daniel the horrific news about the woman he loved, she risked alienating him, for no one liked the bearer of bad tidings. And how likely was it that he would turn for consolation to the person who had gone to such lengths to discredit his beloved? No, Juliette had foreseen all those things and structured her plan so that all the blame would fall on Zenobia.

Zenobia dragged herself to the kitchen and thrust the letter into the stove and watched it burn. Time was running out.

Eighteen

Zenobia continued to yield to Daniel every time he laid a hand on her, but she knew with an ache deep inside that it couldn't last much longer. She agonized each day, wracking her brain for a way to end it before Juliette Archer ran out of patience and ended it for her, but she could not think of a way to say the unthinkable to Daniel Whittaker.

Tell him she didn't love him? She'd learned to lie well—her whole life was a lie now—but when it came to Daniel, she found herself unable to repudiate what they had. She let the days slip by, counting each one like gold added to her precious small store, living in abject fear but concealing it with a desperate effort after that one lapse.

The day after Juliette's letter arrived, Nathanial Evans came into the restaurant during the lull between dinner and supper.

"Heard you were thinking about leaving town," he said, his bloodshot eyes focused on her with special intensity.

Zenobia recoiled. She'd intimated nothing of the sort to anyone.

"You're quite mistaken," she said. "Why would I? I have thriving businesses here."

Nathanial squinted against a strong ray of sun coming in the window. "That's just what I heard," he said, shrugging, "that you might sell up and leave."

"Well, I'm not going to," she said shortly.

"So you didn't sell your laundry to them Chinee?"

Zenobia paused in stacking dirty tin plates on the tray. "How did you know that?" It should have been between her and Wing Loo and the lawyer who'd drawn up the agreement of sale. It was confidential.

Nathanial shrugged again, "News travels. It might not be such a bad idea, you packing up and leaving town."

Coldly furious at his presumption and harboring a nasty suspicion that he wasn't speaking for himself, Zenobia scraped food into the slop bucket vigorously.

"Well, I'm not planning on it," she declared.

The door swung open and Dog trotted in, finding her unerringly with his nose twitching. Zenobia grabbed at the chance to break away from Nathanial.

"You'll have to excuse me," she said, gesturing to the wolf. Dog sat down and watched her with his golden eyes. "Dog has to be fed."

Nathanial's features twisted unpleasantly. "That's no dog, you know. It's a by-God wolf. It's got no business living here among people. You never know when it might turn against them."

"I daresay you're right. I don't know much about wolves, but it seems to me that it would be dangerous not to feed him if that's the case. I feed all sorts of pitiful creatures and I never know when they're going to turn on me," she added, with a glance in his direction.

Zenobia set out briskly for the back of the restaurant with Dog moving easily in her wake. She already had his tamale wrapped and ready in the pocket of her apron, but she kept her back turned so that Nathanial Evans would not realize she had used the feeding of the wolf as an excuse to get away from him. He wasn't drunk but he wasn't sober either, and she felt him watching her back resentfully.

Nathanial had obviously been sent to hasten her departure, and by whom Zenobia could easily guess. He evidently had no compunction about taking Juliette's money and following her orders, even if it meant stabbing Zenobia in the back. Juliette must have learned from her father that Zenobia had sold the laundry to Wing Loo. The weak link in the chain of secrecy must have been the law firm of Thurston and Meyer, or more specifically, Mr. Thurston. Zenobia felt sure James Archer must be a client of his.

It was a complicated world and she was playing a complicated game in it, and her opponent had all the earmarks of a master tactician. Zenobia picked her way through her days with even more care after that, mindful that the ground could open in front of her feet at any moment, never quite sure whom she could trust.

When Charles Merrick came to her later that week with a business proposition, she invited him to sit down, but she kept her guard in place. Only the fact that he had not been involved in the sale of the laundry and was therefore blameless in the leak induced her to listen to him. She offered him coffee, reminding herself that he had never done her any wrong, and that she stood in need of those who would be her true friends. But she did not relax entirely. Her encounter with Nathanial Evans had proved that you never knew who might be on the Archer payroll.

"I was wondering if you were looking for another investment opportunity?" Charles Merrick inquired.

Zenobia nodded warily. "It's possible."

"Well, it's different than those you've been making, but its attraction lies in the fact that it will probably prove very stable over the long term. It would be a good addition to balance the businesses you already have. Since you're one to look at the larger context of an investment and not just leap into things based on emotion, I thought you might be interested."

"I believe you are buttering me up quite shamelessly, Mr. Merrick. Why don't you tell me about this investment without any more flowery speeches about my shrewdness as an investor?"

"Touché," declared the real estate broker, "but really, this is a good opportunity, and when I learned about it, I immediately thought of you."

"I thought we were agreed that you would stop trying to turn me up sweet," Zenobia said.

"Why, yes, we did. Well, there is a man who happens to be German who has been coming to town for some time now for the purpose of visiting Madame Bettina's establishment—for the chance to speak his native language, you understand, and to reminisce about the country of his birth."

"Certainly," Zenobia said solemnly, "no other purpose."

"Laugh if you like, Miss Smith, but I am assured that his visits are entirely innocent, and I have no reason to question the integrity of my informant. As you may remember, I myself am an admirer of all things German. What a cultural contribution that race has made to the world—Beethoven, Goethe, Mendelssohn, Schopenhauer, Freytag, Wagner! Well, I could go on, but I won't! Suffice it to say that I have discovered a young lady of impeccable education and refinement who is the very model of Teutonic perfection who shares my enthusiasm for such things. I speak, of course, of Miss Dulcie Mueller, Madame Bettina's niece. We meet to talk on a regular basis."

"I see," she said, trying to conceal her amusement at the notion of men going to a whorehouse to exorcise their passion for Schopenhauer and Freytag.

Merrick saw the light in her eyes and smiled sheepishly. "I fear I have betrayed my feelings for Miss Mueller."

"That's quite all right," Zenobia said straight-faced, "but perhaps you wouldn't mind getting to the part about the investment."

"Oh!" The sun glinted off his pomaded hair—a recent change—and he took off his small spectacles to polish them. "Yes, of course. Well, this German man who has been coming to Madame Bettina's is homesick and wants to return to the fatherland, but he has not been on his claim the required seven years and therefore doesn't own it outright. He needs to find a buyer who will pay him for the house he has built and the flock of sheep he imported, and file a new claim to the land when he vacates his. Claim stakers typically come for the free land

and don't have the money to buy a house and livestock right away, so he is quite desperate to find one who can."

A place where she might live and yet be able to see Daniel Whittaker every so often. "Where is it?" Zenobia asked carefully.

"Thirty miles west of here, a daunting distance, I admit, but if one could find a foreman—I thought perhaps one of the Chinamen who works for you might take on the job—"

A good four or five hours drive away—not close but not impossibly far either. "Have you seen the house?"

"Yes, I wanted to see everything myself before coming to you. It is remarkably snug and attractive, the very best that German workmanship can produce."

She could ride quite ably—she could see to moving the sheep about and checking on their welfare from horseback. And she could pull a trigger as easily as a man. It didn't require great strength, so she could protect herself if need be. She wouldn't have to worry about going to a new town, about wanted posters, about detectives and lawmen, about people questioning her background. She would still have to break with Daniel, a pain beyond belief, but she did not want to go away where she would have no hope of ever seeing him again. Even if Daniel married the odious Juliette, she would want the chance to see him, if only from afar.

"Find out how much he wants."

"I have already ascertained the price and obtained a list of what is included."

It would cost her all that she had set aside, including Wing Loo's down payment on the laundry. Could she support herself off the profits from the wool after he stopped making payments at the end of a year? Zenobia sat down to carefully review the figures Charles Merrick had provided to her the next evening, after the restaurant closed.

"Pardon, missy."

Zenobia looked up to see Ah Tup holding his black skull cap

and used apron in his hand. Fan waited by the door, hunkered down, head drooping with fatigue.

"Oh, you're ready to leave?" Zenobia started to rise, to go and lock the door behind them. Rosita had gone already.

"Pardon, not go yet, have question, if you please."

Zenobia sat down again. "Certainly, Ah Tup. What is it?"

Ah Tup folded his hands and bowed. "Thank you, most kind lady boss. I wish say to you, if you want sell restaurant sometime, you tell me please?"

Zenobia set her pencil aside and gestured to the bench opposite her. He nodded and bowed again before sitting.

"Why do you wish to know?"

"See missy talk to land man. He no have magazines this time, think missy maybe want sell restaurant, like you sell laundry. Ah Tup like work here."

Zenobia smiled. True. Charles Merrick had come and it had been a business meeting, without the usual *Harper's Weekly* between them. Wing Loo and Ah Tup were remarkably clever, observant individuals. She'd been half afraid for a moment that Juliette had managed to buy Ah Tup's services so that he, too, would suggest to her that she sell out and move on.

"Are you saying that you would consider buying the restaurant?"

Ah Tup nodded enthusiastically. "Yes, yes! I like cook, I want make money, have wife, all things good. I save all time, work hard. So missy say if she want sell?"

So Ah Tup was interested in buying Smith's Good Luck Restaurant. "How much could you pay?" she asked gently.

Ah Tup got serious, dropping his usual ingratiating, smiling demeanor. "Now? Missy think sell now?"

Zenobia nodded. "It's possible."

Ah Tup looked worried. "Know restaurant make plenty money, so missy want plenty money for it. Ah Tup glad pay plenty money but not have so much now." He brightened as a thought struck him. "Missy take money each month, like with Wing Loo?"

It would solve two problems, thought Zenobia. It would provide needed income until she could make the German's place show a profit and it would relieve her of the burden of trying to run a restaurant from a distance.

She instructed Ah Tup in the deciphering of the restaurant's accounts and gave him the ledger to examine overnight. She told him to come back with an offer based on his new knowledge of exactly what things cost and how much was coming in. She locked the door behind him when he left and stood in the darkened restaurant, feeling lonely. Smith's Good Luck Restaurant had become the hub of her new life. It was where her work, her home, her friends, and Daniel all converged. Selling the laundry had been easy. To sell the restaurant meant divesting herself of the best parts of her life and conceding defeat to the past and to Juliette Archer.

The next day, Nathanial Evans walked in again and sat down as if he owned the restaurant. Zenobia tried to ignore him, but she had to pass him in order to serve the other customers. He lingered until the midday crowd had thinned. When she came near to clear a table, he smirked at her.

"Mutual friend of ours says you're overstaying your welcome in Gila City."

"We have no mutual friends," Zenobia said, declining to look at him.

"Seems we do, Miss Smith."

Zenobia didn't want to hear.

But she sent word to Charles Merrick later that day to make an offer to the German, and to coordinate the vacating of his claim and the filing of hers for the same one-hundred-and-sixty-acre parcel. The answers came back swiftly. The broker had been right about the German—he wanted a signed agreement at the earliest opportunity. In all, the purchase took only two days to conclude, and the requisite paperwork went off to the territorial capital via stagecoach.

When next she saw Nathaniel Evans's by-now hateful face coming through her door, she told him coldly that she was selling up and moving out of town. He grinned and limped out of the restaurant, anxious to take the news to the one who had been waiting for it. Zenobia had never hated anyone so much in all her life.

Daniel began to feel that the world treated him mighty well. His beautiful Zoe had not had a recurrence of the mood that had beset her a few weeks ago, and she didn't question his love again. If she seemed preoccupied now and again, he had to think it might be the heat. For an easterner, it could be shocking to learn how hot it still was along the Gila River in September.

The only benefit of the heat was that the adobe bricks for the new jailhouse cured quickly and it began rising rapidly from the ashes. Daniel had insisted on wood floors and a wood front again, and glass windows in it. The Businessmen's Benevolent Association had agreed to the expense readily enough. Money alone, however, could not provide the necessary labor, but he found help in an unexpected quarter.

Walter Connolly grumbled and belched and carried on so about helping plaster and saw that Daniel just plain cut him loose. A man who couldn't work cheerfully just demoralized the rest of the crew, and Daniel felt he'd assembled an excellent one. He made Walter walk about town all day and every night, just to keep him away from them.

The first to sign on was Reverend Bob. He owed Daniel a favor, since it was Daniel who'd discovered Molly B'damn wandering into town by herself about a month before, and it was Daniel who'd unsaddled her and thought to wonder what had happened to the reverend. Thanks to a recent cloudburst, retracing Molly's route proved dead simple. When Daniel and Blue set out to follow her tracks, they'd found the reverend sitting in the great big back of beyond with a sprained ankle.

Since Daniel hadn't been of a mind to try tracking from a wagon when it was so much easier to do it from horseback, he only had limited transportation to offer. He himself rode Blue and he'd brought along a tired-out white draft horse named Sugar that he'd talked Ned into lending him, rather than Molly, whom he had suspected of being the cause of the reverend's failure to appear in Gila City.

"Reckon you're either walking or giving one of these cayuses a try," Daniel remarked as he finished wrapping the reverend's ankle.

"I'll walk, thank you all the same," Reverend Bob said with dignity.

"Uh-huh." Daniel pushed his hat up and peered at the sky, squinting hard. He could have gone for another cloudburst to temper the merciless heat out on the flats but none seemed forthcoming. He tried to muster his patience until the reverend could screw up his courage to get on the mare. The alternative, to roast to death by inches, didn't hold much appeal. The reverend, being stout, had had his fill of the heat while waiting for rescue. Before long, he had overcome his habitual terror of horses sufficiently to clamber onto Sugar.

It took a passel of doing to get him up on her, but after that, Reverend Bob accepted the necessity for riding Sugar. Blue had fallen head over heels in love with the big white mare, and rarely got more than three feet away from her. She dwarfed him, neat little cow pony that he was, but Daniel had to admit that all the signs were there—Blue was partial to large women.

It encouraged and comforted Reverend Bob to see how Daniel's horse reacted to the mare. "He always has seemed such a sensible beast," the preacher admitted, "at least, for a horse. Perhaps, since he deems her worthy of his devotion, she will prove to be likewise worthy of mine."

Daniel just adjusted his hat and said, "Uh-huh."

Reverend Bob clutched the saddle horn most of the way to Gila City, growing ever more cheerful as it became clear that Sugar had no intention of bucking him off like Molly had. He asked for the canteen of water Daniel had brought, but he grew visibly alarmed when Sugar bore off to the right when he raised it to his mouth to take a drink.

"Make her straighten out, Sheriff!" he said, his voice rising an octave.

"Well, drop that right rein, Reverend Bob, and I expect she will."

Reverend Bob stared at the canteen and the rein in his right hand. "My word," he exclaimed softly when he dropped the rein and Sugar stopped turning.

"Now give her a pull on the left rein, so's she'll come over thisaway, toward Blue," suggested Daniel. He did and she did.

"My sainted mother," Reverend Bob said on a worshipful exhalation. "Do you mean to say she'll go any direction I want her to if I pull on these leather straps?"

"That's the case."

They resumed walking and several moments passed. Reverend Bob finally cleared his throat.

"Do you suppose Ned would consider selling me this horse, Sheriff? I must admit, being able to choose my direction of travel would be very helpful. I've rarely been able to do that with Molly."

Daniel adjusted his hat to buy a minute during which to collect himself and keep from laughing. "Well, I expect he might, Reverend, and old Molly could go back to pulling a wagon."

"Oh, I couldn't sell her, Sheriff, as cross as I am with her. She shall have a suitable retirement."

Daniel resisted the urge to tell him steers that had been retired were referred to as steaks.

"I would be most obliged," the preacher said, "if you would help me negotiate the purchase of this fine animal from Ned, though how he could bear to part with her, I'm sure I don't know."

Ned was more than happy to be rid of the old draft horse because she was so slow. The money changed hands and Reverend Bob had been thrilled with his new transportation ever since, and looking for a way to repay Daniel for everything he'd done.

Jacob Aleksandrov came to help, too, for as he told Daniel,

"It is said in the Tractate of Aboth, 'Separate not yourself from the community.' And besides, I *am* a deputy."

Jacob had developed a devoted following in Gila City, mainly among men who had been the recipient of his letter-writing services. He had become known as a man with good penmanship, a sense of discretion, and a fine, flowery way with the language. He charged for the paper he used and the necessary sealing wax only because he couldn't afford to supply it for free, but it was a rare man who didn't slip the rabbi something extra when they asked his fee and were told it was a modest five cents, "just to cover the cost of supplies."

Men would write letters to inform family and friends of good luck or ill, or plans to marry a prostitute or to travel on and seek their fortune in new places, but the real dividend of rendering the service was that men were grateful for his counsel as they stood at the major crossroads in their life that had precipitated the letter writing. So when he came to help build the new jailhouse, Jacob brought his writing supplies with him, and every so often he would pause in his labors to write a letter for some waddie or miner or gambler who came looking for him.

The jailhouse neared completion in surprisingly short order. Daniel felt life could not be much finer, not when he could let himself in the side door of Smith's Good Luck Restaurant with his own key each night and climb the stairs to his darling Zoe. It was bliss of unexpected proportions between them in bed and he assumed it would be only a matter of time until they wed.

He seldom found her fully asleep when he came in, no matter how late it was. She would be there, smelling of violets or lavender or rose petals in the warmth of the late-summer night, and they would talk in the dark and lay naked on top of the sheets. Sometimes it felt too hot to make love, as if the sweat and the heat might chafe the skin right off them, but it seldom stopped them.

Daniel stretched out next to Zoe on such a night in mid-September and felt for her hand across the bed. She stretched and made a long sound in her throat. Just that fast he wanted her.

"You asleep, darlin'?"

Zoe rustled as she rolled over to lie next to him, the cloud of her hair whispering like silk across the pillow. Knowing that she was naked just inches away from him put Daniel into a state of ferocious tension. He could envision the slopes and contours of her as easily as if it were daylight, although there was only a half-moon hanging in the sky outside the window. The firm, heavy breasts that sank into his hands when he lifted them, the hard peaks that tightened at his merest touch and made her gasp when he manipulated them, the little rounded waist from which she flared out below, to the soft belly in front and the cushiony behind in back—he know her as well to the touch as he knew his own skin. He could picture the exact cloudy shade of blue her eyes turned when her breath came almost too fast and she pressed her fingertips into his back, hard.

She laid her warm forehead in the space between his neck and shoulder. "No, not asleep," she mumbled.

He chuckled and swept up the mass of her hair, letting it play out across his hand and arm. It fell to her back and he did it again, releasing its rich aroma to the air. A light breeze played across them and he kissed her cheek. He drew light circles on her shoulder with the tip of one finger. She shivered and it rippled down the length of her.

"Can't a person get some sleep around here?" she asked, but he could hear the smile in her voice.

"No, darlin', I sure can't, not seeing as how I'm laying next to the most beautiful woman I know, and she's not wearing a stitch of clothing."

"Oh, I expect you say that to all the girls," she replied sleepily.

Daniel felt his heart constrict as he reflected on the truth of what he had said. "No, ma'am," he said softly, raising himself on one elbow, "that I most assuredly do not, because it wouldn't be true." He kissed her shoulder. "The truth is that I love *you*. You're the only woman for me."

She rose to him then, swift and silver in the faint moonlight, warm and substantial against his chest when all that he could see of her was gray and shadow and coolness. He took the core of her, what she was beneath his hands and not the paltry phantom that was all the moon would have given him. He held the heat and it was not the heat of desert sun, but of enduring feeling. He brought his own heat to hers and thought of putting a child deep within her. The heat turned to flame.

Daniel touched her with his tongue to incite the same flame in her. She flared beneath him, bright skin and hot hair moving over him, mouths together as they imprinted their shapes on each other. He wanted to say what was in his loins, that he wanted to bring forth a child out of the fire that raged in his blood, but he was mute with pleasure. The sinuous thrusting of her limbs beneath him left no room for words.

He pressed his hands all down her, over the full hips and dense springy curls, coarse to the touch compared to the velvety skin inside the parted thighs. He remembered a promise made to himself in a saner moment and lifted himself high, so that he could lay his mouth against her knees and kiss them. She sighed and came up to pull at his head, curling up over herself like a piece of paper put to a lit candle.

Daniel felt strength surging in him, bold, hot strength that would yield a baby. He started up the length of her again, sliding his hands beneath the bends of her knees, with their rigid tendons the opposite of the dimpled tops. His forearms rode up the underside of her legs, his palms generating heat as they pressed across the sheet bearing his weight.

Zoe found her own purchase on him, locking her cupped hands around his underarms and pulling him up as she arched her back. He knew what that stretching, straining pressure meant. The answer to her need jutted between his legs, feverish in its seeking. He coursed upward and her feet rode up over his shoulders, her legs forming a chute to channel his flesh and his energy into her.

The backs of her knees came to rest on his shoulders, laying her open wide to him.

Daniel inhaled hard and heard her take a deep, seeking breath, too, as his hardness touched her. He held himself up, pushing, working joyfully against the weight of her calves and feet across his back. She let out a small cry as he drove forward, putting all the power of his legs into a thrust that penetrated her. He felt a commanding need to invade her deeply, to plant his seed at the highest point he could reach within her. He rocked against her and searched out her shoulders with his hands, pulling her into his thrusts. She drove back against him with strong hips, as if she felt as greedy to receive what he had as he felt compelled to give it.

Sobs of breath, mere wisps of sound, was all he could hear beyond the roaring insistence in his ears. Her fingers clutched at his sides as he thrust, again and again, and he sensed the pattern of her breath starting to change to the long, rushed sounds of completion coming near, and away from the soft quick whimpers of arousal's beginnings.

He found his voice, harsh and ragged. "Zoe."

Arched high and hard above her, thrusting and rocking with her, Daniel said her name again, knowing the china-blue eyes were misting to a softer hue. He wanted her to feel him in her and hear him above her, to know that he joined her with his heart, too.

It made him strong to hear her answer, even though all she could produce at passion's edge was a pale "yes" on an exhalation, a soft tense sigh. She went rigid against him as ecstasy took her captive. Delighting in knowing how to prolong it for her, Daniel continued to press into her in the same hard cadence, even though she had ceased to return his thrusts. She cried out, in full throat, her head back as he thrusted, again and again. The swell of her body rising around his shaft and pulsing hard against him took Daniel's pleasure out of his control and fused it to hers.

* * *

He awoke with the sense of well-being that came of deep sleep and pleasure unbounded. Zoe wasn't lying next to him, or even in the room, although the sky to the east had barely begun to cast a blush over the bed. He cocked his head and heard water splashing. Quickly, so that he could surprise her, he pulled on his pants and slipped downstairs.

He heard her moving around upstairs, dressing, as he heated the coffee. He fixed two cups rather than take the time to make up a tray. He wanted to get upstairs again quickly, before she was too far gone in her preparations for the day. She pushed her thoughts way out ahead of where her body was sometimes, to all the things she had to do that day, and then it could be hard to tug her mind back to the here and now.

He had a question to ask her. He'd have taken the steps two at a time if not for the coffee, out of anticipation of the relief of getting matters sorted out between them once and for all. Her face, when he went into the bedroom, already betrayed the subtle shading away that happened when she was absorbed by thoughts of the day ahead. He handed her the coffee, fixed just the way she liked it. She gazed at the cup blankly for a moment, from far away, and then took it, thanking him automatically.

He squeezed her neck between fingers made too hot by the pottery mug he'd been holding. "Here now, darlin', you've got to get yourself back here in this room. Forget about that restaurant for a minute so I can ask you something."

She turned. "Yes?"

He smiled to soften her, to signal his need for her to really be there with him. The earnest pucker between her eyes diminished slightly, but she still wasn't in the frame of mind he'd hoped for. But he needed to ask now, today, out of his conviction that they had made a baby in the night. The conviction went bone-deep.

"Zoe, sweetheart, I need to know how you feel about me, and what you mean to do about it." He saw confusion in her eyes and wondered why. It was a simple enough question.

She started to open her mouth and then looked down, blowing

across the surface of the milky brown coffee. Daniel's jaw tightened. He knew she loved him—she'd told him so many times.

"You love me?" he prompted, trying not to sound uneasy.

She nodded, but she wouldn't meet his eyes. Daniel set his coffee down, afraid he was going to do something violent.

"Zoe, darlin'," he said, trying to gentle his voice, "I want us to get married now."

She stared at the mug he'd set down on the corner of her dressing table. Daniel wanted to grab her wrists and twist her body so that she had no choice but to look at him.

"Zoe, look at me, darlin'."

"I can't," she said quietly.

"Can't what? Can't look at me?" His pulse felt sluggish and hard as he watched and waited for her reply—and hoped.

She shook her head and turned back to doing her hair, winding it and jabbing pins in to secure it as she went.

"Zoe, I deserve better than this," he said, and in spite of his best effort, it came out unpleasantly harsh and demanding. She said nothing. Her small, delicate hands didn't pause, twisting and wrapping and pinning the shining hair. "I at least deserve an answer."

"I did answer you."

Daniel jumped to his feet. " *'I can't'*? That's my answer?"

Silence. He was going to break something. He was going to smash the clear red vase he'd bought for her to put roses in. He was going to hurl the wash basin against the wall, and the pitcher. Daniel clenched and unclenched his fists as fury soared through his veins.

" *'I can't'* from the woman who tells me she loves me every night in the dark and makes love with me every way imaginable? I'll be damned if I don't feel entitled to a little something more than 'I can't'!" He tried not to shout, but seeing her sitting there so impassively sent his temper raging. "I want a better answer, damn it!"

She turned and he saw an angry spark in her eyes, although her face was as grave as before and her manner just as evasive.

"Keep your voice down and don't swear at me," she said coldly. "It's a free country. If I don't care to talk about marriage, that's my right."

Daniel felt a hard, shaking temper flowing over his skin and around his heart, taking over where good sense had deserted him.

"If all you wanted was a man to service you, I wish to hell you'd chosen one of the other applicants for the job. I seem to recall there were quite a few. I'm beginning to feel like a bull put out to stud."

"There's no need to be crude," she said sharply.

"All right then, just tell me why marriage is the wrong subject to bring up with the woman you sleep with every night?" He ground out the words in a deadly, low tone.

"If I don't choose to discuss this, I don't have to, and that's all there is to it. Believe me when I say it's for the best." She stood up quickly. The vehemence of her words made her seem taller. "Look, you may as well know, I'm leaving town."

Daniel had to think hard about what she'd said in order to make sense of her words. She was still talking and he struggled to grasp the rest of what she was saying.

"I'm buying a sheep ranch to the west of here. I plan to live there and sell the restaurant to Ah Tup. It's the way I want things, Daniel. I'm not ever going to marry you, but since I can't convince you of that, I think it will be better if we don't see each other at all."

The words came at him like hail, stinging and smarting and slashing away at his flesh. He flinched as she delivered the final words. With a crisp turn, she exited the room and went down the hallway in that ramrod straight, painfully correct way of hers.

Zenobia had done what she had to do. Daniel Whittaker hated her. He wasted no time in gathering his things and moving out, back to the nearly completed jailhouse. She couldn't help overhearing talk among the restaurant's customers about the perilous mood of Gila City's sheriff. He walked the streets, brooding and belligerent to such an extent that there were rumors that a meeting of the Businessmen's Benevolent Association had been convened to discuss the possibility of relieving the sheriff of his gun.

Nothing came of it, though, and lawbreaking reached a new low. Few men wanted to test the temper of a man so obviously looking for a fight. She caught a glimpse of him on the street a few days later and he looked as wretched as she felt, but there was no help for it. She crossed the street so as to pass him on the opposite side.

The next day, she noticed Juliette Archer's big black walking horse tied to the hitching post outside the jailhouse.

Nineteen

Zenobia dealt out steel knives and forks with a swiftness born of practice. Back in the kitchen, Ah Tup was telling a funny story to Rosita, who laughed as she stirred and listened. Zenobia let the clatter of the utensils drown out the happy sounds as Smith's Good Luck Restaurant prepared for another day of business. Ah Tup and Rosita would manage very well together when she was gone.

Wing Loo's cousin had made an acceptable offer for the restaurant, too generous in fact, and Zenobia had made him revise it, comprising smaller payments but over three years instead of two. He had bowed and told her that he was most humbly grateful for her generosity, and for once she had been sure that it was not the usual polite superficiality she saw in his eyes but real emotion.

Young Fan nearly capered with excitement when the sale was agreed upon, and Wing Loo, who had come to make sure that each party understood the other in every detail since his English was better than Ah Tup's, explained to Zenobia that the boy loathed doing laundry but wished to apprentice to his uncle Ah Tup and become a superior cook like him.

"That's very admirable," Zenobia said to the ecstatic young man. "I hope you will one day own a restaurant of your own."

When her words were translated for him, Fan regarded her with deep joy. He bowed low and then did a most unusual thing for a Celestial. He took Zenobia's hand in his and shook it, daintily, as if he held a butterfly in the palm of his hand, and said something in Chinese.

"He is wishing you greatest happiness and thanking you for your most wonderful wish for his future," Wing Loo explained. "He desires exactly what you wish for him, success in business, like Missy Smith."

Oh, she had been a success at business all right, but she was about to be put to a new test. Now she would have to learn to live alone and raise sheep, and not to miss Daniel Whittaker so much that she hurt all over. She had started her life with wealth and then she'd come to Gila City and been rich beyond belief in ways that truly mattered, but it had been all too brief. She felt like the delicate butterfly young Fan treated her as, emerging into the gentle dawn and dew from her cocoon to unfold and try her wings for the merest whisper of time, only to be scorched by the noonday sun, left gasping in a hostile world with her colors rapidly fading.

The sadness of knowing she would leave all these fine friends and proud accomplishments and love behind cut into her composure so deeply that she excused herself and began to hurry around the restaurant, readying the tables. She moved rapidly, quick, quick, to keep her hands and mind busy, so that she could not dwell on the regret and the pain.

And then she turned from a serving stand with a tray full of tin plates and vinegar cruets and salt cellars and saw Eben.

The bottom dropped out of her heart and her hands froze on the tray. It trembled in her hands as she stared at him, as dark and handsome as ever, standing inside the doorway. He walked to the table nearest her and calmly sat down.

"Good day to you, Zenobia. How have you been?"

It reached her ears like so much mush, slow and dragged out and unnaturally deep. *How . . . have . . . you . . . been?* There was one word among all the others that rang clear and sharp though: Zenobia. She had not heard her real name spoken aloud in almost eight months.

"Ebenezer."

He nodded. "I'm glad to see that you remember me, Zenobia. There has been a great deal of concern regarding your mental state."

"What—what—" She sat down abruptly,

"What am I doing here?" Eben withdrew a cheroot, slender, dark-leaved, and aromatic, from the immaculate dark-blue frock coat he wore. "I should have thought that was obvious," he said, drawing the cheroot under his nose appreciatively. "I've come to take you back home where you belong."

"Wh-where I . . . I . . ."

"Really, Zenobia," said her husband, "I do hope that this climate has not adversely affected your speech permanently."

Zenobia reached deep for a breath of air to clear her head.

"I'm not going back," she said. There—that had sounded nearly normal.

"Whyever not?" he inquired politely. "I can't imagine why anyone with any sensitivity or breeding would wish to remain in this town for a moment longer than absolutely necessary."

Zoe was getting into the rhythm and the flow of speaking again, her thoughts taking shape, her tongue forming words. "I have remained here because I do not wish to be hanged."

Eben's face reflected polite puzzlement. "Well, I am sure no sensible person *would* wish to be hanged, but why on earth do you suppose that such a thing might happen to you?"

She had to wet her lips before she could even say the name, and even at that, it still came out barely above a whisper. "Stephen."

"Oh, I gather you are referring to the most unfortunate accidental death of our good friend, Stephen Mayfield." He lit his cheroot and blew out a puff of smoke on a small sigh. "A tragedy, truly, with him being in the prime of his life, too. I gave Sidcup the sack for deserting his post the night Stephen fell to his death. If he had been there instead of taking the evening off with the rest of the servants, he would surely have seen that Mr. Mayfield was in no condition to negotiate the stairs safely and would have escorted him to a water closet on the ground floor of the house. It was the only destination he could have been attempting to reach on the second floor in the opinion of the police."

He paused, his classically even features unnaturally serene given the topic. Zenobia breathed in and out with a deliberate effort, centering her focus on his face, feeling shock lapping at the edges of her mind.

"It took the authorities some time to piece the story together in a manner that fit the facts," Eben continued smoothly. "Sidcup, poor fool, told the police some cock and bull story about my having given him and the rest of the staff the evening off, but I assured them that I had never done such a thing in my life. I told them that you made all the domestic arrangements." He leaned forward, avoiding with distaste any contact with the rubber tablecloth in front of him.

"And you, my dear, your disappearance caused us all such worry. While we were saddened by the loss of Mr. Mayfield, it was you whom I and your parents grieved for most, you who were at the center of all our lives, a perfect daughter, a perfect wife." He shook his head, the smooth high forehead faintly furrowed for an instant. "We considered whether Mr. Mayfield might have been the victim of foul play, and you also, taken by his attacker and with God only knew what result." He shuttered his eyes for a moment, as if pain clutched at something vital inside.

"But the detectives I hired suggested that we offer a reward for the recovery of the jewels discovered missing from your room. They were distinctive and quite expensive pieces, as I'm sure you must know, so we felt we might succeed. When a jeweler in Independence, Missouri, answered our advertisement, he claimed to have bought them from a lady matching your description. It was the first intimation, the first welcome evidence we had that you were yet alive. Your parents were beside themselves with relief, as was I, but please, tell me—I have been so worried all these many months while we searched for you—what was it that made you leave our home? Did the sound of Stephen's fall awake you and the sight of his lifeless body overset your reason? I confess, it is all we were able to conclude after we knew that you were still alive, and yet we heard nothing from you."

"Overset my reason?" she exclaimed. "I should say my reason *was* greatly disturbed, but it was not that which did it but—"

"I thought so," Eben said. "I thought your mind must have been disordered by the horrible experience of finding yourself alone with a dead man. It is what I said to the police all along."

The restaurant revolved around her in slow circles that made Zenobia's stomach twitch uncomfortably. She felt as if she might have been dropped on her head recently, for what Eben said made no sense, no matter how she strained.

"But—but—but that's nonsense!"

"Of course it's nonsense," he said soothingly. "To those who do not know you, it would seem nonsensical for you to flee from the bosom of your loving family, no matter what had happened, but to those of us who know you best, it was perfectly understandable. I had to explain to the authorities that yours was an excitable, high-strung nature, coupled with extreme tenderness and delicacy of feeling."

So she *wasn't* wanted for murder? Zenobia's temples ached with the effort to cut through Eben's copious and persuasive explanations. But she kept pulling herself up short. No matter what he said, Eben knew the truth.

"Why?" she said. "Why have you come to find me?" She know it was the question she should be asking, the question that would cut through all of his lies.

He smiled ever so slightly. "Oh, Zenobia, it grieves me to see that you are still not quite in your right mind. I only rejoice that I have found you at last so that you can be fully restored to what you have been in the past. If you cannot be, if your recollection of events indicates that you have suffered some lasting disruption to your mental processes, then at least we can care for you as you deserve."

He reached across the table for her hand and she hurriedly

snatched it away and folded it in her lap under the table. If she tried to tell the truth, he would have her declared incompetent. And with his powers of persuasion, he would induce her parents to go along with his judgment, and together they would lovingly lock her up in an asylum somewhere and lovingly throw away the key! Would Eben stop at *nothing* to keep his hands on the Strouss fortune?

Eben withdrew his pocket watch. "It lacks twenty minutes to eleven. The eastbound stagecoach departs on the hour." He glanced up with a light lift to his brows. "I have booked two inside seats. I suggest we go to the depot right now, so that the booking agent does not sell our seats." He stood and proffered his bent arm. "Shall we, my dear?"

"No." Numb she might be, in danger of being declared a lunatic she might be, but she had not lost her senses yet. "You must be mad if you think I'm coming with you."

"You can, you must, and you will, Zenobia. I am your husband and I know what is best for you. There is simply no other alternative to your coming home. Even you must see that."

"No, I refuse. I don't care what you say, I won't go. You know what really happened that night."

Eben pushed his lips together briefly and then the chiseled mouth relaxed again, as if her mulishness were of no consequence. "It is as I feared: you are still quite delusional. Fortunately for all concerned, there is at least one person in this town who recognized that you did not belong here and notified me of your presence. I thank God for her intervention."

Zenobia didn't even have to ask: Juliette Archer! She had played an even cleverer trump card than simply telling Daniel she was married. She had let her husband know where she could be found.

"It's not going to work, Eben. I'm not going back, not after all that's happened, and pretend to be your good, obedient wife—or your mad wife either, for that matter."

Eben clucked gently. "Then I shall just have to exercise my authority as your husband."

He moved like a snake striking, taking her arm in a grip that made her gasp, and before she knew what had happened, he had her out the door. Zenobia fought, but he wrestled her along under the bright, hot sun, mastering her easily with his superior size and strength. It seemed a repeat of the night she had pushed Stephen down the staircase, a mundane setting, ordinary in all ways except that something unspeakably *un*ordinary was happening in the midst of it. Once again a man was presuming to use her and twist her to his own dark purposes by force. In the midst of ordinariness, a second nightmare was taking shape. Zenobia's pulse beat hard and fast as she struggled to be free, no less stunned by the sudden turn of events than she had been the night when Stephen had attempted to rape her.

Hot dust puffed at her feet as she kicked and spun and tried to wrench her arm from Eben's grasp. Eben imprisoned her arm with a fury utterly unbelied by his serene expression. They were halfway to the Wells Fargo depot now, and Zenobia grew desperate. The skin of her forearm burned from the rubbing and pulling and her hair had begun to loosen. Attempts to stamp on Eben's foot proved fruitless, for he strode along with her bobbing unevenly beside him and she could not take aim effectively.

"I am not getting on that stagecoach," she said through teeth gritted with effort.

Eben ignored her. She managed to slip one foot behind his leg as he stepped forward on it and he stumbled. Zenobia jerked hard to free her arm and felt his grasp slip where someone had been sweating, probably her—Eben never sweated. But that was as effective as she managed to be and they were almost at the stagecoach office now.

"Let me go!" she panted, and again, louder, "Let me go!" Maybe someone would come to her aid. She couldn't see anyone she knew—there seemed to be a lot of strangers milling about, not unusual when the stage was expected.

People *were* looking at them, but indulgently, as if anything happening in broad daylight on Main Street couldn't be so very serious. But as far as she was concerned, the situation was getting very serious indeed. If she didn't do something effective and fast, she was going to find herself on that eastbound stage and once she left, there would be no one, *no one* who knew her and would take her side.

Zenobia waited until she rotated in her struggle to just the right point and drew her foot back and planted her knee in Eben's crotch. Teresa had taught her the trick, saying she needed to know how to protect herself, and like everything else she'd learned from Teresa, it proved to be wonderfully helpful.

Eben pulled her off balance with him as he descended to his knees. "You bitch!" he gasped through clenched teeth. But he didn't loose his grip on her enough for her to wrest free.

Several men nearby let out howls of laughter and stopped to watch the confrontation. Others slapped their thighs and made sympathetic noises, intended, much to her fury, to console Eben, not her. Hot and breathless from exertion, Zenobia couldn't even draw enough air in to ask for help. Damn their eyes! Couldn't they see she was in trouble?

From the corner of her eye, Zenobia saw one shocked face, a young man who stared at them with mouth open and eyes popping. She hadn't seen Tommy Daly since the day he'd offered her five dollars for a glimpse of her face. She doubted he'd even realize who she was, since she never had lifted her veil for him. Daniel had said then that he was a good man in a pinch, but would he recognize this as a pinch? He turned away and her hopes deflated.

Any minute now she would hear the rumble of the big Concord coach and Eben would pull her aboard as they changed horses and she would be on her way back East to face a nightmare life where truth was lies and lies were truth.

Twenty

"Some miner jest grabbed hold of me and says there's some whore fightin' with her customer in the middle of Main Street down near the Red Dog Saloon, Daniel."

"Well, can't you handle it? Doesn't sound too tough," Daniel remarked. He hadn't sleep well the night before and he was tired. The truth was, he never slept well these days.

"I was about to get me some dinner, Daniel," Walter Connolly said plaintively. "Today's the day the Swede over at the hotel makes them meatballs and gravy I like so much."

Daniel stood up. "Aw, hell, all right, go get your chow."

Daniel jammed his hat on his head and pulled the jailhouse door closed behind him and locked it. Just then, Jacob Aleksandrov came running down the uneven plank sidewalk, the ringlets at his ears nodding and the strings on his prayer shawl flying.

"Sheriff! There's a big fight down the street! Many men have gathered to watch and now the eastbound stage is being held up by the crowd and the jehu has pulled out his rifle and is threatening to shoot people if they don't get out of his way!"

"Well, he's a fool, then," Daniel said crossly, "but he's not the first one I've dealt with today. Look here, Jacob, run in and get my Winchester from up on the wall and come on up there. I may just need to show it as a little persuader for that driver to put *his* rifle away." Daniel handed the jailhouse key to the rabbi. "Much obliged," he said. "See you there."

Daniel stormed off toward the crowd he could see the edges

of now. He wondered which whore it was who had no more sense than to fight with a customer in the middle of the street. And the stagecoach driver was going to get an earful from him, too, and a stiff fine for daring to pull out a gun in Gila City. It just went to prove his contention that there was no problem so bad that some fool couldn't come along and make it worse.

A glint of sunlight on metal drew his eye to the rifle the stagecoach driver had out. He waved his hat and caught the jehu's eye.

"You put that damn thing away right now or I'll make you sorry your mother ever gave birth to you!" he shouted. He wiggled his badge at the driver and gave him a meaningful quirk of one eyebrow. The jehu slowly lowered the gun with a sheepish look. Behind him, perched in the cheap seats atop the coach, was an assemblage of black-haired females craning and weaving for a better look at the spectacle beyond the stagecoach driver's big hat. There must have been seven or eight of them, all Chinese amazingly enough, in frothy, voluminous dresses in the most extraordinarily vivid shades of puce and fuchsia and poppy red and grass green that Daniel ever hoped to see, though not, preferably, when he was hung over.

He tried to push his way through all the men formed up around the fight, but they were so fascinated by what was going on that he couldn't break their concentration long enough to get them to make way for him. He heard the sound of angry words being exchanged at the center of the crowd by a high-pitched, shrieking female voice and a deeper timbred male one.

"All right, let me through," he said with exasperation. "Damnit, make way!"

But when he finally battled his way past all the gawkers and gapers to the opening at the center of the crowd, Daniel's jaw dropped. It was Zoe, not some whore, who was screeching like a fishwife, and at a man Daniel had never laid eyes on before. She was flopping and flipping around, trying to get her arm away from him, and her hair was half undone, flying around her shoulders like a brunette battle flag as she screamed at him.

"I will *not* do as you say!" she cried. "Let me go or I'll kick you again and this time you'll never get back up!"

"Like Stephen?" the man snarled. "By God, Zenobia, I gave you an easy way out and now you do this to me!"

"Let me go!" she shrieked, her face going red with exertion. "It always comes back to you, doesn't it, Eben? What does Eben want? What does Eben need? Never mind what it costs anybody else—Eben's the only one who matters, isn't he? Everybody bow down to Eben, everybody go along with what Eben wants! Well, no more! I am not getting on that stagecoach with you. For God's sakes, won't somebody make this man let me go!"

Daniel blinked. He'd been so immersed in the sheer unexpectedness of what he'd found that he had forgotten for a moment that he was the one who should be doing something about it.

"Take your hands off that woman, mister!" he roared.

The man nearest him jumped and glared over his shoulder at Daniel, rubbing his ear, but the man for whom the message had been intended took no notice of it.

Daniel strode forward. "I'm the sheriff of Gila City, mister, and I said to let go of that woman! If you don't, I'll arrest you for kidnapping!"

The man, who was dressed in the most beautifully tailored coat and trousers Daniel had ever laid eyes on, sent a withering glare in his direction.

"You can't charge a man for kidnapping his own wife."

Daniel went still. Everything around him went still.

His wife? Zoe was this man's *wife?* Daniel saw spots sprouting across the scene in front of him and realized he'd stopped breathing. He took a deep, shuddering breath and the sound of the crowd came back with a rush.

"—want a divorce, do you hear me, Ebenezer Sinclair?" Zoe was screeching. "If I had a gun, I'd shoot you, and then I wouldn't *need* a divorce!" She was shaking with fury. Daniel could see her whole body vibrating with it. "You're a villain and a liar and a—"

"And you're a murderer!" said the man she'd called Eben. "If I had my way, you'd be swinging from a rope instead of being invited to come home to Philadelphia as if nothing had happened!"

Daniel stared at them in wonderment. She was his *wife?*

A shivering, quaking, unspeakably intense joy was spreading through Daniel. She was married! At last he had a reasonable explanation for why she wouldn't marry *him!* And what was even better, Daniel thought, grinning as he watched the noisy, venomous fight pick up steam again, was that she obviously didn't want anything more to do with her husband. Problems like that could be worked out.

"You're the one who sent Stephen to our house," she screamed, panting for breath. "With *your* key! He'd still be alive if it wasn't for you and your dirty, disgusting plan to get me pregnant! *You're* the real murderer!"

A ripple went through the crowd as she leveled the charge. Wing Loo had appeared on the far side of the open circle with all the young Chinese ladies from the stagecoach in tow. He appeared to be translating for them, clicking his tongue and shaking his head as they stared in wide-eyed wonder at the goings-on. The jehu stood next to them and the other passengers from inside the coach, and none of them seemed to be in such a hurry to leave anymore.

Someone tapped urgently at Daniel's shoulder.

Daniel didn't bother to turn around, drinking in the sight of Zoe—with her eyes flashing cobalt sparks—and digesting the highly agreeable news that she was married.

"Sheriff Whittaker, here's your rifle," Jacob Aleksandrov said breathlessly. "I loaded it the way you showed me."

Daniel nodded. "Hang on to it for me, will you, Jacob?"

"With gladness. What's going on? Who is that man with Miss Smith?" Jason whispered from behind him.

"Her husband," Daniel said happily. "And he says she's a murderer."

"Blessed be the true Judge," Jacob gasped. It was his standard response to bad news.

"Now don't go getting all worked up over nothing," Daniel said placidly. "She says *he's* the one who's the murderer."

"Blessed be the . . ." Jacob started to say again and then, for the first time since Daniel had known him, the young rabbi lost the power of speech.

"Well," Daniel said, uncrossing his arms, "I expect it's time for me to step in."

He ambled over to the two combatants, who had not ceased yelling at each other, and with a deceptively mild-looking gesture, took Ebenezer Sinclair's arm and twisted it so that the other man cried out and immediately dropped Zoe's wrist. She jumped back a pace and rubbed it angrily.

"You cold-blooded, self-centered, son-of-a—"

"You lying, murdering, mealy-mouthed, spoiled little—"

"Shhh." The very mildness of Daniel's rebuke got their attention.

In the silence that fell, everyone in the crowd strained forward to hear what came next.

"Now," Daniel began in a slow, easy voice, "as I understand it, you—Mr. Ebenezer Sinclair, I believe I heard your name is—you accuse this lady of murder." He held up his hand as Eben started to speak. "It wasn't a question. I'm just reviewin' the facts. And you, Miss Smith, accuse Mr. Ebenezer Sinclair of the murder in question. Is that correct?"

"He *is* guilty!" she cried. She looked so damned adorable with her hair all loose and her cheeks so pink and all that Daniel had to work at not smiling fondly at her. "He's the one who—"

"Now, now," Daniel said comfortably, "we aren't going to solve this out here in the middle of the street. I'm just trying to make sure I understand so that—"

"We need to hold us a miners' court!" Tommy Daly whooped from the back row.

A chorus of lusty yells greeted this notion. "Yeah, let's get to the bottom of things!"

"I don't like the look of that Ebenezer feller," someone else shouted. "He looks too damn clean by half!"

Daniel caught sight of Teresa up on the landing of the Red Dog's second floor. She had her hands braced on her hips and she was scowling as she came down the stairs. A Cousin Jack that Daniel knew by sight came down after her, pulling up his suspenders. As Daniel quieted the crowd, Teresa waded through it. She faced Zoe with a questioning frown.

"Is that what you want, a miners' court?" she asked. "Or do you want to go back East and get this all sorted out in a proper way?"

Zoe pursed her mouth. "Well, I'm not going back East, no matter what, not with him, so I guess it'll have to be the other, but what *is* miners' court?"

"It's all elected—judge, jury, somebody to represent each person. Everybody gets to vote on them, but only the jury says what happens in the end. Some rough justice gets handed out sometimes," Teresa cautioned, "but it's generally pretty fair, and mainly what else it is, is fast."

"Well." Zoe glanced around.

"You've got a lot of friends here. You're not likely to get any fairer a trial anywhere else than you'll get here," Teresa allowed.

"Yes, all right."

Cheers went up and the Red Dog Saloon was emptied of tables and chairs in record time. Daniel saw Zoe and Ebenezer being swept in through the door by the crowd, and he saw the murderous look on Ebenezer Sinclair's face. No one had asked *him* if he agreed to the trial, but that was just fine and dandy with Daniel. He wanted things settled.

Charles Merrick emerged as a clear favorite for judge. He looked the part, with his smoothed-down hair and spectacles and quiet elegance, and he was known to be a reader. He accepted his appointment with suitable gravity and ascended a chair set on a whiskey keg behind the bar. Dog settled on the bar in front of him and was promptly voted bailiff, although it was felt that on further reflection, they also ought to have a real bailiff to keep order, since Charles Merrick's first suggestion as judge was that Daniel Whittaker, being somewhat personally involved with one of the two feuding parties, should set his gun under the bar and temporarily vacate his post as sheriff and peacekeeper.

Jacob Aleksandrov, shouldering the big Winchester rifle against his thin shoulder, stepped forward to act as bailiff, but then Daniel proposed that he act as Zoe's advocate. Teresa nodded in agreement.

"He's a good talker," she said, "and that's what you want in a legal man."

It got put to a vote and everyone agreed that Jacob would represent her interests well. As Jacob went to stand next to her at one end of the bar, Daniel hissed into his ear, "Keep it short, and no quoting from the Tractate of Aboth." Jacob nodded solemnly, too absorbed by the importance of the task before him to be offended.

Clarence Trilby, the only other deputy present, accepted the Winchester and stood proudly by the judge's chair, ready to quell any riots that might arise.

Then they came to the thorny issue of who should represent Eben Sinclair. He glared at them all, marring his dark handsomeness, although some of the sporting girls—who had been arriving late, owing to having been asleep when the brawl started—regarded him with obvious approval. A general discussion about his advocate ensued, out of which arose several names, including Dog's.

"I have a suggestion," Teresa said in a loud voice. Everyone quieted. "I propose Sell Tarr."

A buzz of questions followed this, for most people didn't recognize the name. Sell Tarr stepped forward when Charles Merrick asked if such a person was present. "Well, sorr, and I am," said the compact, muscular Cornishman, "and I should be most amenable to performing the job. I don't side with either party, not knowing either of them, and being a Cornishman,

I'm naturally blessed with a fine command of the language, so I'll represent Mr. Sinclair as well as anyone can."

Not a single objection was heard when Sell's name was put to a vote, but Ebenezer Sinclair looked at him scornfully. "I assure you, I need no championing by such as yourself. I am a graduate of Harvard College and there is nothing you could say on my behalf that I could not say better."

"Ah, thee've got a little to learn about miners' courts," said Sell. "Modesty will serve thee better than that fine chip on thy shoulder."

A jury came next, and over the objections of some of the men, the doves prevailed on Charles Merrick to make the jury half men and half women, since that would reflect the parties involved. Mama Rosa marched forward and demanded to be included, and since no one felt inclined to argue the point with her, she was the first juror impaneled. Rosita, who had arrived late, with Paco bouncing on her hip, hung back, declining to serve on the jury in case the baby should need to be fed.

Red, the Scotsman who ran the Red Dog, took the next seat, since he had to be there for the whole proceeding anyway, to see that no one helped themselves to any liquor. Madame Bettina stalked to the bar and turned regally, her black curls perfect as always.

"I shall be another participant," she declared. "I have the advantage of a superior mind and good, sound reason, as do all those of German extraction."

No one saw any flaw with that, and the majority also agreed with Madame Bettina's suggestion that her niece, Miss Dulcie Mueller, should serve as a juror for possessing the very same qualities, in addition to which she had received a fine education. The men stared goggle-eyed at the statuesque blonde, whose complexion was somewhere between that of a blooming rose and a lily at sunrise. Not a single objection to her inclusion on the jury was heard, nor even many "ayes" when the vote was taken, since so many men had been struck dumb by her beauty.

Walter Connolly erupted through the door, a smear of gravy

still on his chin, and took in the room, packed wall to wall with Gila City's citizens. "Hell's bells, Daniel, I just heard we was havin' a court! What in tarnation's goin' on?"

"Walter Connolly! I vote we have him on the jury!" someone yelled. Walter looked around uneasily, his mustache quivering, but his fate had been sealed by his dramatic entrance.

It was decided that Walter had qualified for jury duty by his demand to know what was going on, proving as it did his complete lack of knowledge of the case, therefore eliminating any question of prejudice aforehand toward either party. Ned, the blacksmith, chose that moment to come in search of the driver of the stagecoach, to inquire what he wanted done with the horses left hitched to the coach now abandoned in the middle of Main Street.

"Tie 'em up and come get on this jury, why don't you?" yelled the jehu, "so's we can get on with this trial. I got a schedule to keep!"

Ned, being too shy to demur in front of so many people, went out and reappeared a few minutes later, silently taking his seat on one of the ten chairs saved for the jury.

Wing Loo and Reverend Bob were voted in, too, bringing the total number of men to five. A hasty search around the room turned up Silver Sally and Contrary Mary to round out the female jurors.

Charles Merrick borrowed the Winchester from Clarence Trilby to use as a gavel. He pounded the bar with the butt of the rifle and there was a pow and a whizz-zip as the gun went off. The more seasoned among the onlookers immediately hit the floor as the bullet struck a metal sheet overhead labeled "Daisy." It went clean through, and Daisy herself gazed in annoyance at the hole it had made as Dog scuttled out the front door at a lope.

"And to think I've taken comfort in knowing that steel plate was there," she said. "Teresa, I've changed my mind about that room. I want the one back over the storeroom."

Teresa nodded at her from the jury area. "All right, Daisy.

We'll wait until someone newer and dumber comes to town and give her your old room."

Daniel leaned against the wall by the door and watched Zoe—or Zenobia, which was what her husband had called her—standing next to Jacob Aleksandrov. She looked nervous but composed, her small hands folded neatly in front of her. One of the working girls had tidied up her hair during jury selection and she looked just lovely. Daniel couldn't wait to marry her.

Charles Merrick handed the Winchester back to Clarence Trilby. "Well, I don't think I shall be needing *that* again," he said with a slight tremor in his voice. "Perhaps my fist will make a loud enough noise if everyone is paying sufficient attention." A little shaft of light coming through the bullet hole overhead made a warm yellow spot on the bar. Merrick pounded on it.

"There. Now we'll begin. Miss Smith, did I overhear you at some point declaring your desire for a divorce from Mr. Sinclair?"

"You did," she said decisively.

"Well, I propose to follow the general principles of law now prevailing in the United States of America, and from what I know of them, husbands and wives can't testify against each other. If we proceed with the divorce first, it will make everything which follows, relating to this murder, easier."

Eben sneered. "This isn't the United States. You can't issue a divorce decree that would be legally binding there. What a damned pack of yokels."

"Well, I reckon we could write down the decision of this court today and I believe the territorial governor would sign it—"

"Whoever he is this week," Eben interjected snidely.

"—and I do believe that on most civil matters," Charles Merrick continued with dignity, "the Territory of New Mexico has a reciprocal agreement with the United States of America. We could send the paper on up to the capital for a signature and it could be filed back East in the relevant jurisdiction."

Everyone murmured approval. No one liked to feel as if they were somehow inferior, which was what this city boy had implied. Sending papers to be signed and filed made it sound as if the people of Gila City could be just as official as anybody.

"Miss Smith, what grounds do you propose for the granting of a divorce?" Charles Merrick inquired.

"He sure, by damn, sounds like a judge, don't he?" someone near Daniel said admiringly.

Daniel had to admit that while he had not always been able to think rationally where Merrick was concerned, the man *did* make a fine judge.

Zoe faced him and with an accusing glance in Ebenezer Sinclair's direction said, "On the grounds that he conspired with another man, his friend, that this other man should come to our house and . . . and *assault* me." Her face colored up. In the heat of the argument out in the street, it had been easy to be more specific.

"His intention was to get you with child, I believe you said before . . ." Charles Merrick suggested gently.

"Yes." She held her chin up, the neat little figure quivering with indignation. "Because he wanted to assure his claim to my father's fortune."

Heads swiveled, conversation swelled, and the assembled masses examined Eben with extreme interest before turning to look at Zoe Smith with even more interest. A fortune! The word buzzed around the room as men mopped their foreheads with handkerchiefs. The already hot day had grown even more oppressive with so many bodies packed into the Red Dog.

"That's's a lie!" Eben snapped.

Jacob cleared his throat. "If I may . . ."

"Yes, by all means," Charles Merrick said.

"We are asked to judge events which happened far away, and it will be the word of one individual against another," Jacob said. "Therefore, we must judge how these two individuals have conducted themselves in the experience of those assembled here today in order to distinguish between their two characters and who may be more easily believed about past events."

"Makes good sense to me," declared Clarence Trilby and then snapped his mouth shut, remembering that he was an officer of the court and not a spectator.

"First, we take the character of Miss Smith." Jacob clasped his hands behind him. "What is desirable in a woman? What is undesirable? Does she have a loud voice, that she would talk in her house and her neighbors can hear what she says? Does she go into public with her head uncovered? We have not observed Miss Smith behaving in any of these unseemly ways."

"She sure put on one hell of a show today." Eben pointed out with a smirk. "I would say that every neighbor in town heard her."

"That was only today!" cried Zoe. "And only because of what *you* did."

Jacob nodded sagely. "Which brings me to my other point. It is said in the Trac—" He stopped abruptly, darting a guilty look at Daniel. "Ahem. When a man does not honor his wife, then she shall be released from her obligations to him. Today we have seen this man, Miss Smith's husband, call her vile names and humiliate her in public."

"Mr. Tarr? Have you anything to say on behalf of Mr. Sinclair?" Charles Merrick asked.

Sell raised his eyebrows and took a little turn around the room. He sighed. "Oh, sorr, I cannot say thee different. I myself saw this, what Mr. Aleksandrov speaks of. And women, the beautays, are such wonderful creatures, to be spoiled and fussed over, and sorr, as thee well knows, there be too few of them out here anyway, and those we have needing to be treated with special consideration." He nodded and hooked his thumbs in his suspenders as Eben looked thunderbolts at him. "I expect that Miss Smith is the more to be believed."

"What kind of argument is that on my behalf?" Eben exploded.

Sell Tarr turned and fixed his keen dark eyes on him. "Well, sorr, I believe I did tell thee that thee had one or two things to learn about a miners' court. Thee ought not have derided my silver tongue before it were ever pressed into thy service. I can speak free, as my heart dictates, in miners' court. We be after truth and not the fancy telling of lies, as thee may be accustomed to."

"This is ludicrous!" Eben raged. "I'll have nothing more to do with this abomination of a trial! You can't keep me here." He started toward the door.

Daniel stepped lazily in front of the double swinging half doors. "I think you'll find that we *can* keep you here, at least until we're finished."

Clarence Trilby scurried around from behind the bar, brandishing the unloaded rifle at Eben. "That's far enough!"

Eben snorted in derision. "What are you going to do? Hit me with it?"

"If I have to," Clarence said stoutly.

Charles Merrick intervened. "I believe we have enough manpower by the door to prevent Mr. Sinclair's departure, bailiff."

Clarence Trilby retreated to one side uncertainly.

Merrick adjusted his spectacles. "Ladies and gentlemen of the jury, do you have an opinion regarding whether Miss Smith's request for a divorce should be granted?"

Mama Rosa, who had been sitting with her huge, muscular arms crossed over her chest, arose with an expression of disgust on her face. "Of course she should have her divorce! He is a pig. All men are pigs." Her face softened. "Except Lester Cooper—he is a good man, I think."

"And so say you all?" Merrick inquired amiably.

The rest of the jurors nodded with varying degrees of enthusiasm. Walter Connolly nodded, too, although he looked like he'd have preferred it if the word "pig" hadn't been mentioned in the verdict.

"Now as to the murder, perhaps we should begin with your

version of events this time, Mr. Sinclair," Charles Merrick said equitably.

Eben ground his teeth, his feet braced wide apart and his fists clenched at his sides. The pose spoiled his good looks. "She's out of her mind," he spat out. "She's been spoiled and indulged and given everything she ever wanted all of her life and had people to wait on her hand and foot since she was an infant. It's a wonder she ever learned to walk, what with all the people fawning over her and ready to carry her everywhere and do her every bidding."

The miners and waddies and gamblers and working girls, the bartenders and bullwhackers and cooks and clerks and shopkeepers—all of them studied Zoe as Eben launched his attack, but it was plain to be seen that this description of her background did not at all offend or repel them. Rather, being generally of modest to poor backgrounds, they appeared to be fascinated by it.

"Does this have a bearing on the murder?" Charles Merrick asked in some confusion. "I was under the impression it had happened in the recent past."

"It does," Eben said, turning on him with a snarl. "The only thing she ever had to do all by herself was have a baby, and she couldn't even do that!" He stopped speaking suddenly and his face tightened, as if he'd said something he hadn't meant to.

"I see," Merrick said, sending an apologetic glance in Zoe's direction. "I'm sorry if the discussion of so personal a subject distresses you, Miss Smith. Mr. Sinclair, I must ask you to limit yourself to those facts which bear on the murder."

Daniel smiled to himself. So, Eben hadn't managed to get her pregnant! Well, *he* had. He just knew it. The only thing he wasn't quite sure of yet was whether it was a boy or a girl, but he'd know soon enough. Daniel grinned. What an amazingly wonderful day it was turning out to be.

"These are the facts of the murder!" Eben said. *"She* was the one desperate for a baby, not me. She tried to seduce my best friend when he came to our house one night, and when he refused, she pushed him down the stairs and killed him!"

Daniel saw Zoe take a deep breath. Two red spots burned on her cheeks. "And why was that friend—*your* friend, not mine—at our home? Because *you* sent him there and gave the servants the night off and gave him a key to let himself in," she countered. "You said he should try and get me pregnant since you couldn't. He told me, Eben—he *told* me it was your idea!" She advanced a step, her eyes boring into him. "And when I wouldn't let myself be raped, he laughed at me, Eben. He laughed at me! And when I defended myself, he fell down the stairs. I knew what would happen. I knew you'd put the blame on me, just like you're doing now. You're so good with words, Eben. You can think on your feet. I've watched you do it. I knew you'd make a fine politician, always able to talk people around to your way of thinking."

Tears pooled in her eyes. "I *loved* you, Eben, and you sent your best friend to rape me! If you hadn't, Stephen would be alive today. That's why I say you're the murderer and not me." She wheeled and buried her face in her hands, muffling the abrupt onslaught of tears.

Daniel went to her then, and pushed his handkerchief between her fingers. "Hush now, darlin'," he said softly. "It's all over now."

Twenty-one

Eben Sinclair's last view of Gila City was from the back of the eastbound Wells Fargo and Company stagecoach. By popular decree, he was pronounced a scoundrel and lashed to the luggage platform of the big Concord coach, where the driver pledged he would stay at least until they reached Fort Smith, Arkansas.

"Never you fear, ma'am, he'll feel like eggs that's been scrambled," the jehu said. "And don't you worry none about that feller you—that died, ma'am. He needed killing. That funny little feller that was helping you, that rabbi, that letter he's gonna write to the governor is going to set everything straight, I just know it will."

The jehu slapped his huge hat on his head and climbed up to the driver's seat. The coach had fresh digs and scrapes along the top, thanks to Molly B'damn, who had chewed through the hitching rail, freeing the stagecoach horses that were tied to it. The devilish old steer had led them to Ned's livery stable, where they tried to get through the barn door, stagecoach and all, to reach the hay inside.

Fortunately, no damage had been done to the luggage of the Chinese brides. According to Wing Loo, he'd prepared them for the fact that the West was wild, but arriving just in time to witness the fight on Main Street had proven to them just how wild. They'd been traveling for weeks, sailing from China and then traveling overland by coach via the Bradshaw Road from

California, their fares paid for by Wing Loo and his relations. All that remained now was to hold seven wedding ceremonies.

As the last of the crowd piled out of the Red Dog Saloon to watch the stagecoach pull away, Daniel tucked Zoe's hand over his and suggested they take a stroll. She agreed readily. All the good wishes and congratulations being heaped on her as people milled around in the street were starting to make her feel just the tiniest bit shy. Daniel pulled her closer.

"Now, first things first," he said, as they walked. "What do I call you now? Zoe or Zenobia?"

"Oh, Zoe, please," she said earnestly. "I've always hated the name Zenobia."

"Now about those other names of yours," Daniel went on, "Smith and Sinclair. Would you like to change them too? I was thinking along the lines of Whittaker."

"Were you?" She looked up at him from under the sweep of her lashes, with those melt-your-heart china-blue eyes full of humor.

"Will you, Zoe? Will you marry me now?" He tried not to sound anxious.

She pressed her lips together and a tiny ridge formed above her eyes. "Well," she said slowly, "on one condition."

Daniel stopped, consternation making his innards gyrate. "What?"

"The goat has to go," she said solemnly.

"The goat?" he echoed.

"The goat at your place," she explained patiently. "We don't get along. Or, I had another idea." She pulled him to her side and resumed walking. "You see, I'm quite good at business, and I was thinking we might give your homestead to Rosita and Lester and live on that piece of land I bought. There are sheep on it, Daniel, did I mention that?"

He shook his head, bemused and adoring.

"Well, there are, and I've been asking questions and doing some reading, and I have begun to think that sheep are the future. That's where the money's going to be if you want to raise livestock in country like this."

"Sheep?"

"Yes, I know, sheep aren't very *romantic,* not like Texas longhorns, but they don't get nearly so many diseases, and they do better on less fodder per pound of body weight than cattle, and they can tolerate drought better. *And* you don't have to worry about losing money if you can't get them to market at just the right time. You can hold the wool as long as you need to—it doesn't deteriorate or lose value over time."

"Sheep?"

"Really, Daniel," she said, smiling up at him, "you'd think you'd never heard of them. Four legs, fluffy, white, very stupid?"

"Sheep? I ask you to marry me and we're talking about sheep."

"Oh! You want to talk about getting married? Well, why didn't you say so?"

Sometimes there was only one way to get her to stop talking and pay attention. Daniel decided that now was one of those times. He turned her to face him as she opened her mouth to say something else.

"Oh, little darlin'," he said

And kissed her soundly.

About the Author

Pamela Caldwell has lived and worked all over the world, attending universities from Manchester to Cape Town, earning a summa cum laude degree in history along the way and membership in Phi Beta Kappa.

Her past titles for Zebra include *Passion's Bold Caress, Stormswept, Scandalous, Knight's Beloved,* and *Desire's Song.*

DANGEROUS GAMES (0-7860-0270-0, $4.99)
by Amanda Scott

When Nicholas Barrington, eldest son of the Earl of Ulcombe, first met Melissa Seacort, the desperation he sensed beneath her well-bred beauty haunted him. He didn't realize how desperate Melissa really was . . . until he found her again at a Newmarket gambling club—being auctioned off by her father to the highest bidder. So, Nick bought himself a wife. With a villain hot on their heels, and a fortune and their lives at stake, they would gamble everything on the most dangerous game of all: love.

A TOUCH OF PARADISE (0-7860-0271-9, $4.99)
by Alexa Smart

As a confidence man and scam runner in 1880s America, Malcolm Northrup has amassed a fortune. Now, posing as the eminent Sir John Abbot—scholar, and possible discoverer of the lost continent of Atlantis—he's taking his act on the road with a lecture tour, seeking funds for a scientific experiment he has no intention of making. But scholar Halia Davenport is determined to accompany Malcolm on his "expedition" . . . even if she must kidnap him!

Available wherever paperbacks are sold, or order direct from the Publisher. Send cover price plus 50¢ per copy for mailing and handling to Penguin USA, P.O. Box 999, c/o Dept. 17109, Bergenfield, NJ 07621. Residents of New York and Tennessee must include sales tax. DO NOT SEND CASH.

ROMANCE FROM FERN MICHAELS

DEAR EMILY   (0-8217-4952-8, $5.99)

WISH LIST   (0-8217-5228-6, $6.99)

AND IN HARDCOVER:

VEGAS RICH   (1-57566-057-1, $25.00)

Available wherever paperbacks are sold, or order direct from the Publisher. Send cover price plus 50¢ per copy for mailing and handling Penguin USA, P.O. Box 999, c/o Dept. 17109, Bergenfield, NJ 07621. Residents of New York and Tennessee must include sales tax. DO NOT SEND CASH.

ROMANCE FROM JANELLE TAYLOR

ANYTHING FOR LOVE   (0-8217-4992-7, $5.99)

DESTINY MINE   (0-8217-5185-9, $5.99)

CHASE THE WIND   (0-8217-4740-1, $5.99)

MIDNIGHT SECRETS   (0-8217-5280-4, $5.99)

MOONBEAMS AND MAGIC   (0-8217-0184-4, $5.99)

SWEET SAVAGE HEART   (0-8217-5276-6, $5.99)

Available wherever paperbacks are sold, or order direct from the Publisher. Send cover price plus 50¢ per copy for mailing and handling to Penguin USA, P.O. Box 999, c/o Dept. 17109, Bergenfield, NJ 07621. Residents of New York and Tennessee must include sales tax. DO NOT SEND CASH.